$\mathcal{P}$UBLIC AFFAIRS
PRIVATE $\mathcal{R}$ELATIONS

Have a good time
with this ———

Letitia Baldrige

PUBLIC AFFAIRS

PRIVATE RELATIONS

LETITIA

BALDRIGE

DOUBLEDAY

NEW YORK · LONDON · TORONTO · SYDNEY · AUCKLAND

PUBLISHED BY DOUBLEDAY
a division of Bantam Doubleday Dell Publishing Group, Inc.
666 Fifth Avenue, New York, New York 10103

DOUBLEDAY and the portrayal of an anchor
with a dolphin are trademarks of Doubleday, a division of Bantam
Doubleday Dell
Publishing Group, Inc.

This novel is a work of fiction. Any references to real people, events, establishments, organizations, or locales are intended only to give the fiction a sense of reality and authenticity. Other names, characters, and incidents are either the product of the author's imagination or are used fictitiously, as are those fictionalized events and incidents which involve real persons and did not occur or are set in the future.

Library of Congress Cataloging-in-Publication Data
Baldrige, Letitia.
    Public affairs private relations: a novel / by Letitia Baldrige.
    —1st ed.
       p.   cm.
    I. Title.
PS3552.A447P8   1990
813'.54—dc20   90-33298
                                                                     CIP

ISBN 0-385-26563-8

Printed in the United States of America

November 1990
First Edition

RRC

I dedicate this book to Marika, my Hungarian-born roommate at Miss Porter's School. I always loved her *and* her name. (The Americans say "Mar-*ee*-ka," but the Hungarians say "*Mar*-ih-ka.")
From her prematurely reached perch up in heaven, I hope she realizes that I have fulfilled a promise— to write a story, not about her life but about a woman named Marika.

Many thanks to the valiant people who stood by me—my husband Bob, our children Malcolm, Clare and her husband Jim.
Thanks also to my wonderful agent Perry Knowlton and the enthusiastic Doubleday crew both past and present: Nancy Evans, Loretta Barrett, and Morgan Barnes; Steve Rubin, Janis Vallely, Ellen Archer, Estelle Laurence, Dan Maurer, and Marty Lijek. Another *merci* to literary consultant Sandi Gelles-Cole, who also edited my *Complete Guide to Executive Manners* (Rawson Associates).

CHAPTER

1

The telephone buzzed softly in the seafoam green and white bedroom in the penthouse on Sutton Place. Since Marika always left her draperies only half closed, the lights from the East River, and particularly the red glow from the neon-lit Pepsi-Cola sign across the river in Long Island City, made enough illumination for her to be able to rouse herself from sleep, sit up, and take the telephone receiver into one hand with ease. With her other hand, in the semi-darkness, she picked up her green malachite clock and strained to see the numbers to which the little gold hands were pointing. It was twenty minutes past midnight.

"The White House calling you, Mrs. Wentworth." Familiar words.

"Thank you, operator."

There was a pause, and then a low, cool woman's voice came through into Marika's ear.

"Marika, it's so late. I'm terrible to do this to you."

"That's what friends are for."

"No, I take advantage of you. You're a very important part of my life."

"In the first place, you don't take advantage of me. In the second, nothing is more flattering than to have an old college pal and one's best friend, who just happens to be the wife of the President of the United States, declare that I am an important part of her life."

Evangeline Watson laughed on the other end of the line. "Marika, I really was unaware of the hour until I looked at my watch just now. Sorry. But I just had to talk to you about something. The rumors have started flying that Mac's and my marriage is in trouble. Isn't that just awful?"

"I've heard them but pooh-poohed them, because they simply couldn't be true. How did they start, for heaven's sake?" Marika was now sitting straight up in bed, with the light turned on, and she was furiously plumping the white lace-trimmed pillows as a back support behind her as she talked. She had a feeling this might be a long conversation. "Well, let's have it. Is there any truth to the gossip?"

"No!" The voice on the other end of the line was full of anguish. "We're not exactly going around in a lovey-dovey manner, but there's nothing wrong, except that Mac is working too hard. Someone must have just surmised there was something wrong. But there isn't!"

Marika, unsure if this was the case or not, put on her most soothing voice. "Then we'll do something about it. Just who is saying what and where?" She absentmindedly fingered the pale peach satin bow streamers on her lace nightgown as she talked, her mind speculating on just what Washington luminaries might be discussing something like this. Sand was suspicious, but Marika knew she had not yet reported anything amiss in the presidential bedroom.

"I don't know. The press secretary looked very concerned, when he mentioned it to me this afternoon. He said, 'Mrs. Watson, I don't want to worry you or anything, but we must dispel these rumors. They are not going to help the President get his job done.'

Can you imagine him saying a thing like that to me, as if I didn't know how hurtful such a rumor is?"

"Look, I'm coming down for the state dinner in a couple of days, remember?"

"Marika, have lunch with me that day, will you?"

"Of course I will. I'll even take you to a new restaurant you haven't been to before, in Georgetown."

"It will be great to get sprung from the prison for a couple of hours! I can't wait to see you."

Marika laughed. "Do you realize how shocked Americans would be to hear their First Lady describe the hallowed White House as a prison?"

"They don't have to live here."

"That's true. Eve, where's Mac right now?"

"Working in his study next door, as usual. He usually comes to bed about two."

"Sounds like your sex life must be at a low ebb." Then Marika caught herself, because even if they were talking on a secure line, someone might be listening.

"You can say that again. There isn't another *woman* in Mac's life. It's the whole damned country that's in it!"

"Tough competition." Marika suddenly brightened. "Look, Eve, cheer up. No one's printed any of these rumors yet, and every time Sand asks me about them, I head her off at the pass by calling such stories totally ridiculous. I don't think you have anything to worry about. It's not as though they were public."

"I hope you're right. At night, when I can't sleep, problems exaggerate themselves. I guess I'm overreacting."

"Look, you're doing a great job down there. So is Mac. The press on you both has been fantastic; Mac's televised press conference last week was his best ever, and your project with youth education is really taking off. And I know it's not just a photo opportunity. You're doing wonderful things!"

"I think one of the reasons God put you on this earth is to make your old buddy feel good when she's down."

"Don't be down. I love ya. Mac loves ya. We all love ya."

"Thanks, Marika. See you in a couple of days. Lunch away from the White House. Two canaries out of the cage."

"Buona notte, bella."

"Every time you say good night in Italian, you remind me of our escapade on Capri in our senior year, remember?"

"Yeah, when you were ready to cut graduation, stay in Italy, and marry that handsome devil Luigi."

"Until you pointed out to me Luigi was gay."

"That was my job in life when we were growing up, to keep you safe until you married Mac Watson and became First Lady of the Land."

"Well, I haven't done such a fantastic job of taking care of you, Marika Wentworth, have I? I haven't found a guy yet for you, to replace that fabulous husband of yours."

"No one will ever replace David."

"I know that! As usual I've put my foot in my mouth without meaning to. Of course, no one can replace David. But there are other men around, and David wouldn't want you to be a widow forever, for God's sake."

Marika was intent on getting back to sleep. "Now get some sleep. With or without Mac beside you."

"And you get some, too. I promise I won't wake you up again—tonight."

Two telephones clicked simultaneously. Two bedside lamps were extinguished in the cold nights of Washington and New York. Tomorrow would be another day in the lives of two Boston friends, both prominent, attractive women, intent on keeping the world around them and the people in it neat and tidy.

Le Cirque's aristocratic-looking owner, Sirio Maccioni, swept his eyes around the dining room with the movements of a rapid lawn sprinkler, taking in every table in the room. The excitement quotient was high this November noon. For a moment, Sirio's eyes rested on the lady in red at table two. Signora Marika Wentworth was lunching with one of her important clients, Signor Miller, the important home furnishings manufacturer. She looked striking—a red Adolfo suit with her thick brown hair highlighting her exquisite complexion. Everyone of importance knew her and liked her. *Una donna di qualità*. Sirio thought the phrase quite suitable for her. And she never made a fuss about where she was seated. If only all his clientele were as gracious and unassuming.

Sidney Miller had insisted on Le Cirque for meeting with his public relations counsel to discuss the renewal of her contract. Because of time pressures, Marika had countersuggested some place closer to her office. Sidney, however, was adamant.

Marika had arrived punctually at twelve-fifteen, an unfashionably early hour, so that she could avoid the later traffic jam of people waiting to be seated. By twelve forty-five there would be chaos in the entrance, the women either guiltily or proudly sporting their ecologically unsound but luxurious furs and creating further havoc with the hatcheck woman in her tiny coatroom. Marika despised the symphony of women calling out loud *Dahling!* greetings to no one in particular, and air-kissing anyone actually recognized. The fumes from their lavishly applied expensive perfumes always overpowered the trays of delicate salmon, white asparagus, and raspberries that were beautifully displayed just inside the front door of Le Cirque.

She had found Sidney already seated at their table. Sirio Maccioni always sat him well, in a prominent banquette seat, which was one of the reasons Sidney liked to come to this restaurant. As the CEO of Millerhomes Company, a conglomerate of companies manufacturing luxury home furnishings, he was the success story of the year. The son of a Russian immigrant kosher butcher, Sidney put himself through Princeton and the Wharton School of Business. He had educated himself in art and music. His table manners were as impeccable as his English suit. Exceedingly bright, he was one of the whiz kid darlings of bedeviled Wall Street. He was also a very good client of Marika's firm.

Today was the annual review of the PR account, but Marika was anything but worried. The only special effort she had made, along with having all of the salient facts and figures memorized in her head, was to wear her red success suit to the restaurant. Her agency had accomplished wonders in getting Sidney and his company good press.

"Marika, you look absolutely fantastic!" She saw the eyes behind the Cartier gold-frame glasses go back and forth over her like a computer printer in action, sweeping over every detail of the red suit, black blouse and the unusual jeweled fish on her jacket. He appreciated good-looking women and wasn't afraid to let them know it. Once the complimentary greetings had been exchanged, they had asked about each other's families, and their order of grilled pompano had been taken by the captain, business began.

Marika handed Sidney a folded list of all the media successes created for him by her agency and told him to "read and be impressed by it when you have a minute."

"Thanks, Marika, I'll read this back in my office." He tucked it inside his breast pocket, too much of a self-taught gentleman to open a piece of business mail at the table with a woman guest. He kept scanning the room, Marika noted, his eyes searching for someone he knew or at least recognized. It was a trait she particularly disliked, but she was fond of Sidney, so she suppressed her critical thoughts.

She began to enumerate additional services her company had performed for Millerhomes, but he interrupted her, suddenly excited.

"Isn't that Sand over there?"

Following Sidney's gaze, she saw the gossip columnist alone at a table, obviously awaiting a tardy guest.

"I wonder who has the nerve to keep her waiting?" Sidney remarked.

Marika restrained a sigh and resigned herself to Sidney's distraction. No one had ever quite discovered why the gossip columnist had borrowed half of the pen name of George Sand, the nineteenth-century French writer. It wasn't because she dressed like a man, as her namesake did, though her clothing did have eccentricities. Today, Marika noticed, she was dressed conventionally, in a battleship gray, mannish suit. In the evening, Sand's wardrobe was, well, idiosyncratic—the "shroud look," as one of Sand's rival gossip columnists had dubbed her nighttime attire. The clothing was nothing more than a piece of luxurious fabric Sand wore draped around her anorexic body. The creations— obviously made by her own "little dressmaker" (no one ever asked Sand for the name)—were inevitably cut so low that anyone who cared to look could get a view of Sand's two shrunken breasts sitting atop her sunken rib cage.

Sand caught Marika's eye and waved with the one hand not wrapped around her ebony cigarette holder. Marika could see that Sidney was enjoying the little tribute to his table. Marika waved back discreetly and turned to the business at hand.

Though he was obviously more intent on surveying the scene than listening to her, Sidney kept nodding his head in feigned interest and agreement with the contents of her proposal. When Marika then presented him with a printed copy of everything she had just discussed, he immediately added the envelope to the other one in his inside pocket. It was time to mention the necessity of raising the annual retainer not only because of the rise in the cost of doing business, but also because of the recognition she felt her company merited for its acknowledged successes in attaining this year's previously set goals. However, Marika could tell something was on Sidney's mind. He just wasn't listening to her with his usual attention. She suddenly felt tired from trying to read him.

"Sidney, you have something on your mind. What is it?"

"It's Rachel, Marika. She has a request to make of you."

Marika registered surprise.

"Oh, it won't cause you too much work or time," he said defensively, "and I'll pay you well for it." He paused, reflected on his words and then added, "Very well."

"Sidney, for God's sake, what is it you're trying to tell me?"

"First," he said, "you ought to know that we are renewing your contract."

Marika sat back on the banquette with a sense of relief. Well, at least that was set. "Thank you, but I would like to ask for an increase in the renewal."

"You deserve it. How much is this going to hurt me?"

"It's not a question of hurting you. It's a question of a fair price for our services. We are asking for a two-year contract at three hundred thousand per year, plus expenses, of course."

"That's an increase of a hundred thousand a year!"

"Do you want me to send over to your office a station wagon full of scrapbooks filled with press clippings, taped television and radio interviews, and special-promotion data? And of course the interior designer spreads, using your named products, in the top shelter magazines? Do you want me—"

He interrupted her. "Stop! You get the increase." Then he swallowed some water. "But now to the other matter."

Marika thought to herself, here it comes, whatever it is.

Just then Sirio moved quickly to the restaurant's entrance, and Marika cursed the timing of this next distraction. Joan Bolder was arriving, her jewels so gaudy that they flashed beneath the restaurant's subtle lighting.

The owner led Joan Bolder and her young escort past Sand's table, still lacking the columnist's tardy guest, and on to one situated farther from the door. Marika chuckled to herself. Mrs. Henry Bolder would be quite annoyed at missing her favorite spot, near the door and facing the room, where she could see everything. But Sand was there and everyone knew that the reporter had priority at Le Cirque no matter who wanted that table, except perhaps for the royal family of Great Britain or Mac and Eve Watson—the First Family of the United States.

"I know that man," Sidney said. That's Demetri Guardevecchia, the jewelry designer. Rachel loves his things. Do you own any?"

"No," Marika said almost curtly. She was desperate to get back to the conversation and wrap whatever was on Sidney's mind. The image of papers stacked up in her office, and the phone messages Hortense was bound to be piling up, started to feel like an actual weight on her neck.

But Sidney was taking his time. "Mrs. Bolder over there is always photographed wearing Demetri's things."

Joan's overabundance of jewels was no compliment to the

designer, Marika thought. She absentmindedly fingered the Jean Schlumberger brooch on her jacket that Great-Aunt Victoria had given her—a graceful fantasy fish, made of sapphires, diamonds, and green peridots set in eighteen-karat gold. The fish was her only piece of jewelry—no necklace, earrings, bracelets—just the fish thrashing against the red wool of her jacket, vibrant with life. Marika's collection of jewelry was modest. Like most proper Bostonians, her family was not comprised of gem buyers, and David had certainly never overinvested in jewels. But what she had received from her aging Great-Aunt Victoria was valuable. The fish was probably Marika's favorite piece, after her diamond wedding band.

Joan Bolder decided to table-hop, an act that made the waiters, operating in a small space, very irritable. The crowd was growing more hectic at the entryway, and Marika wanted to conclude lunch before the noise level threatened the ease of their conversation. By now they had finished their entrée and were on to the espresso, no dessert for either one. Marika urged Sidney back to the conversation. "Please, Sidney, I can't stand the suspense any longer. You sound as though you were about to reveal a state secret."

He laughed, obviously flattered by her attention. "No, nothing quite so grand, I'm afraid." He sighed and ran a hand through his thick head of hair. Marika noticed that he had developed a liver spot on his hand. Sidney had always had big, broad, healthy hands, those of a confident, competent man. No weak handshakes from him. The spot made him seem vulnerable. Well, they were all getting older, weren't they? Marika thought. Anyway, more mature.

"Rachel thinks we have arrived on the New York scene, but that no one is aware of it." He looked guiltily down at his plate and continued. "Arrived to the point of taking our proper place in New York society, that is."

"Of course you've arrived," Marika said firmly. "You're successful, you're known to everyone, you're respected in the industry—"

He interrupted her. "No, we haven't arrived in the way Rachel wants. She's talking about being in society."

Marika decided just to listen. The conversation was becoming unpalatable.

"Rachel thinks we . . . we should get out, go where the Beautiful People go, appear at the same benefits where people are seen. We should be written about in Sand's column"—he peered thoughtfully in the direction of the columnist—"in *Town and Country, Vanity Fair*, in places like that."

As Marika sat there in silence, he continued, "Rachel thinks, you know, that when the *New York Times* runs a photo story on some big event at Lincoln Center or the opera, for example, our picture should be there. We usually buy more tickets to these benefits than those who are photographed. The photographers don't know us. There's something wrong here."

It was obvious to Marika that Rachel had rehearsed him and made him memorize every painful detail of this discomforting speech. He tugged at his collar. He was even sweating, and a red flush swept like a henna rinse over his Florida-tanned face. She had never seen him like this.

"Rachel also feels that she or I should be on one of the prestigious boards like the New York Public Library, the Metropolitan Museum, the Memorial Hospital, or maybe the New York Philharmonic."

Marika felt she could not let Sidney continue unabated. This was surrealistic, not just unpleasant.

"People are invited to serve on these boards," she interrupted, "when they have done a lot of service and contributed a great deal of money over a period of time. They also have many personal friends already on the board when they're tapped."

"We have given a great deal of money to a lot of things. And we're prepared to give a great deal more. There are no qualifications fulfilled by the present members of New York's great institutional boards that Rachel and I don't match. We're as good as they are. We're as civic-minded. We care as much about our city."

"But, Sidney, this sort of thing is not what my firm does. It's just not up our alley."

"To me, it's a perfectly logical function of a public relations firm with a well-connected management, like yours."

Marika realized she had to find some way of persuading him tactfully that this assignment was not one she could—or would or should—undertake. He read her mind.

"I'll compensate you more than generously, Marika. I will pay a great deal more than your retainer if you do something on our behalf—even if it doesn't work at first. We need a social champion."

"But why? You are already so well respected. Why do you feel the need of this? It's insecurity. Sidney, I never thought of you as insecure."

"In plain and simple language, it hurts that people like us— well motivated, capable, deserving, and eager to help—are not part of New York society."

"But what you're talking about is not the *real* society. It's café society. It's nouveau-riche society. It changes every five years."

"To us, it's the real society. Your old WASP establishment is passé, Marika. It is no longer a factor in New York or in the business world. Our new money society is the one that counts, and I couldn't care less if it's nouveau riche in your eyes, or if it is based solely on who has the most money. I could own half the real estate in this city, if I wanted it."

"I'm sure you could."

"You know everyone," he pleaded. "You could get us the right kind of exposure. You could suggest one of us for a board. We'd work our balls off, you'd see. You'd be proud you recommended us."

She looked at his tanned, handsome face. He was the leader of the entire home furnishings industry, with enormous international investments. Yet, Marika noted, he was also totally insecure. He wanted to become part of a group of much photographed, often vacuous people who were rich instead of interesting, and newsworthy because of hired press agents.

"Sidney, the people whose friendships you crave are not my friends. I just know them to speak to. I don't have the time or the inclination to lead the kind of lives they lead."

"Don't sound so pious and disapproving. It's unbecoming to you."

"Their entire focus," she continued, "is to be seen and pho-tographed at the same time. Nothing else matters."

"You know them and they know you," he said crossly. "I don't see why you are acting this way when I have asked you for such a small favor."

"I can't—I absolutely will not begin a feeder operation for you and Rachel to join that group, Sidney. It's not my way of working."

"Marika, you obviously don't realize how much this means to us." He sounded pathetic, and suddenly she felt a twinge of sympathy.

"How would you react," he said in a strained voice, "if I told you that this means more to us than what you do for the com-pany?"

This last statement pulverized Marika. She suddenly began to hate the entire field of public relations. It had become a demeaning profession. How dare he compare her agency's work in public relations and marketing in the same breath with a social press agent's flackery?

She knew this lunch had to end before sheer rage governed her movements. "It's late, we both have to go, and I can only promise you this, Sidney. Tell Rachel I will try to find a way. But don't ever again denigrate the work my agency does for you. We have done so much for your company! We have been part of your success, even if you don't understand that. Don't put us down— ever—like that!"

He was surprised at the strength of her outburst. "Think it over, Marika. I will ask for the check, make a telephone call, and then you and I can say good-bye. After you've given careful con-sideration to my request, you can call me from your office and let me know what you think. I don't think you've given it *careful consideration* as yet." He was obviously referring to three hundred thousand dollars' worth annually, of careful consideration, mean-ing that the entire account depended on her acquiescence.

He left the table, and Marika, depressed and angry, decided she would use the time to say a quick hello to Mimi Wellton and Daphne Johnston, who had just sat down at a nearby table. She noticed that Sand's guest still had not arrived. Poor Sand, she thought to herself, she must be humiliated to be sitting waiting for so long, when she, Sand, thought that everyone should wait for her.

Daphne Johnston, a tall, rangy woman from Chicago who was a cabinet officer's wife in a previous Democratic administration, was one of the national leaders in the literacy movement, while Mimi Wellton, also involved as a member of the Literacy Volunteers of New York, was one of Marika's old friends and, like Eve Watson, a Vassar classmate. Standing in the crowded restaurant aisle, Marika gave both women a warm hug. Then they were joined by Sand.

"Your guest hasn't arrived," Marika noted sympathetically.

"No, Gretchen Schultz's plane has been delayed." Sand waved her ebony cigarette holder in the air by way of explanation. "I thought in the meantime I'd stop by your table to see if anyone has any news of special import." Her black eyes burrowed holes in Marika's green ones.

"What do mean by that?" asked Marika innocently.

"You know what I mean," the columnist answered.

"If you're hinting that I'm going to gossip about the Watsons, forget it," Marika said simply. "Sand, you must trust me. If there were any truth to the rumor of marriage problems, I'd be upset, flushed, embarrassed, and chagrined at your even mentioning it. I'm none of those. There's nothing to it. That's a plain and simple fact."

"Oh," Sand replied, patently disappointed. "Well, ladies"— she addressed all three women now—"nice to see you all. And Mrs. Johnston," Sand added before returning to her table, "I will put something nice about the literacy movement in an upcoming column."

Daphne Johnston brightened perceptibly. It was difficult getting social publicity—the kind of story that everyone reads—on the grass roots literacy movement. "Thank you. We'd appreciate that."

"I'm not an ogre, you know," Sand whispered in Marika's ear as she left, but Marika's heart sank when she noticed the tardy

Swiss ambassadress, Gretchen Schultz, rushing to Sand's table, full of apologies.

Please, dear God, Marika said to herself, don't let Gretchen Schultz have anything juicy to say to Sand about Eve and Mac. She saw Sidney waiting for her to say good-bye at the front entrance, so she picked up her handbag from the banquette seat, saluted Sirio, told Sidney she'd "do her best" to handle his request, and rushed through the open door of the Lincoln Continental awaiting her on Sixty-fifth street. She sank back against the cushions and proceeded to suffer acute indigestion pains all the way back to Stuyvesant Communications, Inc.

CHAPTER

2

*B*ack again in her office, Marika pulled out a newspaper article from her overloaded In box of unread mail. Hortense, her assistant, had clipped it from the business section of a Kansas City paper and carefully marked it in red pencil. Having just returned from her lunch with Sidney, Marika began laughing at the irony of the reporter's quote from a speech she had given in Kansas City just two days ago: "We are becoming a nation of social climbers and worshipers of opulent lifestyles— which is totally nonproductive in the marketing of our products or ourselves." She contemplated for one second sending a photocopy of her remarks to Sidney, then realized she would probably lose the account if she did.

Hortense had affectionately, even proudly, labeled Marika a snob. She could not contest that label thinking to herself that she is probably one of the biggest snobs there is. She coveted the secrecy of her social life, because she carefully edited every social and business invitation she accepted. If it involved a client, she would accept; she considered such a social occasion a necessary sacrifice . . . She knew that sometimes her clients used and abused her social standing—even in an introduction. "Of course I know you have heard of Marika Wentworth, President of Stuyvesant Communications, Inc. We're her client, and she's been trying to rub off some of her old family class on us for years . . ." The other person would inevitably laugh and say, "It's plain to see it hasn't rubbed off on you, Joe," and Marika would always manage a smile, its falseness disguising the fury she felt beneath it.

She avoided accepting other important business invitations, always making a personal call to explain her regrets, and making the host feel that "Marika Wentworth *really* wanted to come tonight but couldn't." She would send a high-ranking executive from her company as a substitute. "It will be good experience for you," she would explain to the recalcitrant executive, and it usually was. Her staff came to enjoy the glamour of the splashy business parties held in famous hotels and restaurants, on board chartered cruises, and in offbeat places like the gardens of the Cooper Hewitt Museum, the J. P. Morgan Library or the medieval Cloisters. If the parties were failures from any point of view, the executive she chose to go in her place enjoyed reporting that fact back to Marika, too. ("Our company would *never* have done it that way.") For any social occasion she chose to avoid, which meant most of them, she inevitably spent the evening in bed propped up against a galaxy of pillows, going through her baskets of required reading. She was always behind on these papers and periodicals. To her, not being able to read for pleasure was one of the serious drawbacks of her profession.

Marika's feelings about social standing were based on her inherited niche in the Old Eastern Establishment into which she had been born, and it carried over into her professional life. If the Old Eastern Establishment had become increasingly less important to the social press—by virtue of a quest for privacy and a reluctance to make material possessions the number-one priority—it still counted for a great deal. Its members knew who they were, whence they had come, and who was not one of them. Marika was decidedly one of them. She and her peers had been given many advantages, without having earned them—including a superior education, foreign travel, exposure to the world of culture (which some of them rejected), and stimulating conversation around the dinner table (to which some of them were not bright enough to contribute).

Marika was grateful for having been taught the tough discipline of good manners, a natural part of the background in which she was raised. It was a bigger asset than anything else in her career. It had made her poised, confident, and able to walk through the world of business or society with total self-assuredness.

She put the newspaper clipping into her Out box, feeling guilty about what a bloody pretentious statement she had made in Kansas City about social climbing. Swiveling around in her comfortable blue chair she watched the fading afternoon sun reflected in gold and silver rays on the building across Madison Avenue. The insidious, accelerating worship of money in New York had started getting to her, making her mouth taste a little sour. The attitude was like a new overlay of the worst kind of grime on this beautiful, exciting city. She observed that in the last few years social prestige had become nothing more than a vulgar litany of the names of the recent rich, those most often photographed and mentioned in gossip columns, the big spenders on clothes, houses, and press agents.

In her business life Marika talked with ease about money matters every day, but her upbringing had taught her that "in social situations you don't talk money or ask questions concerning the price of anything or how much someone lost or won in a venture." Lately in New York she had noticed that it had become very declassé to show any modesty or even honesty about one's financial position. One night, Marika's dinner partner, whom she had never met before, offered her some gratuitous advice. "If you want to succeed in this town, and I know what I'm talking about, you gotta talk rich. That's the way to make your agency business grow. Talk big, talk rich!" When she asked him about telling the truth as an alternative, he shook his head and Marika was positive he was thinking that her agency probably wouldn't last another month.

In the quiet of her office, with the door closed, the muffled

New York noises in the street below were strangely soothing as she worked on reports and gave the final sign-off to her staff's press releases and background material prepared for clients. She puzzled over the less than good news on her company's latest profit-and-loss statement and made some notes.

To keep down the noise of voices and clattering office machines, she had installed pale blue carpeting with a design of small white carnations throughout, and pale blue acoustical-tiled ceilings. The cool blue silence of her office was welcome as she worked, but it didn't stop the familiar stabbing sensation in the back of her neck, a pain that quickly traveled across her shoulders as if carried on electric wires. She buzzed Hortense and asked her to withhold all calls for five minutes. Then she began the routine of stress-relieving exercises, swinging her head slowly around in a circle, her jaw hanging loose, her eyes closed. She was aware of faint, odious, cracking sounds of floating cartilage in her neck. She frowned. Good Lord, probably signs of arthritis to come. But then she stopped her rotating neck movements and smiled at herself in the big Venetian mirror hanging on the wall opposite her. There might be a lot of tension in her neck, but there was nothing wrong with her body. She gave a firm thigh a congratulatory slap. She had worked on that body every morning of her adult life—exercising patiently, boringly, on the floor of her bedroom, without benefit of Jane Fonda or anyone else on tape or TV. She was always amazed by the people she knew who frequented gyms and spas. She did not know what magic recipe of time management they possessed that permitted them such an option.

Marika admired the executives like Jim Robinson of American Express who could afford to install snazzy gyms in their corporate offices to improve their employees' "morale, health, and productivity." All Marika had ever managed to do for the morale, health, and productivity of her staff was to supply a fold-up plastic exercise mat from Macy's in the little coffee room and an extra supply of deodorant in the men's and women's restrooms.

She was used to people saying that she looked in her twenties, not forty-four years old. She glanced in the mirror again and wondered what those compliment payers would say now if they could see her, rolling her head around like an idiot, listening with despair to the cracking noises in her neck.

The late afternoon sun had moved and was now reflected in the Venetian mirror, tossing prisms of crystal light like monster diamonds all over the blue and white office. It was disconcerting enough to do the head rolls, she decided; to watch herself in the mirror was like watching a simian mimic her.

Marika knew that some women might envy her "perfect life," with a beautiful daughter, success in her business, and such a great social life that she was asked everywhere. What all those women did not know was that her perfect life was substantially flawed. She had lacked the love or closeness of a man since the death of her husband six years ago. The smiling, chic, well-known Marika Wentworth, independent, sure of herself, was a very lonely woman.

Yes, she had her daughter, Lisa, the living, growing, dynamic proof of David's genes. As long as Lisa was alive, David was, too. But if she did not have Stuyvesant Communications, Inc., if she did not have this group of thirty-six human beings all pulling together with her, she would have a very small family indeed. Her company completed her.

And if there were no company, there would be no Hortense either, no black-eyed, black-haired, Fu Manchu guardian dog at the front gate. Hortense, her right arm. Every woman who was trying to be many things to many people should have a Hortense in her life. Hortense, her protector, her fiercest supporter, and also her most honest critic.

Marika leaned her head back into her crossed hands in the big blue leather swivel chair, smiling at the thought of Hortense sitting straight-backed, with an air of intense authority, at a black leather executive desk outside her door. No little secretarial niche for Hortense. She was an important part of her boss's success, whether gauging Marika's success as a mother, businesswoman, or heavy-hitter on the New York social scene. Hortense was a presence without anyone having to express it. People were in awe of her, realizing they had better watch any joking remarks or snide comments about Number One. Hortense's saucer-like black eyes, generously framed in black mascara, could pierce the eyes of anyone like a laser beam. She wore her thick long black hair parted in the middle and combed back into a stylish bun. Two silver streaks framed the part of her hair, which some of the staff felt had been put there artificially to increase the deference she demanded from the younger members. As one of the young ones, Kristen, once phrased it, "Gray hair would never *dare* grow naturally on Hortense's head. It would exist only if she had *summoned* it."

Hortense, living up to her role as gatekeeper, always dressed with drama, and only in black—a perfect foil for the large, expensive, heavy sterling silver artifacts, designed by American craft artists, that she favored. At times she wore enough jewelry to fill a department store display case, but somehow, in the black sea of her attire, it was never too much.

She was exotically attractive, somewhere in her fifties, had never married, was suspicious of men, and was totally devoted to her job. Sergio, Lisa's Milanese friend, referred to Hortense as "*la cara schiava*," Marika's beloved slave. Marika paid her well, sixty thousand a year, but the salary did not make up for the fact that Hortense's entire life, seven days a week, was devoted to making her boss's existence efficient, comfortable, well organized, and protected. When *Working Woman* magazine had asked Marika the one major secret to her success, Marika had replied, "Hortense O'Malley," without hesitation. Hortense knew how to handle people, how to address them, how to cajole anyone into obeying her wishes. One small example: she could read her boss's mind; a two-minute conversation with Marika on "how the dinner party went last night," was sufficient for her to compose an appropriate typed thank-you note for Marika on her good personal stationery, which would be waiting on her desk, so that all she had to do was affix her signature. Hortense also knew how to keep someone away from Marika without the person's thinking that he or she had just been given a "no."

There was one person Hortense could not control—Marika's father, Charles Russell. Her assistant's oversized eyes would become illuminated studio lights every time he called his daughter on the telephone. Marika had chosen to ignore the existence of the snapshot of her father in its little easel-back frame on Hortense's desk. Asking her about it would be stepping too far into the deeply personal side of her assistant's life, but she knew of Hortense's strong attraction to Charlie. Marika smiled again, realizing she never had the courage to tell her father about the snapshot on Hortense's desk. It would have embarrassed him, perhaps even put a strain on his relationship with her assistant. Then again, Marika thought, perhaps not. Who knows? Had Hortense and her father ever had an assignation? *Anything* was possible in this life.

Marika had made the decision to move her business from Boston to New York within a month of her husband's death. With lightning speed she had signed the lease on the Madison Avenue space, the movers had brought her furniture to New York, the stationers had delivered fifteen varieties of printed and engraved stationery with the new address and telephone numbers, and she was hard at work interviewing potential account executives and clerical assistants. When her father had cautioned her against making such a major move without thinking it through properly, Marika had replied, "I would never have the courage to do this if I didn't use the extra adrenalin and energy that God or someone has given me because of losing David. Don't discourage me from this, Daddy. I know in my heart it's the right thing."

Hortense and Anthony made the move from Boston with her, and she recruited two other men, Greg Willis and Stephen Lamton, within two weeks of the change. Charlie Russell had advised her to "make your agency strong on men, so that as a woman president, you won't be accused of running a clucking hen house—either in reality or in other people's perceptions."

It was always understood that intelligent, quiet, conservative Anthony, perpetually meticulously groomed, with his brilliantly polished black shoes and thick dark hair, parted on one side, would someday take over the reins of the company. Thirty-five years old, soft-spoken, and with a legal degree, he ran the business side of the operation with a firm, steady hand. He was forever being teased about his closet of Tripler's dark pinstriped suits. Anthony described his job as "putting a cap on the raging excesses of creativity in this incredible company."

The number-two executive, Greg, dark-haired and dapper, irritated Marika with his penchant for black, opaque sunglasses, which he wore indoors and out, in daytime or at night. "Greg, people can't see your eyes," she told him one morning in a fit of pique. "They don't know what you're thinking."

"Fine by me," was his frank reply. "I don't want them to know what I'm thinking most of the time." A special creative talent, he had successfully adapted the look of a Hollywood director. He often wore Glen plaid double-breasted suits, cashmere turtleneck sweaters, and dark brown suede English shoes. Hortense, no fan of Greg's, remarked to Marika that he was obviously impersonating Cary Grant, "which should be enough," she added bitterly, "to cause Cary Grant to return from the dead to fight for his reputation."

Marika had countered with "Down, down, Hortense!"

"I don't care," Hortense muttered. "I don't trust him. There's something sleazy about that guy."

Stephen, who reported to Greg in the creative end of the business, was Marika's favorite. Lean and lanky, with an unruly mop of sandy hair and a mustache that continually changed in shape—from an apologetic topiary bush to a pair of giant antlers—he was one of the best creative talents in New York. He dressed in jeans and sneakers, and wore a large Western silver and turquoise rodeo buckle on his leather belt. Only in his late twenties, he accepted with ease his place of third in command under Marika. But in the eyes of the staff, he was first, because he was kind and gentle, and blessed with an eternal sense of humor.

And then there was Sarah, head of graphics, who was an ex-ballet dancer, but who also served as the resident astrologer, fortune-teller, tarot card and tea leaf reader. Her desk was cluttered with a changing collection of crystals, any one of which she would pick up and feel when she was worried about something. She saw the world in mystical terms. She would make a prediction on any subject, ranging from telling Bill, the controller—in advance of the court's decision on his divorce settlement—the size of his alimony payments (and she was right on the nose), to informing Jenny, one of the secretaries, that she was about to be asked out on a date by a new man—which, of course, happened. She always wore jeans and sneakers. She looked like a Flower Child of the late sixties, with beautiful long, flowing, disheveled hair. Every time Marika smelled marijuana on her and threatened to fire her if she didn't stop smoking pot at once, Sarah would protest like an innocent angel. "It's just my sandalwood essence, Marika—you know that." Marika had answered that if she wore her "sandalwood essence" to the office once again, she would still be fired. All the staff knew of Marika's intolerance of drugs.

Marika often wondered what her staff really thought of her. They knew so little about her private life, which of course made them curious. She imagined the lack of a man in her life was a subject of endless conversation. She wondered if people thought of her as glacial? Probably. (She had heard herself being described as *"La Freddissima"* by a male voice in the duplicating room, but she was not certain just who had said it, and she was too embarrassed to look in and catch him.) She suspected her staff thought of her as someone who was uptight, and overly conscious of her public image.

Every time Marika became uneasy with these thoughts, she would automatically look over at the one photograph that dared to occupy space in that cluttered mess of papers. It was a snapshot of a wonderful blond head, a face smiling at her out of its Chinese cloisonné frame. David. Her husband. Just a quick glimpse of that smiling face would give her a sensation of comfort. It was a beautiful Praxitelean head of curly hair, she thought . . . Youth, strength, beauty, and intelligence personified . . . A smile so impish, it lit up a large area of darkness in her office.

All that remained of David Wentworth materially was the snapshot in the cloisonné frame and some scattered photographs around the apartment. Death is merciful in only one respect. It forces the survivor to survive, to choose options, to find a substitute reason for living. She had her daughter, her father, and her agency. They were good reasons for living. She could not feel sorry for herself . . . there was a plethora of blessings in her life.

Being married to David had given her the first confidence she ever had. The only child of two very handsome parents, she had grown up loved—but shy and unsure, particularly after losing her mother when still a little girl. She assumed marriage to David meant the joy of starting a family, but he encouraged her, after working for two agencies, to open her own public relations and marketing company. David was the one who suggested that she christen the agency with her mother's maiden name, Stuyvesant. He made her feel she was good in everything she did—a success as a wife, mother, a businesswoman, and lover. He had been so loving and even-tempered, with a glance or a word he could simply diffuse any imminent explosion of her temper. He always talked about "the good and the bad energy juices that flow through us," and when she was hurting or acting in a vindictive manner toward someone, he would remind her to "get rid of that negative flow." He would make his tempestuous young wife "huff and puff and blow that house down" to banish it. They would both break up laughing, because she looked so ridiculous huffing and puffing— and then the sensual side of their relationship would take over— and her world would become safe and serene again. All she needed to motivate her was the sound of his voice, to feel his presence in the same building. There was no need for stress-relieving exercises when David Wentworth was alive. Marika wondered many times if he *were* still alive today, would their marriage be the same as it was then? Do all widows and widowers wonder that? So many factors can alter what two people perceive of as their own perfect marriage. Something like a fatal car crash puts such definite limits on any perfect marriage, but the memory of a union that ended in death begins to shine, glow, and magnify in rosy reflections, so that the one left behind finally no longer can remember how it really was. Six years ago: a car crash in the middle of the night, David was on his way home from a business trip. When he called from the airport his voice was full of excitement and happiness with news of a successful deal just completed. He asked about Lisa. Marika could picture him smiling in the stand-up telephone booth, as he anticipated opening his young daughter's bedroom door and seeing her sleeping form, just to make sure she was still there. Before he hung up, his voice dropped down to a husky whisper. "Warm the bed for me, Marika. *Be* in the bed waiting for me." Then she heard a dial tone. When she saw the reflection of car headlights slash across the bedroom wall an hour later, she wondered why he was so late. But then the doorbell was ringing. He wouldn't be ringing the doorbell. David was the kind of person who never lost his keys. He was too organized.

The soft-spoken state trooper said that death had been instantaneous. David's car had been hit by a truck going the wrong way at high speed, right at the exit ramp from the airport. There had been no suffering, "and you should remember that, Mrs. Wentworth," he had said, "when it comes time to view the body."

Ever since, life had been a series of constant reminders to herself to maintain in Lisa the spirit of David's amazingly affirmative philosophy on life. It had kept Marika going.

One day, as though David were prescient, he had talked about a mutual friend who had lost his wife. "Some people never have known even for a day what a great love is." She remembered how he had interlaced his fingers with hers and squeezed hard. "Lucky people like us must accept the real happiness that is on our plate. No matter the size of the portion."

For six years of widowhood she had not forgotten what he had said that night. They had had thirteen years of marriage. She was convinced that once you had a fantastic love like that, it wouldn't present itself again. You never fell in love again. You forgot about marriage.

She had made the required effort, had made herself go to parties, go on dates with men who found her basically cold when it came even close to a discussion of prolonging the evening in bed. She felt no desire for any of them. If no man had touched her in all this time, it was her wish. Except for one man at one time, there had been no sudden awakening of lust during the past six years, no mad desire to make love with someone and then to lie in the darkness, exhausted, triumphant, still tasting each other's mouths and bodies—with the contentment of challenged, pleased connoisseurs. She knew she would have made a comparison of any man's performance to David's, and that performance would have been, of course, inferior to his. Except for a few men who had had too much to drink, the men she went out with seemed to know that sex with her was a taboo subject. That was why they did not press for future dates. They were old enough to be frank with her. They explained they worked too hard, and did not have enough time in life to seek out attractive, compliant women. The compliant women usually sought *them* out. They took it for granted that when two people had a very easy, compatible time at the dinner table, a sortie into sex was as logical as drinking coffee after dessert. Their rapid disappearance from her life was what she wanted and what they wanted, too.

Only once had she decided it was time. An advertising agency president, Connor Morton, had begun to court her, and she was beginning to feel the stirrings of a deep physical attraction. He was fun to be with—intelligent, dynamic, and gifted with a sense of humor about everything in life—including his clients. There was a certain mysteriously hyper atmosphere with which he seemed to enshroud himself—like a fog that moves with the wind. It made her slightly uncomfortable, but she knew many people in advertising who were hyper, so she pushed it out of her thoughts. He was after all, an attractive, exciting, and gifted man in her creative world.

She felt that Connor sensed, in the short time they had known one another, that it was now time for her to love and be loved again. It was time for that body of hers to come alive again, to be appreciated the way David had revered it. She had worked hard and long and too successfully since David's death to keep his memory alive and to shut out other men.

Connor was as busy as she, and the few hours they could spend together began to be treasured by them both. They laughed the entire time they were together. They had fun. He had kissed her when they said good-bye the last two times—just kissed her —but the physical contact of their lips and bodies had grown suddenly intense. She was aware that he was being deliberately gentle. He was waiting. It was as though he knew that this prize was to be had only by going slow.

Hortense informed Marika that she approved of Connor, but then Hortense approved of any successful, attractive, single men who came along—for Marika that is.

One night, after having to cancel dinner three times, Marika and Connor managed to have a late dinner at Mortimer's. They greeted Glenn Birnbaum effusively, and ordered the *paillard* of chicken, served with its broiled tomatoes and tiny shoestring potatoes, and a bottle of well-chilled Montrachet.

"Just trying to get you to have dinner with me is exhausting," Connor said, putting his hand on top of hers and caressing her fingers with his own warm ones. The side of his leg under the white tablecloth was now gently touching hers, and there was suddenly no further doubt. Tonight would be the night. Seated opposite each other at a small table against the south red brick wall, they felt a mutual warmth and electricity passing through them both. Conversation was suddenly difficult and awkward. They ate silently, sipping their wine, and watching the crowd of young executives standing at the bar—slim young girls with long hair and obligatory little black dresses, the men in their dark suits, talking to their dates but mainly watching the front door to see if someone new and exciting was walking through it.

"Dessert tonight?" Connor asked her absentmindedly, after the waiter had cleared their dinner plates.

"No thanks," she answered. He motioned for the check. "I have some champagne waiting for us at my apartment," he said. She laughed, "I guess that decides it. I do not have anything in my fridge other than Mandarin Orange Diet Slice, and Lisa and Sergio have probably consumed that."

"I think what I have in my fridge will sit better on the *paillard* than Mandarin Orange."

They took a taxi from Seventy-fifth and Lexington back to his Trump Tower apartment. In the back seat he reached over only once to kiss her, but then pulled back and said, "This is better saved than wasted on the driver, who has been looking in his mirror the entire time."

"He probably was hoping to see something raunchy."

"Well, if we don't get there soon, he will," Connor replied, pulling himself away from her.

Connor's apartment was a well-lit, contemporary, cool environment of floor-to-ceiling glass walls, oriental rugs, black and brown leather and chrome furniture, and dramatic nineteenth-century bronzes of animals on pedestals—spotlit from the ceiling.

He put down on the oval black marble coffee table in front of the deep leather sofa two perfectly chilled Baccarat flute glasses. Then he brought in a bottle of Dom Perignon champagne in a chrome tub packed with shaved ice, opened it, poured two glasses, handed her one, and in a silent toast, saluted her with his eyes. They both drank, licked their upper lips, uttered a few words of appreciation of the taste, and sat silently for a few minutes, watching through the glass wall in front of them the pattern of lights interwoven throughout the tall buildings. When they began to kiss, they were two tired, relaxed people, with lips meeting pleasurably, but seemingly too weary for fire. But then the fire came, and their kissing became more and more urgent. Suddenly, Connor arose from the couch and left the room. Marika felt jolted by this sudden interruption, but she decided it was for a good cause—he must be doing something in regard to safe sex. Thank God for that.

He came back with something in his hands, smiling like a little boy with a toy. "Wait until you join me in this," he said excitedly, placing a small crystal container in front of her on the marble table. It contained a small amount of fine white powder, and he put down a straw next to it.

Marika looked at it and a shudder passed through her body. He had reached for her, to take her in his arms, but she pushed his arms away, stood up, and said, "Connor, I don't believe this. You are offering me dope. You are expecting me to snort this stuff with you."

He protested immediately. "The purpose of this is dual joy, Marika, because it makes the beautiful thing we're about to have that much more sensational." He got up off the sofa, pulled her up, and then pushed down the top of her off-the-shoulder dress—hungrily kissing her bare skin.

"I don't need this," she said angrily. She pulled her dress back into place and pushed him so hard he fell back on the sofa. "Why, Connor, why?" Her voice sounded dejected, pleading.

"Because—it makes it so much better!" He reacted in a hurt, defensive way. "Sex—me—it makes me much better at it—you, too. I'll give you much more pleasure!"

"You make me sick." And she strode quickly to the heavy cherrywood front door, calling over her shoulder, "You know, Connor, when I go to bed with a man, he doesn't need coke, speed, heroin, or *anything* else to make it better. It can't be any better than just being with me." And dramatically, as if she had rehearsed it, while saying her last two words she slammed shut the door of his apartment with tremendous force.

She heard him calling after her, protesting, striding toward the door of his apartment, but luck was with her. The elevator had just stopped on his floor. There were three other people in it, going home after a dinner party. As the elevator began its descent, she suddenly couldn't stifle her laughter. She had just intimated to Connor that when she slept with men, they didn't need to be stimulated by dope, and that she was enough stimulation all by herself. "All" those men she had slept with!

She kept her hand on her mouth to quiet her laughter, her shoulders shaking from the effort. The other three people, very aware of her, began to smile, too, as if drawn into the sphere of her personal amusement. One of the men, an older gentleman wearing cowboy boots and a well-tailored gray suit, said, "Well, pretty lady, that must have been a good story you just heard. Wish you'd tell it to me. I need a good one to take back to southwest Texas."

"You wouldn't want to take this one back," Marika replied, as the elevator doors opened to the lobby of the Trump Tower. "It's really not all that funny. Good-bye." Then she grabbed his hand, shook it, and departed the elevator.

So she had closed the door on an entire storeroom of her own passionate physical feelings and needs and then twirled the combination lock shut. It didn't matter if she didn't open that door ever again. She had her daughter—her work—her friends.

Enough on her plate. She could not feel sorry for herself. Great-Aunt Victoria had taught her that. The octogenarian had spoken sternly to her a year after David's death, telling her to snap out of it, that she had more going for her in her present and in her future than multigenerations of women had going for them in their entire lifetimes. Instead of feeling sorry for herself, she should feel completely blessed, fortunate, coddled by that Supreme Being, whoever He, She, or It might be.

Marika shook her head as if to shake herself out of her reverie. David's picture in its enamel frame was still in her fingers. She had been turning it occasionally, sitting at her desk for the past half hour, feeling as though she could touch his face, right through the glass.

She began to peruse the pile of folders and clipped papers before her. In spite of what Great-Aunt Victoria says, damn you, David, she thought to herself, leaving Lisa and me when you did. No warning, no preparation for the loss. Just death. I am *not* superwoman, she thought, frowning at David's picture—and Lisa is not superwoman junior, either, in spite of your legacy, David, of all that good positive thinking stuff.

She checked her mini-personal computer entries for the day. The name "Lisa/Sergio" was under her "Urgent Action" file. She must have a talk with her daughter tonight—that irrepressible, charming, exasperating, vulnerable young creature. "A beauty, just like her mother," people kept saying, but then she thought to herself that she was never as ill-prepared for life as Lisa seemed to be. Was it her fault? Would Lisa be more mature if she had been a stay-at-home mother instead of a dedicated career woman?

Those were questions to which no one knew the answers, she decided, except for the Management Upstairs, and He obviously had more pressing problems with which to cope at the moment.

Lisa was in the "Urgent Action" file because she had called this morning from Columbia to announce in a voice black with drama that her romance with Sergio had suddenly been terminated. It was *finito*, and she was now contemplating entering a nunnery. Since Marika was familiar with Lisa's propensity for exaggeration, and for her Sarah Bernhardtian flair for drama, she told her to hold the convent idea until the two of them could talk about it at dinner tonight. Lisa had quickly agreed, because she was now late for her French class and could not argue any longer ... Deep breath, very slowly, exhale slowly, too. Deep breath, exhale. Roll to the right. Roll to the left. The pain was almost exquisite. It had now passed from her neck to the base of her skull. Marika checked for the rest of today's schedule in her mini-computer. The staff meeting was at six this evening, with serious business to be discussed. Not one, but two important new potential clients had been lost to competing firms this past week, because of inexcusable sloppiness and the bad timing of her company's proposals ... Push the head back on the neck, swing the head down on the left, then roll it over to let the chin sit on the breastbone ... Well, at least Sidney Miller had renewed his contract with a generous increase, even if she did have to act like a whore and she had really promised to get Rachel "socialfied" in New York ... Head roll up on the right and back down toward the spine ... There would eventually have to be some hurtful cost-cutting in the firm, too, which she would announce at today's staff meeting.

Hortense buzzed her. No more time for relaxation exercises or self-contemplation. Marika picked up the telephone.

"Boss, it's Mathilde Kauffman on the line."

"Mathilde Kauffman? What does *that* woman want? We've had enough of her for a lifetime."

"I don't know. She was insistent on speaking to you—now."

Mathilde Kauffman and her husband Luke were the heads of a very large Swiss food conglomerate, LUXFOODS. One of Marika's big disappointments this past week was losing the big-dollars Kauffman chocolate candy account to Hill and Knowlton. Even if Stuyvesant Communications, Inc., deserved to lose it, Marika had not enjoyed the experience of spending a lot of time on the Kauffmans only to lose out to a rival firm. Before her business trip to London she had worked hard on the overall creative concept of the Kauffmans' good quality chocolate product, and left the roughed-out draft of ideas in Greg's office for him and Steve to complete. She had gone on her trip secure that the proposal would be prepared in the usual Stuyvesant Communications buttoned-up, perfect form—a proposal that stated the goals up front, and then dramatically relayed how the firm would reach those goals. It meant spelling out every step of the way and (with Anthony's fine hand here) the costs of taking "every step of the way," so that there would be no illusions as to how expensive it would be. But somehow the proposal had ended up substandard, sloppy, with out-of-focus artwork. PR was a business that was all about image and appearances, and this had cost them the account.

Marika thought of Mrs. Kauffman's pillow-puffy body as she waited for her to come on the line. Both the woman and her husband were overweight. She imagined Mr. and Mrs. Kauffman munching on their chocolates, their clothes fitting dangerously tight. "Hello, Mrs. Kauffman," she said, trying not to sound too disinterested.

"Mrs. Wentworth," the other voice whined into the telephone, "Luke and I are very sorry your company did not get our chocolate account."

"Not half as sorry as I am, Mrs. Kauffman."

"You were the only one of the eight companies who were unsuccessful in making a pitch for our account who wrote us a thank-you note. It was a beautiful letter, one which we did not expect to receive."

"I'm glad you liked it, Mrs. Kauffman." Marika, who always sent thank-you notes to everyone, even when they had rejected her, felt almost lulled to sleep at this point.

"That letter—so, so well bred—made Luke and me say to each other that we would like to give your company another chance. We would enjoy working with someone of your—your refinement."

Marika was now sitting upright in her chair. She could sleep later tonight.

"Are you talking about our making another pitch on the chocolate business, Mrs. Kauffman?"

Her voice with its slight Swiss accent was coy. "No, something even better. It's a secret new product. It's an introduction of an entire new line we're talking about, not a strengthening of an existing product. It's very exciting, but we cannot discuss it over the telephone. I'm sure you understand, Mrs. Wentworth. We are a very big corporation, and this kind of news must be kept very much between us."

"It will be, it will be, Mrs. Kauffman." Marika hoped the Swiss woman would not notice how changed her tone of voice was, now that she had picked up the scent of important new business just waiting to be dropped into someone's lap. Marika knew it was urgent to get a date firmed up to meet and discuss the new business.

"When would you like to see us?"

"We're going to Zurich for a couple of weeks. How would Tuesday the twelfth be? Here in our White Plains offices?"

Marika checked her mini-computer. "The twelfth would be fine. Early in the morning?" She wanted to be fresh and clear-headed, with a high energy level.

The voice whined its good-bye. "See you at 9 A.M. then. You already know where to come. We'll give you a nice cup of hot chocolate when you arrive. All you slim, stylish ladies never touch hot cocoa, but ours is something—very dee-licious." Marika could imagine her salivating on the other end of the telephone as she pictured a fragrant cup of cocoa in her own chubby hands.

Mrs. Kauffman, Marika said to herself, I will consume an entire liter of it, if that's what you would like me to do . . . I will drink cocoa with you until eternity.

Marika did not like to use the big conference room for informal meetings with her staff. She felt that it helped establish a formal, business-like atmosphere with clients by meeting in this room, but it was not the place to meet with her own staff. It was a twenty-yard stroll to Anthony's office from hers, where the senior staff meetings were held. Anthony had an endless supply of collapsible director's chairs stashed in his coat closet that could materialize in a second to accommodate any number of people who wanted to meet in his office. The fact that they were all of Yale blue canvas, with his alma mater's white crest and motto *"Lux et Veritas"* on the back, was fortuitous. They harmonized with the blue color scheme that ran throughout the offices.

Hortense had warned Marika that her quick ad hoc meetings were viewed with alarm by the staff, since they knew they had no choice but to attend, regardless of their other plans at that moment. Hortense said further that these quick meetings were referred to, rather untenderly, as "Marika's BA's" (meaning "bugler alarms"). Marika responded that she didn't care, as long as the initials weren't changed to something less attractive.

As usual, Marika knocked and entered Anthony Garrett's office at the same time. Her senior vice president was seated comfortably, leaning way back in his swivel chair, in his usual pinstripe suit, his feet in his well-polished black-tasseled loafers up on the desk. When Marika made her entrance, he took his feet off the desk and rose, giving her a mock salute. "You can save it, Anthony." Greg, dressed in one of his Glen plaid suits and brown suede shoes, sat in one of Anthony's black and chrome Marcel Breuer chairs. Sarah Fischer and Steve Lamton, were both lolling in their director's chairs, pushed back against the wall, balanced precariously on the chair legs. Marika noticed they were dressed in today's version of "slum attire"—battered khakis, T-shirts, and torn sweaters. Hortense sat upright in her chair, as she always did at every meeting, ostensibly to "take notes when necessary," but everyone knew she just could not bear to miss anything. She was dressed today in a black leotard with a black suede overskirt. She wore three large silver brooches, and somehow they looked like they belonged.

Marika noticed that Greg's foot was conspicuously tapping in a nervous tic gesture. He was cleaning a fingernail with an unfurled paperclip, as though the proceedings were of no interest to him whatsoever. For someone who had major stock in the company he was certainly in a negative mode. But he was good, and she depended on him. Marika watched Hortense's face blacken with distrust as she, too, became aware of Greg's tapping foot and fingernail-cleaning operation.

Marika decided to give it to her staff straight. "The bad news is that we cannot afford to mess up the way we have been doing recently. Our cash flow is not healthy. It's ailing. We had a fair chance on two new business proposals while I was away, but we lost these two golden opportunities to other agencies that are no better than ours. That's what hurts. If this keeps up, we're going to have to take a hit in our staff and expenses very soon. We're down in billings and up in expenses. It's sloppy! I can't understand what's going on around here. If someone knows why this is happening, will he or she speak up?"

The staff had felt the sting from her words. The boss wasn't fooling around today. Anthony spoke first. "We have been—you used the word, Marika—sloppy. I think each one of us has let you down. I feel personally responsible, and I can tell you right now, Marika Wentworth, I'm going to do a hell of a lot better. I won't let a proposal go out of this office like that ever again."

Steve interrupted. "I feel I should take the blame, Marika. I was, after all, the last one in the office who saw the proposals before they went out, because I checked the artwork and design. I should have realized they weren't right. I'm beginning to feel very responsible."

"You can't take all the blame," interrupted Sarah. "I was with you when we packed up all the material. I didn't read the final draft. I just didn't bother. It's my fault, too."

"I did the final word processing on both projects," Hortense said grimly. "I've been in this office since the beginning. I can recognize a half-baked presentation as well as anyone in this business. I should have studied it, read it, and brought it to Anthony's attention. It's my fault, too."

Marika looked over at Greg. It was his turn to speak. Instead, he looked out the window, detached from this conversation. Everyone in the room was now aware of his silence, but he did not react. Steve looked particularly dejected, rubbing a nonexistent spot on the rug with his sneaker toe and nervously stroking his mustache, which presently was handlebar-shaped.

"My feeling," Marika said solemnly, "is that we all should take the blame. We're a team, for God's sake, and we just haven't been pulling together like we used to. And that means you, too, Greg. You had the overall creative responsibility."

"Now just a minute, Marika." Greg spoke harshly after his self-imposed silence. "Don't pass this one to *me*. You were away, and you gave me five other projects to marshal through. Don't lay this one on me." He looked directly at Steve.

Marika ignored his outburst. "You're all such talented people! And I've always been so proud of your professionalism—your individual pursuit of perfectionism. What has happened to this team?"

There was only silence. She spoke again. "It was not my fault that I was out of town when those two proposals were drawn up and sent out. And yet I should have arranged to have them faxed to me in London. I should have seen them before they went. We have all done a lousy job of coordinating our efforts lately."

There was a sense of shame in the room. Marika could tell by looking around the room that they agreed with her.

Anthony spoke first. "We needed that blast, Marika, and I hope I speak for everyone here when I say that we will shape up and not let something like this happen again." Then he smiled and lowered his voice. "You said, Marika, that there was bad news first. We've had that given to us, it seems. Now is there really any good news to relate?" He had begun sucking on his empty pipe, a familiar habit when he was feeling ill at ease.

"Our Swiss chocolate friends called me this morning." There was a look of surprise on the others' faces.

"Have they decided after all not to pick Hill and Knowlton to handle their account?" Sarah was all smiles at the prospect.

"No, and Hill and Knowlton will do an excellent job for them. But they are going to give us another chance."

"How come?"

"Because I sat down and wrote a little letter, a simple little letter."

"Go on, go on, please explain." Anthony was becoming impatient, and had absentmindedly begun to light his filled pipe, something Marika had made him promise not to do in the office. She reached over and took the lighter from his hand.

"Mathilde Kauffman has a very important new product—or line of products, still a deep secret. She might let us have the account." She could see the others in the room making eye contact with one another at this news. A new product launch backed by big dollars was every marketer's dream.

"I still would like to know what happened," said Steve, "just why she came back to us."

"I'll tell you why," answered Marika. "Because when we got the letter saying Hill and Knowlton had won, I wrote her my usual thank-you note for having allowed us to make a pitch. It impressed both of them."

"Good God." Steve's voice sounded disbelieving, or was it sounding weak? Marika had noticed he was looking a little down. Also, he had not been up to snuff lately in his work, as though he were fighting problems of his own. She realized that somehow he had been off his peak working condition for some weeks now. She had always considered Steve a dandy, even if he never wore a suit. But lately—even the slum-attire clothes were worn with an attitude of not caring as much anymore.

As the meeting broke up, Marika lingered in the hall and softly asked Steve to come into her office. She shut the door and sat on the edge of her desk. "Steve, something is wrong, and I feel it is physical. You don't look well, and you don't seem to have your usual energy."

"I haven't been feeling too great." He looked down at his feet and traced over a part of the design of the blue and white Chinese rug with his toe.

"Will you make an appointment immediately for a complete physical? Call Dr. Postman and make it your annual company physical."

"If you think it would do any good."

"I want you to do it right away."

"Okay. I'll do it. And—Marika . . ." He had started out the door, but he hesitated.

"Yes, Steve."

"I feel awful about the new business. I feel God awful about letting you down."

"It was a joint snafu. I wish some of the others had felt as bad about it as you."

"Did you mean what you said, about the possibility of there being a hit in the staff?"

"Yes."

"I feel I should be one of the first to go."

"You'll be one of the last to go. You're my creative muse, after all. Just what would I do without you? You make all those ideas I'm supposed to have originated flow forth. Half the time I think they're your ideas and not even mine."

"No, they're *yours*," Steve said in obvious admiration. "You can give all the credit you want to everyone else, but the real idea person around here is *you*, and you know it damned well."

She put her arm around his shoulder and walked with him to the elevator. Then, realizing she had forgotten her briefcase, she told him good-bye and dashed back into her office. She was already late for her evening appointment.

Hortense looked up and queried Marika as she rushed back into her office.

"What did you think of that performance in there tonight?"

"Whose performance, Hortense? Mine? Was I too tough?"

"Did you notice Greg welch out of taking any blame?"

"I noticed."

"When you left for Europe, you put the early draft on the Kauffman matter and also on the savings bank on his desk for action. Yet he took no responsibility whatsoever for what happened."

"I'm aware of that."

"He's working against us, Boss. Not only that . . ." and she stopped speaking because Marika, obviously late, was impatient to leave.

"Go on, go on," said Marika, her curiosity now raised to the point where she did not want to leave without hearing Hortense's last comments.

"I hear via the grapevine that Greg is looking for better opportunities elsewhere. He obviously thinks it should be he and not Anthony who's your heir apparent. And that's not all."

"Oh, for heaven's sake, Hortense!" Marika's voice was edged with impatience and disbelief.

"I also hear via my very authoritative grapevine that Greg is taking kickbacks from our press kit materials suppliers."

"Hortense, you have been reading too many detective stories lately. You don't trust anyone anymore!" And with those words, the elevator doors closed on Marika. She could not be one second later for her literacy volunteer meeting. Besides, Hortense was making no sense. No sense at all.

Ten minutes later Hortense heard the unwelcome sound of Sand's voice on the telephone. Those two women shared one thing in common—a mutual dislike for one another. When Sand learned Marika was not there, she announced brusquely that she needed some information on a "cocktail *dansant*" one of Marika's closest friends was giving that evening. When Hortense explained that Marika had left to do her volunteer job, Sand sounded irritated and incredulous.

"Isn't Natasha Vanderlippe one of her intimate friends?"

"Mrs. Wentworth never accepts engagements on Tuesday and Thursday nights," Hortense said with the solemnity of a judge handing down a decision. "All of her friends know and accept this fact. She takes her volunteer work in teaching reading with great seriousness. She feels that people who are successful in their businesses are supposed to give back to their communities." Hortense, having finished her speech, drew a deep breath.

"Well, I had hoped for some news of the Vanderlippe party," said Sand, obviously disappointed.

"So that you wouldn't have to attend the party yourself?" asked Hortense with a malicious tone.

"Perhaps you can help, Hortense dear. Do you know if she's been in touch with the White House?" Sand spoke in a warmer, more cajoling voice.

"Oh," replied Hortense with an air of boredom, "if you want comments on that from Mrs. Wentworth, you might have to wait a long time."

"Like how long?" pressed Sand.

"Like forever, Ms. Sand," replied Hortense.

"Don't call me 'Ms. Sand.' My name is *Sand.*"

"Sorry, Sand"—Hortense waited a beat—"*dear.*"

The gossip columnist slammed down the receiver in Hortense's ear.

Marika was tired; it had been a draining day. The walk from her office to the bank, where the Literacy Volunteers of New York held their classes, required a special effort tonight. Normally, she made the trip with exuberance, rejoicing in the pull of the muscles and the feeling of well-being that went along with the rhythmic strides of her long legs.

She suddenly remembered she was still wearing the jeweled fish on her lapel. She would certainly not appear wearing a piece of flashy jewelry at a literacy class—even if no one there knew the significance of a Jean Schlumberger design, and even if no one there would know it was real. She stepped into the dark doorway of a small building, turned her back to the street, quickly undid the safety clasp on the brooch, and then slipped it into an inside zippered pocket of her handbag.

Some of the teachers and students were already there. She knew them all, and everyone greeted each other cheerfully with broad smiles and first names. Soon others began to wander into the donated space of the bank's cafeteria. Groups of two and three began to form at the tables, the tops of which were now covered with notebooks and books. There was an air of camaraderie in the room. The students were all there for a very serious purpose—to learn how to read and write, something that they missed in their lives that had become unacceptable and unbearable.

The supervisor, Grace Forman, walked over to Marika, shook her hand warmly, and said, "You did such a good job with Alonzo, we're giving you another young man who's coming tonight for the very first time. The tall one over there, hanging up his jacket on the rack."

"Happy to have a new pupil. What's his name?"

"Bill Carver. Comes from Kentucky hillbilly country and he

just never got the printed or written word in school. He's a janitor now of a building in Queens, but he's afraid he'll lose his job because he can't read the instructions the owner hands him every now and then."

"Is that the only reason he wants to learn?"

"That's for you to find out. He's married and has a little girl in second grade."

He was coming toward them, smiling at Miss Forman, the one person he knew in this room. When he shook hands with Marika, she felt the sweat and nervousness of his body transmitted right through the damp palm of his hand. He was obviously a nervous wreck from having to face this ordeal tonight.

"Sit down, Bill," she said matter-of-factly.

He first tried to help her with her chair as she sat down.

"You don't have to do that, Bill," she said kindly. "Not here."

"Oh," he said, his face crimson now. "My wife told me—she told me that I—well, she said I should act kinda well-mannered here."

"I can tell you're *very* mannerly, so just relax. I would like to hear about you. I'm going to ask you some questions, and let's just have an informal talk—all right?"

She asked him where he lived and questioned him about his family and job, taking notes of every answer. Sitting across from him, she could not help but notice his earthy attractiveness and superb build—that of a natural athlete. He had a wonderful head of dark brown hair. His eyes were big, brown, and bright as Christmas tree bulbs, and when he smiled, there was a flash of pure white. He was terribly handsome—but he did not know how to read and write.

She felt she should stop admiring his looks and get into his motivation for coming to this class.

"Why does it mean so much for you to learn how to read, Bill?"

"Because I feel dumb. I can't get no good jobs. I don't even know what the traffic signs say." He looked utterly dejected.

"That's a very important reason to learn how to read," she said, reinforcing him. "Anything else?"

"My little girl is learning how to read in school. She's been asking me for lotsa years to read to her at night. I give her lotsa excuses. 'Get your mama to do it,' I say. She don't know that her mama can read but that I can't. But now . . ." He suddenly stopped and looked down at his hands clasped nervously on the table.

"Go on, Bill, but now what?"

"She said to me last week that she was goin' to read to *me* now. She got me to sit by her on the bed, and she had a little book and she started to read some words from it. It almost done kill me. My baby readin' to her daddy, because her daddy couldn't read to her. It almost done kill me." He stopped because the tears were coming down his cheeks unabashedly. Marika put her hand on top of his for comfort, but he looked at her strangely. She withdrew her hand immediately, because she knew she had upset him with an overly familiar gesture. She chided herself for reaching out her hand so instinctively, so naturally, to anyone in need of sympathy and support.

"You know something, Bill? You're going to learn how to read. You're going to learn because you have the most important prerequisite." She stopped herself, because she knew he might not know what that long word meant, but then again, he could probably sense it, because she could tell he was intelligent. "You know why you want to learn how to read. You have good reasons for going through all of this hard work ahead. You're going to make it."

"Yes, ma'am." He was smiling. "Can we start now—I mean tonight? Or is this just a meetin' or a folks-get-acquainted time?"

"No, we start right now." She gave him a notebook, took an alphabet magnetic board and letters from her briefcase, and they began.

CHAPTER

3

here was a surprise awaiting Marika when she reached home by taxi at eight-fifteen, to have dinner and a chat with Lisa. The subject was to have been Sergio, of course, and the surprise was the presence of Sergio himself. "I knew you wouldn't mind a guest for dinner, Mom."

"Of course not. I'm delighted."

Sergio kissed her hand in a practiced fashion. "Signora Wentworth, this is a great pleasure." His voice was slightly husky, aristocratically accented in Italian. He was undeniably handsome, with gray eyes encompassed by the longest eyelashes she had ever seen on a man. And something else, he was obviously intent on sleeping with her daughter. The way he stood protectively next to her now told Marika this. She couldn't help wondering if she could have nipped this hot romance in the bud if she had pulled in Lisa's reins sooner, or at least been around to talk it over.

Lisa had not brought Sergio home in the two months they had been dating but over the months, Lisa had told her bits and pieces about him.

Sergio, his brothers, and his sister had been raised on Alfa Romeos, skiing vacations in Cortina d'Ampezzo, summers on an estate in Portofino (with Magnum Marine power boats to take them to and from races with the Aga Khan in Sardinia), and a complete lack of understanding of the work ethic. Sergio had never held a job and he was taking an inordinately long time to complete his graduate work at Columbia.

Marika knew about these attractive young English and European titled visitors—"Eurotrash," the press had dubbed them. Sergio was one of them, the kind who looked great in a dinner jacket. Tonight he wore a beautifully tailored black Italian number with a white silk dress shirt, jeans, and brown loafers. Such a young man wouldn't have to worry about paying his own way. If his family fortune was not at his disposal, he could always inveigle anything he needed from American friends—and that included meals, theater tickets, taxis, even a young woman's bed, if he needed it.

As the three went into the dining room, Marika thought quickly about what she and Lisa had discussed before on the subject of safe sex. *"Urgent Action/Lisa/Sergio"* her mini-computer had reminded her this afternoon. Lisa's laughable threat of suicide over the breakup with Sergio seemed a mild emotion compared with the sensual atmosphere threatening to explode right here in the dining room. Now *that* was urgent!

Before leaving that evening, Geneviève had left in the kitchen a heaping bowl of *pasta al pesto*, slices of rare roast beef, and a mixed green salad for their supper. Lisa made some rye toast and the three sat at the mahogany dining table, eating, talking, and watching the barges go by on the East River. The young couple looked unbearably handsome in the candlelight, Marika thought. She pressed Sergio to talk. Perhaps she was overreacting to his good looks. Would David have found his sensuality as threatening as she did?

She asked Sergio about his studies, his family, his length of time in the States. He answered politely but briefly, because he was much too engrossed in Lisa. Once in a while he would lean over to feed her morsels of food from his fork, as though it were an expected, intimate habit of theirs at the table.

"What brought you to New York?" Marika asked, then realized she had already asked the question and had received the answer "I was destined to find your daughter," in reply.

Oh, David, Marika thought for the third time since the meal began, I need you. Tell me what to do.

Sergio leaned over Lisa and, disregarding his own wineglass, drank from hers, making sure, Marika noted, to drink from the same spot her lips had touched. That was too much. Marika put a hand over her mouth, afraid she would laugh. He was suddenly just a young boy pretending to be an Italian lover, and was no more sure of himself than Lisa. Beneath his facade, he was also vulnerable and maybe a little scared in the big city, far away from home. Marika breathed a sigh of relief. *Thank you, David,* she whispered in her heart.

After that, the evening sped by fairly painlessly. As the two youngsters, which was now how Marika plainly saw them, bid each other a lingering good night, Marika stayed in the living room pretending to read a magazine, while she thought over how to handle Lisa and Sergio. The boy was vulnerable, but he was still definitely not husband material for Lisa—not that Marika's opinion would count for much. She would simply have to spend more time with her daughter, guiding and helping her make better decisions about her relationships with men. The threat of the sexual tension between them was a worry, but so, too, was their new habit of going to nightclubs that threatened Lisa's health and studies. Getting Lisa to "think school" with Sergio around was going to be an arduous task. Marika flipped a page of her magazine. I should have had sons, she thought to herself. But then she thought about the young man who had made such a spectacle of himself tonight and realized his parents obviously had their hands full, too.

"He is so divine, I don't know whether I'm coming or going," Lisa sighed as she flopped down on the couch next to her mother.

"That I could tell."

"Well, how did you like him?"

"He's uh—very attractive."

"We're in love."

"You can't be, you're a freshman in college. Infatuated yes, but don't call it love. Besides, this morning you told me it was 'all over,' which I must admit, made me very happy."

"I'm a grown woman!" Lisa's voice was angry and determined.

"You're eighteen, on the threshold of a college degree, and Sergio is—well, he's not a particularly serious person."

"Mom—'serious'? What do you want him to be? A judge with a long beard? A scientist with a test tube stuck on the end of his nose? A Wall Street M&A crook? A lawyer hunched over permanently from carrying too many law books?"

Her mother was laughing in spite of herself. Then she grew serious.

"I've been noticing how much of your life he has been absorbing in the last two months. You are spending more and more time with him, and I never seem to know where you are. It really concerns me, Lisa."

Her daughter did not answer, only studied her fingernails.

"I hope you're not having sex," her mother continued.

"Cripes, Mom, you're not serious!"

"I'm very serious. Someone of Sergio's sophistication—well, not really sophistication, but rather, experience from playing around all his life—you're just not in his league."

"Women are much more mature than men."

"Lisa, *you* have yet to show me these great signs of maturity."

"Mom, don't worry, okay?"

"I do worry, okay?" she answered, mimicking her daughter's words and tone of voice. "I have to be your mother and your father, too, Lisa."

"If Daddy were alive, we wouldn't be having this conversation. He would know better."

"What would he know? That you *are* or are not sleeping with Sergio?"

"Well, he'd know that we haven't yet, but that Sergio wants to very much, and so do I, so it's—it's . . ."

Marika waited for her daughter to continue.

"Inevitable," was the final word.

"If you have held out this long, which I think is wonderful, Lisa, can't you do it for a longer time?"

"If Daddy were here with us, he'd be more understanding—of Sergio's impatience."

"I don't think so. I know he'd think of you first, Lisa, Sergio, and his macho desires long afterward."

"Oh, Mom, don't call it 'macho desires,' whatever you do. You know what my friends would say about this whole conversation, if they were here? They'd say the whole thing sucks."

"Well, I'm glad they're not here, then."

"I talk differently around them. That's hypocritical, isn't it?"

"No, it means that you're all being immature, even infantile, when you talk like that with each other, and that when you talk with your mothers, you become more mature."

"Mom, exactly what are you asking of me, other than to refrain from using words like *suck* around you?"

"That you hold off on sex with Sergio or anyone else until you're older."

"And if I can't?"

"That you make Sergio use condoms, and that you do everything in your power not to contract a sexually transmitted disease. I'm scared to death for you."

"Okay, I promise."

"Promise what?"

"To adhere to your first request, and if I can't, to adhere to the latter."

Marika put her arm around her daughter's slim shoulders and gave her a hug as they walked upstairs from the living room. "If David Wentworth were alive today, he would be very proud of his daughter."

"Maybe of his wife, too," Lisa added, turning to give her mother a high five with her hand. The discussion was finished, and Marika went straight to her room, in the direction of a bottle of Tylenol. She could feel one large headache coming on.

The shuttle trip from La Guardia to National Airport in Washington seemed to go faster than usual. Marika tried to peruse the contents of her briefcase, but she couldn't help worrying about the Watsons. She was used to nocturnal telephone calls from the White House, but never so late as the last one. And Eve had sounded so strained and depressed.

She was glad they would have lunch together quietly. A White House secret serviceman had called to check out the name and address of the new little restaurant where she would take Eve. She had begged the agent to keep the news away from the restaurant owner that her guest was going to be the President's wife. "Sorry, ma'am," was his answer. "There's no way the owner won't know it's someone from the White House when we arrive to check it out the day before your lunch."

Hortense had thought of a solution. She had called up the restaurant owner and told him that if he breathed one word of the First Lady's visit before Mrs. Watson had left the premises, she, Hortense, would personally see to it that every media restaurant critic heard what a terrible place the restaurant was.

Lunching away from the White House was important to Evangeline Watson. It gave her a taste of freedom and normalcy, a brief escape from the constant public scrutiny she endured in her home. And this lunch with Marika provided a reunion of two very close friends from childhood, each of whom was riding a very different, although rapid train to success through life.

Marika was not even tempted today on the shuttle to eavesdrop on the earnest conversations around her. She usually did, and as a result had picked up some very interesting scoops on this gossip-riddled plane—such as which Washington senator was sleeping with which Washington hostess, what major company was in trouble with the SEC on its recent merger, and which lobbyist was about to have the whistle blown on him or her because of undue influence on a congressman. She had once told Sand that if she were to ride the early morning shuttle to and from Washington weekly she'd have enough for her gossip columns for the month.

It was only a short walk from the Hay Adams Hotel to the North Portico of the White House. Marika confounded the White House police each time she arrived on foot at the entrance, even though she was expected by the Chief Usher's Office, and was properly credentialed for that gate. People coming to visit the

President's family always arrived by limousine—never on foot. And, unless they were heads of state, never at the North Portico of the main house. But when Eve had become First Lady, she had asked security to bend the rules for Marika. The thought of her dearest friend restrained by security made Eve feel trapped. Now Marika was permitted to walk from her hotel to the closest gate and enter through there.

It always gave her a star-spangled jolt to pass through the portals, past the little guardhouse, and up the curving driveway to the majestic North Portico. It was her habit at this point to glance over in the direction of the West Wing, where there would often be a TV news crew standing in the driveway, interviewing some exalted personage who had just seen the President.

Even if most New Yorkers suffered from an acute case of *blasé-faire*, Marika considered Washington a very exciting city. She explained to Eve once "that in Manhattan we're accustomed to our mayor showing up everywhere in his shirtsleeves like a jack-in-the-box, or our Broadway stars rushing to media interviews to promote their shows, or Hollywood personalities hawking their fragrances wherever they can get a crowd and a perfume counter to stand behind." Celebrities being interviewed in front of the West Wing of the White House were quite a different matter. For them, Marika would halt and stare—a little—even if she didn't know who they were. Her nostrils could sense an aroma of importance, of real substance in the air. In New York, the aroma was usually one of puff pastry baking in someone's hot air!

The Chief Usher, having been signaled by the North Gate policeman, was waiting for her at the door. The two made their way to the small, hidden, private elevator behind the Usher's Office, slipping by a crowd of tourists in the great marble hall who were finishing their tour of the public rooms of the house. The cleaning people stood by, patiently waiting with their equipment, ready to rush to work the minute the last group could be hurried out at the noon hour, when the mansion returned to a modicum of peace and decorum. There was to be a state dinner tonight for the President of France, which meant that at noon, the household staff assumed battle positions in a coordinated rush to clean house and move into the State Dining Room thirteen round tables of ten with little gold ballroom chairs—so that the butler could then supervise his staff's arrangement of 130 place settings for the guests who would dine there that night. Marika laughed to herself, thinking of the logistical nightmare tonight's place settings would bring. For the President of France, many crystal goblets would be needed—white and red wineglasses, champagne and water glasses. Four times 130 guests equals 520 glasses to be set on the tables!

She was accustomed to riding in the little presidential elevator, probably the world's most prestigious one, which carries only the family, heads of state, and top VIP's to and from the private quarters on the upper floors. She entered it now.

After she'd graduated from Vassar and opened her small public relations company, Marika and David Wentworth were married. Eve's and Mac Watson's wedding followed soon after, and they rented a house a couple of blocks away from the Wentworths' in Boston. David and Marika worked almost full time on Mac's successful campaigns for lieutenant governor of Massachusetts and then United States senator.

They were friends in the good times as well as the bad. The first telephone call Marika made after the policemen left her house the night of David's fatal accident was to Charlie Russell, her father. The second was to Eve and Mac, who raced up to Boston to be with her. Congress was in session, but Mac knew his and his wife's place was at the side of their friend, to help her get through what would have to be the worst time in her life.

The Watsons stayed with her in the house for three days. They simply took over—notifying family members, coping with David's aged parents, giving special attention to Lisa and Charlie Russell, supervising the telephone calls in and out of the house, listing all of the flowers and sympathy cards that flowed into the house during the day, getting the meals organized, dealing with the minister and the funeral director, notifying the family lawyers, and arranging to have all out-of-town relatives and close friends picked up at the airport and delivered to the funeral in time. Eve even managed to organize a memorable *fruits de mer* lunch after the funeral services at Trinity Church and the burial. One Boston matron, holding her dessert plate of *profiterôles au chocolat* in one hand, and her glass of excellent port in the other, remarked that "There's something wonderful about going out in style and leaving behind good friends who are enjoying themselves so much in your memory!"

In Marika's memories of that sad time, her father and the Watsons were the supports that propped her up through the entire trauma of David's death. She and her daughter had been uncomprehending, anesthetized by what had happened.

When Mac Watson ran for President a year later, Marika and her now New York-based firm entered the New York political battleground. It was good therapy for Marika to become involved again in the fray. Even though she did not wear white gloves, except to weddings, to the campaign staff she became known as "White Gloves," almost a code name. When she complained about this "discriminatory and unflattering nickname," one of the political organization men she most disliked told her to "get off yah high horse. Ya' look like Grace Kelly, ya' get treated like Grace Kelly." She stopped complaining.

When Mac won the presidency, he offered Marika her choice of two important, highly visible jobs, but she declined them. It was not the time to leave her company; she did not wish to suffer the income differential loss of two hundred thousand dollars a year; and most important of all, Lisa was happy and had close friends at her Chapin school in New York.

The rise of Evangeline Watson to an exalted position in the land did not change the closeness of the two women. Every time Marika was invited to a state dinner or any important White House function, she made extra time to see Eve privately. Marika had noticed that Eve was beginning to show evidence in public of the physical strain of her job. The smile was not as natural and enthusiastic as it had once been. She didn't walk down the White House corridors with the usual energy and spring to her step. The stuffiness of the White House was obviously beginning to get to her.

As she made the trip up in the private elevator to the second-floor family quarters, Marika couldn't help remembering what fun the two women had had in planning the *Salon de Beauté Présidentiel* where both Eve and the President would be coiffed by their respective hairdressers. Mrs. John F. Kennedy had had a room fixed up as a hair salon near the Oval Room, facing the South Lawn, when she was in the White House. Subsequent First Ladies took it out, put it back in, took it out, and put it elsewhere. When Mac said, "I'll be damned if I let any of the voters know I use a bloody unisex hair salon," Eve soothed him and told him it would be much better if he had his hair cut and styled away from the White House barbershop—away from prying eyes and whispering rumors of hair loss or hair dye.

Marika managed to sneak her favorite architect into the White House one day. There the Chief Usher showed him around and went over the plans of the mansion with him. He managed to take one of the old beauty salons and make it perfect for the Watsons. To make Mac comfortable in the room, they mirrored one wall, and covered the others in a Yale blue linen, with white ceiling and moldings and white rough-textured linen draperies. The carpeting was a houndstooth check in royal blue and white; a pair of white enamel basins and hair driers were installed.

Marika had robes made for Eve and Mac—royal blue, with their respective initials embroidered in white on the pockets. "I'll be damned if I ever wear this pansy thing," sputtered Mac, but, of course, by the second time he used the *Salon de Beauté*, he was happily wearing his robe. The Watsons concluded, rightly or wrongly, that by referring to it as the *Salon de Beauté*, no one would know what they were talking about, and Mac wouldn't be embarrassed by the existence of the room in the family quarters.

On the second floor, a footman stood at attention as Marika passed by. She nodded a greeting and found the First Lady in the sunny yellow and coral Oval Room, the main family sitting room, with its sweeping vista down to the Potomac, the Washington Monument, and the Jefferson Memorial. The lemon-yellow curving walls and the white ceilings and moldings made this majestic room, as Eve once described it, "a precious space." When the light shone through the glass doors that led onto the balcony, it also illuminated the pale yellow tapestry carpet with its field of spring flowers, the French armchairs covered in green and yellow silks, and the sofa and easy chairs abloom in an apricot and green floral chintz.

Marika found Eve rearranging a group of two dozen or so family photographs on a large round table covered to the floor with a fringed apricot velvet cloth. A maid stood next to her, watching her intently. Each photograph was encased in a handsome sterling silver frame—all of different sizes and textures—basketweave, ribbed, stain-finish, some monogrammed, others engraved with the presidential seal. Eve gave Marika a big hug, and then her guest waited silently until Eve had finished angling the photographs in the exact way she wished them. Marika noticed that Eve was thinner than the last time she had seen her, a month ago. Her famous, photogenic, shoulder-length ash-blond hair was held back by a cocoa-brown velvet ribbon. She looked so young that way, but her eyes told a different story. There were charcoal gray shadows around them. Tired eyes.

"Lucia," Eve was now addressing the little woman by her side, "this is the way I want the frames lined up on this table—*siempre. Entiende?*"

"*Sí*, Señora Watson."

"Dusted every day, polished every three days, but always put back in this order, *entiende?*"

Lucia nodded, was dismissed, and slipped out of the room.

"Thank God there are *some* emoluments with this job of mine," Eve said. "The silver gets polished. For the first time in our marriage, the silver gets polished. Constantly."

"Is that the main advantage to being the First Lady of the Land?" Marika queried, laughing.

"Just about."

"How you have time for me," Marika said, "when you have a state dinner tonight for the French President, is more than I can possibly understand."

"Tonight's dinner is courtesy of the White House staff," Eve replied, "I've had little to do with it because Madame Guerin didn't make this trip—just his teenaged daughter. This means I'm off the hook during the daytime. I do, however, have a surprise tonight for the daughter."

Marika inspected Eve's suit—a warm beige wool crepe with a coffee-colored silk blouse. "You look so slim and chic."

Eve grinned. "You're sweet to say so. Oh, Marika, it's so good to see you!" She gave her friend another hug. Then she took a large silk scarf and tied it into a turban, completely covering her recognizable hair. She added a pair of large, dark sunglasses and an old raincoat. She was suddenly no longer the First Lady, she looked like Mrs. Anybody.

They descended in the elevator to the ground floor, and walked quickly through the Diplomatic Entrance and out to her car, with its ever-present shadow containing more agents behind it. None of the people passing through the White House ground floor corridor had looked at them. Only the White House policemen, who knew her disguises, had given Eve an inconspicuous salute. In a matter of seconds, they had left the White House behind and were headed for the little restaurant in Georgetown. Marika laughingly told Eve of her assistant's ploy to keep the press away.

The owners greeted them quietly. The Secret Service had thoroughly checked their premises that morning. Two of the agents, looking like young executives about to have a business lunch, came into the restaurant and sat down at a discreet distance.

"I don't have one cent with me," Eve laughed. "I hope you can pay for this lunch."

"Don't I *always* pick up the check? You and the Queen of England never carry any money."

"Listen, don't complain. You're getting a four-course dinner tonight at my house—free."

They both laughed, and Marika acknowledged that she would buy Eve lunch any day in return for a state dinner.

"This is such a surrealistic job. You lose track of all normal things, like shopping in a store, and paying with a credit card, tipping people, and going to the hairdresser like anyone else. All of a sudden, you have no freedom. People are always peering at you, trying to touch you. The agents never leave my side for one minute. I can't even go to the john anymore in peace." She looked over at the two secret servicemen who were trying to look non-chalant, their eyes like flashlight beams constantly searching the room, paying particular attention to the windows and doorways. They were also watching the occupants of the one other occupied table.

"I've heard you complain before, Eve, but never this much. Is something getting to you? Those agents, after all, have a big job protecting you and your husband. Don't take it out on them, for pete's sake."

"I know, I know. They're the greatest guys in the world. It's this—this life we lead. We have no private time anymore—ever. Mac has the affairs of state to occupy him. They almost anesthetize him; his worries are deep, constant ones, and when he gets back to the family quarters at night, he just falls into bed, wiped out. I, on the other hand, get pushed around by everyone on my staff, Mac's staff, even the chef's staff in the kitchen. All I do is keep changing my clothes, smiling, doing works of mercy, and muttering 'SHIT' behind closed teeth—oh, here I am complaining again!" Mac doesn't have time to listen anymore. It's no longer —a partnership. Until now I've never missed not having any children. Our marriage was complete without them. Mac was always so full of fun, so in love with me, so fascinating a person —he occupied all my time and my thoughts. I ran just to keep up with him. But now, we seem to be running in opposite directions. We share nothing anymore. He has his own schedule all day, late into the evening, and that's that." Eve spoke so softly, Marika could hardly hear her.

"Eve," Marika whispered in return, "I had no idea you were going through all this. Why didn't you tell me sooner? I have never seen you this depressed—and here you are, the number-one woman in our country, the envy of women everywhere."

"I've been pushing away how I feel. I can't even have conversations with our dogs anymore, because someone on the staff would surely hear me." They both laughed at this, because all her close friends knew that whenever she and Mac had a fight, Eve would slam the bedroom door and talk to her two Jack Russell terriers. They always took her side and not Mac's, she claimed.

"I never wanted the presidency for us. It was Mac who wanted it. What I need is for my husband to understand how really tough life is for me within the confines of 1600 Pennsylvania Avenue—the house that's *certainly* not a home. He ought to realize that this job is of his making, not mine. I deserve at least a crumb every now and then from his table. Is that asking too much?"

"No, but there's another person to whom you should be telling all this right now—and his name is Mac."

"Ha! We won't be alone for months to come, and he has more important things on his mind, I assure you."

"Nothing is more important to him than you. When did you last talk to him about how you feel about things?"

"I never talk to him about it."

"That's your fault, not his. Do it the minute you get back to the White House this afternoon."

"The President of France is here, remember?"

"Isn't Mac lunching with the French President right this minute?"

Eve consulted her watch. "In fifteen minutes."

"Then as your ad hoc chief of staff, I am going to make an appointment for you with the President through proper channels so that you two can have some unfettered time together—the minute he ushers *Monsieur le Président* out the door."

She laughed. "You're nuts, Marika. You were crazy in college, but the condition has worsened."

Marika excused herself from the table, went over to talk to one of the secret servicemen, then went out to talk to another agent who was standing outside the car. She got into the front seat, and with the agent working the White House radio, she got through on a secure line to Nathan Stoughton, the Appointments Secretary, whom she knew well from past Massachusetts campaigns. After speaking a few minutes with him in a kind of code that they had used before—and which no one understood except the two of them—Marika thanked him and went back into the restaurant.

"Eve, let's order right away. We must have you back at the White House by two-fifteen sharp."

"For what?"

"The President's schedule is empty between two-fifteen and three-thirty, and he wants to spend that time with you *alone*— discussing the horticultural improvements of the Rose Garden."

"You're mad, Marika!" Eve was grinning now unabashedly. "It won't accomplish anything, but I love you for what you just did. You have just arranged for me to share the first waking hour I've had with Mac in two months."

"Don't you have some time together at Camp David on weekends?"

"That's even worse. He gets up and jogs at 6 A.M., and I see him only at meals when we are joined by anywhere from four to eight staff members or cabinet officers. He gets to bed even later at Camp David."

"Sounds absolutely fascinating to me," Marika said lamely.

"It's hell," and that was the end of that. They each ordered a Virgin Mary and an endive, arugula, and bacon salad. The owner put down in the center of the table a basket of miniature, freshly baked biscuits and sticky cinnamon buns, and a mother-of-pearl shell dish packed with sweet butter. They ate quickly and hungrily, including the complimentary mango sherbet the owner presented to them for dessert. They talked of their mutual Boston friends and the latest gossip tidbits from New York and Boston that Marika always saved for Eve.

As Marika paid the check, Eve said, "Do you realize how much I need that ear of yours, what good therapy you are?"

"And how about all the glamour and excitement you let me in on by having me at the White House all the time?"

"You always add to any group. You always give. I know that tonight, for example, there will be at least one table in the State Dining Room where everyone will be having a great time—your table. You're always responsible for that."

"That's a nice compliment, Eve."

"And I have sort of a surprise for you tonight. After what you did for me this noon, you really deserve it."

"What? Am I allowed to sing the "Marseillaise" before the soup course?"

She laughed. "No, I'm not going to be blamed for a rupture in Franco-American relations. I have a real man for you tonight. For once you're not going to be sitting next to a non-English-speaking official bore."

"My God, a single, eligible man who speaks English?"

"His name is Jonathon Scher, and I, for one, think he's very attractive. He's what I guess you'd describe as a *very successful* Jewish businessman, forty-two years old, recently divorced after ten years of marriage to an awful woman whom everyone hated. He's CEO of a group of venture capital companies. Lives in Chicago but flies around everywhere. He's been a big party contributor, too."

Marika laughed at the very quick bullets of information Eve was giving her about one of her dinner partners tonight. "What if I like the man on my other side better?"

"Jonathon has a great sense of humor. Need I say anything further?"

"No, I'm sure he will be pleasant company."

"You'll see that Jonathon is a pretty warm, sexy guy. I warn you, now that he is divorced, every woman in his circle is after him."

"Eve, I don't need a man all that much, you know. I'm not desperate."

"The heck you're not! Aha, we're being a little on the defensive, aren't we?"

They both laughed, locked arms, and thanked the restaurant owner, who stood wringing his hands with emotion and gratitude. The future of his new restaurant was now assured. The discreet motor cavalcade took off in the direction of the White House, stopping to drop Marika at an office building on Connecticut Avenue where she had an appointment with a client. Marika watched as the First Lady's car proceeded with its Secret Service escort car toward the White House. She was confident the President of the United States stood waiting at that very moment in his office for his wife—wondering why this mysterious appointment and just what was on her inscrutable mind.

CHAPTER

4

On a party night the White House always seems to cast an extra glow on the horizon, like a brilliantly lit, freshly painted Acropolis. There was the smell of Christmas to come in the crisp early December air, and Marika remembered that in another week the mansion would be transformed into a Christmas wonderland with decorations inside and out. The stream of cars discharging passengers at the East Gate had begun well before the party hour of eight o'clock. Like one's own wedding, one is not supposed to arrive late at a White House dinner. Even film and rock stars, famous athletes, and others not known for their manners, try to arrive on time.

Marika was not shy about arriving unescorted, so the First Lady never arranged an escort for her, but she did, however, always send a White House car with a driver for her friend. Marika had been there so often, she knew many of the White House police force by sight, as well as the ushers, who wear black ties on party nights, and the doormen, who wear white pique bow ties with their black dinner suits. The White House car dropped her off in the small driveway in front of the East Gate doors, where her ID was examined and her name was checked off on the dinner guest list. Already there was welcoming music in the air at the east entrance as the lovely sounds of a harp filled the air. The woman harpist, trim in her Marine Band uniform of a bright red tunic top and dark blue long skirt, sat strumming cheerfully, smiling at the arriving guests.

Marika greeted members of the First Lady's Social Office as she passed through the ground floor corridor that joins the East Wing and the Mansion. One wall of this corridor was glass, facing the garden and South Lawn. The other wall, shared with the President's private movie theater on the interior, was accented with a group of framed photographs and text, which told the history of this great house. During the weekday morning tours, tourists by the thousands walk through this passageway, but tonight there was only the occasional click-clicking sounds echoing the women guests' high heels tapping on the tile floor.

She was now inside the Mansion, the doorway flanked by two large Remington bronzes on pedestals—figures of rough-riding cowboys on their fast-moving horses. She handed her coat to a maid, who checked it, and then she began to mount the stairway to the main floor, past a huddled group of Washington press corps members, armed with scruffy looking pads and pencils. The journalists recognized only top government officials passing by, while CEOs of the top *Fortune* 100 companies, whose incomes were ten times higher than those of powerful senators and other government potentates, walked by unheeded. Everyone recognized Marika as Eve Watson's great friend from New York, and they called out questions to her, hoping to get some "pigeon droppings of gossip," as Eve had once described it. Marika walked by them faster than usual tonight, because she feared a question on the state of the Watson marriage.

The Associated Press photographer recognized Marika and said admiringly, "Marika, that's a terrific dress! Who was the designer?" His camera began to flash as he put her in the center of his lens frame. "I made it myself, Jerry!" she said, knowing it would give everyone within earshot a good laugh. Then, realizing she had made him the butt of a joke, she whispered, "It's Oscar de la Renta's, Jerry." He now had a complete caption for the photograph he would move tonight over the AP wire.

"Thanks," he said smiling again, "you sure look pretty." As she climbed the stairway, she was pleased that she looked well tonight. She wanted to, particularly since somewhere in this throng there was a man Eve wanted to introduce her to. Her off-the-shoulder sapphire blue velvet dress fit her slim body perfectly. She knew it looked good because Lisa had tried to borrow it. She gazed around at the unaccompanied men filing past up the stairway, men of all sizes and descriptions. Eve had not described the man to her physically, so she could not identify him.

At the top of the stairs on the first floor she was greeted warmly by one of the ushers, "Mrs. Wentworth, so nice to see you again." He handed her a small white table card, which had "Mrs. Wentworth" on the top fold and "Table No. 4" on the inside, all done in a flourish of calligraphy. Then she was offered the arm of a handsome young officer, one of the social aides assigned by his military service to the White House to assist at social functions. When Marika had once asked such an officer what were the requirements for the job of social aide to the White House, he had replied, "He or she should have good manners, know how to stay cool, and know enough not to blow the nose on a jacket sleeve." Eve had more formally described the group of military men as "attractive young people who escort single women into the East Room and make sure everyone has a drink and someone to talk to. On rare occasions," she added with a smile, "they have also been known to put a drunk and disorderly guest into a homeward-bound taxi."

The Marine Band musicians, looking like a covey of scarlet-coated quail in their chairs in the large hall on the first floor, were playing "Dancing Cheek to Cheek," a favorite of the Watsons'. Marika looked at the nice young blond Marine officer who had offered her his arm. Although young enough to be her son, she noticed that he wasn't so young that he did not throw her some admiring side glances. Her Great-Aunt Victoria had once told her she had "very good shoulders, an important asset, Marika," and the Marine seemed to be aware of this asset, too. Good, she thought to herself. Better than good.

Once inside the white and gold East Room, she thanked the Marine and bade him good-bye. She couldn't help but be awed by this room and its history every time she entered it. It was an emotion that far surpassed the excitement of being part of the present social scene. The enormous windows were dressed in heavy gold damask, and the low-slung ornate chandeliers glittered from every crystal drop, reflecting the golden glow of the highly polished light parquet floors. She almost felt the presence of the presidents who had danced here in this room, the presidents who had listened here to great concerts after dinner, the presidents who had lain here in state here after their assassinations, with flag-draped coffins guarded at four corners by fresh-faced young guards at attention.

The Marine Band was now playing a medley of Viennese waltzes, and she noticed two couples out in the hall, moving in waltz steps, a breach of etiquette to dance before the presidential arrivals. She took a glass of champagne from a waiter's passing silver tray and tried to figure who was who tonight. Which suit in this sea of black dinner suits encased the body of one Jonathon Scher? A hopeless task.

Then she noticed Jan Alcott, the Social Secretary, scurrying about, wearing her "uniform," one of her many evening gowns. She looked stately and beautiful tonight in an iridescent green taffeta. She greeted Marika with a cordial smile, then rushed off to confer with the Chief of Protocol from the State Department about last-minute changes in the seating list. These changes were the scourge of her life, Marika knew, because every little drop-in or drop-out of a guest on a state dinner list could mean a major protocol reshuffling and perhaps the reseating of from twenty to thirty people, all of whom already had their table numbers in their pockets. Of course, when the table numbers changed, the guests had to be located and given new ones.

Jan Alcott and Joe Needham, the Chief of Protocol, had laid out the seating lists and the precedence list of the French and American officials on top of the famous oversized grand piano in a corner of the East Room. The French *Chef du Protocol* had now joined them, Marika noticed, lending his own needed assistance in the reseating of the official French party. He was muttering *merde* under his breath to himself as he passed her by, and she understood perfectly why.

Marika sipped her champagne and surveyed the people who were surveying everyone else. She recognized the French ambassador, several famous media figures, two cabinet officers, the head of the Smithsonian Institution, a champion boxer, two movie stars, three famous corporate CEO's, two senators, two congressmen, a baseball star, two of Mac's special assistants, a ballet dancer— *and a partridge in a pear tree*, she hummed to herself. Finally she ran into someone she could talk to—Nathan Stoughton.

"You did me a favor this afternoon, Nathan, but then you owed me one."

"I know I did."

"How did it turn out?"

"Well. The President was extremely nervous waiting for his wife, not understanding why I had booked this time as an 'emergency' appointment. Then she came, and they went out on the South grounds, arm in arm, and didn't come back from their walk for almost two hours. He kept the Secretary of State waiting, too. We all watched them. They would stop and talk earnestly, frown, laugh, then start to walk again, then stop. All I know is that when they came back, they both looked—well—happier than I had seen them for a long time. And the proof of the pudding, Marika," he paused, with a very pleased expression, "is that they gave each other a big juicy kiss when they separated. Right in front of the Secretary of State. Reticence be damned. I haven't seen them do that since before the presidential campaign."

The Chief of Protocol and the Social Secretary were now in the dining room, juggling place cards, while their assistants substituted for them in the East Room, lining up the guests into a single line, "in order of precedence"—in other words, as Marika explained to a curious couple from Wichita, who were obviously big party contributors being paid off this evening, "in order of the importance of the officially appointed, ranked, or elected people in this room." The people from Wichita, more confused than ever, thanked Marika nicely for her kind explanation.

The Marine Band abruptly stopped playing in the hallway, and the Kansas couple asked her what that meant. "It means the President, First Lady, and the President of France are about to come into this room, but first we'll hear the 'Ruffles and Flourishes,' followed by 'Hail to the Chief,' the President's own ceremonial arrival song." She explained that the press—television and newspaper reporters—were now filming and photographing the official party at the bottom of the stairway in the great hall, and in two minutes everyone would see them.

The East Room was now hushed into total silence. The guests gave their champagne goblets to waiters who passed by with their great silver trays. The guests were learning from each other that "one does not go through the receiving line in the President's House holding a drink."

Then came the awesome sounds of the "Ruffles and Flourishes" and the rhythmic shuffling of the color guard. First came the military color guard with the flags tilted before them, followed by Mac and Eve Watson, flanking the President of France. The latter's daughter followed on the arm of the Vice President, and other leading American and French dignitaries filed in behind them. The guests burst into applause, and the wife of a prominent French diplomat stationed in Washington burst into tears at the sight of her *Monsieur le Président*.

The French President's daughter, a pretty seventeen-year-old, wore a fairy princess kind of pink tulle dress—strapless, with large pink satin roses adorning the sweeping full skirt. Marika explained once again to the visitors from Kansas what she had learned from Eve at lunch—that the young daughter was substituting for her recuperating mother on this trip, and in her honor, there was to be dancing, with young Washingtonians invited to come in after dinner for a special reception to meet *la belle jeune Française*.

As the principals took their places in proper rank in front of the fireplace, so that the receiving line could begin, Marika noticed that Eve looked terrific tonight. The dark circles framing her tired eyes from this noon seemed to have disappeared—probably be-cause she's "onstage, doing her job," Marika decided. Eve's splen-did figure was poured into a gold and black lamé ballgown by a French designer—in honor of the French President's visit. The fashion scribes who stood with the photographers in the hallway to witness the grand entrance of the heads of state were still writing on their notepads twenty minutes after the official party had gone into the East Room. They would not leave, either, until the harried Press Secretary procured for them the names of the designers of Eve Watson's and the French President's daughter's ballgowns. "Givenchy" and "Christian Lacroix," he told them, completely mispronouncing both names, but the fashion scribes needed no assistance in identifying them properly.

As Marika waited patiently in the long single-file receiving line, she stared at the Watsons standing straight and tall alongside the French President and his daughter. How handsome they are, she thought, Eve looking like a goddess and Mac like a movie star with his perfect physique and his thick head of black hair. His chiseled features, strong chin and nose made him look rugged and manly. What a great bronze equestrian statue he would make in the middle of a Washington rotary traffic circle after his death, she decided. "The Malcolm Watson Circle" instead of "Scott Circle" or "Thomas Circle." Then she giggled out loud at such an image.

The Watsons both kissed her on the cheek when she reached them. The warm grasp of their hands and the way they were looking at each other told her what she needed to know about how their afternoon meeting had gone. Sand can darned well wait for another fifty years, she thought to herself, before getting any proof of trouble in this marriage. When she reached the French President, she greeted him in his tongue and brought a wide smile to his face when she expressed her best wishes for the rapid recovery of his wife from her operation. Then she complimented him on his beautiful daughter.

"Madame," he said after kissing her hand, "it is a pleasure to have someone like you go through this line, speaking such im-peccable French." Then he turned to Mac and whispered, "You should appoint this woman as the next American ambassador to France."

"I've already tried and failed to persuade her," Mac replied with a wide grin.

Marika next took the hand of the daughter, Mademoiselle Agnès, telling her in French that the entire White House was mesmerized by her beautiful pink dress. The girl's face lit up. "I have trouble with English, you know," she said apologetically. Marika told her quickly that she wouldn't need to struggle with English after dinner. "You won't have to talk. There will be lots of handsome young men coming to the White House, all trying to dance with you." Agnès laughed with pleasure and made a parting A-okay gesture with her fingers in Marika's direction.

Within a half hour all guests had been hurried through the receiving line and were then shown the way through the Green, Blue, and Red Rooms of the White House and into the State Dining Room. There was the usual confusion of finding one's proper seat—particularly difficult for those who had not brought their glasses and could not read the place cards. The last people into the room were supposed to be the two heads of state and their ladies. Marika rechecked her table card, which read "Table No. 4," proceeded to the table bearing a discreet stanchion with the number four held aloft, and found her place. Her name was written in calligraphy on a handsome white place card, embossed with the gold presidential seal at the top. Each place card had been laid on top of a white damask napkin, which was handsomely embroidered in white with the presidential seal. The napkin in turn had been laid in the center of the rich cobalt blue, gold, and white place plate, also adorned with the gold presidential seal. A menu card, matching the design of the place card, sat on the table to the left of each place setting, listing in calligraphy the various courses and their accompanying wines.

A cheap-looking, large-breasted blonde, also at Marika's table, had plopped herself down at her place, and was already consuming the tiny breadsticks on her butter plate, making a mess of crumbs all around it. Marika decided she didn't like this woman, but she was going to help her out anyway. "Just thought you would like to know," she whispered very quietly in her ear, "that you're supposed to remain standing until the two presidents and their party have entered the dining room and taken their places."

"Shit!" she said, not in a whisper, but then, with an irritated air, managed to push her chair back and stand up again.

The Watsons and the French came in, took their places, and remained standing while an incredibly handsome, much-decorated French army chaplain officer, traveling with his President, said a short prayer of grace, first in English, then in French.

Everyone sat down and the conversation began to fill the room. Marika unfolded her large white damask napkin in half, spreading it on her lap. The man on her left spoke to her at once, introducing himself as "Ambassador Tuffier," a member of the French party, so she was immediately engaged in conversation with him. She could not help but sneak a glance to the right at Jonathon Scher but all she saw was his back. He had turned in the other direction, obviously engrossed in conversation with the buxom blonde. That bodes ill, she thought.

Marika also quickly glanced at her menu card. She had learned long ago that in official life, one speaks to one dinner partner for the first course and to the other dinner partner for the next course, and then one continues alternating conversational partners at the beginning of each new course. She would have Ambassador Tuffier all through the smoked trout and *mousse de foie gras en gelée,* then Jonathon Scher for the *faisan Fontainebleau,* Ambassador Tuffier for the salad and cheese course, and Jonathon again for the *bombe glacée rustique* dessert. She could manage.

She stole another glance in Jonathon's direction, but was stopped by the sight of the blonde, who had leaned way over for Jonathon's benefit, exposing her vast décolletage. Her contortions were not lost on Ambassador Tuffier either. He asked Marika in French if she agreed with him that "both masterpieces will probably pop completely out of her dress by the salad course, *n'est-ce pas?*"

Marika, audibly chuckling, replied, "*Monsieur l'Ambassadeur,* with that sense of humor, I'm really glad to be sitting next to *you.*"

"And where did you learn your excellent French, Madame?"

"A junior year abroad at the Sorbonne, and two summers with a family in Normandy, working as an English tutor for the children."

"How was the Normandy experiment?"

"From my point of view, excellent. I learned good French, but the children alas, learned almost no English."

"Mieux pour vous, chère madame."

The hum in the softly lit dining room was pleasant and relaxed. The figure of the pensive, seated Abraham Lincoln in his monumental portrait over the marble fireplace seemed to gaze down on the scene with approval. The room was bathed in a rosy glow from candlelight reflecting on the ruby velvet seat cushions, tied to the chairs with gold tassels—and from the round silk moiré floor-length tablecloths in shades ranging from the palest of pinks to the deepest of garnet reds. The centerpiece vermeil baskets were filled with white tulips and roses in many shades of pink. The white-gloved, tail-coated waiters threaded their way through the narrow passageways between the tables with skill and grace.

Ambassador Tuffier explained to Marika that so far his President's visit to the United States was going encouragingly well. Then he sighed and told his dinner partner she could not know how much he appreciated being able to speak to her in his own tongue. *"On se fatigue,"* he said, "one becomes exhausted speaking another language hour after hour, without respite." He told her how no one in the French party had slept on the plane, but had gone right into conferences, and they were now dizzy from fatigue and jet lag. She was full of sympathy, and he sighed again how lucky he was "to have such a beautiful, understanding woman as a dinner partner."

Out of the corner of his eye, Jonathon Scher noticed that the French diplomat's hand was now resting on top of his other dinner partner's. The jerk, he thought disparagingly, predicting that hand would probably go down lower, too, under the table.

Jonathon didn't have much love for the French, and he frankly wondered why Mac and Eve had asked him to this particular state dinner. Still, he was anxious to speak to the woman on his left—a very handsome, classy kind of female. He would enjoy talking to her, if he could ever detach himself from the The Chest on his right. God, what a front on her! Normally by now he would have had fantasies of drowning himself in the white seas of her breasts, which she kept shoving at him, but tonight was not the place, and it was certainly not the time.

He had noticed that the dinner partner on his left had taken a couple of sidelong glances at him. Encouraging. He knew nothing about her except that Eve Watson told him in the receiving line that she had put him next to a lovely widow, Mrs. Wentworth, who was very elegant and smart. Jonathon had replied, "so you think that's what I need, Eve, a woman who's elegant and smart?"

"Yes," she had replied, "the opposite kind of person from the one you married."

Jonathon decided that Eve had seated him tonight between these two totally different women to make the contrast between the two even more startling. Smart Eve.

There was a sudden new energy in the air. The main course was being served, and people were dutifully switching their conversational partners. Ambassador Tuffier expressed regret at having to leave Marika, turned to his left, and Marika turned to her right. Jonathon Scher was still talking to the blonde. She decided to act.

"Heh, how about me? I can talk, too." He laughed and abruptly turned to her and away from the blonde.

"Lady," he said, "you have NO idea how grateful I am to hear that. I have been having tough going conversationally with her from the beginning."

"Yes," Marika said sarcastically, "it must have been really tough—eating, talking, and enjoying that frontage all at the same time."

"Well, if you're going to be crude enough to talk about frontages in the White House, I'd much rather discuss yours," and he looked quickly over her shoulders and down into the top folds of her blue velvet dress. She blushed furiously.

"Don't worry. I promise to behave." He took her hand, shook it, and said, "The name's Scher." She laughed and said, "The name's Wentworth."

"Do you mind if I ask you what you were doing to that Frenchman on your other side? He looked cross-eyed over you. Were you trying to draw Élysées Palace secrets out of the old guy?"

"He's not old," she whispered, "and he's an important member of the French Foreign Office, and I wasn't spying. I was being polite."

"What does a man have to do to get your attention—act like that frog? Be a diplomat? Kiss hands in the proper way?"

"I'm no diplomat-chaser," she said in mock anger. "I'm just a plain old American girl."

"Yeah, I can see that."

"I was just sympathizing with him over the rigors of these official trips—the changes in time, diet, and water—the strain of speaking another language all the time—"

He interrupted her. "I'm broken-hearted thinking about what these frogs have to go through over here on this visit." He noticed the frown that creased her forehead. "I mean what the *charming French* have to go through on a trip like this."

He picked up her place card to remind himself of her name. "Mrs. Wentworth, tell me about yourself."

"It would be easier if I had my office send you a copy of my résumé."

"No need for such a major rebuff. I was just curious, that's all."

They moved to casual conversation, discussing the menu, how the dining room looked, and how they would hate to be the president of any country. Marika took physical stock of her dinner partner. He was not tall, but he was powerfully muscular. His hairline was receding quickly, but what hair there was Marika liked. It was a very nice reddish-brown color. He had a wonderful ruddy complexion—freckles, too—but what she really liked were his unbelievably blue eyes, bright even in the candlelight. She wished her eyes were backlit and clear like his. She asked him if he was wearing colored contact lenses, and he answered in an exaggeratedly offended way, "Absolutely not. Those are for male models. I wear these for reading—" and he whipped out of his breast pocket a pair of ordinary spectacles. She knew he was pleased she had noticed his eyes.

She asked about his business, and he told her about recent mergers his Chicago-based company had engineered, as well as small companies he had bought and was "bringing along" with new management and stricter financial controls.

Jonathon was careful to ask her about her company as many times as she asked him about his. Their conversation went back and forth, seeking, probing, each business mind trying to find out as much as possible about the other, without overprying.

"You know, it's very flattering, your interest in what I do," Marika finally said.

"You're an interesting woman in a field I know little about, and I find it fascinating. You're giving me an education."

"I usually have to do that with every businessman I meet. PR is a misunderstood profession."

She liked the way Jonathon was dressed. It's ridiculous to care so much how a man dresses, she told herself, but she had felt this way since she was eighteen years old. She didn't like herself for it, but she judged a man by his clothes as well as his personality and reputation. His black dinner suit was beautifully tailored, his cream silk dinner shirt was simply pleated. His studs and cuff links were small black pearls set into gold acorns. Tasteful. But every now and then she saw the flash of what she recognized as a wafer-thin, diamond-studded platinum man's evening watch. Handsome but very expensive and showy. She winced. He also wore a heavy gold ring, with a good-sized, square-cut custom-shaped diamond in the middle of it. Each time she saw it, she looked away. To her it was vulgar. Once when she was a little girl a Boston "hood" had come to the house for dinner, someone she knew even then that her father disliked. He had worn a ring like that.

Jonathon, in the meantime, had been carefully observing the lady on his left—even her perfume got to him. He never before had particularly noticed a woman's perfume, unless it was too strong. Marika's was titillating to his nostrils. He noticed the graceful movement of her beautiful hands, with their carefully manicured nails and the handsome jeweled rings, one on each hand. Turning to the side to see her, he was most conscious of her wonderful creamy bare shoulders and the rising curve of her lovely small breasts in the blue velvet dress. His ears were enticed by the cadence of her voice with its melodious, pleasing sounds and cultured accent. He was aware of her body—taut, lean, but not bony or sharp-angled. He wanted to touch her, but of course could not. He had a desire just to run his fingers quickly over her arms, hands, and those beautiful shoulders. He told himself, Scher, watch out. This is no time to be horny. You haven't met this kind of woman before. She's a no-touch person. Probably cold and haughty away from the spotlight of society. He laughed at himself. How long had it been since he had been in the same room with an overbred woman? There had been so many more women like The Chest, offered to him on a platter.

"I want to ask you the ultimate question," he said.

"Which is?"

"How did you rate a seat at Table 4 tonight?"

"I'm just an old pal of the Watsons." She would be, he thought. "And you?"

"My checkbook's an old friend of the party's." She knew he was being modest, because Eve had let drop the fact that Mac sought Jonathon's advice on business matters.

"I have a feeling you're more deserving of a seat at this dinner than I am," she said. "I know that the President values your advice. . . . Tell me something," Marika found the courage to ask, "since we're talking about why people earned the right to be here tonight at dinner, what did Madam La Zonga on your right do to deserve this dinner invitation—and particularly a seat next to you?"

"I'm flattered by the last question. I think I probably got her on one side because the Watsons know how I love Reubens paintings."

She laughed. "All right, understood, but what about the first part of my question? Surely, you have talked so much to her tonight, you know why she is here."

"Because she is the mistress of Ronny Schilden, that's why."

"Mr. Big Bucks himself."

"Mr. Big Contributor to the party."

"It only cost him two hundred thousand dollars."

"But why isn't Schilden here with his wife?" asked Marika, feeling disappointed that the Watsons would have to go this far in their political payoffs.

"I can read your face, lovely lady. I'm sure Mac and Eve don't know about this bimba, why she is here. I'm sure the patronage people put her on the guest list, and knowing Schilden, he's too smart to show up here with her instead of his wife. And knowing Schilden's predilections for—for—"

"Big balconies," she interrupted.

"Yes, he had to keep his mistress happy, so this is the way he shuts her up and keeps her happy for another year. Socially happy, that is."

"There's something so immoral about all this," she said, breaking a small piece of roll with her fingers and studying it.

"Not really, lovely lady. It's been ever thus, since ancient Egypt. George Washington's first administration. It's the political arena."

The blonde next to him was now wrenching his arm.

"I've GOT to have the answer to one more question," he said to Marika with dramatic urgency in his tone.

"Quickly, what?"

"What is your first name?"

"Couldn't that have waited until dessert?"

"Positively not. I want to be able to say it over and over to myself when the lady on the right drives me nuts with her chatter."

"It's Marika."

"What kind of name is that?" he asked. The blonde was now furiously pulling at him and talking to him in an angry, high-pitched voice. "Marika doesn't exactly match 'Wentworth,' does it?"

"It's Hungarian," she smiled. He rolled his eyes heavenward

and turned to the woman on his right. "Tell me," Marika heard him saying, "do you like Hungarian goulash? I do."

All through the salad and cheese course Marika talked animatedly to Ambassador Tuffier, but her mind was definitely on her next-door neighbor on the right. When they were back together again during the dessert course, Jonathon got his entire spoon enmeshed in the silvery blanket of spun sugar woven around the melon-shaped ice cream mold. "What am I supposed to do with these cobwebs?" he whispered in Marika's ear. "When, in doubt, *eat!*" was her whispered reply. When she saw the impish expression in his eyes, she knew that he knew perfectly well what to do with the spun sugar.

Marika finally felt she could maneuver conversation to a more personal level. But each time she tried to insert a question about his private life, he would make a witty remark and change the subject. At first, Marika felt he was a master at the art of evasion, which made her nervous. After all, if he had to evade, there must be a reason, but then he began to talk a little more about his divorce and she sensed that his personal life cut very close to his heart, maybe too close to discuss at the White House over spun sugar. He basically described his life as that of a hermit. "I really don't have the time or opportunity for pursuit, if you know what I mean"—Jonathon looked directly in her eyes—"unless I meet someone of quality, someone worth pursuing from one end of the earth to the other."

"Do you have any children?" she asked.

"No. No, very unfortunately." Such a simple, straightforward answer, but the look in Jonathon Scher's iridescent blue eyes turned to fire, then to ice. Marika unconsciously put her hand on top of his arm for a fleeting second.

"Let's talk about something less serious, shall we?"

"Now, wait a minute, not so fast. Now it's my turn. Your daughter? Lisa you said her name was?"

Interesting, Marika thought to herself, she had mentioned Lisa's name just once.

"Yes," was all she said, not wanting to push too far, seeing how the conversation about children might upset him. She

wouldn't blame anyone for envying her for the relationship she
had with her daughter.

"Is she as smart and beautiful as you?"

Marika felt herself blossom into a smile. "More so, in every
department."

"Hm—this I have to see."

Marika waited a beat. The momentary silence between them
seemed to command a response. "Yes, someday, you'll have to
meet my daughter." Jonathon smiled at the idea of a possible
invitation.

What did she like to do in her spare time, he wanted to know.
And where did she like to vacation? Play tennis? He shot questions
at her so fast, she would have been intimidated if it were not for
his kind and admiring eyes—eyes that told her he was really
interested, not just a curious gossip. She decided he was really
very amusing—and bright. Eve had been clever to think of introducing the two of them. He was a diamond in the rough in
some ways, but an interesting man—with an undeniable, in-con-
trol sexual energy. He probably took out only young women in
their twenties. Well, even if he was a well-practiced flirt and there
would be no postscript to tonight, she would always remember
it as a very enjoyable evening.

Something else at the table had made a big impression on
Marika. It was a diamond ring—a big, gaudy, but absolutely
beautiful diamond ring on the left hand of The Chest. Every time
she waved her hand in the candlelight, which was often, the ring
threw off a fireworks display of flashing light. What fascinated
Marika was not the size of the stones, but the design of the
ring—two diamond bees, one larger than the other, set in gold.
The bees reminded her of the ones she had seen woven into French
Empire fabrics; the "Imperial Bees" were a design motif seen
repeated throughout the decorative arts of Napoleon's Empire
period. At one point she leaned across Jonathon, admired the
ring, and asked its owner if she was a fan of Napoleon's, and if
her ring was based on his bees. When the answer came, "What
bees?" Marika decided to drop it.

The blonde, however, was waiting for Marika to say something more, because Jonathon had pulled back his chair between the two women. He sat back relaxed, his fingers interlaced over his chest, grinning like a mischievous Peck's Bad Boy.

Marika realized the conversational ball was in her court, and she decided to go for it—to go for the bees, that is. Any woman with that many carats of diamonds in the shape of bees should darned well be interested in the subject!

"Did you know that an apiculturist tends a beehive on the roof of the Paris Opera House?" she asked.

"A *what*?" the blonde asked in a loud voice.

"Someone who tends beehives is an apiculturist," Marika explained, warming to the subject. "The one at the Paris Opera House has been tending three hives on the roof for more than a decade. He sells the honey in the Opera boutique"—she smiled at the man from Chicago sitting between them—"and he sells it to Marshall Field's in Chicago!" Marika watched the blonde for a reaction. "Naturally, the bees make great honey up there on the roof, with that magnificent view of Paris!"

The blonde's mouth now hung open in a wide "O" in utter astonishment, as though she were about to hit an important note at her concert.

"It's very complicated tending a beehive, you know," Marika continued. She couldn't stop herself now. The Napoleonic bees were one of her idiosyncratic interests. She could see Jonathon grinning unabashedly. "A beehive is very passionate, and the apiculturist must be very careful to keep things well regulated, or the honey will be affected." On that note Marika took the woman's hand, inspected the diamond bees, muttered, "Very beautiful, those bees should make great honey for you," and then just as quickly dropped the woman's hand.

The toasts of the two presidents were exchanged at the beginning of the dessert course. A standing microphone suddenly appeared from nowhere, which Marika knew was thanks to a signal corpsman, and the room fell into a respectful silence the minute President Watson rose to his feet. At a certain point Jonathon put his arm over the back of Marika's chair, and one finger of his hand accidentally touched her bare skin. Or was it accidental?

The finger stayed there, just grazing her, and it sent a series of shivers all through her body. She was furious at herself, calling herself a juvenile teenaged idiot, chastising herself to the point of forgetting to listen to the President. She was mortified with even the possibility that Jonathon might be able to feel the surge of electricity, or whatever it was, right through her skin. Finally, she began to concentrate on the speech.

President Watson was, as usual, superb in his welcoming message to the French, in his anecdotes on the great bonds of friendship the two countries had enjoyed through history, and in his summation of the effects of the two-hundred-year-old French Revolution on the world and on the new Europe in particular. The French President was as humorous as Mac Watson in the beginning of his remarks, and then grew more substantive when he expressed his hopes for the cooperation of the two countries in the new millennium that was dawning.

As the applause died down and President and Mrs. Watson prepared to rise and lead their guest out of the dining room, the French teenager guest of honor rose from her chair, asked the permission of President and Mrs. Watson to speak, and then gave a toast to an utterly spellbound audience. Agnès had memorized her short remarks in English, and delivered them in a strong young voice, with a charming accent. Jonathon whispered in Marika's ear, "I've changed my mind about the French." The young woman ended by saying, "Président and Madame Watson, I am grateful for one more reason, and that is that I won't have to wait much longer for the dancing!"

The guests then moved out into the hall and reception rooms. Jonathon and Marika were separated in the crowd. Butlers passed among them, serving demitasses and glasses of liqueurs and brandy. Marika enjoyed strolling at random, her demitasse cup and saucer in one hand, watching people and smiling at everyone who smiled at her. The air was filled with the sounds of excited chatter, mixed with the romantic music of the Air Force Strolling Strings—smartly uniformed violinists who managed to play in perfect precision whether they were standing or walking around. When they began playing passionate Hungarian music, she felt

Jonathon's hand on her elbow, pushing her toward the Red Room. "You're so tall," he said, "how in hell did I lose you?"

They sat down on a sofa upholstered in a fabric of crimson silk with gold medallions that matched the solid crimson fabric on the walls of the Red Room, and Marika gave him her usual guided tour lecture about the magnificent American Empire period furnishings in this high-ceilinged historic room. They looked at the massive portraits of presidents stacked up like postage stamps in an album on the walls and finally Marika finished her art lecture. "I now know more than I want to about this room, Marika—but I also know more about *you* than you could possibly imagine."

"Why? And how?" Her curiosity was piqued.

"You are well known in New York. I've heard about you more than once. I know two of your clients well."

After he had cleared up that mystery, she answered some more of his questions, always demanding more information from him in return.

"When I first sat down at our table tonight," he said, "I thought The Chest was the woman Eve and everyone had raved about."

"Were you sad when you found out the truth?" she teased.

"Didn't you hear me shout 'Hallelujah' when I found out her name wasn't Wentworth? His eyes twinkled at his own rather silly joke. "Do you think Hallelujah is an expression of sadness?" He reached over and took her hand. "I like you, Marika. I enjoy just sitting here with you, just the two of us. I like not having to share you."

She was embarrassed again. He was coming on strong and she liked it, but it was quite a new and unfamiliar feeling for her. She was used to holding back on any display of her emotions. She had been trained all her life that a "nice girl" never admitted an attraction for a man this fast. She was so used to holding herself in, to controlling herself, that the fact that someone was speaking frankly of his attraction for her bewildered her—even if it pleased her.

The young people—Washington socialites and sons and

daughters of Administration and congressional officials—invited for dinner dancing had started to arrive. Their excited chatter filled the great entrance hall. Agnès, her father, and the Watsons formed a new receiving line there to greet them. Then the real surprise the Watsons had arranged for Agnès materialized. Into the hall walked the hottest international music group of the moment—a shaggy Irish musical band called the "Cro-Magnums"—Agnès literally screamed when she saw them, then gave each of the Watsons an enthusiastic hug. There was no way in which a receiving line could continue. Agnès was too excited, and so was every other person in the White House under the age of thirty. The group took their positions on the portable bandstand the National Parks Service had built for the East Room, and the Cro-Magnums swung into action. Within two minutes the sound system, turned up to a high volume, filled every corner of the White House and out into Pennsylvania Avenue with a pounding beat that transcended history and tradition. From the family quarters on the floor above, the Watsons' two Jack Russell terriers began howling in unison to the music, but only the President's valet and Eve's personal maid working on that floor were bothered by it.

Finally, even Jonathon and Marika found they could neither talk in peace anymore nor resist joining the Cro-Magnums. "Let's show 'em how," he said, leading her by the hand into the East Room to join the others. Eve, in planning the Cro-Magnums' appearance, thought the older generation would want to absent themselves from the noise level and go into the other rooms to talk—leaving the young to dance to the ear-splitting sound in the East Room. Instead, every member of the dinner party, from the most exhausted French official to the sleepiest CEO, was out there doing his or her stuff on the beautiful waxed inlaid floor. Some of the older couples were watched with fascination by the younger generation, because of their ingenuity and dancing skills. The styles of the different generations, not to mention the two countries, were different, but the enjoyment and energy output were similar. The portly French President, dancing a fast foxtrot with Eve, managed to keep time to the pounding beat, and Mac moved speedily around the floor with young Agnès, her pink tulle skirts fanning out as she moved. Soon four of the young men who had been eyeing the dancing young lady, but were obviously shy about cutting in on the President of the United States, solved their problem by forming a group and all of them cut in on Mac Watson at the same time. He relinquished her with a flourish, then watched to see how she would select who would be her next partner. The four young men solved the problem by all gyrating around and with her. Each one managed to do some close dancing with her, but never for too long. There were too many others of their peers who wanted a chance to dance with her.

Jonathon and Marika danced apart and then closer, and decided that closer was better. She felt comfortable in his arms; he danced smoothly and well. It didn't matter that she was a little taller than he. Then Jonathon felt a tap on his back. Mac Watson cut in and said, "Jonathon, I hope you don't mind."

"I can't very well object, Mr. President, even if I do." He stepped away with a small bow.

"Let's go to a quiet place for a minute," the President said, leading Marika into the deserted Green Room, where they sat down on a green damask-covered Duncan Phyfe sofa. A butler, picking up used demitasse cups and saucers and putting them on his tray, discreetly left the room the minute they entered.

"Mac," she said with pride, "you did more for Franco-American relations tonight with the surprise for Agnès than any amount of high-level negotiations could have accomplished."

"I know," he laughed, "and it's all Eve. It was her idea. It's Agnès's favorite music of all. Eve has a touch of genius. And she kept it a secret—even from the White House press corps. They're going to be brought in now for a few minutes—to look and listen to the scene in the East Room. Rather a historic night!" His face became serious. "I hope you realize how much I appreciate what you did for me—for us—today, Marika."

"Oh, come off it!"

"No, I mean it. You *made* me take the time to talk to Eve alone. I had no idea how serious the situation was, how strongly she felt, how upset she was."

"She needs you, Mac. Your time and attention, at least a little bit."

"I know. I've taken her daily concentration on my needs and her contribution to my job for granted. I've been so engrossed in my own life, I've been just plain selfish. She never asks for anything for herself, so I just shut her out—thinking she was a staunch, brave soul who would understand."

"I don't think you realize what a tough job she has, and what a cold, impersonal environment this is."

"I know. But now I know a lot of things I didn't before this afternoon. And things are going to change."

"Don't let your marriage disintegrate, Mac."

"Marika, what are you saying? Our marriage 'disintegrate'? There's no chance of that. Why would you even suggest it?"

"Because people are saying it outside. The press in New York is checking out rumors that you're splitting up."

He was angry. "You're completely out of your mind!"

"I'm not. Sand is trying to get the story any way she can. She badgered me, though you know how pointless that is. Then I saw her lunching with Gretchen Schultz at Le Cirque. She obviously now has a Washington spy working on it."

"It's a goddamned lie. Our marriage is not breaking up."

"Sometimes, Eve looks so sad, it seems like it's true."

"I can't believe this. What are you trying to tell me?" He was quiet then, thinking.

"No one loves you two more, and no one can get to you these days, and so tonight, when you asked me to talk, I just forgot myself—and—I talked. I hope you don't mind."

They arose from their easy chairs and walked back into the East Room. Mac squeezed her hand and whispered, "You and David were always our best friends. Thank God at least one of you is still around."

She watched him cut in on his wife on the dance floor. Four photographers caught the scene and took more pictures as they danced close and looked into each other's eyes. Marika hoped that Mac's romantic actions were not just a photo opportunity.

Jonathon came up behind Marika, put his arms on the top of her shoulders, and whispered in her ear, "What presidential conversation could possibly be more fascinating than mine?"

"Well, it was a big bore, but to be polite, I just had to listen to him spell out all the military plans for the next five years."

He laughed and took her arm. "Would you like to split this place?"

"We can't!" She was horrified. "We can't leave until both presidents have left the room. It would be a terrible breach of protocol."

"Hang the protocol. We can pretend we're breaking out with chicken pox, and then everyone will be happy to see us leave." Taking her by the hand, he threaded his way through the dancers, out into the hall, and into the open door of the Ushers' Office.

"I have a serious business emergency," he announced gravely to J. B. East, the Chief Usher. "Mrs. Wentworth kindly agreed to assist me."

"I see," said Mr. East, as he and Marika exchanged amused eye signals.

Jonathon continued in a serious tone, "We don't wish to be seen by everyone—breaking protocol."

"Of course. We'll send you down in the private elevator, Mr. Scher, and in this way no one will see you." He called a doorman, who took them down one floor, and they made their way out of the East Gate without being seen by any of the guests.

Jonathon's car was summoned, and a big white stretch limo pulled up. She gave an audible gasp. He noticed it, and later, when they were sitting in the bar of the Pisces Club, he asked her about it.

"That's the limo I keep in Washington. I'm often here, you know."

"Yes," was all she could say.

"You don't like it."

"I guess I just like smaller—well—more unobtrusive transport."

"You mean, my car smells of 'new money'?" She was astonished at how quick he was, how perceptive he was in reading her mind. She decided to be frank. Why not?

"Yes, either new money or inner insecurity."

"Ouch!" He gave a false moan, clutching his stomach with pain. "You know how to hurt a guy. Below the belt, too." He laughed, and she suddenly felt mean. She took his arm and snuggled close to him.

They sat for a long time, talking, sipping cognac in enormously tall brandy snifters, and sinking into the pillows of their own private sofa. The lights were low, he held her hand, and soon they were alone in the club except for the staff.

"I find you absolutely fascinating," he said, again in that husky tone. "I've been lonely for a long time. But I promise you I'm not one of those guys whom all women hate because they talk all night about their divorces and try to extract sympathy at every turn."

He took out a cigarette, lit it, and then angrily put it out before taking another puff on it. "My wife and I have been separated a long time, even if only recently divorced. In all these years I never found another woman who could make me feel good." He turned to look at her. "Until tonight."

"There are plenty of women worth feeling good about," she said, laughing. "You just haven't opened your eyes. And you have, I feel compelled to tell you, the most beautiful blue eyes I've ever seen in my whole life." The cognac had given her a spurt of courage.

"You'd better watch it, green eyes, saying things like that to me, you never can tell what I might suddenly do."

They sat in silence for five minutes, ignoring the waiter who was clearing his throat. Their bill sat on a little tray nearby, awaiting his signature.

"What kind of a marriage did you have?" he suddenly asked. The awkwardly posed question abruptly cut into the silence.

"Wonderful. Happy. Contented. Loving." She spoke in a slow cadence.

"A very tough act to follow."

"Very."

"But you've had lots of men making—I mean—trying to get close to you ever since then."

"No. Since David died, there hasn't been one single man in my life. Plenty of homosexuals, playboys, lightweights, or drunks. No one else." He drew back, studying her face, as though he didn't know whether or not to believe her.

"I can't believe that a successful, beautiful, intelligent, sexy woman like you could be—would be—"

"You mean, without a man all this time, is that what you were trying to say?"

"What is really ironic here," he said, interlacing the fingers of her hand with his own, "is that you had such a good marriage you haven't felt like marrying again, and I had such a lousy one, I haven't felt like marrying again. Of course, I could change my opinion. A beautiful woman with very white skin, brown hair, and green eyes could change all that."

"You're going too fast, Mr. Scher."

"I'm known for quick decisions. I take risks."

"One shouldn't take risks in marriage, that's my philosophy."

"Quite obviously. But to never take a risk in any matter of the heart is—well—"

"Sage. Very sage."

"How can such a glorious-looking female be so sage?" She found herself blushing for the second time that night. "Let me ask you something," he continued. "You're not used to men letting you know how sexy you are, are you?"

"Frankly, no."

"Your dukes are up. I'm too close, aren't I?"

"It might be better if you backed off a bit—just a bit," and she turned and smiled into his eyes. "Do you think," she asked him, "I could learn to relax and not be skittish when a man talks to me the way you do?" She felt a little embarrassed at her own brash flirting. It must be the cognac. She felt it was opening her up like a newly fixed zipper—fast and easy.

"Very possibly," he answered. He was tracing his finger around her neck, and she felt that razor-sharp bolt of electricity again. It was his touch. She offered him a sip of her cognac, and he brought her hand to his lips. "You have the most incredible, velvety, fragrant skin. Let me try some skin elsewhere." Then he kissed her neck, chin, nose, and finally her lips.

The waiter cleared his throat loudly. "Sir, it is 4 A.M."

They got up from the sofa, Jonathon signed the bill, and they got into the "odious" white limo, a name Jonathon would always use for it henceforth. They remained quiet all the way back to the Hay Adams Hotel.

"You know I want to come up with you."

"No, not tonight. It's—too—fast."

"Marika, I'm a patient man. I'll wait for as long as I have to. I want you badly. When you want me badly, let me know, will you?" He laughed, because the dialogue was somewhat like a B movie, but neither of them knew how to change it.

He accompanied her to the hotel elevator. "I mean it, I will be seeing you every chance my travel schedule will allow, and don't forget, when you are ready to change your mind about my making love to you, call me—even tonight at my hotel?"

She pushed him away, laughing. "Maybe I'll get through to you some morning in Chicago, on your car phone, when you're on your way to close a big deal, and I'll say, 'I'm ready, Jonathon.' What will you do then?"

"Take a cold shower and get on the next plane for New York."

She blew a kiss at him as the elevator doors closed.

He was on the telephone from Chicago late the next evening, and they talked long into the night.

"I should let you go to sleep, but I feel—"

"You feel what?" she said, stifling a happy yawn.

"I'm not going to tell you what I *really* feel," he said, "because it would embarrass you. Let's just say I want to see you soon—often. Let's make that *all the time*."

"That's nice," she said. She suddenly knew what it felt like to be a purring cat. Half asleep, she curled up in a fetal position on the green silk bedspread.

"I wish I were there," he said.

"I wish you were, too."

"If I were, you'd be wide awake. You wouldn't get any sleep for a while."

"There's no nicer wake-up than that."

Every morning Marika opened the office at seven forty-five, an hour and fifteen minutes before the others arrived. And though today it was hard to keep her thoughts entirely on business, she still disciplined herself to start the day with this important private time, when difficult mail could be digested and important writing could be tapped out at high speed using her personal computer's word processing software. These were the moments in which she could study her schedule, settle the day's priorities, and then enter all such decisions and reminders into the mini-computer-organizer that she carried with her at all times.

This early morning time was the only period free of time-wasting telephone interruptions. The clients' demands were incessant and often unreasonable. After all her years in business, Marika still wondered why they always had to "talk to the boss. The account executive won't do"—even if the account executive knew much more about current matters than the boss. Marika heard the same question implicit in every call. "What are you doing for us *today*, Marika, to merit that big retainer we pay you? The fact that you got the story of our new product in *People* magazine and the *Wall Street Journal* as well as on Channel 5 News last week is all very fine, but what are you doing for us *this week*, Marika?"

At times, the boss wanted to respond to such a client with a "go stuff it," but that would not fit the cool, well-bred image of the firm. And besides, today nothing could rattle her. She was sure of it. And Jonathon Scher was the reason why.

When Hortense arrived, Marika asked her to book her client meeting with Illinois Bell in Chicago—for the soonest possible date.

"I thought you told me that wasn't a rush meeting? That you could do it in January?"

"I'd better make that trip before Christmas, like *right now*." Marika thought for a moment. "Make it a day trip. Oh, and

Hortense, leave my lunch free in Chicago. I can take the four o'clock back to New York."

"Why this sudden interest in Chicago, and in the middle of the Christmas rush? What's this lunch date? What's his name?"

"You're too darned smart."

"Come on, Boss, you can't fool me. Someone you met in Washington at the state dinner?"

"Why must you know everything?"

"I already know everything. I listened in on your answering machine, like a good assistant should, and I heard his voice and his message. That wasn't any business call. That was no potential client. That was a man who is infatuated, if I ever heard one."

Marika smiled but did not continue the conversation further. She had a feeling that Hortense felt justified in maintaining a certain editing function for her boss's love life in the same way she did in her business life. Whether Hortense had arrived at this part of her job description duties all by herself, or whether Charles Russell had asked Hortense to keep a watchful eye over his daughter's affairs of the heart, Marika could not say. It didn't matter anyway. Hortense had always known everything that went on in her life, short of being present at the parties where Marika met and flirted with possible suitors. Marika not only tolerated it, she rather enjoyed it. Hortense had become like an adult Nanny in her life, and her assistant's curiosity felt comforting more than intrusive. She was lucky to have someone who cared that much about her.

After a week of receiving Jonathon's welcomed twice-daily, telephone calls, Marika made her one-day round trip to Chicago. Clear, sunny weather without strong winds made the trip in and out of the La Guardia and O'Hare airports blessedly easy. She spent from nine-thirty to noon at the Illinois Bell offices, going over the prototype her firm had designed for a new promotional brochure aimed at working women. At twelve-thirty she arrived punctually at the Drake Hotel, and found Jonathon already waiting for her.

"You're a cagey one," he said. "You come out here for a morning meeting, and I get to see you for lunch only. You fly away back to New York, your virtue absolutely intact."

"Ah, but lunch is such an important time, such a revealing time."

"You're an expert at manipulation through the art of tantalization," he said, sipping some wine and watching her eyes carefully over the rim of his wineglass.

"Look," she said, "I wish it could have been longer, but it's such a busy time, and I happen to know you don't have one single second on your schedule, so I couldn't have seen you even if I had stayed longer."

"And how do you know about my schedule?"

"For one thing, you told me you were trying to buy that company in Louisiana that manufactures parts for industrial machinery. As I recall, you had to have the deal sewed up this week, or you might lose it. I happen to know you haven't gone to Louisiana yet this week, so I surmise that you are probably going to leave at least by this evening. I also remember that you are off in a day or two for two weeks in the Far East."

He laughed. "I can't get away with anything with you."

"Remember that," was her answer.

The conversation meandered gracefully, moving from his mother, who called him often from California, to Lisa's romance with Sergio. He told her about a small failed thrift he was trying to buy with two other people, because he felt it had promise and with the proper management and a little bit of luck, it could come back. When she asked why, he explained that the bank and its branches were well situated in an affluent part of the community.

They began to argue over politics, but when Jonathon interrupted her impassioned defense of some subject or another by telling her that her green silk dress matched her "luminous green silk eyes," she laughed with pleasure and forgot what she was in the middle of saying. Then, when she disagreed with yet another of his political peccadilloes, he said "When you hold my hand like that under the table, how can I disagree with anything you say? If you say I'm wrong, well, then, I'm wrong. My God, you've got *some* touch, Marika."

Suddenly it was two-thirty. "Time for me to leave to catch the four o'clock from O'Hare," she said. He sent her out to the airport in his ridiculous big white car after apologizing for it and giving her a lingering good-bye kiss. They would not see each other until more than two weeks had passed. It seemed like an eternity.

On the way back to New York she tried to read her notes from the meeting with Illinois Bell, but at a certain point, she put the reading material down and looked straight ahead at the ugly seatbacks in front of her. She was falling in love with Jonathon Scher. There was a delicious ache inside of her, so she continued simply to stare straight ahead at the turquoise polyester fabric, smiling her own secret smile.

Marika was nervous. Lisa and Sergio were sitting in the living room, drinking club sodas. She had asked them to stay for a few minutes before they went to join their friends for pizza and a movie. It was time for Lisa to meet Jonathon. Her daughter had obviously noticed the effect this new man was having on her mother's life. Lisa had even said to her, "Mom, are you aware that not only your face but your tone of voice changes when you mention this Jonathon guy? He must be really something."

Marika was feeling pangs of insecurity. What would she do if the two didn't like each other? And tonight she and Jonathon would finally make love. He had been talking about it enough, Lord knows—and she would welcome it. In fact, her body longed for him, even just a touch of his hand. She had denied him—and herself—so far. Would they be right for each other?

She smiled at her own girlish actions tonight in preparation for his arrival—the long soaking in scented bath oil, the wild splashing of eau de cologne over her entire body, and then, when she was dressed, an additional application of strong perfume on her neck and wrists. She grinned at herself in the mirror, as she dabbed perfume in between her breasts. The perfect *Cosmo* girl, she laughed to herself. Lisa reacted when she saw her, "Mom, you smell like a dozen perfume counters at Bloomingdale's stuck together," but Sergio was more gallant. *"Signora, stasera lei è proprio un giardino di Paradiso!"*

The doorbell rang right at the stroke of eight. Jonathon stepped into the foyer and was about to take Marika into his arms when he saw the figures of the two young people right behind her. Instead he gave her a kiss on the cheek and said in a low voice, "My God, it's good to see you again. You are so beautiful." Marika turned and introduced him to Lisa and her friend, suddenly realizing that the presence of the young ones had made them both a little uncomfortable.

"I'll get you a drink. What would you like, Jonathon?"

"Believe it or not, a club soda."

He sank gratefully into the big white sofa, rubbed his red eyes, and made polite conversation with Lisa and Sergio. When Marika arrived with his drink, she noticed his fatigue. "You look really bushed."

"Thanks." He laughed and said to Lisa, "There's nothing like walking in the door after many days of forced labor in the Far East and being told that you look like a tanned, rested Adonis."

"How long was your flight?" Sergio asked sympathetically.

"A mere twenty-two hours, with no sleep, and no sleep from the night before either."

"You deserve to look—a little tired," Marika said. She longed to touch him, hold him. She wanted to feel his whole body interlaced with hers, but she could not show any of these feelings to her daughter and Sergio. She did not want them to know the depth of her attraction for this man—not yet, anyway.

"I hope you appreciate, my dear," he managed to say in a light tone, edged with fatigue, "that I overflew Chicago and made my flight even two hours longer, just to be with you tonight."

"I'm well aware of that."

Lisa noticed how her mother's eyes reflected Jonathon's smile every time she looked at him. She was wearing her new wide-legged white crepe pajamas with a halter top that showed off her beautiful figure. (Lisa had tried them on before her mother had the chance to do so when they were taken from the Saks box a week earlier.) A diamond rose sat on her mother's only draped shoulder; the other, with its firm, slim upper arm, was left provocatively bare. Hot stuff.

Lisa rose from her chair, taking Sergio by the hand. "Good

night, Mom. Good night, Mr. Scher. It was very nice to meet you."

Marika's dinner, courtesy of Geneviève's advance preparation, was as delicious as she had hoped it would be. The table looked gracious with its white mother-of-pearl place mats, linen napkins, and the Imari orange, blue, and gold dinner plates. Jonathon tried to talk about his trip, but finally said, "Look, I told you more about what I was doing every night when I called you than I could possibly remember tonight."

There was a momentary silence and then Jonathon said quietly, "You're so far away from me." He got up from his chair, picked it up, and brought it around until it was very close to her chair on her side of the table. She laughed and reached across the table for his wineglass, flatware, napkin, and dinner plate, now well heaped with Geneviève's mild curried chicken and rice.

"I just wanted to be able to smell you," he said, sniffing her hair. "It's been a long time, and I love the smell of you. Not even the curry can touch it." At the touch of his face in her hair, she could feel a warm pink flush of embarrassment suddenly appear in her cheeks—shyness over what she was feeling inside at that very moment, which was simple passion.

Whoa, she told herself. It's going to happen. But let him start it.

She noticed he had eaten hardly anything, and it suddenly made her concerned.

"Jonathon, you haven't touched your food. Are you feeling all right? Geneviève will be so upset." He excused himself, saying that he had consumed too much bad airplane food in the last day and night. She then realized he was having trouble keeping his eyes open. They were rimmed red from exhaustion. He kept blinking them in a kind of daze, then shaking his head as if trying to regain his concentration. "Jet lag," he apologized.

After dinner she brought the silver coffee pitcher and two demitasse cups on a tray into the living room. They sat down close to each other on the oversized white damask sofa, with its deep cushions, and she put two pillows behind his back to make him comfortable. Then she jumped up again, going into the kitchen to bring him some sweetener. When she returned, two minutes later, he had slumped to one side and was in a deep sleep.

"So, my wild, passionate lover," she laughed, speaking softly to him, "you have gone to sleep—and without me." She pulled off his shoes and put his legs up on the sofa, adjusting a pillow behind his head. He did not wake up. She found an afghan in the closet off the foyer, and covered him. She left a note on the outside of the apartment door, warning Lisa not to disturb him when she came in. Then she turned off the living room lights and climbed the stairway to her bedroom.

The telephone rang at seven while she was doing her exercises. It was Mrs. Matthews, Jonathon's secretary, asking her if she knew where Mr. Scher was. "He has an urgent eight-thirty breakfast meeting this morning and he doesn't know where to go. I—er—tried to reach him at his hotel."

"I can get the message to him," Marika replied.

"Wonderful, Mrs. Wentworth. Please tell him he should be at the Regency at eight-thirty with Mr. Danforth. Tell him the company jet is not yet back in service so I've made a reservation on American Airlines' ten o'clock back to Chicago. If he misses it, he also has a reservation on American's eleven o'clock flight."

"You're very efficient. I'll get these details to him."

She put a robe over her leotard and went to wake Jonathon. "My God, Marika, I'm so sorry about last night. Did you slip me a mickey?"

She laughed and gave him his secretary's message. "This way to the guest bathroom. There's a new toothbrush, some toothpaste, even a razor in the cabinet."

"You're the perfect hostess." His eyes played over her form, making her aware of the clinging robe.

As he started to close the door of the bathroom, he added, "If I never do another thing in my whole life, I'll make it up to you for last night."

"Don't worry. We have time—and I think your secretary is shocked and thinks we had a wild sex orgy last night."

"Just you wait, we will have one." He winked one gorgeous blue eye and closed the bathroom door.

CHAPTER

*H*ortense buzzed her boss on the intercom with more vigor than usual. "The world's most attractive man wants to speak with you." Marika thought at first it must be Jonathon. Then she smiled, remembering her secretary's crush on her father. Hortense had made a declaration more than once that if she were lucky enough to meet an eligible man cut of Charles Russell's fabric, she would "mount a campaign to entrap him that even Napoleon Bonaparte would have found ingenious."

"Daddy, what a pleasant surprise!" Marika said into the receiver. "Your voice is so much more welcome than those I usually hear so early in the day."

She noticed his voice was edged was seriousness. "Are you busy tonight?" he asked. "I'm taking the five o'clock shuttle from Boston this afternoon. I need to see you about something."

She shivered from a sudden sensation of cold. He didn't need to say that something was wrong. She could sense it. Her father was totally direct—forthright.

"Lisa and I will be thrilled to see you," she said eagerly. "But aren't you going to tell me what's up? Don't I get a hint?"

He tried to sound reassuring. "Nothing of any great importance. But it's something we should discuss."

"Will you have dinner with us at home?"

"There's nothing I would love better. But I need to see you alone for a few minutes before dinner, without Lisa present. Can you arrange that?"

She was now totally perplexed. This was so unlike him.

"Of course, Daddy, I'll arrange that. I can send Lisa off to listen to her sad music tapes before dinner. She's the one who's feeling a little low. Trouble in the romance department, but nothing that about twenty-four hours won't cure."

"Good." She could hear him chuckle at the mention of Lisa's love life. "We'll cheer her up at dinner. In the meantime, I'll come directly from La Guardia. With luck—and you always need that on the shuttle—I should reach your apartment by six forty-five."

The mysterious conversation her father wished to have with her tonight had an ominous cast. She looked at the stainless-steel Tiffany clock tower rising like a miniature skyscraper from the pool of cluttered papers on her desk. She turned the clock at an angle to be able to see the hands. She had exactly six more hours in which to accomplish an office workload that would normally require twelve hours. She also had to order the food for tonight's dinner, get Geneviève to set the table and prepare the salad and dessert, warn Lisa to be home or else, and last but not least, there was the matter of Lisa's temporarily broken heart. She had to get home in time for a chat with her. Maybe they could have a talk while she was preparing the scaloppine for tonight's dinner. She couldn't, after all, ignore that young broken heart. But everything had to be completed before her father's arrival at six forty-five. It was time for some high-pressured juggling again.

She felt a sudden compulsion to open her top right-hand desk drawer. A motto written in calligraphy was pasted on the side of the drawer. It read: "Never Substitute Complaining for Doing." She meditated on the thought for a moment and went about her business.

. . .

Marika was late. As always, when alone and behind schedule, she talked to herself at a normal volume but at a rapid rate. "That's all right," she consoled herself, "just five more minutes for the scaloppine, then the table. Oh, and I mustn't forget to decant the wine." Her out-loud thoughts helped organize her.

Lisa arrived, laden with books from the library, and heard her mother's familiar muttering sounds. She walked into the kitchen, pulling off her dirty gray sweatshirt and pulling on a pink ski sweater at the same time—her one concession to her grandfather's presence at dinner.

"What about changing those dirty gray sweatpants?"

"Mom, be cool! Grandpa's not going to notice."

"Lisa," there was a touch of guilt in her voice now, "I—I seem to be behind schedule on this veal. Your grandfather is about to walk in the door. Now is—sort of—not the time for us to have our talk about Sergio. There just isn't time."

Lisa said she would be glad to wait until after Grandpa had left before telling her mother the latest horrible news about her fight with Sergio. A juggling bonus, Marika decided, hallelujah! The doorbell rang just as she was finishing the sautéeing of Geneviève's veal scaloppine in the heavy iron skillet, and was beginning to simmer the lemon-dill sauce. The herb-flavored rice was already made. She would slam the lid on the skillet and keep the veal and its sauce ready for a reheating later when they sat down to dinner.

She heard the sounds of her father greeting her Haitian housekeeper, who was on her way out the door, headed for home. "*Bonsoir*, Geneviève," she heard him say in his familiar Bostonian-accented French. "*Ça fait plaisir de vous voir.*" She heard Geneviève greet him with affection, and could picture the dark face wreathed in smiles—the tight black curls of her wig bobbing in unison with her courtly little bows. Geneviève knew how to usher someone in with deferential bows while simultaneously backing out of the door, which required a certain skill. Marika heard the bantering of the two voices. Geneviève loved Charles Russell as much as Hortense did. My father, the lady-killer, Marika thought, smiling to herself.

When she walked into the black and white foyer of her Sutton Place duplex, wiping her hands on her apron, her father had already hung up his gray Chesterfield coat with its dark gray velvet collar in the hall closet. He held her in a silent embrace, confirming Marika's fear that this was not just an ordinary meeting. My God, she thought to herself, as she hugged him, how thin he has become. Even with the fewer pounds on his frame, Charles Russell was tall, handsome, and aristocratic-looking. Not even aging could change that. His grayish-blond hair was as thick as it was in Marika's earliest memories of him. Everything about him was always *just right*. Then she noticed again how terribly thin he had become in the seven weeks since she'd last seen him. His suit hung on him, almost apologetically. His shirt collar, usually fastened at his neck with perfect snugness, was loose. His Adam's apple sat like a small ball imprisoned in the thick veins of his neck. He was gaunt and looked like another person. It frightened her.

Lisa, having heard the front doorbell, leaned over the stairway railing from the second floor and called down, "Grandpa, a big kiss! See you later, and don't talk too long. I've already tasted the scaloppine. They're great, so don't procrastinate, you two."

Without asking, Marika fixed him his usual scotch with ice, motioned him into his favorite wing chair in the living room, and sat down to listen. He was wearing a beautifully cut dark gray suit and a fashionable white shirt with wide pink stripes, a stiff white collar, and French cuffs. Charlie Russell always dressed better than the men in *GQ* magazine. Maybe it was the contrast of the cheery red silk paisley tie and red silk pocket handkerchief that made his skin so pallid. She decided he looked gray all over, matching the color of his suit. The black circles under his eyes were startling.

"Marika," he began, his voice cracking very slightly, "it seems I'm not all that well."

Instinctively, she arose from her chair and pulled a little pale blue satin stool right next to his chair. She sat down on it and took his hand. His voice hung in the air with that pronouncement, and there didn't seem to be anything to follow. "Daddy, go on," she urged, feeling a sense of panic and a rush of blood to her head. She knew something terrible was to come.

"My doctor gave me the final report this morning. I've been going through a lot of tests. I have colon cancer. I go into Massachusetts General tomorrow. They are going to operate in a few days after a lot more tests, but they told me that the risk is"— he stopped and took a quick breath— "major. I told them to hell with it. No operation, if it's a major risk. They told me to hell with it right back. They told me I *will* have the operation, and any chemotherapy afterward they decide is advisable, but I've been told the prognosis is poor. I let it go too long. The tumor is massive and has probably spread. I was a damn fool. I had symptoms of pain and blood that I ignored for a long time."

"Daddy," she protested, "you've always been in perfect health! You've never had a thing wrong with you." This must be something he was imagining. He was overreacting to what the doctors told him. He had never really been sick, never went to doctors. His friends always teased him, calling him "Charlie-the-Invincible," the man who kept himself in perfect physical condition, who never even succumbed to the common cold, who had stopped smoking cigarettes, who never drank too much, and who, it was rumored, used to break Olympic records in his Harvard days by making "memorable love" to three women separately during the same night. He was able to keep the reputation going even *after* his Harvard days, it was said.

"Of course," Marika said matter-of-factly, "you'll pull through this operation with flying colors. I know you, Daddy." The buzzing in her ears got louder. Somehow, Marika thought, if she just kept talking, it would be all right.

"Maybe yes, maybe no. I hope to God I don't survive if it means being an invalid the rest of my life."

"You *will* survive, Daddy, and you'll lick colon cancer like so many people have, and you *won't* be an invalid." Marika felt as though she and her father were on one end of a tug-of-war rope, with death on the other. She and Charlie Russell could take on anything together in this fight, and *win*.

"Marika, I don't have much energy. I'm not in good shape. I had the feeling for several months that something was terribly wrong, but—"

"But you felt it would go away without having to see a doctor." She finished the sentence for him.

"Let's don't argue now," he said with a terrible sadness in his voice, "about either the prognosis or my stupidity on medical matters. They are both givens. There's—there is something else I must tell you that's difficult to say, but it must be said. Just for a second, please don't interrupt me, like you always do."

For God's sake, what more could there be in addition to telling her that he was dying? What could "something else" be?

"Daddy," she broke in, "I won't interrupt. Just get it out, whatever it is, quickly."

His tired eyes crinkled up in a resigned smile, because, of course, she had just interrupted him again.

"Marika," the words came slowly and in pain, "I'm not—I'm not your blood father."

It was like the blurb for a novel on the dust jacket. "I'm not your real father," he told the heroine in a strained voice. . . . There was a complete stillness in the room. It was a time to recover from the shock of getting something out that had lain trapped for many years in one person's subconsciousness. For the other, it was a time to face the unacceptable.

Marika remained on the little footstool by his chair, feeling like the little child who would sit dressed in her nightie on the stool next to him in the library, his favorite room in the Boston house, listening to bedtime stories. He had just told her another make-believe story, even though she was no longer a child. At the exact same hour every night her nannie would come fetch her for bed, a signal for the wonderful Daddy stories to cease, right then and there. There was no deterring Nannie from her rigorous nursery schedule, except for Marika and her father's evening story hour. She remembered that even if Daddy had a dinner party to attend, he would first tell her a story, sitting in his chair—slim and handsome in his black dinner clothes—like a royal prince. She loved to admire his evening shoes—black patent leather pumps with black grosgrain bows, shiny enough to be able to see your face. Or sometimes, when he had guests for dinner at home, he would wear his black velvet slippers with embroidered peacocks of splendid colors. "Peacock" had been one of the earliest grown-up words she had ever learned.

It's amazing, how many thoughts can fly through the brain in a moment of silence. Marika began thinking about her mother's death when she was only five. There were confused, somber memories of days that were shadowy and gray, when strangers seemed to be wandering all over the big house, speaking in quiet tones. People were all dark in their clothes and faces. It was like being in an ancient church at twilight, when only the smallest shaft of light could penetrate the stained-glass windows. They say death has a smell, she thought, and then she suddenly remembered the scent of many kinds of perfumes mingling in the air—friends of her mother, beautiful and sad in black, their perfumes wafting through her house. Her mother wouldn't have liked it. Not in her house. All those fragrances of death . . .

Her mother had died suddenly of pneumonia. "So young, so tragic," were words that Marika remembered people saying over and over. She remembered going to a church to say good-bye to her mother, but she didn't really remember it. She did remember that afterward when they were home again, Charlie Russell had picked her up and whispered, "You and I are going to do just fine, Marika. And in a while," he added, "we will even learn to have fun again."

He had kept his word. They did have fun while she was growing up. He was everything to her—mother, father, brother, sister, all rolled into one. He and Nannie managed to fill her days with sunshine. When she graduated from the eighth grade Nannie left to work for another family with small children. Father and daughter became like a "couple of old shoes," her father often said. "We run this house almost as well as if your mother were with us."

Lord, how the ladies loved him, Marika thought with a smile, and how they tried to entrap him. He was Boston's most eligible, attractive widower. They invited him to dinner, concerts, weekends at their country homes. They were all over him.

Marika suddenly remembered one night, after she was supposedly asleep, when she had tiptoed downstairs to the sounds of Frank Sinatra singing "A cigarette that bears a lipstick's traces . . . These foolish things remind me of you." She peeked into the living room where she saw one of Boston's most famous society figures—a jazzy divorced woman—dancing around like a snake, while she removed all of her clothes. As Marika watched, galvanized, the jazzy lady proceeded to tear at her father's clothes, ripping them off. At first Marika thought he was in danger and wondered if she should call the police, but then an eight-year-old's common sense prevailed. Her father was laughing and obviously liking it. Perplexed, she went back to bed, but didn't sleep all night. At breakfast the next morning, she confronted him. "Daddy, what were you doing with the naked lady in the living room last night? You both looked awfully strange . . ."

Her father at first chuckled, then laughed outright. "There are certain things, Marika," he said, mopping the tears that rolled down his face, "that you will have to learn about when you're older." He always dismissed anything he did not wish to answer directly as something she would learn about when she was older. She accepted this unquestioningly, as she always accepted anything he told her.

They sat together peacefully in her Sutton Place living room, in a wing chair and on a little stool, not needing to make conversation at this particular moment, but feeling closer than close as father and daughter. She suddenly could not help but notice the great wall of books against which her father's body was now silhouetted. This particular group of books was jammed floor to ceiling in dark mahogany bookshelves—favorite editions that dated from her childhood in Boston. The most favored ones had been saved for Lisa, as Lisa would save them for her own children. They were childhood books that told of happy lives—and they spoke to Marika, too, of loneliness, of life growing up without a mother, but with a father who loved her more than anyone else ever could.

She had a sudden flashback to twenty-six years ago, when she was eighteen, on the night of her private debut dinner-dance at the Ritz in Boston. She had come down the stairs of their house in her bouffant white tulle ballgown and found Charlie Russell waiting for her, leaning against the stairway, smiling like an admiring swain. He was wearing his black top hat, white tie, and tails. She decided he looked much handsomer than Fred Astaire ever had wearing the same regalia in his movies. Her father had whistled his appreciation when he saw her, and suddenly his expression had changed to a very melancholic one. Marika remembered now that they had talked about her mother. He spoke about her all the way to the Ritz. He held her hand and told Marika that she was every bit as beautiful as her mother on this night. He told her that she had consoled him through the years since her mother's death, more than she could ever possibly understand.

"Why haven't you married again, Daddy?" Marika had asked him. "You've had so many chances. You've had so many proposals. I'll never receive as many as you!"

He just laughed at that, and told her that no one could take her mother's place. "Your mother made me feel like such a fantastic man," he said sadly. "No one else can make me feel that way. I prefer to remember what the two of us had together for a short time, rather than settle for anything less."

He whirled his daughter around the dance floor in a waltz, ignoring the young men in white tie and tails trying to cut in on them. "Remember, Marika, nothing is more important than making the one you love feel like the greatest man who ever lived." Then he had given her hand to one of the young men and gone to greet friends. He never had the chance to dance with her again all evening. In fact, she had repeated this statement to Jonathon in one of their conversations about Charlie. Jonathon—was it only yesterday he had been here, lighting up her life, and now, here was her father, telling her he was a man with a death sentence hanging over his head and that he was not even her natural father?

Marika felt at that moment that life was a roller coaster, carrying her on a bumpy ride over its valleys and hills, and that it was important that there was Jonathon at this moment in her life to help her hold on. It seemed to her that her father's face, that beloved, thin face, was growing grayer every second. His fingers, almost skeletal in their boniness, clasped his glass of scotch carefully, as if there was not enough strength in them to do the job.

He began to talk again, speaking slowly, haltingly. "You remember," he paused for a second, "how your mother and I met again in London during the war? We were in the prime of our youth, we had known each other as children, but we had not seen each other since our freshman year in different boarding schools."

Marika certainly did remember the London part of their lives. There were photographs in three different places in her parents' house, taken at the time of their wedding in England. Both young, aristocratic, blond, the world seemed to be lying in the palms of their joined hands, even in wartime. The lovely Alice Stuyvesant in her Red Cross uniform, with a visored cap crowning her thick, naturally curly blond hair. And Charles Russell, movie-star handsome in his Army Air Corps uniform. My God they were beautiful, she thought, both of them.

She pulled up with a start. She had been reminiscing with such speed covering such a long period of time, she had stopped listening to her father.

"Before your mother and I saw each other again in London at Christmas in 1944, she, uh, she—" He suddenly stopped, unable to continue. Then he took a gulp of scotch, and the words began to tumble out hoarsely, quickly, one after another, as though he were tossing them over a cliff into an abyss.

"Your mother had been involved with someone just before I saw her," he began again. "She had been very much in love with a Hungarian named Istvan Bokanyi who was working underground to help the Jews in Hungary. He had come to London to raise some more funds for his group. He met your mother, and two weeks after they were together, he—he had to go back. The Nazis got him. I'm not sure of the circumstances, only that your mother got word of his death around the time she learned that she was pregnant."

"Good Lord!" Marika got up from the stool and began pacing the floor in front of him, not knowing how to contain her own feelings. Her father's hands were visibly shaking now. The ice cubes rattled against his glass. She kissed his forehead and enclosed his poor fingers with her own, to still them.

"Go on, Daddy. Get it all out." The fact that he had kept this secret from her seemed an impossible burden for either of them right now.

"From the moment I laid eyes again on your mother as a grown woman at the Officers Club, I was intoxicated by her. Perhaps it was the war and the drama of what was happening to both of us that made our shared childhood and Boston roots even more important. Or maybe it was because we needed each other so much at that point. I was damned scared of going down in my bomber with a piece of ammunition in my skull; she was frightened about being pregnant, and then losing the man she thought she had loved. She was such a cool, beautiful woman but that first night she had tears in her eyes the entire time we spoke. I just sat drinking in that chiseled profile, wanting to dispose of the tears in those incredible blue eyes. I just wanted to hold her, and tell her she would never have to worry about anything again for the rest of her life. I had never seen anyone or anything so beautiful in my life. I must have frightened her too—professing my love so quickly—and so—urgently.

"I guess I was persuasive. She left the party at Tooey Spaatz's headquarters with me and we spent the rest of the evening talking in my room—sharing my one glass and a bottle of liquor. You know," and he laughed as he said it, "two people don't really need more than one glass." Marika nodded and urged him by her expression to continue.

"I saw her again the next night, the second I could get off duty. I couldn't help myself. I used every cliché in the book. I told her she was the woman I had dreamed of all my life, that we would marry and live happily ever after, and that I had fallen madly, passionately in love with her. I was leaving on a bombing mission over Germany in three days' time, and when you hover so nonchalantly between life and death as we did in those war days, you say things you would never have the courage to say otherwise. I was amazed how articulate I was—me, a typical uptight, repressed Bostonian. But Marika," and the smile came into his eyes again, "your mother always told me I was pretty damned good with my flowery speeches, and there were some good actions, too, speaking louder than—"

Marika could only smile and tighten her hand over her father's. The tears slid uninterrupted down her cheeks. She made no attempt to find a handkerchief. Her father smiled. "You're just like your mother—no emotional control whatsoever." He continued, as quickly as his ebbing strength would allow. "I held your mother in my arms after that proposal, and she broke down and sobbed uncontrollably. I have never seen anyone cry so hard, for so long. I thought it was because she had fallen in love with me, too, and was afraid I was going to die on that next bombing mission. It made me love her and want her even more. I was beside myself with longing for her." He stopped to catch his breath and took a sip. It choked in his throat.

At this point Marika got up, found some tissues, which she had brought for both of them to use, and made herself an unusually large drink. Then she returned to her perch on the little stool, her body turned toward him, her hand protectively laid once again on his arm.

"Your mother was someone so honest, so pure, so straightforward, Marika."

"I know, Daddy, I know." They both were snatching the tissues at the same time and stopped to share a laugh.

"She told me she could learn to love me, but that I had to know that she had just found out there was a baby on the way— Istvan's child."

Marika was frantic to learn more from her father. He was talking so slowly again, trying to collect his thoughts, emotions, and words, and having great difficulty in sorting them out.

"What about this Istvan?" she asked. "What did Mother tell you about him? What did he look like? Where was he from? What did he do before the war? Where did he go to school?" She was almost cruel with her barrage of urgent questions. The figure of this shadow father reverberated in Marika's head. She needed instantaneously to give him substance, specifics.

"Your mother told me nothing about him. I don't think she knew the answers to any of those questions. He was a sudden *coup de foudre* in wartime London—a love story that ended tragically and quickly. And after we were married, Istvan's name simply never came up. It was as though she wanted to wipe out his memory for my sake, and for your sake. You were," he touched Marika's hair, "our pride and joy. I considered you my own flesh and blood. If your mother had made you aware of your Hungarian background, it would have broken our deal. In our eyes, you were *my* daughter. Our one deference to your Hungarian parentage is that we gave you a Hungarian name."

"Mother told me that I was named for the heroine in a Hungarian folk tale she read as a little girl."

"Yes, you were, but did it ever strike you strange we would give you such a name in the Boston environment in which we raised you?"

"Go on, Daddy."

"Our deal was that I would raise you, love you, protect you, and make it unnecessary for you to know the identity of your real father. My name is on your birth certificate as your father."

"Your mother," he paused, "had only been with Istvan a total of two weeks. Your mother and I were married for—almost six wonderful years before she died. Istvan simply did not exist in our lives."

Marika looked her father in the eyes, and softly said, "But Istvan exists in *my* life now. Why did you tell me this secret now?"

He didn't answer, but instead continued his reminiscences again. "You can't imagine how I felt when I chalked up enough missions to be granted some leave. Your mother and I were married as soon as we could get the papers in order, which required the genius of General Spaatz to help us. Marika, it was the most wonderful wedding anyone ever had."

She remembered the photograph of them standing outside the

exquisite eighteenth-century Grosvenor Chapel in South Audley Street. There were framed photographs, too, of wedding guests who were famous figures in London during World War II, people like Averell Harriman, Generals Ira Eaker and Spaatz, and OSS figures like David Bruce, Evangeline Bell, Frank Wisner, and Dick Helms.

"We had at least a hundred people—your mother's Red Cross friends, my Air Corps buddies, some English friends, and some OSS pals." He suddenly gave a small cough, but it seemed to shake his body like a child shakes her rag doll. He looked so ill. Alarmed, Marika put her hand again over his, trying to instill some of her warmth, energy, and strength into his body.

"Go on, Daddy. I love hearing about this." But what she was burning to hear about was more information on Istvan Bokanyi, the man whose blood was running in her veins. There was no picture of him, no letters—nothing to make him a real human being. There were so many unanswered questions, so many doubts . . .

"All of us walked from the Grosvenor Chapel through the quiet streets just a few blocks away to Claridges for the wedding reception. We made a happy, boisterous parade to the hotel. It may have been wartime, but champagne never tasted so much like divine ambrosia.

"The news of our wedding pleased my parents." He laughed. "My bride was 'suitable' in their eyes. The Boston papers, the *New York Times*, and my Groton and Harvard alumni magazines carried the story and photos. My family was pleased that a beautiful young Stuyvesant had joined the Russell family."

Get on with Istvan, Daddy, she wanted so badly to say. Let's get back to Istvan!

"Once your mother announced her pregnancy a month after the wedding, the Red Cross sent her back home immediately. It took me another year to finish my missions and get home myself, and by then, you were not only born, but you were a beautiful little girl with the whitest of skin, green eyes, and the brownest of curls framing your face like the angels in the Fra Angelico frescoes. You were certainly not a blond, English-looking Russell or Dutch-looking Stuyvesant, Marika," and he laughed, "but I didn't mind. We raised you as a Bostonian, not as a Magyar."

The Hungarian word startled her, but her father did not notice.

"Neither your mother's family or mine," he continued, "ever brought up the fact that my wife had produced a baby after seven, not nine, months of marriage. After all, we were married in Europe, and I don't think anyone in our families wanted to count!" The corners of his mouth turned up in a sweet smile at this. That was a different era. Marika knew that in those days the Stuyvesant and Russell families could never have coped with a scandal, nor could they have accepted the fact that Charlie Russell's daughter was in reality the daughter of another man. Since such a thing was impermissible, it was also inadmissible, and therefore would be totally dismissable in her grandparents' eyes.

"But why—I mean how—" Marika interrupted, "did you handle the fact in your own mind that you weren't my real father?"

"It didn't matter to me that she had become pregnant with another man's child. He was gone and I loved her—oh, I loved your mother and you so much. If I didn't feel I had to tell you now, you could have gone through your entire life not knowing about Istvan. You really were *my* child. All of these years, I never admitted—even to myself—that you weren't. But now, in fairness to you and to Lisa—"

"But what about my real father's family?" She saw him flinch as she asked this question. She had hurt him by conjuring up the image of Istvan's family.

"Your mother did not even know their names, their addresses, anything about them, and they certainly knew nothing about her—or you. Her affair with him had been an impetuous one; there was little communication. Your mother knew no Hungarian, and he spoke only a little English. They saw each other only for two weeks, and for very few hours at any one time."

She pictured her very proper mother, a well-behaved Red Cross girl, losing her virginity and thrashing around in bed with her lothario, unable even to speak in a common tongue! Marika smiled to herself, titillated by the idea, shocked, too, but also frankly amused.

Then she wiped out that image with the one she always remembered best—her beautiful mother looking crisp and sunny-faced in her white piqué tennis dress with an embroidered green frog on the skirt, her blond curly hair tied back in a ponytail with a green velvet ribbon. In the evening Marika's mother would change. To the little child she appeared almost as a fairy princess in a pale pink satin evening gown, with a pink satin rose tucked into her décolletage, and her hair swept up into a chignon, with a small, perfect diamond brooch tucked into its back fold. Marika could almost smell a whiff of her wonderful perfume, and delighted in the thought that this woman whose every shining blond hair was always in place, who fit so perfectly into the constrained Boston social life, had experienced a passionate, tempestuous love affair—with a foreign "prince"—her father!

Her beautiful, graceful, moral, and pure mother, who appeared more of a Boston Brahmin than her father, had allowed herself to travel down Passion's street. It was wonderful to contemplate.

"Why, Daddy," she asked, "should you be telling me this now—forty-four years after I was born? I don't understand. Why did you feel compelled to tell me this?"

"Because I am probably going to die, Marika, and I think it's important that you know from where you have come."

"I come from *you*, Daddy." She suddenly felt insecure, buffeted, as though the very heritage in which she had been so secure all her life was suddenly being pulled out from under her like a rug being picked up—so the floor can be mopped. She tried to force back the tears, but they came anyway, at first gently, then unapologetically.

"You are the only one who matters to me, Daddy."

"You had to know the truth, Marika. Half of your blood is Hungarian, even though," he laughed, "you seem very American to me."

"Or at least Bostonian." Charlie knew his daughter well enough to know that if she was teasing, then she'd found her courage.

"Someday you must trace that Hungarian ancestry of yours," he said solemnly, "and find your roots on your father's side. I can't help you, because your mother had nothing of Istvan's to go on—no names or addresses. He was under deep cover when he was in London. He left no traces. Your mother only heard him mention a little town once or twice—called something like Szentendre or a similar name."

"Look, Daddy, as far as I'm concerned, the only thing that matters right now is that you get through this cancer fight and get well again!" She wrote the name Szentendre on a nearby notepad.

She had to help him up from his chair to walk into the dining room. She called Lisa to come down to dinner. Charlie Russell was already seated at the table when Lisa arrived and Marika was thankful that she would not have to see how frail her grandfather was in his movements. Lisa kept him company while Marika gave a quick reheat to her scaloppine and special rice, tossed the salad, heated the rolls, and brought everything to the table. A bottle of red wine, decanted, already sat on a Georgian silver coaster. Marika brought in a half bottle of chilled white wine and placed it on the other coaster.

Somehow Charlie and Marika managed to get through their dinner with Lisa. They did not even have to talk, but listened instead as Lisa lamented the trauma of her breakup with Sergio. As always, her grandfather was ready with sympathy and advice.

No one said a word when it appeared that Marika had burned her usually magnificent dill-flavored wild rice that always accompanied her usually splendid scaloppine. When her father rose to leave, she whispered in his ear, "I'll be there before your operation. I'll call to find out the exact time. Will you be all right taking the shuttle back alone?" He nodded and they hugged each other good-bye a little longer than usual just before he stepped into the limo that would take him to La Guardia. Lisa remarked in jest when Marika stepped off the elevator to come back to the apartment, "Heh, Mom, you two acted as though you were never going to have dinner together again."

Perhaps not, my fair Lisa, thought her mother, perhaps not. Marika put her arm around her daughter and they walked slowly back into the living room and sank into the deep white sofa. The soft pale grays, warm beiges, and cocoa colors of the two-storied room had turned rosy pink in the light from the dimmed table lamps.

"Tonight's heart-to-heart was supposed to be for you," Marika pushed back a strand of Lisa's strawberry hair, "but although your heart is breaking over Sergio, mine is too, over your grandfather. He's very sick, Lisa."

"Mom, I knew it. I could tell. How sick is he?"

"He has colon cancer. They are operating in three or four days at Mass General. Naturally, I will go up to Boston beforehand to be with him. I hope you will come up, too, on the day. You will be a great comfort to me. The prognosis is not good, he told me."

"Mom, we can talk about Sergio another time. In comparison to Grandpa, it's very unimportant." The two women sat silently in the deep recesses of the sofa, each immersed in her own thoughts and absentmindedly stroking the other's hand. Everything seemed insignificant in the face of this news—a direct attack on a stable support system that had always been there, provided by Charles Russell. It had been there for the duration of each of their lives—and neither knew just how to cope with the idea of such an immense loss. Even though he lived in another city, Charlie Russell had always, ever since David's death, been the man "around the house."

A half hour later, they climbed the staircase to bed, both leaning wearily on the graceful, black wrought-iron railing—which normally neither used. Marika tried to sleep for a half hour, then turned on the light and dialed a Chicago number, wanting to hear the warmth of Jonathon's voice. When he answered, she told him about her father's illness and they talked quietly for an hour. There was a new relaxed tenderness that now touched their relationship. They both felt it without saying anything, but they sensed it in each other's voices. She did not tell Jonathon about the other thunderbolt her father had hurled during the cocktail hour—the news of her Hungarian father. It seemed immaterial and unimportant in the light of her father's illness. Thanks to Jonathon's reassuring words, finally she was able to lapse into a troubled sleep.

CHAPTER

6

She knew she could not keep it from Lisa any longer. She could not bear the burden of knowing about Istvan one more hour alone. She had to tell Lisa. Lisa was her flesh and blood.

She had a car coming at six o'clock to take her to the seven o'clock shuttle to Boston. At five-thirty, she woke her daughter.

"Mom, what are you doing? It's only—it's—" She squinted hard at her clock, trying to bring the hour into focus.

"I know, I know," Marika said soothingly, "but there's something you must know. It's another little missile your grandfather threw at me last night."

Lisa wrinkled her nose, squinted at her mother, and finally pulled herself up into a seated position, with her back resting against the tufted, flower-splashed headboard of the bed. "Well?"

"It's, it's—let me put it this way," Marika was trying very hard to clothe her feelings with words.

"Mom," Lisa said impatiently, "I'm going back to sleep. You're having a premenopausal flap, or something."

Her mother laughed. "At the very worst moments in my life, you can always make me laugh." Lisa began to slump back down under the covers.

"Your grandfather is not your real grandfather." Marika threw out the words into the air with the speed of a fastball in a baseball game.

Lisa sat up straight again in bed. "Mom, you're losing it. Are you on drugs or something?"

"Certainly not. I have to go in a few minutes, but in case my plane crashes or something, you are the surviving member of this family, and you have to know."

"What's this about Grandpa? Mom, get ahold of yourself. Talk sense. You're just overly concerned about Grandpa. He's going to be all right."

Marika took both of Lisa's hands in hers, for support more than as a gesture of comfort for Lisa, and told her the story of her mother and Istvan. Lisa listened incredulously, then burst out laughing.

"I fail to see the humor in all this," her mother said coolly.

"It's so absurd, so 'Saturday Night Live,' I just don't believe it."

"Well, believe it. And file it away. And let me get through my father's illness before we have any further discussion of it. Is that all right with you?"

"Sounds like you've decided for me," Lisa turned suddenly into the child again.

"You'll need time to digest it all anyway," her mother said kindly, as she heard the driver of her car service, honking out in the side street for her.

"Digest it?" Lisa answered abruptly. "It's given me indigestion already. But *you*, Mom. What does this do to you?"

"I don't know. My father said last night that someday you and I would have to go to Hungary and seek our roots. I guess that's something we'll have to do."

"Yeah, someday," Lisa said slowly, "someday when we don't have anything too much better to do." She slid back under the covers as her mother softly closed the door. "Grandpa," Lisa said aloud to herself. "Grandpa Charlie and Grandpa Istvan. My God!"

Jonathon had arranged for a car to meet Marika's shuttle in Boston, enabling her to go directly to the hospital. The driver was instructed to take her baggage to the Russell house on Beacon Street.

Charles Russell's room at Mass General Hospital looked like a laboratory in a science fiction film—a jungled mass of machines, tubes, and people. She found him surrounded by a conferring circle of peering, low-murmuring doctors and nurses. It seemed as though each one was thinking aloud to himself. She could feel the tension in the room. There was so much equipment and onerous-looking paraphernalia around the pathetic figure in the bed; she felt that, in a way, Charles Russell was already gone from her. The senior physician took her aside. "It doesn't look good, Mrs. Wentworth. We were planning on some simple tests prior to the operation, and he—he suffered a heart attack."

Charles Russell suddenly realized his daughter was in the room. He smiled wanly at her and tried to hold her hand, but she knew the strength lay in her hands, not his. With her free hand she dialed Lisa in New York. "Don't wait two days before coming up for his operation. I think you had better come *now*."

Lisa did not make it in time. Charlie Russell, the prince of princes to his daughter and granddaughter, an aristocrat personified, and a warm, loving man, died a half hour after Marika reached his bedside.

Before he died, Charlie said, "I'm not afraid, you know. I'm going to join your mother, and that is my heart's desire. Marika, even though you are not of my blood, no one could have asked for a finer child. I have loved you so much all these years." His voice was a whisper, but she leaned close and heard him clearly.

The only person Marika called at first was Hortense.

"Hortense," was all she needed to say.

"He's gone? So quickly? Oh, Boss. Do you want me to come?"

Such a good friend. Charlie Russell's hand lay close to Marika's on the bed. She reached out to cover it, thinking that it still had life, that any moment, he might speak again. She thought back to the day he had met Hortense for the first time, so many years before, in the Boston office. "O'Malley," he had teased, "my goodness, with a name like that, you should go into Boston politics." From then on, he had taken to calling her Madam O'Malley, the nickname Marika used as well. Charlie always swore Hortense was as tough as Margaret Thatcher and twice as astute a politician.

"Boss?" Hortense's soft voice brought her back to the present.

"Sorry. No, stay there, until the day of the funeral. Handle the New York calls and file the obituary with the *Times*. Mrs. Kerry will consider it her right as Daddy's secretary to help me organize the funeral."

"And Lisa?"

"She's on her way. She doesn't know yet."

"I'm so sorry, Marika." Hortense's voice cracked then and Marika knew that at that moment, her friend was crying for herself, as well as for Marika. Hortense had loved Charlie, sometimes Marika suspected she cared for Charlie in ways her father wasn't aware of. It was not something she and Hortense would ever speak about. But it was there all the same. And now that he was gone, Hortense had to do her own grieving.

"I have to go. The administrator is hard to find around here and I need to sign the papers—the whole dismal business."

"Call me if you need anything, please. I'm here."

"I know you are, and Hortense—take care." Marika hung up and without letting herself dwell on the sight of her father's body, she left the room.

Later Marika thought to herself that someone who has experienced death in the family a few times should be able to take it in stride. It didn't always happen that way. She had lost her mother as a little girl, her husband as a young woman, and now her father. Past experience with grief doesn't make it any easier, she decided. There's no cram course for this kind of exam to help one get through it.

When Jonathon called Charles Russell's room two hours later, Marika was in the administrator's office. A nurse who answered gave him the news. He then called every half hour, trying to reach her at the hospital or at the house on Beacon Hill. When he finally made contact, the conversation lasted half an hour, with remarkably few words spoken. There were long silences, a few garbled words from Marika and some quiet reassurances from Jonathon, as well as questions from him on who was in charge and what kind of staff support there was at the house.

"You are so kind to think about those things, Jonathon. But actually I'm well taken care of. Lisa will be with me, my father's secretary, and his maid and cook of twenty-five years."

"Good. Have you talked to Hortense?" He knew how much she depended on the other woman.

"Oh yes. She is handling calls to inform people who should know—all around the country. She's handling the obituary for the *New York Times,* and the secretary here is handling the funeral notice and obituary for the Boston papers."

"Can I do anything?"

"Yes. And you're doing it. Just being supportive, the way you always are, my friend."

"You can count on it, Marika. Lean on me. I'll be there."

And Marika felt as though she'd seen the sun peeking through the clouds before the rain comes again.

The organizational aspects of a funeral which leaders of Boston officialdom and society would attend required every ounce of Marika's energy and managerial talents during the three days of preparation. Her father's secretary, Mrs. Kerry, although emotionally unstrung by the death of her boss of many years, found comfort in having to concentrate on the details and on the intricacies of Massachusetts protocol problems.

Marika had assigned both Lisa and Mrs. Kerry to handle incoming telephone calls on two lines in the house on Beacon Street, and she commandeered the third with her outgoing ones. She had placed an early call to Eve, hoping she and Mac would be able to attend the funeral, but they were already in Mexico on a state visit. In a way, she was glad, because the presence of the President and First Lady, with all the accompanying White House security and communications details, plus press entourage, would have shut off the streets of Boston, created total gridlock, and turned Charlie Russell's funeral into a circus performance.

Her next call was to Great-Aunt Victoria in New York, who said, "My dear, I loved your father very much because he made your mother, my niece and a beautiful representative of the Stuyvesant family, so happy. I will come for the funeral."

"You certainly don't have to, Aunt Victoria! It's too much of a trip for you. I just called to let you know we love you and we do not expect you to make this trip."

"Nonsense. I will motor up. I'll reserve a car and driver at once. I ask only one favor, that you make a reservation for me the night before and the night of the funeral at the Ritz Carlton."

"Aunt Victoria, you haven't been back in Boston in so many years!" Marika was touched that the octogenarian would go to these lengths to honor her father.

"Don't tie up this line for one more second," her great-aunt commanded. "You have much to do. Make the reservation for me, and I'll see you in church. The services, of course, will be in Trinity?" It would not possibly have been otherwise, her voice seemed to say, and Marika assured her that the funeral was being properly handled.

Charles Russell, an eighth-generation Bostonian, had been both a civic and a business leader of the city. His prominence and fine reputation in the community were enhanced, he once confided to Marika, because he never ran for public office. Flowers and messages arrived from his friends, a cross-section of politicians, including the governor and the mayor, two United States senators, one congressman, various members of the consular corps, labor leaders, denizens of Boston society, and executives of the philanthropic organizations in which he had been active. Mrs. Kerry tearfully typed up all the names, titles, and addresses of people who called, sent messages, Mailgrams, or floral offerings. The flowers which arrived at the funeral home and the house were noted and then dispatched at Marika's instructions to nearby hospitals, except for the prettiest of all, in Marika's estimation, which came from the White House—a bouquet of white gardenias and lily of the valley, tied with a white satin ribbon and with a card that read simply "Eve and Mac." She put the bouquet in a silver vase, next to her bed upstairs.

Marika hired a car and driver and moved quickly from the funeral home to the church to the stationer's during the days prior to the services. She ordered white notepaper narrowly bordered in black, on which to write close friends, and for the rest, she ordered black-bordered white cards to be engraved with the message: "The family of Charles Seth Russell greatly appreciates your kind expression of sympathy." Later she would scrawl a sentence or two on each card to personalize it before mailing it. The message of appreciation would be too cold by itself, she decided, and if there was one thing of which she was certain, it was that Charlie Russell would want a warm message of thanks hand-written to all the little people as well as the big shots who had touched his life in some way.

Marika decided against a viewing or visitation at the funeral home. The funeral and lunch afterward were enough to endure. With great tact, Mrs. Kerry guarded the door of the Russell house, and sent away many people who wanted to pay their respects to Marika Wentworth, but who mainly wanted to see her again out of curiosity. Bostonians had really not seen her in years—except in newspaper and magazine photos.

Marika was also concerned over Lisa, because once again Sergio had abandoned her. But a few hours after Lisa's arrival at the house, she received a telephone call that instantly changed her mood. Sergio had learned of her grandfather's death from a close friend of Lisa's. A sentimental family man in the true sense of the word, the young man had rushed to the nearest pay telephone and, tracking her down through information, had called his "*Beata Lisa*," collect.

Their conversation was a long one, dramatically followed by Lisa bursting like a spinning frisbee into the study where her mother was now conferring with her father's distinguished white-haired lawyer. "Mom, you won't believe this. Sergio and I have made up."

"All this on the telephone?" Marika remembered her own quick highs and lows as a young woman, which enabled her to cope with Lisa's. Then she laughed and asked, "and all this, collect?"

"Yes, and he's coming up to Boston tonight to be with me."

"I'm delighted for you," she said in a voice garnished with as much enthusiasm as she could muster. "I think at times you're more theatrically emotional than Italian opera, Lisa. But I do think you might acknowledge the presence of Mr. Thurston."

"Hello, Mr. Thurston, glad to see you!" She moved quickly across the room to shake the hand of her grandfather's lawyer, her face as illuminated as the top of New York's Chrysler Building. She must have become aware of the wide grin on her face. "Is it wrong of me, with Grandpa having died, to feel so happy?"

"No, your grandfather is probably glad to be responsible for this reconciliation, wherever he is. How is Sergio paying for his airfare, by the way?"

"Oh, the way we always do it," she replied without guile. "He has your American Express number."

"My God, Lisa. I don't believe it! You mean Sergio can fly free anywhere in this world? Sort of like he's won a hundred thousand Frequent Flyer miles, all charged to me?" She made a mental note to check the accounting department at Stuyvesant to see why nobody had caught these discrepancies. "We'll deal with my credit card later," she said. Marika knew she should be more motherly, whatever that meant, but she couldn't help catch some of the rays of enthusiasm emanating from the figure now dancing in a happy aerobics rhythm to some mysterious music playing in her head. "I'm glad for you that he's coming, even if I'm paying for it. He can stay in one of the fourth-floor guest rooms."

"Mommmm—" Lisa stopped dancing.

"He will stay in one of the fourth-floor guest rooms," she said firmly. "I'm sure this conversation is fascinating to Mr. Thurston, but he really does have a lot to do after he and I finish our business. Why don't you and I continue our discussion of your houseguest later?"

Lisa hesitated. She wanted Sergio taken care of in her own way right here and now. They had begun to sleep together; it would be terrible to be separated while sleeping in the same house! But she shrugged in acquiescence, and pulled down her pale pink and blue ski sweater tight over the top of the skinny jeans that covered her unendingly long legs—an innocent gesture that revealed her perfect body. Marika noticed the lawyer eyeing Lisa up and down, carefully and appreciatively, as the young woman left. Gilland Thurston, she thought to herself, *you dirty old man*.

Marika and the lawyer reimmersed themselves in the papers that had been laid in neat lawyerly piles on her father's oversized antique English partner's desk. It was hard to concentrate on legal material when she was surrounded by so many memories in this, Charles Russell's, study. She remembered what fun it was for her as a little girl to steal into this room and pull all the shiny brass pulls on the many drawers on the four sides of the great desk. She would peek into one drawer after another, enjoying her father's "exotic" treasures. One drawer inevitably released the mysterious aroma of pipe tobacco every time she opened it. Another contained a sterling silver box, all covered in lacy, delicate carvings; this one held his stamps. He told her it was a Victorian box, but she didn't know what Queen Victoria had to do with a silver box. There was a collection of shiny lacquered boxes from India. Each bore beautiful scenes of flowers, or rivers, or funny-looking people and occasionally animals in a landscape. In each box there was a fascinating visual treat such as a wormy mass of rubber bands, or a glittering cluster of paper clips, or a crisp pile of white labels with red borders.

How strange to be sitting now at this very desk, face to face with a lawyer, discussing her father's death, when it didn't seem so long ago that as a child she watched her parents occasionally use the desk in tandem in the evening hours. It seemed like such a distinguished, overwhelming piece of furniture to a small pair of eyes. Her mother, she remembered, would be writing personal notes on beautiful cream-colored stationery, her fancy monogram engraved on the top in shades of blue, or she'd be working on her household accounts, bothering her husband every few minutes with her questions. Her father, she remembered, would be involved in his business papers. Occasionally he would reach into the tobacco drawer to replenish his pipe, and she remembered the ghostlike figures of smoke that inevitably hung in the air above him.

Mr. Thurston kept talking, but instead of listening to him, she tried to remember when her father had actually stopped smoking his pipe and cigars. It was long ago. Her mother had always hated it, and wouldn't let him smoke it anywhere except in the study, this room, which had been *his* room—although he complained jokingly that everyone in the family wanted to use it all the time. The beautiful dark mahogany-paneled walls were still fragrant with a delicious woodsy smell. The draperies, hanging on fourteen-foot-high windows, were made of a heavy linen fabric of an East Indian design of tobacco, ruby red, and ocher yellow. A gold damask Chippendale sofa sat at one end of the room facing a carved mahogany fireplace at the other end. The desk chairs were covered in the same East Indian fabric, and French antique bouil-lotte lamps sat on the desk and end tables. The overhead eigh-teenth-century brass chandelier and matching wall sconces were never lit. Once she had asked her mother why and her mother said, "No matter how beautiful a chandelier is, never light an electrified one, only one with candles. Pretty light comes from lamps on side tables, never from the ceiling." She had never forgotten that, and had never lit an overhead lighting fixture in her life.

When Marika and Charlie Russell sat on opposite sides of this desk one evening a couple of years ago, her father, enjoying his afterdinner brandy, admitted that he and her mother used to break the monotony of their work at this desk on occasion by "playing footsie" with each other in the space beneath the desk. Marika laughed, "Daddy, how wonderfully wicked!"

"It didn't matter who started it first," he reminisced, "but the activity of one foot under the desk inevitably resulted in an im-mediate cessation of all paperwork and a hasty retreat to the bedroom." She smiled, imagining her handsome young parents engaged in a prelude to sex with their feet under this distinguished old desk.

Mr. Thurston was saying, "Well, that's all we can do today,

Marika. We'll have more legal sessions yet to come." Her father's estate was complicated, but meticulously organized. The will had been opened by Mr. Thurston shortly after Charles Russell's death. His wishes for the funeral were carefully detailed. Other than certain generous bequests, to his alma maters, Groton and Harvard, to charity, his secretary, and office and household staff, everything else was left to his daughter and granddaughter.

One other bequest touched Marika deeply. He had written by hand, "To Hortense O'Malley, $25,000, a small sum of appreciation for the warm, caring manner in which you have improved the quality of my daughter's life for so many years." She knew how much his gift would mean to Hortense, though knowing Hortense, she would probably be moved by the sentiment rather than the money. He also left "$3,000 for a celebration lunch for Marika's staff, at '21,' after someone has rung the bell at Stuyvesant Communications to announce a big account."

Little things were left to specific friends, such as "my fishing rods and other gear to Jeff Fessenden, because perhaps now he won't be able to excuse his total lack of fishing success on his inadequate equipment." His barber received the sterling silver cigar box he kept in his study as well as his well-stocked supply of cigars, because he and his barber shared a love for their smoke. He left, along with a thousand dollars, "the piece of scrimshaw on my partner's desk to my longtime caddy, Jimmy McElligott, because he admired it so thoroughly and now he can start his own collection." Little things that had meant so much to him would now mean so much to those mentioned in the will. Her father had always been a person of heart.

Once, while rummaging through scrapbooks and memorabilia in the house on Beacon Street, Marika had found an old diary of her mother's. She knew her mother would forgive her for picking the little lock with a hairpin. She savored every word of it, including tiny secrets that had been dropped into the text. One of these entries read:

"I have admitted only to myself, and never to anyone else, that although Charles was known in his youth for being hyperactive in regard to getting pretty young women into the nearest available beds, in actuality he is quite clumsy as a lover. This shortcoming could have bothered me were it not for his total kindness, his goodness, his shining spirit. I feel in awe to live with such a man. I have the best of what is spiritual in him. It makes the physical very unimportant. And he is such a wonderful-looking man!"

Marika had put that diary in her lockbox at the bank. Some day she would give it to Lisa. It was too precious to be consumed by a young person who might not understand certain things. At that time she wondered if her mother had ever known really terrific sex in her life. Now, of course, after learning of her Hungarian father, she knew the answer was *yes*.

Sergio arrived the day before the funeral, and she saw little of Lisa for the next twenty-four hours. Marika continued working on the planning of the funeral and luncheon, and she saw them only at meals. She overheard Sergio explaining to Lisa that he "felt like a jerk for having taken a walk when he hadn't meant to at all." Her grandfather's death had "brought him to his senses." Marika couldn't help wondering to herself if the thought of Lisa's handsome inheritance from her grandfather had any bearing on his having been brought back to his senses. Then she caught herself. She was being unfair to Lisa—and Sergio. She wouldn't believe Lisa would be so shallow as to fall for just another piece of "Eurotrash."

On the morning of the funeral, Jonathon, in his usual thoughtful way, arranged to give Anthony, Greg, Steve, Hortense, and Sarah a ride in his jet from Teterboro Airport in New Jersey to Boston. They arrived at the door of the house on Beacon Street just in time to join the procession of black limousines from the house to the church for the service. Despite the sadness of the occasion, Marika felt excitement quicken her pulse when she opened the door and found Jonathon waiting on the stoop with her staff standing behind him.

Jonathon rode in the front limousine with the Wentworths and Great Aunt Victoria to Trinity Church. Marika felt content just to be holding his hand—unobtrusively so that no one else could see. Marika watched the church come into view and began to reminisce about this edifice. Her mother's burial service had been held here. Lisa had been christened and confirmed here and, of course, she had married and buried David here. Charles Russell had stipulated in his will that his burial service be held here. She wondered how many generations of how many Boston families had celebrated the ceremonies of life—like the Stuyvesants and Russells had—within the walls of this familiar edifice.

The candles on the altar of the fine old church cast sparkling reflections on the shiny bronze and silver casket. It was hard to think of her father inside that cold, impersonal box. Six years before she had sat in this same pew attending David's funeral, but she couldn't remember the words of the service or the music that was played for him. She had been given Valium by the family physician, and it blissfully removed from her consciousness details of what had transpired. Today there had been no Valium. Her grief was clear and intense.

Marika sat between Jonathon and Lisa. She tried to visualize her father in heaven—up, down, inside, out, off to the side—wherever heaven is. She pictured him in his gray flannels and wonderful tweed sports jackets, one of his ever-present silk handkerchiefs tucked jauntily into the pocket. She heard the minister's words about how happy Charlie Russell was now, free from pain and worry, then she felt the gentle squeeze of Jonathon's warm fingers on her arm, a gesture of comfort. She saw him absorbing every aspect of the interior of Trinity and particularly of the altar, the majestic pulpit, and the soaring archways overhead. She noticed him looking at the red and blue blaze of light coming through the stained-glass window, but she also could feel now and then his eyes turned toward her.

Marika had found a black crepe coatdress, buttoned up the front with black buttons, in her closet in the Beacon Street house. She had left it during one stay over or another. It was perfect for the funeral. Lisa had brought from New York the only black dress in her wardrobe that wasn't something to wear nightclub crawling, a black linen shirtwaist, and she was worried the summer dress would not look right in cold December weather, but Marika had assured her no one would notice the fabric, and that it was very suitable. Lisa was bent over the pew, too immersed in her own thoughts to pay attention to what was transpiring on the altar. Her grandfather had been her only relative, other than her mother and Great-Great-Aunt Victoria. He was the only man in her family; he had been much more than the patriarch, too. He had been Lisa and Marika's adviser, "support system," and most of all, friend.

Marika caught a glimpse of Sergio's blond curly head between Lisa and Victoria Stuyvesant. His gray eyes were cast down, unable to mask the few escaping tears from beneath the long eyelashes. Though he had never even met Charlie Russell, he was emotional . . . *Italianissimo*. His blood surged with a strong and sincere sense of family. For this, Marika respected him—perhaps he wasn't all wrong for Lisa after all.

Behind them sat the rest of the "family"—some of the staff of Stuyvesant Communications, Inc. Anthony, Greg, and Steve wore dark suits, white shirts, and appropriate black and white ties. Hortense, in total disarray, partly because of her own feelings for Marika's father and partly because of her worry over her boss, was an abject figure. She wore her black suit and blouse, without even a touch of her silver jewelry today to relieve the starkness. Her hair, parted in the middle, now fell straight and long, a shower of black that made her look severe, unrelenting, like an old-fashioned Spanish peasant widow who would cast herself into an aura of black mourning for the rest of her life. Sarah wore a borrowed navy faille dress, modest and chic, with several rows of pearls. It was the first time she had worn a dress since Marika could remember. No one was wearing sneakers. She was very proud of her staff.

As the eulogy, hymns, and prayers continued to resonate through the loudspeaker to the four corners of the church, she thought what a sad Christmas this was going to be. Her father had always been the centerpiece of Lisa's and her celebration. He would come down from Boston and stay with them for two and a half days, never longer. He would take them to dinner every Christmas Eve at "21," generously tipping the Salvation Army carolers in the restaurant who appeared as regularly as turkey on the menu the week before Christmas.

Charlie Russell would never open even one of his own presents until "his ladies" had opened all of theirs. He would enthusiastically enjoy Geneviève's Christmas lunch, too, prepared Haitian style, with some of her many relatives from Brooklyn in attendance in the kitchen. He would always say grace at the beginning of the meal, and at the end of the meal he would call in Geneviève and her relatives from the kitchen for a "toast of appreciation to the chef for *un repas magnifique.*" Georgiana and Chauncey Wilkins, Stuart and Mimi Wellton were due to join them at lunch this year. Jonathon had already declined, because he had promised to spend the holidays with his mother on the West Coast this year.

What was she doing, planning Christmas lunch? It was out of the question. Charles Russell would be elsewhere.

She started to think about how her father—her Boston father, that is—was up in heaven, and how she and Lisa would hopefully be there, too, one day. She would rejoin her family. It made the separation of death so much easier to bear. She really did believe in the next life, accepting it completely on faith, but it also seemed logical to her. "You're put on earth to do God's will." Her parents believed that, and she did, too. Suddenly, she began to puzzle over the problem of which group of loved ones would she join when she, too, died? Her husband David and the Wentworths? Her mother and Charles Russell and the Russells and Stuyvesants? Where would Jonathon's family be in all of this? Would Jonathon's ex-wife be hovering around up there, or, if she was such a witch, would she not make it at all?

She began suppressing short, stifled laughs under her breath because of all these ridiculous images of little human figures, shuffling back and forth in heaven, weaving patterns of family relationships. Jonathon protectively took her hand, a gesture that could not have been lost on her staff and the guests behind them. He later explained to her that he had done this because he thought the laughter was a signal of oncoming hysteria.

Then ten men in dark suits, white shirts, and black ties

marched down the aisle, two by two, nodding to Marika as they filed into the front pews on the left. These were the distinguished and lifelong friends of Charles Russell whom Marika had telephoned personally and asked to serve as honorary pallbearers.

The casket had already been in place, with only one floral offering in front of it—the family's. This was in accordance with Charles Russell's instructions. Marika had ordered shooting sprays of white lilacs and tulips, mixed with roses of various shades of pink, arranged in a tall white basket. They were Charlie's favorite flowers.

The Trinity Church service was short. Marika had requested the shortest one the pastor could arrange, and the service afterward at the cemetery was even shorter. The family reached the house on Beacon Street just as the first people were arriving to greet Marika, offer their condolences, and have lunch. She was happy to see her own old friends, too—classmates from Winsor School and later Farmington, who had made their debuts at the cotillion the same year she did, and who joined the Vincent Club and the Junior League in the same years she had, handing down their Chilton Club memberships from female generation to female generation.

Millie, her father's longtime cook, a tall, regal black woman with hair now almost completely white, performed her usual great culinary achievements for those who came for lunch after the church service. The Beacon Street house was ablaze with pink and white flowers; small tables and chairs had been set up all over the house for those who wished to sit down during lunch. The tables were covered with white cloths printed with pink flowers. Her father's and her own friends wandered through the rooms of the house, reminiscing over the many memories they all shared of this great early nineteenth-century red brick mansion. At her father's request, the pianist from the Ritz played the baby grand in the salmon and apple green-colored living room. Lisa and Marika circulated among the seated groups, each sitting down at a table for a chat when there was an empty seat.

Jonathon remained quietly in the background, not fitting in, but not wishing to distract Marika from her important mission. The friends of Marika's family were conservative, and rather timid, and Marika knew that they would not easily bring Jonathon into their group, preferring to reminisce and share their emotions with those they had known for years. In the meantime, Jonathon kept himself busy poking around, perusing things. As she watched, he picked up a nineteenth-century Russian gold-trimmed malachite egg that had been kept for years on top of a table in the living room. The egg had been a gift to her father from one of his partners, Winthrop Steadhurst, and had been there for so long, Marika had forgotten its existence. Jonathon absentmindedly threw the egg from one palm to another and she couldn't help but be amused as she saw Winthrop Steadhurst wince, watching the valuable piece thrown to and fro like a hard-boiled Easter egg. Marika studied Jonathon, watching how he handled himself in this crowd that must seem strange to him, and he to them.

Eventually, Marika excused herself from the conversation she was having with the minister and joined Jonathon and Lisa, who were talking in quiet tones in the corner.

"I see you two are taking good care of each other."

"Lisa was just filling me in on who's who—or who's whom, you know what I mean."

Marika smiled at him, and her eyes found the jeweled, razor-sharp-edged object, now in his hand, that usually sat upon her father's desk.

Jonathon was handling it in his nonchalant way.

"Do you like my father's dagger?"

"I was wondering what he used it for. To clean fish? Protect the women in his family?"

"He opened letters with it."

"Hmm—classy way of opening bills." Marika watched him weighing the opener, studying it as though it would somehow tell him more about her and her family. "You're observing us, aren't you, Jonathon Scher?"

"They're observing me, aren't they?" he said somewhat defensively.

"You're right." She turned to Lisa. "Do me a favor, sweetheart. Go check on Great-Aunt Victoria. She's been huddled in that corner for an hour with Mrs. Daley. Make sure she sits down and doesn't stand too long."

"I'll go with you, Lisa. Maybe your Great-Great-Aunt Victoria would like a sherry or something."

"You're a dear, Jonathon."

"Even if I'm not in the Social Register?" His smile did not quite reach his eyes. He replaced the jeweled object on the desk and traced the gadroon edge of her father's antique English silver inkwell with his finger. "Nice little Georgian piece of silver," he said, turning to follow Lisa.

"How did you know that?" she asked him.

"I remember everything I see or read," he answered simply.

Later Marika would learn that Jonathon didn't forget anything—not an object in her house, if it gave him clues about her, and not a word she said—particularly an unkind one.

CHAPTER

7

The night air on this December day had a chill in it, and the furnace was not on. Theresa lit a fire in the library before leaving the house. She, Millie, and the extra staff had cleaned up after the last people had left. The house was sparkling clean again. One would never have known there had been a hundred fifty people for lunch that day. Marika embraced Theresa and Millie in a sad farewell. She would see them briefly in a few weeks, but they were already, suddenly, part of her past.

Jonathon followed Marika into the library. Although there were no lights on, there was enough glow from the fireplace to illuminate the rich red and blue oriental rug on the floor and the mahogany Chippendale and Queen Anne furniture in this large room. Ten years before, Marika had hired a specialized European painter to finish the linenfold-paneled walls of the room in a high-gloss dark cherry color. In the firelight, the room glowed a ruby red. Books, some of them old and rare in fading leather bindings, lined the copious floor-to-ceiling built-in bookcases.

"These books!" Jonathon exclaimed. "If you weren't so important to me, I'd be spending the entire evening with them instead of you."

"Some compliment—I win out over a bunch of books," she said teasingly." They sat for a while on the dark blue velvet sofa, not speaking, gazing into the fire.

"What does one say after a day like this?" asked Jonathon, "that it was a 'beautiful funeral'? A 'successful funeral'? I heard your Boston friends thanking you and saying 'how lovely it was' as though they had just been to your debutante dance."

She laughed. "No, they were just being polite. They had already told me during the day how sorry they were about Daddy. They were just thanking me for lunch—and for their last glimpse of this house. I will be selling it right away, of course. The people who came today knew they were saying good-bye to memories of my mother and father, and all the Russells and Stuyvesants before them. They know I'm not coming back here to live. Lisa won't come back here to live. Daddy's death was the end of our bloodlines in this city."

She stopped herself at this point, suddenly remembering that one of her bloodlines—that of her Hungarian father—had nothing to do with Boston.

"I've never understood about these WASP dynasties," he said wryly, "but what you just said makes me kind of sad."

"It is sad. It's the end of an era. My father had no brothers and no sons. It's the end of his line of Russells. Maybe we should celebrate the finis with a flourish. Daddy would like that. At least there won't be any dissipated, depraved heirs ruining the good Russell name!"

He didn't know whether she was serious or kidding. He didn't know this woman well enough—yet—to know whether she was being brave or funny—or hysterical.

"Let me see if there's any champagne left," Marika said brightly. "Daddy would want us to see him off to the very last minute in a proper style." She went out to the kitchen and returned with a chilled bottle and two champagne flutes she had found in the pantry. "Typical of dear Millie and Theresa to have left this for us."

Jonathon opened the bottle, poured each a glass, and then raised a toast. "To us, but particularly to the memory of Charlie Russell."

"To my father—and to us." She drank with her eyes looking straight into his, over the rim of her glass.

"It may not be appropriate on this day, but I have to say it. You are a very sexy woman, especially with those wonderful eyes of yours." He wondered if tonight was finally going to be the night, or if it would be forward and disrespectful of him to even think about it. He was longing to make love to her. But though her eyes seemed to be giving him a signal, he had to move carefully. She was a woman of appearances. He was damned well not going to screw it up by making too fast a move the night of her father's funeral.

"The house seems so quiet. Where are the two young love-birds?" he asked.

"Lisa and Sergio took the shuttle back for tomorrow's classes at Columbia, and I told Millie and Theresa to take tonight and the next two days off. They have worked without even going to bed ever since Daddy died."

"You have had too much experience with death, little one," Jonathon said, caressing the side of her cheek.

"I guess I have."

"Was David's funeral like this one?"

"I was so doped up, I can't recall many details, but yes, it was the same size and shape as this one, you might say. It's something you go through like a dream. It doesn't have much reality—until later."

"Has the—finality . . ." He stopped in mid-sentence.

"The finality of what?"

"I shouldn't have started the question. I had no business to."

"You mean, has the finality of Daddy's death hit me yet?"

"Exactly. I should be shot for making you more depressed than you probably were."

"No, you can ask me about that. You see, I have a deep faith in the next life—the one in which Daddy is already living. I know I'll see him again. It makes death so much more acceptable. I know someday I'll be joining him, David, Mother, everyone. It makes death a lot easier to take when you believe that."

"I don't have that kind of faith about the afterlife. I guess I don't spend much time thinking about it. Perhaps I should. But for me it's always been the here and now that counts."

"It's a question of faith, Jonathon. You either have it or you don't. If you lose the ones you love, and you know they're happy in heaven or whatever it is, wherever it is . . ." She couldn't finish. She had started to cry, very softly. He placed both their glasses on the coffee table and pulled her over to him, so that she was inside his arms, her head upon his shoulder. He smoothed back locks of her hair, quietly kissing her cheeks and eyes every now and then. They sat for a half an hour, not moving or speaking, half asleep. Marika felt safe in his arms. She felt protected, warm, as though there were no obstacles to surmount, as though every problem had a ready solution.

Then he began kissing her neck—gently—as though he had just awakened from a deep sleep, and she felt the same awakening, too. He heard her sigh with pleasure from the contact of his lips on her skin, and it was the signal he needed. His lips found her mouth, and at first his lips barely grazed hers, then pressed more firmly, and soon she was kissing him back hungrily.

The room was dark, except for the flickering firelight. "I want to comfort you," he said, his hands caressing her breasts.

"I've been wanting this a long time," she said in a husky voice. He laughed and said, "You've taken my line."

She kissed the top of his fingers and his hand began to open the top buttons of her black crepe dress. Then she bit his chin. "You could go a little faster, you know."

He knew her just well enough to realize that when she was embarrassed, she would make a joke. It drew him to her more quickly. She said nothing more, grateful for the sure movements of his warm hands. She saw in the firelight that he was smiling as he slowly undressed her, kissing her with tantalizing little kisses as each part of her body was revealed to him. Then he stood above her, looking down at her beautiful naked body on the sofa—watching the play of shadows and topaz light from the fire on her creamy skin, and on her beautiful breasts.

He undressed himself quickly as she watched him from the sofa. He looked beautiful to her with his muscular body, covered with reddish-brown hair. She reached out for him and found that he was ready for her.

Now he spoke, his voice low, husky, like hers. "I have wanted you since the night I sat next to you at dinner." He lowered himself quickly down onto the sofa. "You're the most beautiful woman I have ever met. Your intelligence, personality, spirit— My God, Marika, what did I do to deserve you?"

When he kissed her this time, his mouth was more insistent, demanding more of her. Her body found his rhythms on its own and when he penetrated her, they remained locked in complete oneness, exulting in a joint ecstasy. For Marika, it was a feeling of fire and lust and a satiation that she had never even imagined before. This was such a new set of feelings. It had been so different with David. She had been young then—inexperienced in both her body and her heart. Their lovemaking had never evolved to its full potential. Now, she was mature, ready to return all levels of loving. And Jonathon had become this very minute the perfect man with whom to share these complex emotions.

Jonathon put more logs on the fire, they found more champagne, pâté, and French crackers in the kitchen, and they lay on the sofa sipping, eating, and making love through the night. When the grandfather clock chimed six hours, they were both asleep, but it awoke Jonathon. He arose and picked up his clothes. "I have to be at the airport in ninety minutes, Marika. Are you going to point me in the direction of a shower in this stately house?"

"It seems to me I'm always doing this," she said, arising to show him the bathroom upstairs.

"Well, at least I hope last night made up a little bit for my performance that night in your apartment."

"You are more than exonerated."

"I remember that sensational white crepe job you were wearing that night."

"It was meant to be a seduction spectacular."

"I shouldn't have been *that* tired!"

She showed him to one of the guest room bathrooms, he took a long careful look at her body in the morning light and then pulled her laughing and protesting into the shower with him.

Finally, they both managed to get out of the shower and Jonathon started dressing quickly. "If I'm late, who knows when my pilot can get a clearance to get out again?" She sat on the bed on a towel, watching him. Then she followed him downstairs, without any towel, to the front door.

"You're completely shameless. Is there a little bit of whore in this nice Boston girl?" He took her in his arms and started to enclose her nipples in his lips, and she felt a shiver run through her again.

"Before I miss my plane, let me say one thing."

"What?" She was giggling and nuzzling his neck, careful to pull him behind the door, mindful of the driver and the neighbors. "I love you," he said simply, "and I'd better get the hell out of here."

She called out after him. "You'd better stop by the Ritz and get your suitcase."

"I'd better stop having my driver check me into hotels I never see."

The door closed. Marika went up the stairs of the house on Beacon Street, rubbing her hands gently over her body, trying to recapture the feel of Jonathon's warm hands on it. It was the first time in her life she had walked around this great old house without her clothes. And it would be the last time. She would return to New York that afternoon to go back to work at her agency. She would return here to this house within a few weeks to dismiss the staff, give them large bonuses, and find them jobs. She would put the house on the market and arrange for the shipment of certain furnishings to her in New York and other things to a warehouse—to save for the apartment Lisa would have one day. The one thing that she was moving to New York was the antique partner's desk. It meant so much to her. The rest of the exquisite furnishings would be put up for auction at Christie's in New York.

That would be one auction for which she would surely arrange to be out of town.

Oh yes, and Jonathon had said "I love you," this morning, right before he walked through the door.

"How goes it?" The voice of Sam Merriweather, the CEO of one of America's largest utilities was warm and jovial. Sam had been a longtime friend of her father's, who had remarried a younger woman and begun a new family late in his life. She loved him, particularly his soft Georgian accent, but he always talked on and on, and she was in a real time bind today.

"Well, Sam, well." Marika tapped her gold pen against the blue telephone console, making an impatient staccato. She could tell just from his voice that he had a favor to ask. She had no time for chitter-chat today. "What can I do for you?" she asked in an urgent, crisp manner.

He was not to be hurried. "I've got the smartest, brightest, best-looking . . ."

"Daughter," interrupted Marika. This was going to be another request to help someone's daughter find a job. It was the hundredth call of this kind she had received since she'd moved the business to New York. All the college graduates of last June had completed their graduation present trips abroad and were still cashing in their daddies' chips to get job interviews.

"Her name is Jennie Lee, and, Marika, you jest would'n' believe how smart a young lady she is!" The Southern drawl was burning hot with enthusiasm for its mission.

"Yes, she is, Sam. I've already met her, remember?" Marika had to be polite because Sam used her agency every so often, turning the meter off and on according to project needs for his company. He was a good client, even if he only threw her company a bone of profitable enterprise every now and then.

Marika remembered meeting his daughter, whom he dubbed "The Viscountess." He had stopped into the office when he was taking her to lunch one day. She was home from school for vacation, and looked like a Southern belle in the classic sense. Marika remembered her long sweep of eyelashes that Hortense was positive were the result of creative makeup, not Mother Nature's handiwork. Then she remembered that after she and Sam had left, Hortense had pronounced her a "fashion disaster of *powdah blue*," complete with plaid skirt, sweater, velvet hair ribbon, eye shadow, and enamel earrings, all of the same pale blue. "Thank God for black," Hortense had muttered, eyeing her own somber self appreciatively in Marika's Venetian office mirror.

As Sam continued today's ode to his daughter's attributes, Marika decided to interrupt. "Sam, I know what a busy guy you are, and I wouldn't think of delaying you. What exactly do you want me to do about Jennie Lee?"

"Give her a job, Marika, an unpaid job. Let the Vicountess be an intern in your office. It would be the best damned exposhah to business that lil' girl could have."

"I can't use an intern right now. We're busy, thank heavens. We have so much business in-house that there's a body sitting in every chair, at every desk, in every cubicle in this office."

"I'll pay you to take her on. I know she will be trouble for y'all to train—time and effort—so we'll call it a consultin' job for a fee. She needs experience. She needs to see what the real world is. She graduated last June from a small Southern women's college, and she needs some sophist'cation."

"What did she get her degree in?"

"Boys." They both laughed at this, and Marika asked, "Look, I've meant to ask you this before. Why do you call her the Viscountess?"

"Because it's a title higher than countess or baroness, just under a marquess."

"Why don't you just call her princess or something? Just curious."

"Because," Sam's voice grew slightly stentorian, "she'll have to work her way up to becomin' a duchess or a princess. I don't want to spoil my little girl. I want her to have goals to strive toward."

"I see," said Marika, impressed that the farm boy had learned enough about royal titles and the peerage to have them all straight in his mind. Henry James would have loved Sam Merriweather!

"Marika," he pleaded, "take her on for six months as an unpaid intern, and I'll pay your firm three thousand dollars a month for her training. You don't have to spend all your time with her. Just let her sit and learn, kinda quiet-like. Maybe an account executive might let her go along on a client visit or somethin'. Give her lottsa dirty work to do. She knows it's not s'posed to be a picnic."

"You mean, you've already told her that I'd take her on?"

"Sort of," he said, now embarrassed. "I felt we were good enough old friends, and I knew you take summah interns, and I thought she could just help out as a messenger, go-fer, whatever."

"I just don't know, Sam. We're so busy around here."

"Please, Marika. I want her exposed to the greatest li'l lady in the public relations field. I know just watchin' y'all in action will inspire and mot'vate her. She'll be able to observe and learn from the smoothest operation this heah side of those pearly gates."

"Gosh, you sound like you're going to fire all your other PR firms and use us alone! Don't worry, Sam, only teasing. I'll take her, on a monthly fee basis. Have her call my assistant, Hortense O'Malley, tomorrow."

"I'm much obliged, li'l lady."

"And there won't be any of this viscountess stuff around here."

"I know, I know," he said, embarrassed again. They both hung up, and Marika began to tap her blue telephone console once again with the gold pen, this time chuckling to herself over how Ms. O'Malley was going to react to the news that she was now fully in charge of the training of a new hire, "Ms. Powdah Blue."

Hortense, who believed her vocation in life was to take great care of Marika Wentworth, felt no empathy whatsoever for "Powdah Blue." For two weeks, Hortense shunted Jennie Lee off to Anthony, who kept his door closed the entire time, with the air clouded over like a giant fog chamber from his pipe smoke. The young intern's mission in Anthony's fog chamber was to throw out several hundred old files he had marked with an orange marker as being out-of-date and destroyable. Twice a day he had Jennie Lee open the windows to the cold to air out his office, and he had Hortense, a special favorite of his, warn him of any possible entrance to his office by Marika, who so heartily disapproved of his pipe smoke.

Jennie Lee later confided to Hortense that Anthony taught her all kinds of things about the company while she was perusing the files she was throwing away, and Anthony later confided to Hortense that the young woman's intellectual curiosity made him think there was hope for her within the agency.

Hortense then shunted Jennie Lee to Greg, knowing that he would get rid of her quickly, which he did, within two days. He persuaded her that the most exciting thing she could ever do in her life would be to stay in Sarah's tiny office, learning her operation. Jennie Lee happily dabbled in the occult for several days, spending her time studying astrological charts, picking up and dusting Sarah's crystal objects, and awaiting the occasional prized lunch hour during which Sarah would read the tea leaves for her or make some predictions based on tarot cards. Jennie Lee wrote a memo to Hortense on the importance of understanding New Age philosophy, so Hortense, thinking of what Sam Merriweather would make of all this, suggested to Marika that it was time to take her young intern to lunch.

"I'm going to take you this noon to a Women's Forum lunch, Jennie Lee, and then let you accompany me afterward when I make my final presentation to the top brass of Flairhotels, Inc."

"Thank you, ma'am," the young woman said in an awed voice.

"Look"—Marika's voice was tired—"I've already spoken to you three times about your incessant use of ma'am. That just doesn't go up here in the North. It goes in the South, but nowhere else. It sounds subservient. Agreed?"

"What'll I say," she asked, quite abashed, "if I can't say ma'am?"

"Call me by name—Mrs. Wentworth or Ms. Wentworth—or don't call me anything. Just make a flat statement, like 'Thank you very much,' with nothing following it. Is that so hard to do?"

"No, ma'— I mean, no, Mrs. Wentworth."

"Good," Marika said in a warmer voice. She wondered what on earth could be in Jennie Lee's bulging red felt tote bag that she was lugging along to lunch. Then she decided not to ask. It was really none of her business.

Once at the Regency Hotel on Park Avenue, they checked their things and entered the crowd of people in the anteroom of the ballroom. The sound of mainly female voices was loud, high-spirited, and equally high-pitched. Marika bought them both diet sodas at the cash bar, greeting everyone around her and introducing Jennie Lee as she went along. "When I don't come up with a name," she said in a low voice to her young sidekick, "it means I don't have a clue what it is. That's the cue for you to quickly stick out your hand, give your own name, and they'll quickly give theirs back to you, and I won't be left with egg on my face for having forgotten their names."

"Oh," Jennie Lee replied in a voice that denoted awe at learning such an important lesson in coping with big decisions in life.

"Marika darling!" Aggie Furth, the editor of a leading fashion magazine, was heading in their direction, a great mass of teased brassy blond hair on top of a beautifully tailored beige and caramel wool Bill Blass suit. She smelled as though she had just taken a bath in someone's newly launched fragrance. Marika whispered in Jennie Lee's ear, "She probably has the head of that perfume company as her guest today. She must want the company to advertise. That's why she's overdosed on his perfume."

"It's been ages, sweetie," Aggie was saying, having pulled back to get a good perspective on Marika, head to toe. "Love the aquamarine suit. And with a deeper aqua crepe blouse—heaven! Divine!"

Jennie Lee in the meantime had been standing by Marika's

side all this time, her hand limply extended, expecting Aggie to take it in a handshake. When that did not happen, Jennie Lee simply held it out awhile longer, until Marika finally pushed it down to the girl's side with brute force.

As Aggie and Marika continued talking, Jennie Lee interrupted them brusquely. "Jennie Lee Merriweather, ma'am!"

Aggie Furth drew back again and inspected the interloper as though she had her under a microscope and found her to be merely a cluster of most uninteresting cells. "This is my new intern, Jennie Lee Merriweather," Marika explained apologetically. Then she turned to Jennie Lee. "You shouldn't have interrupted us to do that."

Aggie looked at the young woman with a shriveling glance. "Too much eye shadow, dear," she suddenly said, "much too much for daytime. In fact, too much for nighttime, dear," and without missing a beat, she went back to discussing a mutual friend with Marika. Jennie Lee had ceased to exist in her eyes.

As they pushed through the doors of the ballroom to sit down for lunch, Marika reminded Jennie Lee that "you don't interrupt two people who are engaged in conversation in order to introduce yourself. You wait until there's a lull."

"Oh."

"And I hope you heard about the eye shadow. It seems I have mentioned the subject at least twice, haven't I?"

"I just don't know," Jennie Lee said, ready to cry, "what to do and what not to do. Everyone says different things. My boyfriend likes my eye shadow."

"Did I understand correctly," Marika interjected, "that you hope for a career in fashion ultimately?"

"Oh yes!" Her tone brightened considerably.

"Well, then, who are you going to listen to—your boyfriend from Athens, Georgia, or the editor-in-chief of America's most successful fashion magazine?"

"The fashion editor, ma'am."

"You mean, 'the fashion editor,' period."

"Yes, ma'am."

Good God, thought Marika, just let me make it through this meal.

Marika had purchased two tickets to the Women's Forum lunch, in order to give Jennie Lee some one-on-one teaching of the kind of good manners to use at a public business lunch. She had explained to the young woman before that it was the host's responsibility to introduce her guest to everyone else at the table—in this case, to introduce Jennie Lee to eight other women—so that the conversation could then flow with ease.

"I know some of you at this table," Marika began, "but not everyone. I'm Marika Wentworth, president of Stuyvesant Communications, Inc. This is my intern, Jennie Lee Merriweather, from Athens, Georgia. She is just out of college. I'd really appreciate your going around the table explaining who you are, because I know she'll be impressed by all of you. As a matter of fact, *I'm* impressed by all of you!"

With that the women all smiled kindly at the young visitor. Several, sitting close enough to be able to do it, shook her hand and said a warm hello.

"I'm Ruth Greenberg, president of Hawkes Advertising," began one woman.

"Marian Swanson, president of Greenwich Sportswear," said the next woman.

"Hi, I'm Julienne Boyer, designer for France Mode," said the next woman.

"Jane Curtain, The Mayor's Office," nodded her neighbor.

"Ellen Bayard, president of Brennan College," said the next woman.

"June Willard, president of Willard Commercial Real Estate."

"I'm Barbara Teel from Goldman Sachs," smiled the next woman.

"Judge Dorothy Greenough from the Federal Court of Appeals," said the last one in the circle.

"As you can see, Jennie Lee," said Marika, "you are sitting with a veritable powerhouse today."

"Wow!" was all Jennie Lee could muster. Between the hearts

of palm salad and the *pêche Melba*, the conversation flew fast and furiously around the table as the women networked, caught up on one another's lives, and discussed who had just lost her job or received a promotion.

The main luncheon speaker, New York's new mayor, talked about business opportunities for women professionals in New York. When he had finished and it was time for questions, Marika whispered a quick apology to everyone at the table and spoke in Jennie Lee's ear, "Get up quietly but fast. We are late."

The Flairhotels presentation was only two blocks away, but Marika wanted the time before the 2:30 P.M. presentation to go to the ladies' room, apply some perfume, and run through her notes on her pitch one more time. She knew that Greg and Sarah would already be there, with her slides all in order. As soon as they could enter the room, they would check out for her the machinery, lights, flip charts, and sound system.

"Did you have a good time at the lunch?" she managed to ask Jennie Lee on the way over, hopeful that her intern had seized upon the Women's Forum lunch as a tremendous learning experience.

"Oh yes, ma'am," was the enthusiastic reply. "I mean, oh *yes!* It was wonderful."

"One thing I always ask my interns to do after an experience like the one you've just had is to write a short synopsis of what they observed—of what they learned from that meeting or program. Do you think you could do that, Jennie Lee?"

"I'd be delighted to," was the drawled response.

"You were with some of the leading women in business, education, and the arts in the entire country. They have all made it to the top."

"They certainly have," was the respectful response with nary a "ma'am" in sight. Marika was grateful.

They had reached the Park Avenue offices of Flairhotels, Inc. "What you are going to see now, Jennie Lee, is my company's attempt to grab an additional piece of Flairhotels' business. We are already involved in a considerable number of PR assignments for them, but they're on a great expansion kick, and it would be profitable for us to add a nice extra chunk to the business we already have. We're in competition with at least three other firms who want to handle Flairhotels' huge new resort to be developed on the island of Maui."

"Who will be there from the agency?" Jennie Lee drawled.

"Greg and Sarah."

"Miz Wentworth, how do you decide who goes on these— these . . ."

"Pitches?" Marika finished for her.

"Yes, pitches." Jennie Lee shifted her red tote bag and her handbag to opposite hands, making a mental note, Marika felt sure, of a new word of jargon just learned.

"Everyone in the agency has a hand in these new business quests, Jennie Lee. Anthony, the lead member of the team, has already made a guess projection on all the costs of execution of our project, plus our fees and expenses. Greg, Steve, and Sarah worked on the creative preparation of the proposal, but Steve isn't feeling that great today, so I told him not to come."

"Is he sick or somethin'? He just doesn't look too good."

"You're right," said Marika thoughtfully.

"Well, anyway," Jennie Lee continued, "you probably don't want too many of the Stuyvesant team heah anyway. It might look like overkill."

"Right," Marika echoed. The girl had actually made an intelligent observation. There was hope yet for this intern.

Jennie Lee wasn't finished with her questions. "Who gets the major credit for winnin' the account, if you win it?"

"The praise and accolades go to everyone on the senior staff —but to the support staff, too, Jennie Lee," said Marika in her best textbook fashion. "We're a team. We don't take individual credit when we win, and we don't take individual blame either —when we lose."

Not true, not true, Marika thought. What a phony statement I just made. Greg will take full credit if we land this piece of Flairhotels' business. He always does. He pushes the others' contributions right off the proposal's pages. He's a thief who sneaks the credit with the agility of the cat burglar.

She suddenly remembered David's teaching her to consciously switch from negative to positive thinking at times like this. An image of thief Greg, clad from head to toe in a black leotard and mask, scrambling over the rooftops, was not a healthy, positive one.

Marika joined Greg, Sarah, and Jennie Lee in the foyer of the hotel chain's offices. The plush room was overheated or maybe it was her own nervousness. No matter how many presentations Marika made, she always got psyched up and had a few butterflies in her stomach beforehand.

"I just hope," she murmured to no one in particular, "the air in there is clean and cool, and that the Flairhotels' people aren't all tired out of their skulls by the time we can seize their attention."

She suddenly noticed Greg was wearing his trademark sunglasses. "Take them off, for God's sake," she said rather sharply, "you look like the Godfather in them." Jennie Lee laughed outright. Marika was more uncomfortable, as she noticed his eyes seemed as dark with the glasses off as on. Hortense's warnings about him were getting to her. She was becoming testy and suspicious around him. It was the sign of a bad manager that she had reached the point where she really did not want to go out on presentations with him anymore.

All three continued to pace back and forth on the plush teal blue carpet, with Jennie Lee watching them and catching the rays of nervous tension in the air. Suddenly the heavy teak doors to the conference room swung open, and five people from another agency walked out, silent, but looking smug and pleased. Too bad, thought Marika, they look as though they had a successful presentation. I hope we still have a chance.

A marketing staff member from Flairhotels ushered them into the big room. A large burled elm oval contemporary table dominated the room, with giant dark teal leather swivel chairs crowded around it. Small sidechairs upholstered in teal wool were lined up against the walls, to provide seating space for the underlings. Jennie Lee started to plop herself down in one of the big leather swivel chairs, but Marika caught her by the back of her dress and whispered, "Sit against the wall, not around the table, for Pete's sake! Those chairs are for the directors of the corporation."

Marika whispered to Greg as they waited for everyone to sit down again. "The atmosphere in here is dark, dank, tired, down, heavy." He whispered, "Yeah, but we can change things fast."

Marika smiled brightly at the CEO's signal to begin. She greeted him by name, said hello to the other senior officers, and introduced her staff, including "Ms. Merriweather, our new intern. I would like to thank the chairman for allowing me to bring her with us here today." Marika then nodded to Sarah, who was working the wall switches. The dimmer was suddenly turned all the way up, flooding the room with light. The down, oppressive atmosphere changed immediately. Marika and Greg stationed themselves by the two standing easels holding annotated flip charts in the front of the room and began the outline of their marketing hopes for the new resort. Their diction was perfect and they spoke in upbeat, enthusiastic voices, moving deftly on well-rehearsed cues back and forth between the flip charts. Then Sarah darkened the room again and the dual slide projectors were turned on— showing romantic, magnificent color views of resorts all over the world. Marika described mellifluously how all of the assets of the Flairhotels Hawaiian resort would be developed to the media. At a certain moment Sarah, who had brought along a cassette player, started a new hula rock music tape, keeping it low on volume, as a further buttress to Marika's voice in describing the colorful resort experience.

In the still room Marika continued detailing the scenario—of what would be the experience of the widespread target market for this resort—families, honeymooners, business convention delegations, tourists, sportsmen and women, single swingers, women traveling alone, and older people in search of a rest. Each type of guest would have his or her own personal, delightful and pampered time. Marika could feel her audience listening with intensity. Their faces were relaxed and smiling. That was *good*. She looked over at Greg and he made a very small A-okay sign in the air as she continued to use her pointer like a magic wand, revealing the wonders of the complex in its many facets—gardens, myriad restaurants, sporting facilities, lounges, pools, hanging fountains, nightspots, and above all, creative services. As she talked about the remarkable athletic facilities, she was swinging a golf club one minute and making an overhead serve on the tennis court the next, her body language now an important part of the monologue. "This is how we will be presenting this property to the media," she said, suddenly aware of an annoying, intrusive sound in the room. What could it be? What machine or human being was making that awful click-click sound? Was it our projector? A telephone? No, Sarah's and Greg's faces were nonplussed, too. Had someone's beeper jammed? What electric device was it?

Finally, Marika had to stop her presentation, because quite obviously, everyone was uncomfortable and questioning. The click-click did not stop. It came from the other end of the long room, up against the wall where Jennie Lee Merriweather was sitting. Marika addressed her. "Jennie Lee," she said, leaning on her pointer, "may I ask just what you are doing?"

"Just sittin' here knittin'," drawled the answer, "knittin' on a sweater for my boyfriend." She held up the long cable-stitched sweater on large wooden needles against her, so that the entire room could see in the dim light of the projectors just how far she had come with her creation.

The entire room then went into convulsions. Bob Tewkes, the CEO, had his head in his arms on the table trying to control himself. Greg had turned to the wall, fists clenched, his head bent on his arm in exasperation, but shaking from laughter. Marika bent over her pointer until she could control her own laughter. Jennie Lee flushed hotly and stuffed her knitting back into the red felt tote bag.

Marika apologized for the interruption and announced that Greg would now give the costs and budgets for the firm's media plan for the resort. Five minutes later, Marika summarized the major points of Stuyvesant's proposal, adding "there is no question but that our firm is positioned to do this job better than anyone else." Her last words to her audience, said gravely and forcefully, were, "And I hope, Mr. Chairman, that no matter what other retail operations you plan for this property, you will not fail to have a knitting shop in the lobby of the hotel. It is a hot new fad, you know. It may well be essential to the success of the project. Thank you, ladies and gentlemen, for your attention."

The Stuyvesant team walked back to their office on foot.

Hortense was waiting for them. "How did it go? Do I ring the bell for a new account?"

"Not yet," said Marika with a smile, "but hopefully soon." The next morning, by nine o'clock, Tewkes had telephoned to say that "the knitting needles have it." Hortense rang the big ship's bell, mounted above Marika's office door and rung only when new business had been obtained. Hearing the bell reminded Marika that it was time now to plan the celebration lunch at "21" her father had bequested to the staff in his will. She memoed Hortense to take care of the arrangements, and then went into Anthony's office for a quick meeting to announce the new business to the rest of the staff. Staffers filled Anthony's Yale blue director's chairs, his sofa, and the window ledges.

"We just landed another fat piece of business." Marika nodded to Sarah, who, supplying her own throaty Hawaiian humming, performed a creditable hula dance. She had tucked long, thin strips of newspaper into the waist of her jeans, and only a person of absolutely no imagination would not guess that she was wearing a grass skirt.

Afterward, Marika went back to her office and read Jennie Lee's synopsis of the Women's Forum lunch that had been left in her office as directed. It was typed but full of strikeovers.

**Women's Forum Luncheon—Regency Hotel, New York City
January 23
His Honor the Mayor of New York as Featured Speaker**

"Present were women of power, most above the age of fifty, which is depressing to someone of my age. If you have to wait this long to make it, it can't possibly be worth it. I include these comments because Mrs. Wentworth believes that frankness is a sign of maturity, and I am being frank.

"Women of power talk a lot about which hairdresser they go to, whether they have been intimidated by the animal rights protestors over the wearing of their fur coats, and about the pro-choice issues. One thing they have in common: they constantly shift their exaggerated shoulder pads around while eating lunch. They must not have their shoulder pads properly sewn in or something. It looks really funny when a woman is talking and a pad falls off one shoulder, looking as though it's carrying half her body with it.

"Women of power with good hands wear big rings, have long, scary polished fingernails, and look at their nails constantly. They are mesmerized by their own hands and clunky jewelry, and want you to be, too. It is a fixation, and I must grow my fingernails.

"This kind of woman doesn't talk too much about what she does, I find. Maybe she is afraid she will give away secrets another woman of power can use to get ahead of her.

"Women of power are either incredibly thin and wear pants, or they are dumpy and it doesn't matter what they wear.

"My conclusions: As a group, they seem really glad to see each other, but I don't know why they would. They seem very harried and tired and don't talk all that much about their husbands or children. Guess not too many of them have them. Maybe the ones who do don't talk about them in order to be kind to those who don't.

"Anyway, I don't know if I'd want to be a woman of power —and have to sit through boring speeches by mayors and people like that at lunch."

Marika had planned to go over Jennie Lee's paper with her, paragraph by paragraph, after it was completed. As she put Jennie Lee's paper into her "pending" basket, she decided it could wait a day or two. Maybe a month or two. Sam Merriweather's child was perceptive and sharp, but if shoulder pads and scary fingernails were really all she amassed in the way of information from the exceptional women at lunch that day, Jennie Lee should perhaps try her hand at something else as a career, back home. Organic farming, for example.

. . .

That evening, during her usual good-night telephone chat with Jonathon, she had him roaring with laughter over the day spent training Jennie Lee Merriweather.

"If the young woman is hopeless," he said, "my advice is to let her go right away. It would be a kindness to her—and her father—in the long run. But then you haven't asked my advice, and I know better than to give it to someone like you when it hasn't been beckoned."

"I will always beckon your advice, Jonathon. I give you plenty of my own, after all, that is unsolicited."

"You certainly do," he said laughing, "with your 'Marika sniffs' about my table manners, my diamond ring, my evening watch . . ."

She interrupted him, not unemotionally. "I won't do that any more! The way you describe it, I sound contemptible. 'Marika sniffs'—that sounds unbelievably snobbish."

"If the woman I love gives me constructive criticism in small doses, I will always welcome it," he said soothingly. She felt her cheeks flush with color at the words "the woman I love." Then he said, "But let's get back to Jennie Lee."

"I quite like her, you know," Marika said protectively. "She's extremely naive, but there's a sense of humor there, a spark . . ."

"Sounds as though you've already decided to integrate her into the agency," he said.

"Yes, the more I think about that spark of hers, the more I like her. After some more training, I'll move her to the bottom of the totem pole as a paid employee, so that another one of my young trainees, Kristen, can move up one slot." She began musing over and talking out loud her thoughts regarding the table of organization of her agency, disregarding Jonathon on the other end for a brief moment. Then she came back to consciousness.

"I have a feeling that Hortense's dislike and mistrust of Greg may have a solid basis."

"Well, then, even after telling you to ignore my unsolicited advice, I'm going to give some more. Get rid of him!"

"It's not that easy. He owns a lot of the company stock. I've given it to him—as an incentive bonus. He's earned it."

"Get rid of him anyway."

"I have no proof of malfeasance or anything else. What do I say to him?"

"Tell him your woman's intuition tells you that he must go."

"I can't tell him anything like that!" Marika laughed in mock disgust. "Be serious. This is a tough one to call. What excuse could I use?"

"Just be aware, and he'll give you one soon enough. My dear, adorable, Marika, there is nothing in the business world in my opinion that has greater validity than a woman's intuition. I put it ahead of any other prediction source. Find the proper moment, and you'll find the proper words. They'll just come."

"It means a lot to me to be able to talk to you about my company. It must bore you incredibly. My father used to be on the receiving end of all these office conversations."

"Nothing about you bores me. And don't think I don't agonize, too, over my handling of top staff people when something goes wrong. It happens to all of us. You need a fresh eye telling you to follow your own instincts. However, remember, if you don't have a specific bona fide reason to fire him, talk to a lawyer—not Anthony, but an outside firm—before you do anything. Be prepared to give Greg a very generous settlement to go, and then tell him to go quickly."

"We're far from being ready for all that yet."

Jonathon began to sign off, but Marika stopped him.

"You know what's hard?" she asked with a sadness in her voice.

"Well, for one thing, I'm hard, just talking to you."

She laughed. "You're like Lisa, always making me laugh when I'm trying to talk about something that is really serious, even upsetting."

His voice immediately changed to one of concern. "I'm sorry. Go on."

"Have you got the time now for a real piece of theater?"

"This sounds interesting. Talking to you, Marika, is always

fascinating. I get love talk, business problem talk, Lisa problem talk—and now, what drama are you about to relay? You're so much more interesting on the telephone than anyone I have ever talked to in my whole life!"

Marika had decided in the middle of the conversation about Jennie Lee and Greg that the time had come to tell Jonathon about Istvan. She had buried Istvan Bokanyi deep in her heart and had talked about it with no one. Even Lisa, perpetually consumed with curiosity over the subject of her exotic grandfather, knew enough not to press her mother on the subject. It was too soon after Charles Russell's death. Her mother simply could not handle it. Lisa had only said on two occasions after the funeral, "Mom, someday we'll have to go to Hungary, like Grandpa said to do." Marika had answered each time, "Someday, Lisa, we will."

So, Marika Wentworth, who by all rights should have been named Marika Bokanyi at birth, told Jonathon about Charlie Russell's conversation the last night he came to dinner at his daughter's Sutton Place apartment.

Jonathon probed gently, saying nothing during the long pauses in her replies. It was as though he was helping her talk through her guilt. He helped her realize that out of loyalty to Charles Russell, she had pushed Istvan out of her consciousness, and into a maximum security cell in her subconsciousness.

Finally he had the story. She had even given him every detail she knew about Istvan—which wasn't much.

"Guilt is a normal reaction," Jonathon said, comforting her, because he could hear the emotion in her voice. "You're still grieving for Charlie Russell. A heart can only handle one grief at a time."

"But I have to face the fact of this strange, romantic, shadowy figure of a man whose genes are in me, who never knew about me . . ."

"You don't have to face it in the way you would if he were alive," Jonathon interjected. "He's gone, Marika. He was never a concrete factor in your life. Don't give him too much importance now."

"I was my mother's only child!" she protested. "I can't wish away Istvan Bokanyi as though he never existed. He's responsible for my being alive this very minute."

"And for that, I'm undyingly grateful to him!"

"I wish you could see me smiling at you for saying that," she said, "but you can't see it."

"I can feel it," he answered. "It's as soft as a butterfly's wings."

"What a divine man you are, Jonathon Scher," she said softly.

"Let's say good night. I've been thinking, I am going to have to buy AT&T to justify my telephone bills."

"Good night, my darling," she said. And no matter what problems pressed her, she felt better, just knowing he was somewhere in the world, loving her.

CHAPTER

*I*t was one of those tough days. Clients were calling in to complain. They were not satisfied if she got them on the front page of the business section of the *Times* or in the latest issue of *Forbes*. The question was always, "And why didn't the media mention such-and-such?" "And why wasn't my picture in the piece, when two of my competitors' were?" It was the kind of day that made her really want to chuck the whole profession of public relations.

Sidney Miller was one of those "charming" calls. "I recently read your name in the paper, Marika, as having been a guest at a state dinner at the White House. That's the kind of thing you could do for us perhaps, if you would."

"I don't think I can bring that off, Sidney."

"Rachel says it's the dream of her life to go to dinner at the White House. Not one of those tour things, not even a reception, but a dinner, a state dinner, if you know what I mean."

"Sidney, I can't just call up the President of the United States

and command him to invite my good friends the Millers to dinner!''

"You're good friends of the Watsons aren't you?"

"Good Lord, Sidney!"

"See what you can do. All I'm asking you to do is try," and
he said a quick good-bye.

Hortense came in with a pad full of telephone calls for her
boss to return. "Shall we start calling these people now?" she
asked.

"No."

"Well, then, what do you feel like doing, Boss?"

"Throwing up is what I feel like doing." Marika felt the pressure building inside her head. It was time for some neck rolls
again. Jonathon, would you please come and massage my neck
for me? Oh, Jonathon, just thinking about you makes the knots
begin to untie themselves.

"This telephone call will be a pleasure," Hortense announced
grandly over the intercom. "It's the White House!" Hortense
always managed somehow to include the sound of the President's
song, "Hail to the Chief" in her voice tones when she wanted to.

"Eve, darling, how's everything?"

"Good. Marika, good. Are you coming down here for lunch
next Thursday?"

"Yes, and I am looking forward to a good Eve-talk. You know,
every time I think about your genius in placing Jonathon Scher
as my dinner partner, I am more in awe of you than ever."

"Ummm. Sounds good. Is there something intense going on
here that I don't know about?"

"We talk every single day, we're together every single weekend
we're both in this country, and we simply—simply . . ."

"Yesss?" Eve asked with an enormous drawl of the "s" sound.

"We find we . . ."

"Go on."

"We sort of need each other. It's a longing each of us has—
to be talking to the other, to be sharing what is going on in our

lives, to be discussing everything. We spend hours on the telephone at night without even realizing it."

"Sounds like you're enrolled in Vassar's Infatuation 105 course. Marika, tell me something."

"Yes. Go on."

"Have you slept with him yet?"

"I don't care if you are the First Lady, you sure are cheeky. Is this a secure line?"

"Of course it is!"

"I wouldn't want America's enemies knowing about my sex life."

"Cut the extraneous conversation. Have you slept with him yet?"

"And how!"

"I take it things went well? The tone of your voice tells me that."

"Just thinking about him makes me weak, Eve."

"Must be *very good*."

"He's—*wonderful*."

"Is this my stouthearted, brilliant, independent feminist friend talking like a mound of mush over a man?"

"You bet it is! Now what's going on with you?"

"I need some girl talk! What's the gossip, Marika? Seen Georgiana's new place yet?"

"No, but I will at the big dinner dance she and Chauncey are giving on the ninth. She desperately wants you and Mac to be there."

"Impossible. She's nuts!" Eve snapped. Then, "I'm sorry, we're all on too fast a track," Eve added. "And Georgiana should have called me herself, not used you as her messenger girl."

"She was afraid to call you at the White House."

Eve sounded sad. "That's just terrible. Even my old pals are so intimidated by this damn place, they're afraid to call me." Then Eve's voice grew calmer. "Anyway, ignore me. I overreact occasionally—maybe more than occasionally. Well, since you're Mercury bearing the messages these days from Georgiana, tell her that I love her, that I wish I could see her version of Versailles, the new apartment, that I would adore to go to her dinner party, even if Mac wouldn't—no, leave that last part out—but we can't possibly leave Washington to go to a private party in New York. Tell her to use her new *palazzo* for a dinner for a foreign head of state, and then we can come. I'm dying to see it!"

"You'll be missed, Eve. But I have something else to ask of you. I have—well, it's a huge favor to ask. It's embarrassing. I hate this. It's pretentious and awful of me."

"What are you asking me to do?" Eve asked in mock fear, "move out of the White House, or leave Mac?"

"Worse. I'm asking you to invite a client of mine and his wife to a state dinner, a very improper thing to do, except that he is a denizen of big business and a big contributor to the party, and qualifies on the guest list for that reason."

"Marika, you know that's easy for me to do. Of course. We have a boring state dinner coming up that I know you wouldn't enjoy, but I'll ask Mr. and Mrs. Whomever. Call the Social Secretary's office tomorrow, and give them the particulars—you know, name, address, social security number, all that stuff. I'll tell Jan Alcott this afternoon to await your call."

"What a pal you are. I feel ashamed, taking advantage of our friendship like this."

"You never ask me for anything and you give all the time. End of conversation!"

"Jonathon Scher was a gift I'll never forget, Eve."

"I hope it's a gift you never want to exchange."

They started to say good-bye, but first asked each other the solution to a riddle. Not only were they unable to solve one another's riddles, but in each case the one who asked forgot the solution.

"This would never have happened in college," Eve said sadly.

"Yeah, but you wouldn't be calling me from 1600 Pennsylvania Avenue, either, if we were still in college."

Marika entered a reminder in her mini-computor to call Sidney Miller and tell him the good news. Then she decided she would really finish the Millers off by having them invited to Georgiana's dinner, too. The two invitations should "make" them socially, and her social work would be finished for Millerhomes forever. She called her ex-roommate and told her about her conversation with Eve. Then, in a frank and apologetic manner, she asked Georgiana for the favor. Her friend immediately wrote down the Millers' names and addresses for her invitation list.

Marika asked if there was anything she could do for her in return.

"Yes, help me get Sand to come to dinner that night," said Georgiana. She sounded very serious.

Marika laughed. "Does it mean that much to have her come and cover your dinner?"

"It means that much."

Shaking her head, Marika dialed Sand's number, gave her some chatty Washington news, and then added, "I guess I'll see you at Georgiana's dinner."

"Are *you* going to that?" she asked in a disapproving tone.

"I wouldn't miss it. There's going to be an exciting crowd, and Georgiana and Chauncey's new apartment is the talk of the country, not just of New York."

There was a pause, and then Sand said in her curmudgeonly way, "Guess I'll see you there."

Marika filed a note in her computer to buy a thank-you gift for Georgiana. Then she dialed Sidney and, after explaining all the details to him, rang off, saying, "That's it, Sidney. No more of this social arranging. Our company has done enough of that for you for two years' worth of contracts."

Thank goodness Sidney didn't give her any argument on that point. Maybe the day would get better yet!

She had been sitting in the blue chair half asleep, very relaxed, having done her breathing exercises and head rolls. It was difficult concentrating on the press materials she had to approve. His voice on the telephone made her sit bolt upright, electric-charged.

"Where can an ugly guy take the most beautiful woman in the world to dinner for three hours and show her off to the world?"

"I'd tell an attractive guy that normally I'd invite him home, but Geneviève has left, I haven't a drop of food in the house, and no desire to cook anyway. But I'd love to have dinner with you in a restaurant."

"Some place quiet, where we can talk undisturbed, and I can tell you how wonderful you are, and get you all embarrassed and shy."

"I'll have Hortense book us a table at Jean Lafitte on Fifty-eighth Street, between Fifth and Sixth. It's a great place to become embarrassed in. When?"

"In half an hour. I have only three hours. Just got out of a meeting, and my plane leaves New York at ten. I don't want to waste a minute of you."

"What luck you finished with the meeting in time to have three hours free. I feel privileged. I'm also purring."

He made a low purring sound back at her.

"I suppose I should have been coy and pretended I was busy tonight and told you that a guy just can't call me up anytime and get me to meet him for dinner on thirty minutes' notice."

"We're wasting my time. Can you make it to the restaurant in twenty?"

"Yes!" She put down the telephone, asked Hortense on the intercom to book a table in her name at Jean Lafitte, and sat back in her blue chair for one minute. "All right!" she cried out to no one in particular, but Hortense heard it and smiled. If Jonathon Scher elicited such a cry of joy from her boss, he must be the one Hortense had been praying for since the day she had watched Marika bury David Wentworth six years ago. Sometimes prayers did go answered. All right, indeed!

She found Jonathon already there at a table in the dimly lit bistro, with its art nouveau lily-shaped wall sconces. He kissed her hand, they ordered a drink, and one hour later, during a marathon of nonstop conversation, the waiter finally was able to interrupt with the dinner menu. Jonathon suddenly looked at Marika and asked the waiter to come back in two minutes.

"I'm not hungry," he said, grabbing her hand, "for food, I

mean. I'm crazy mad over you, and I want you this very minute, and if you make me sit through a meal these next two hours, I'll never forgive you."

"Just what did you have in mind?" Marika asked, laughing and gathering her purse by its handle from the back of her chair.

"You'll find out." He got up and helped her into her coat. He called the waiter over and handed him a fifty-dollar bill. "Here's for our two drinks and for the dinner tip you would have received if we had ordered dinner."

"Thank you, Monsieur," the waiter said with no little enthusiasm in his voice.

They went to Marika's apartment and made passionate love for the two hours that remained before his flight. She went out to the Marine Air Terminal with him, kept the car waiting, and stayed at the gate until his company jet took off, something she hadn't done since Lisa, at age eight, flew by herself to visit her Great-Great-Aunt Victoria in Palm Beach. They had talked fast and furiously again all the way out to the airport. Jonathon was on his way to Montreal, he explained to Marika, to buy a package of Canadian agricultural real estate deals, which he would then resell to a group of West German investors.

"You're such a wheeler and dealer," she said admiringly.

"I'm a careful one. I don't take inordinate risks."

She realized she had displeased him. "What I meant to say was, you're such a careful, conservative, but successful wheeler and dealer."

Before boarding, he took her face in both hands and kissed her good-bye long and passionately, much to the amusement of the staff of his jet. "I don't know why it gets harder every time to say good-bye to you," he said huskily.

"I know why," she said, realizing she had the last word this time.

Marika came quickly out of her office, with her coat only half on, carrying her briefcase and handbag, and checking her watch. She had only fifteen minutes to make it to Rockefeller Center for a meeting with the company's lawyer. Hortense, holding an opened Federal Express envelope in one hand and a small red heart box in the other, was chanting "A valentine! A valentine for you!"

"Oh, for heaven's sake," Marika chided, taking the box and acting slightly irritated at these unbusiness-like proceedings in her reception area. She removed the glove from her right hand and quickly opened the box, which was filled with an oversupply of tissue paper.

"Hortense, you are so curious, you are practically in the box yourself. I can feel your hot breath on my neck. Would you prefer to open this yourself?"

"No, but hurry, Boss. You're late."

Marika walked out to the elevator and pressed the button. Hortense was right behind her.

"I just might wait to open this package in the elevator."

"Don't you dare!" Hortense was only half-teasing.

Marika opened the last bit of tissue just as the elevator doors opened. Inside was a beautiful little eighteen-karat gold butterfly brooch. Its wings were set with pavé rubies, and there was a strangely familiar, large, cushion-shaped diamond in the center of the body. Marika managed to read the enclosure card in private, for the elevator doors had now closed on Hortense.

"I know you don't approve of men who wear diamond rings and since I didn't have a clue what to do with the diamond in my ring, I thought maybe a butterfly could use it, and that the butterfly could then spend a happy life perching every now and then on the world's most beautiful shoulder. You know you have my love, as well as the diamond, Jonathon."

Marika immediately pinned it on the top of the shoulder of her dark gray flannel double-breasted coatdress. It glistened alongside her large double-strand pearl choker necklace, and all during her meeting with the firm's lawyer, she kept touching it, to make sure it was still there.

At the conclusion of her meeting, she entered a Rockefeller Center candy store on the ground floor and purchased thirty-six small red heart boxes full of miniature chocolates, which she stuffed into a giant shopping bag. When she reached the office, she gave one to each employee of Stuyvesant Communications, saying "Happy Valentine's Day" to each and every one.

Anthony said, "Marika, such a nice, sentimental gesture! I wonder ... Does a man named Scher have anything to do with this excess of sweetness?"

"He might, Anthony."

"Well," he said, taking her hand in both of his, "I just want you to know you deserve it, Marika, and I hope and pray that everything turns out the way you want it to."

"I'm not going to broadcast this all over the place," she said, after they hugged.

"I understand. We shall not gossip. Those of us who know about Jonathon, and that is probably just Hortense and me—we will quietly smile among ourselves."

She plopped a chocolate heart in his mouth and left the office, a spring in her step. Anthony munched on the chocolate as he closed his door, took his pipe from his desk drawer, and carefully prepared it for smoking. He was so fond of this woman whom he had known so well since the day she hired him in Boston. If he were not happily married, he probably would have fallen in love with her himself after David's death. I just hope, he thought to himself, that this Scher is an A-okay kind of man. He'd better be. The forbidden smoke wafted up to his ceiling, making the plant in the corner droop a bit more.

At home that evening Marika was reading press material drafts when Lisa arrived and walked into her bedroom. Her mother was ensconced on her mint green satin chaise, a matching mohair throw over her legs. It was chilly in the room, because the french doors were open onto the terrace and the crisp crystal air made the other side of the East River seem just a few feet away.

"What's up?" Marika's red-rimmed granny glasses were down on the lower bridge of her nose as she peered over them at her daughter. Lisa had sprung in one graceful leap onto the bed, ruffling the pale green silk bedspread into a sea of troubled waves and changing currents.

"Dunno, just bored, I guess."

Marika wondered if Lisa's friends, with little grasp of the work ethic, ever thought of the fact that the older generation, while supporting them, had work to do during the younger one's period of boredom. Then she felt a tiny tightening of guilt in her jawbone. This was no time for criticisms. She was always wishing for more time alone with Lisa. Down with the press materials. Up with her daughter.

"I'm delighted," Marika said with a smile, "that I haven't seen you with a cigarette for months now. What made you really stop? Did all of my scare tactics finally work?"

"No, it was Sergio," Lisa replied matter-of-factly. "He said kissing a girl who smokes is like licking an ashtray."

"Nicely graphic." Marika grimaced at the thought of this young Italian being able to motivate her daughter with a power she had never had, and all because of a threat to withhold his kisses.

Lisa sighed again and slowly began kicking her legs sidewise in a scissors-kick exercise for flabby thighs—a problem not yet affecting Marika's daughter.

"Come on," Marika said, "you have a much too energetic and insane life to admit to being bored."

Lisa was now doing a bicycle exercise in the air, and her words were punctuated with breathiness. "Would you be upset," she asked her mother, "if I did not follow in your footsteps?"

"*What?*" asked her mother incredulously.

"Would you be disappointed if I didn't try to duplicate your career, you know, go into PR and all that sort of stuff?"

"What in heaven's name has brought forth this weighty line of questioning?" Marika was grinning over her granny glasses at her daughter.

"I don't know, it's just that in three more years, I'll be out of college, and everyone thinks I'll be like you."

"Do you want to?"

"I don't want your life, Mom."

"You can have any life you wish—as long as it's healthy, clean, civic . . ."

Now it was Lisa's turn to laugh and interrupt. "Hey, don't

read me a list of Elizabethan virtues! No, I'm serious. I don't want to have to work as hard as you do."

"Is that it?" her mother asked. "My job entails too much work for you?"

"Look, Mom, I see you working on Saturdays and Sundays, all day, all night."

"You have to when you run your own company, and it's small."

"Well, *I* don't want to."

"You don't *have* to."

"I don't want to have to run to catch planes all over, to work late at night on press releases, to always be on deadline, to carry around a briefcase like you do that weighs fifty pounds."

"Lisa, you can carve out any life that you want. You're lucky, you have options. I never asked you to follow in my footsteps. Have I ever *once* even mentioned it?"

"No, but Sergio and I have often discussed it. In Italy, a child is supposed to take over his parents' business."

"Well, you're one child who doesn't have to. Frankly, I've never even thought of your taking over my company one day. That's so far in the future—and you're just finding your way."

"I'm not a public person like you, Mom. I can't give speeches and stuff like that."

"You won't have to. You do with your life what you will— when you're through with college."

"Positive you won't be hurt if I don't want to enter the PR field?"

"Super positive."

Lisa finished her bicycle kicks and bounced off the bed. She started doing knee bends. "Mom, guess where Sergio took me to dinner last night?"

"You mean where *I* took Sergio to dinner last night. That will be the day when he picks up the check."

"I paid for it out of my allowance."

"And your allowance emanates from where, may I ask?"

Lisa ignored this. "We went to a really Hungarian restaurant in the upper Eighties."

Marika took off her glasses, put down her pen, and gave her daughter her full attention. "How come you did that?"

"Because I felt a pull toward it—you know, we don't talk about my Hungarian grandfather, but he's there. You can't shut him out, and I can't either."

"I know," Marika said sadly. "I wish I knew how to handle what I feel inside about all this."

"Do you think about him? Do you kind of tune him in and out of your thoughts all day the way I do?"

"Yes," Marika said, a sad edge to her voice. "All the time. And every time I wonder and imagine and try to reconstruct him, thoughts of your Grandfather Russell come charging in, and my mind becomes an unintelligible jumble."

"Me, too," Lisa said, her strawberry hair flying in all directions from the exertion of her exercises. "Mom, we have to get to Hungary, you and me."

"You and I," Marika corrected her. "Yes, you're right. But it's going to take some time to . . ."

"To get organized? Get real, Mom. You mean you're not ready to deal with it."

"You're right, Madam Freud." Mother and daughter smiled at each other, Marika thinking how Lisa could seem so mature one minute and so hopelessly young the next. "It just would be too tough to face whatever we might uncover in Hungary. I guess I'm not ready yet."

There was silence in the room for a while, as both women sat, comfortable with their own thoughts, frozen as if on a painter's canvas, Marika on her chaise, looking out the window, and Lisa on her mother's bed, on her back and gazing at the painted ceiling of white clouds floating across the blue sky.

"It's strange, both of us thinking about our Hungarian family so often—and not talking to one another about it," Marika finally said.

"I feel it's disloyal to Grandpa Russell to think about Grandpa Istvan." Lisa pronounced the name gingerly, still not used to the sound of it.

"Someday, we'll be able to think about them both—with

ease," her mother said, "when we can handle Grandpa Russell's death better than we do now."

There was quiet again. Then Lisa asked, "Mom, how old do you think you'll be when you stop having a sex life?" She had begun doing rapid leg lifts and the entire bed shook each time she dropped her legs in unison.

Marika had to laugh. "This conversation has taken a 180-degree turn, Lisa."

"Well, these are things I always mean to ask you and never get the chance."

"Are you trying to ask about Jonathon and me?"

"I guess I am," replied Lisa, now embarrassed. "I mean, when you're in your forties, it can't be as good as it was in your twenties, right? You're sort of on a downward curve, right?"

"Look, Lisa, I am under no obligation to give you any details whatsoever of what Jonathon and I do in private. But physically, we are as good as—I mean, some of us have just as strong a drive as . . ."

They both laughed at her confusion and embarrassment. "Look," Marika said in a determined voice, "sex goes on for as long as you want it to and for as long as you're attracted to each other."

"But not—like in your sixties!" Lisa was thinking of the athletic feats she and Sergio undertook, and how you have to be young and physically fit to do it. Then she continued, "When a woman's all wrinkled and old, what man wants to have sex with *her*?"

"How about a man who is all wrinkled and old? Look, just think of your Great-Great-Aunt Victoria, prim and proper—and *very* old." Lisa smiled at the sound of the octogenarian's name, the great old lady, the paragon of the Old Eastern Establishment society.

"You have probably never heard this before," Marika continued, "but she has had a series of lovers all her life, until about the age of eighty."

"But how could she?—I mean, how could . . ." Lisa stopped in mid-sentence, unable to continue embracing such a vision.

"How young and unknowing you are," Marika said gently. "Sex and charm and personality become very much combined in a mature adult. At your age, it's all physical beauty, nothing else. When you become a real adult, you'll find there's much more."

"I'll keep having plastic surgery all the time when I get older," Lisa concluded. "Then I'll be able to stay physically attractive."

"Women who 'keep having plastic surgery all the time' are just that, Lisa, splotches of plastic, collagen, and fakery. There's no substance under the artificial stuff." Marika peered at the lithe form of her daughter, her body with legs together straight up in the air, supported on her upper back by her hands and arms.

"Lisa. My bedspread. For God's sake you're wrecking it!" Lisa's legs obediently came down, crashing onto her mother's pale green silk and white embroidered organdy pillows at the head of the bed, making them fly off in every direction like recently frightened pigeons.

"Don't tell me people like wrinkles, Mom. You don't have 'em, and I bet you'll fight like hell—I mean like heck—when they come along. Jonathon sure wouldn't want you to have them."

"I'm not defending wrinkles per se, but I certainly don't want you to look at life with such vapid eyes. A woman can remain sexually attractive, Lisa—like my Great-Aunt Victoria—well into her older age because she takes care of herself physically and most important, because she leads an interesting life."

"Mom, come on! Leading an 'interesting life' is not going to keep the guys coming on to you. Who's going to get out a magnifying glass and examine some old bird's wrinkles to see if they're interesting or not?"

"A real face—one that is not in a state of continuous renovation at a surgeon's hands—proudly shows wrinkles of experience. Your Aunt Victoria was never slim, nor did she ever fry her face in the sun. Her skin was always beautiful, not desiccated-looking, like the dried fruit you and Sergio keep eating out of those little packets."

"I happen to know, firsthand, that the best thing for the face," Lisa said while rolling over onto her stomach again, further messing the silk bedspread, "is good parallel parking."

"Good what?"

"Ah, Mom, good sex. Like boxing tonsils."

"I'm not even going to ask for a translation of that." So there it was, overtly bragging about their amorous activities. "Your preoccupation with sex," Marika continued, "is unbecoming to a young unmarried girl."

"What else do you expect me to be preoccupied with?"

"You never talk to me about your studies."

"I get A's and B's, don't I?"

"Yes, and I'm proud of you for that. I'm terribly proud of you, and that's why I wish you would share a little more of it with me."

"I'm doing my job at Columbia. It's *my* life after all, and Sergio is my number-one priority."

"I'm not trying to change that. I just think there's too much talk about sex all the time."

"I'm making him use a condom—most of the time. Doesn't that relieve your mind?"

" 'Most of the time'? What good does that do?"

"Mom, I know he's squeaky clean about all that stuff with drugs and homosexuals. He tells me everything. I know about his whole life. He is not going to infect me."

"You know about *every* person that he has slept with?"

"Every one. Since we're on this subject, why aren't you worried about sleeping with Jonathon? He's been around after all. He's had twenty more years of potential danger in the sexually transmitted disease department than Sergio."

"I know everything about his past life."

"Ha! Well, Mother dear, I don't want to worry too much about you getting AIDS or some other disease. Make Jonathon wear a condom, too."

"I can't believe this conversation we're having."

"It's today, Mom," and with that Lisa bounded off the bed, took a satisfied look at her own face in the dressing table mirror, and finding no wrinkles, threw a smile and a kiss at her mother as she left the room.

When Marika reached her office the next morning, the first

matter Hortense brought to her attention was a request for an interview from *Woman Today* magazine.

"They're doing a big issue on successful career mothers as role models for their daughters," Hortense said proudly, "and they said that you would be a great example. They want to do a mother-daughter story featuring you and Lisa. It ought to be great."

"Hortense, I hate to disappoint you, but forget the role-model story. Make your usual wonderfully diplomatic excuses and get me out of it."

Marika allowed herself, finally, thirty seconds to deal with the conversation she and Lisa had had last night—So, Lisa didn't want her life. And Lisa thought about Istvan constantly. And, hardly a revelation, Lisa was enjoying her sex with Sergio. Well, David had always said, "Different strokes for different folks," Marika remembered, and there was no doubt about it, Lisa Wentworth was some different stroke!

CHAPTER

9

She thought it over carefully beforehand, and decided to take only Steve with her to White Plains to see the Kauffmans on the LUXFOODS account. She arranged to have Greg represent her at the very same hour at a luncheon meeting for prestigious leaders in the PR field, hosted by New York's major metropolitan hospitals. The institutions were enlisting the help of the public relations industry pro bono—in combatting their massive problems of overcrowding, fiscal disasters, and nursing shortages. She suspected Greg would see through her ruse immediately and be furious that she had not brought him along to make the pitch to Mathilde Kauffman and her husband.

She also knew she had to show her independence from him. Hortense kept feeding her small pieces of information showing disloyalty on Greg's part—little, subtle things. Such as he had been seen lunching with the president of a rival PR agency at an out-of-the-way restaurant, and he was quoted as having said he was tired of having to do all of the dog work at Stuyvesant Communications. There was a kind of mutiny afoot, and she felt instinctively that it was an evil disloyalty. She couldn't quite put her finger on it. Something was going on behind the impenetrable black lenses of those damned sunglasses he wore all the time.

She also wanted to give Steve's morale a lift. He had been losing weight rapidly and looked so tired. There was even a slight change in his gait. At least on the way to and from White Plains, they would have a chance to talk, and she could try to get to the bottom of his problem. Funny. She really cared about helping Steve, but she did not wish to hear about Greg's life at all. The chemistry was awry on that one.

They arrived exactly two minutes before the scheduled appointment time, and were ushered at once into an ultra-modern conference room, all done in orange and gray, with warm brass accents—the same place where they had made their unsuccessful pitch for the LUXFOODS chocolate account.

Like the railroad trains in their country, the Kauffmans ran their operation precisely, punctually. Marika and Steve were offered some hot chocolate, and then the Kauffmans began. Marika had prepared Steve to accept—and drink—his hot chocolate with gusto. While Mathilde Kauffman spoke, they each made individual notes—which they would later compare and find to be totally different. Marika listened with a manager's ear. Her thinking was structured, and as she listened, she conjectured about market studies, personnel requirements, deadlines, press materials, and research that would be required. Steve's ear was creative, and as he listened, the Kauffman's briefing conjured up fast-moving images, design and symbolic words for delicious, healthful food. He was interested in visual and verbal beauty, Marika in the nuts and bolts first, the visual beauty afterward.

LUXFOODS would be presenting to the American market, and later to the markets of other countries, a whole new line of expensive gourmet products based on different combinations of honey and low-fat cream, emphasizing the health aspects of honey as well as taste. There was to be a new honey, a yogurt, a honey-cream custard dessert. There was even going to be a chewy honey-cream chocolate candy and a honey-cream chocolate sauce. Mathilde Kauffman was convinced that the lead in marketing of the products should come through the public relations campaign, instead of the ad campaign, and that the advertising should reinforce the theme, philosophy, and language established by the PR campaign. Mathilde was a compelling speaker—gesticulating in the air in an almost hypnotizing manner to the rhythm of her words, as her many small gold and gem-encrusted rings glinted on her fat fingers. Her husband Luke sat stolidly by her side, uttering guttural expressions of agreement in his *Schweitzer-deutsche* dialect every now and then—to prove to the visitors that he was still part of the game.

Chocolate had always been LUXFOODS's main product, so that the Kauffman's venture into the world of honey and cream was a very expensive and courageous one. The budget for the marketing and advertising launch had been set for twenty million dollars more than the advertising and promotion budget for all their chocolate products.

"We are counting on you, Mrs. Wentworth," Mathilde said, taking another sip from her Meissen cup of hot cocoa, "to come up with a program that will give us a name and a glamorous focus for these new products. We want all the top hostesses in America to use them. We want the leaders of America to know them—and want them—and we want these products to have the same recognition value as the leading caviar and champagne brands. The new products may be high in calories, but the experience will be worth it. They are also high in taste, and, I sincerely believe—although some nutritionists refuse to accept it—high in energy content from the bee pollen involved in each product. We have no time to lose. We are eight months behind schedule in our launch."

"We can do whatever needs to be done," Marika said firmly. Steve gave her the victory sign as the two Kauffmans talked to each other in German.

"I am sorry to say that you are going to have to pull this together impossibly fast," Mathilde said gravely. Her voice was soft, and not as guttural as her husband's. "There is no other option. We must have the new name for the products, the entire marketing concept must be spelled out, and the first year's suggested PR activities and budget must be presented to us within four weeks."

Marika felt a flash of panic. With all the research and planning that needed to be done, what Mathilde Kauffman had just demanded was impossible. Steve, aghast, threw her a look that said, No!

"We'll manage to meet your deadline," Marika said. She looked over at Steve with amusement. He rolled his eyes heavenward, as though asking God's forgiveness for her enormous lie.

They toured the plant and offices, listened to a detailed briefing on the content of the new products by a nutritionist from the laboratory, and filled the limo with reports, brochures, and research papers. The Kauffmans put a bag of chocolate samples in the back seat with them, then bade them good-bye. The New Yorkers both noticed that Mathilde had burst a seam in the back of her dress. "Too much bee pollen," Steve quipped.

On the way back into town, Marika and Steve discussed animatedly the enormous task ahead of Stuyvesant Communications, Inc. Then Steve seemed suddenly to sag on the seat, like a rag doll when it is disturbed from its resting position.

"Steve, what's the matter?"

"Not feeling too well, really. I just overdid today a little."

"Did you go to Dr. Postman as I asked you to do?"

"Yes."

"Well, yes what?"

"I have AIDS."

"Jesus Christ!"

"Marika, I never hear you swear. It doesn't match."

"I'm sorry. Instead of taking the Lord's name, I should be praying to Him, and don't think I'm not going to start right this minute."

"I know you will." They sat in silence for a while. Steve offered her a chocolate.

"I suppose I should leave the company."

"You darned well will not."

"Some people won't like my staying around—sick—and not as useful as I used to be."

"You stay until you can't stand to stay another second longer. I need every burst of that fertile brain that I can get." She took his hand. "We need you, Steve. Don't desert us."

"To use an old cliché, it's nice to be needed." He smiled and began coughing—not a hard cough, just a gentle one.

"I've noticed you're doing a lot of that lately, Steve—that coughing. Is that—is that part of it?"

"Yes. And when I start to get forgetful, you'll tell me, won't you? I don't want to hang around when I'm not making sense anymore."

"What's the plan of action? Who will take care of you? What can I do . . ."

He interrupted her. "Dr. Postman is going to keep checking me, and I called Bill Davis, an AIDS clinical specialist at Mount Sinai Medical Center. I heard he was great, so I went up to see him. He's going to help me—and he also referred me to the Gay Men's Health Crises."

"Look, do you want to renege on offering to work on the honey-cream products? Won't it be too much of a strain?"

"No, no!" he protested. "Please let me work on it, Marika— please."

"I would like that, Steve, but if you feel you've had enough punishment on this project, just tell me. In the meantime, I need every ounce of your know-how and ideas."

"You'll get it—what I have left, and I think I have *a lot* left," he said sadly. "Look, Marika, tell the others, will you—about my having AIDS? I would just like to get it out, so that when it's apparent later, they won't think they've been duped or anything. If they want me to wear gloves in the office, I will. I don't want to scare anyone."

"We're your family, remember?" The elation of winning the big new account had evaporated with Steve's news. Then she asked, "What about your partner, Steve? Is he around to help you?"

She had always known that Steve was gay, but had never met any of his friends. He kept his personal life far removed from the office, and she thought it strange that she had never met his lover, with whom he shared his apartment. Instead of answering her, he slumped down on the seat, his hands in his jeans pockets, looking so weary, she wondered if he would have the strength to get out of the car. Finally he spoke, "Ray left me when he heard the news. The classic rat leaving the sinking ship."

She helped him out of the car when they reached his place— a charming terrace apartment only four blocks from the office. She walked him to the elevator.

"I appreciate your standing by."

"You know we'll all stand by you until . . ." And then she didn't know how to finish it.

The staff meeting was called the minute she returned to the office from White Plains. Marika kept a perplexed Hortense from ringing the big ship's bell outside her office door, even though there was a new account in the house. With the news of Steve's illness, somehow ringing a joyous bell didn't seem appropriate today. When Marika announced that she had just landed the big new LUXFOODS account, the group of fifteen who had crowded into Anthony's office all cheered.

"Mrs. Kauffman remembered you very favorably, Greg," Marika was careful to say, "from our first meeting. She asked to be remembered to you again and said she hoped you'd be involved with the project. I told her most certainly yes."

"I'm surprised you didn't take me to White Plains," Greg said, his irritation showing, "since I'll be in charge of this account."

"I am in charge of this account," Marika interjected quickly, "and I decided to take Steve with me on an exploratory visit for very good reasons." She looked at Greg with a renewed sense of distrust. It seemed each company victory drew out more of his ugliness.

There was total silence in the room. As Sarah described it

afterward, nervously trying to read the future in her tarot cards, "you could have cut the tension in that room with a hacksaw."

Marika decided to break the silence. "We must give these products an upscale image," she emphasized. "These are expensive gourmet products, so put on your thinking caps—don't sleep all night long—and come in here tomorrow with your ideas."

"When is everything due?"

"I want them to have our bare-bone proposals within two days, so their lawyer can look at it, they can sign it, and we can get our first fat check! Then we have exactly four weeks in which to hand the Kauffmans the first plan, schedule, finished budgets, and even the prototype press kit."

There was a stunned silence. "That will take four months to accomplish, Marika, that is, if none of us goes to bed—ever, for that next four months."

"We can do it, because we have to do it."

"Hey," Sarah suddenly asked, "where's Steve? Didn't he go to White Plains with you? What's he doin'? Goofin' off?"

"No, he's home, because he's very tired." She realized now was the time. She had to do it. "I have something to tell you that is very sad. Steve has AIDS."

No one said anything. Most of the people in the room suddenly looked out the window, as though the darkened New York sky would blot out this moment in time.

"We're going to stand by him," she said firmly, "while he gets through—what he has to get through. We're going to help him —and he's going to help us. He will have a lot of input on the creative plans for these new products."

Each one was lost in thought, but Marika could not help but notice the bellicose stance of Greg Willis, Steve's immediate supervisor. His dark eyes under heavy dark brows flashed with displeasure, and he stood with his feet apart, arms akimbo, in a defiant position. The suede patches on the elbows of his expensive houndstooth-checked sports jacket seemed to jut out in Marika's face, like warning signals. Finally he spoke, "I don't think it's such a good idea to have him work around us."

There was an outburst of indignation in the room, critical cries of "Greg, how can you say that!" Marika looked him directly in the eyes and said, "I choose to forget that remark."

There was another silence. Sarah was crying quietly to herself in the corner. Since she was always smiling and never down, people looked in her direction. She reacted. Sarah always did. She took a small quartz crystal from her jacket pocket, rubbed it in her hand, and then said, "This will help remove the bad emotions in this room and make everything calm again."

There was laughter at this and Marika called the meeting to an end, with the reminder that they would have a meeting tomorrow to assign exact duties for each person in the preliminary planning stages. As for the work on the contract proposal, she announced dourly, "It will leave this office for LUXFOODS headquarters within two days—perfectly presented, inspired in its content, and without typos."

The office emptied quickly. There had been too much for each person to digest.

Marika followed Greg into his office and closed the door behind her. "I said in there just a moment ago that I was going to forget the remark you made about Steve, but I can't. Just how could you react the way you did—to news of a friend and a colleague who's in deep trouble?"

"He's in deep trouble because of his own doing."

"He is probably going to die. How can you talk like this?"

"Don't you care about this company, Marika?"

"I care about this company and the people in it a heck of a lot more than you do," she retorted with real anger in her voice.

"To have him working alongside us, with that communicable disease, to have him languishing around, not doing any real work, to have everyone fussing over him—it's—it's counterproductive. You should let him go."

"You sound as though you're jealous of him, and the attention he'll be receiving."

"Hardly. I'm not jealous of anyone having AIDS."

"He is important to this firm, Greg, and don't you forget it.

He came with me from the start when I opened the office here. He is as important to this company as Anthony or you."

"That's the trouble with the way you manage, Marika. You have no sense of priorities whatsoever."

"Anyone who defies me has no sense of priorities. I'm the boss, and following my orders should be your priority, if you want to keep this job. My orders are that everyone gets behind Steve and helps him through this crisis, right to the end."

"I heard you," but he said it with a half snicker.

She walked out of his office and tried not to slam the door. She hated door-slamming, even if this particular scene warranted it.

Marika tossed and thrashed in bed that night, trying to wrestle with the day's events, calm her emotions, and fall asleep at the same time. It was, she concluded, an impossibility, so she turned her mind to Jonathon, and to their long conversation tonight. Then she began to savor the memories, as she had so many times before, of the night they met at dinner in the White House.

Lazily, she thought of The Chest, who sat on Jonathon's other side, and then suddenly, she had a thought so compelling and strong that it made her sit up in bed. She turned on her bedside table lamp—her mother's—with its base of Sèvres porcelain in the shape of a lady with a white flowered skirt and a large straw hat, held on her head with a pink satin ribbon that tied under her chin.

She quickly began sketching on a little pad near the lamp the wonderful diamond ring worn by the blond dinner partner—The Chest. That was it! The logo for the new LUXFOODS products! The ring had reminded her of Napoleon's bees—a symbol often used on his furniture and fabrics. What more important bees could there be than Napoleon's? The Emperor's bees. Imperial bees. That was it—Imperial Honey Cream products! It sounded rich, royal, luxurious. Powerful. Finally, she fell into a deep sleep, propped up against the pillows in her bed, with the lights on, dreaming of Napoleon eating honey and cream with his berries each morning in the Tuileries, with a swarm of bees set in gold forming a perfect floating emperor's wreath above his head.

She frowned in her sleep when another image inserted itself into her dream, as it often did. A shadowy foreigner. A Hungarian.

The next morning, Marika, her creative juices flowing, and bursting with enthusiasm, arrived at her office by seven-thirty to sketch out the project. Greg was the first to arrive, wearing a semblance of a smile as he passed her open door. The rest of the staff arrived by eight forty-five, stunned by yesterday's news about Steve, but refreshed by a new injection of energy.

"My congratulations," Marika said when they all assembled at nine. "I have never seen such universal promptness before." Steve was present, too, as she hoped so much he would be for many mornings, with his smile, good humor, and gentle teasing of his peers. Marika had told him late last night that everyone in the office knew about his illness, and that relieved him. His color was good this morning, Marika noted, but the way his jeans and sweater hung loosely on his gaunt frame was already testimony to the progress of the disease. After one or two grumblings of dissent, everyone accepted the "Imperial Honey Cream concept," particularly after Marika began unfolding her ideas. They would commission a graphics firm immediately to come up with the perfect logo for the products—to use in packaging, in advertising, and in their promotional activities. There might be a bee, Marika suggested, in the design of some of the textiles used in one of Napoleon's palaces. One of the staff had a sister in Paris who could immediately undertake a thorough research job on the Napoleonic bees in the textile department of the Louvre Museum. Perhaps one of the diamond bees of the ring, as described by Marika on the blonde's finger at the White House dinner, would make a glamorous logo. Marika described with relish the perfect press junket: taking top food editors in the United States to Paris—to eat in great restaurants, but also to attend a grand product launch dinner in Malmaison—Napoleon and Joséphine's home outside the city, and one of the treasure troves of Napoleonic style still extant. Perhaps if LUXFOODS made a big donation to the curator at Malmaison for the house and grounds, it could be done ... There was research to be done—on exactly what kind of cream and honey products were consumed in Napoleon's time. Perhaps a joint promotion could be arranged with Tiffany's—for an exhibition of Empire-style dining room settings set up by famous interior designers. At the store's invitational preview opening of the table-setting exhibition, the new Imperial Honey Cream products would be served. They would be mentioned in gossip columns. Columnists like Sand would write them up as appearing on the menus of well-known hostesses ... Stuyvesant Communications, Inc., would be responsible for educating the American public in French Napoleonic history—and the decorative arts.

By the time Marika had sketched out the ideas she had envisaged in the middle of the night in her bedroom, there was more than enough for everyone to do, working around the clock for the ensuing weeks. She put Anthony in charge of overseeing the formulation of the barebones proposal from a legal standpoint, and getting two sets of signatures on it, so that the first check to Stuyvesant Communications, Inc., from LUXFOODS would arrive up front, right away, before any further work was done. She had learned from her past experience that until you have the client's signature on the contract and obtain the first monies, the client is not completely *dans le sac*, or in the bag.

She felt very uneasy about Greg. There was something terribly amiss there, not just his jealousy of Steve. Rather than accuse him of not having his heart in his work—or worse—she would give him this opportunity to show his good colors. She put him in charge of editorial management of the first marketing launch, press kit, brochures, promotional in-store pieces—everything that would be seen by the future consumers of the products. Marika announced she would initiate the market research studies and would eventually go to Paris for three days to do research on Napoleon's bees to help in the product publicity. Steve and Sarah were assigned the development of the logo for the products, and all of the artwork for the promotional pieces. Two of the best staff writers were to be assigned full time to the writing on this project, and another assistant account executive would be tapped to go out to White Plains, to be officed in the LUXFOODS headquarters, and to serve as a daily liaison between staff and client. Marika also announced that at some point she would go to Zurich to study the LUXFOODS operations at their European headquarters.

"The public should know what a fine company LUXFOODS is," Marika explained, "to ease the acceptance of its products on the shelves and in the cold food cases of America's top gourmet shops and finer grocery stores."

The only cloud on the faces of everyone in the room was on Sarah's, Marika decided, as she broke up the meeting. She followed her into her small, cluttered office.

"You didn't look all that excited, Sarah."

"Oh no, I think it's thrilling! It's just that . . ."

"Go on."

"It's just that your astrological signs are not in harmony right now, and we really should wait a couple of weeks before you start all this. The tarot cards said the same thing."

Marika laughed. "If those are our only problems, we're golden," and gave her youngest vice president a hug on her way out of her office.

"This is a hot romance," Hortense cooed exaggeratedly over the intercom. "Now he's calling from Buenos Aires."

It almost irritated Marika that she was so excited to hear the sound of his voice. She felt an increasing dependence on him, and since she didn't know what was going to develop, she didn't enjoy feeling that way. If this relationship were to sour, the hurt would be terrible. She felt a vulnerability she did not like.

"Jonathon, you sound as though you're in the next room."

"I wish I were. I'm tired of talking to you through a device and dreaming about you, when there's no flesh and blood to squeeze."

"Do you squeeze blood?"

"Must you be so damned literal all the time?"

"Sorry, that was a copywriter speaking. Your line has been polished through so many decades, it must be quite automatic."

"Would you rather I be nasty with you?" He sounded just a little offended.

"No," she laughed, "it's because I'm not used to such niceness during the workday. When did you get there?"

"Just arrived, hot and tired, but already I've been served coffee and all my clothes were immediately taken away to be respectively washed, dry cleaned, polished, or sewn. Wish I lived this well in Chicago. I really need a woman in my life."

"You have a houseman to take care of you! He does a far better job than any woman I know would."

"Somehow, it's just not the same."

"Maybe you should import a young woman from an exotic Far Eastern country to do your bidding."

"You refuse even to conjecture that one day we'll be together."

"Not with me doing your bidding."

"No, I suppose I'll be the one doing *your* bidding. Do you know how long it's been since we've seen each other?"

"I've missed you, too, blue eyes."

"At last, an affidavit of affection!"

"We would be the winners of any international long distance marathon. Do you ever look at your telephone bills?"

"No, it would depress me. The people in the office look at them though and wonder, I'm sure, what the hell we talk about for so long." Jonathon laughed as he said this, surveying the room that he had now littered on every possible surface—the bed, tables, bureau, coffee table, and even the floor—with his neat piles of documents and files.

"Now even I have a guilty conscience about spending your company's money on personal conversations. So I'll ask you a business-related question. How are the deals coming along?"

"On behalf of the shareholders of my company, it's nice of you to ask. The two companies I bought here last year are languishing—more because of bad management than because of the poor economic climate. So I'm working on that, and I think I've located at least two fine people to put in place. Anyone would be better than the principals who are there now, so we can only go one direction with this minerals operation, and that is up."

"And how about the fast food enterprise you want to get into in São Paulo?"

"I must go slowly on that one. I'm up against a lot of tough, very smart Brazilian competitors."

"I can't believe you worry about going up against any one in a negotiation," she smiled into the phone.

"Listen, I'd hate to be up against *you* in any deal." He laughed, and she decided there was no sound she liked better in the whole world than his laughter.

"So what's been happening in Marika's world?"

"Great things and terribly sad things, too. You're not the only one who makes deals you know. I have cut the biggest one our agency has ever been involved with. It's the new product line of LUXFOODS."

"All right, so that's the 'great things' part of it. Now for the 'terribly sad' ones? Is anything really wrong?"

Her voice changed from its upbeat tone. "It's bad news. I don't even like to talk about it. Steve Lamton, one of my executives—"I told you about him—remember? He's been with me since the early New York days. He's important to me, but most of all, a dear friend. He has AIDS."

"God, I'm sorry. What are you going to do?"

"Hang in there with him and help him as best I can."

"How much time do you think he has?"

"Who knows? He's able to function still, thank goodness, for our sake as well as his."

They talked some more and then made plans to have dinner in two weeks, the night of Jonathon's return to the States. "You deserve the most splendid dinner of your life," he said, "so you pick the restaurant and make the reservations."

"How about dinner at my apartment?"

"Just the thought of it automatically makes it the most splendid dinner of my life."

"And think of the money you'll save," Marika said, laughing.

"And think of the time we'll both save because of the short distance from the dining room to the bedroom."

Marika put down the receiver and picked up the snapshot of David in its cloisonné frame. "What do you think of my carrying on about this guy like a love-struck fifteen-year-old?"

Then her thoughts turned toward her father, Charles Russell. "What rotten luck, you never had a chance to meet Jonathon. You would have been so happy to see me in love again. And you would have liked him, too."

Then her thoughts turned toward a man named Istvan. He had been intruding on her thoughts more lately, maybe as her mourning for Charlie grew a little less intense. As Lisa said, the mystery of her "real" father was always on her mind, though now it seemed less background music, more foreground. Soon, she was sure of it, she wouldn't be able to tune him out any longer. And that's when she'd have to pursue his memory.

CHAPTER

10

*H*ortense made a rapid staccato of buzzes, which she always did when it was the White House calling. Marika had told her not to do that several times, but it made no difference. When the First Lady was calling, Hortense felt it only proper for Marika to pick up *at once*—not put down a file folder, not finish sorting papers, not do anything but make an immediate response. It did no good when Marika explained it was never Eve Watson on the line, always the White House operator, and that Mrs. Watson only came to the phone when her party was on the line.

"Marika," Eve's voice had never sounded so elated, "we did it! We did it!"

"Did what? Win the lottery? Patch up the marriage of the Prince and Princess of Wales?"

"Even better. We put one over on the press corps. Can you imagine that? We got away this past weekend and had a honeymoon by ourselves at Dick Frazier's house on his island off the Carolinas!"

"Oh, Eve!" Marika's voice mirrored her friend's elation. "That must have been fantastic! But however did you swing it? I didn't read a word about it in this morning's paper—and it wasn't on the evening news last night."

"Well, it was thanks to a few close-mouthed members of the staff. I told Mac it felt as though we had just been sprung from prison on a temporary leave. We planned it with a small group in the White House who were sworn to total secrecy. They were superb co-conspirators. The Secret Service and the Signal Corps, of course, were with us, and the required number of planes and helicopters—but we didn't see or hear them on the island."

"How could you possibly get away right under the noses of the press?"

"We said good-bye to everyone from the South Lawn, just as we do every Friday afternoon, before boarding the helicopter to Camp David. From Camp David we flew to Paul Morton's airstrip in Virginia, and from there we took a small Air Force jet to the island."

"Where was Dick and his domestic staff during this Fantasy Island weekend?"

"Gone away. Dick left us wonderful goodies in the fridge, enough caviar, champagne, and gourmet frozen casseroles to sink a fleet. The Secret Service checked out Dick's fridge, of course. After they'd pronounced the contents safe, I managed to whip up three great meals for two. Mac even brought me breakfast in bed each morning. Marika, do you realize we were alone for the first time since before the presidential election? I'm so happy, I could burst. We talked all night and all day. We got back to where we were years ago in closeness. It was fabulous."

"You two lovebirds." Marika was amused by the thought of them alone and cooking their own meals as they had when they were newlyweds in Boston, oblivious to the large numbers of White House staff who must have been discreetly hiding behind every tree on the island, trying to give them the privacy they were so desperately seeking. The pilots, Secret Service agents, Signal Corps technicians, medical staff, and others must have had everything with them, from the latest weapons to the most sophisticated communications equipment, and every kind of surveillance gadget, not to mention a garlic press and extra-virgin olive oil for the kitchen and extra toilet paper for the master bathroom. Marika chuckled as she envisaged frogmen swimming underseas offshore, keeping in constant communication with a series of large ships "hiding" in the seas nearby.

"What did you do all day?" Marika asked, knowing full well what they were doing all day.

"Well"—Eve was also laughing by now—"we enjoyed the water and those beautiful white sandy beaches, empty except for us—well, at least, empty-looking in our eyes. We managed to have a second honeymoon, something I would never have thought possible."

"You know," said Marika, "this is the best telephone call I've had from you in many years. But I have a feeling you didn't call just to tell me about white sandy beaches."

"I have a favor to ask."

"Finally. Something *I* can do for you."

"The press—particularly the Washington press, who feel they own us—will be livid when they find out we gave them the slip, and *I want them to find out about it.* I want the world to know that our marriage is in good shape, that we've been on a second honeymoon. Maybe it will put an end to those nasty rumors about us. Would you leak the story to someone in New York for me? I wouldn't dare have it leaked to the Washington press. They're too smart. They would know it was me doing a plant. However, you could give it to someone like Sand, you know, 'accidentally' let it slip."

"Sand will go nuts!" Marika exclaimed, and then let out a whoop. "It will be the high point of her career to put something over on the White House press corps."

"Well let her scoop away, then."

After a few more pleasantries about Mac and mutual friends, Eve asked about Georgiana and how her party was coming along.

"She takes it so seriously!" Marika said, and then added, "but I guess it means a lot to her, and we should look at it from her terms. It's her social launch as Chauncey's wife. She senses that

Chauncey's family feels their fine conservative name has been besmirched by his marrying her. She wants to prove to them that her taste and social skills prove she belongs by Chauncey's side."

"Ridiculous! She doesn't have to justify herself to them."

"Yes, but we both know how sensitive she is on the subject. She's positive that Chauncey's family is waiting for her to fall on her *keester*, so they can say 'I told you so.' Her image isn't exactly what they had in mind for their beloved Chauncey, and I'm sure they're concerned about the family fortune, which rests in his hands."

"Well, damn them for thinking ill of her," Eve said, now irritated for her old college roommate. "I'd take one of her to a hundred of them, any time, and they don't need to worry about their old family fortune, either. Georgiana knows how to spend money, but she's no gold digger. She wants to make this marriage last forever. She adores him, and if she can manage to heighten his social position, well, that's all right, too.

"You know what's sad," mused Eve, continuing on with her random thoughts, "no one loves a party more than I do. Life at the White House is one endless large stage production and media event. I long for small parties—and big, fancy, flossy private ones, too! I wish Mac and I could go to Georgiana's party and help her out at the same time."

"Well you can't, but don't worry. She'll pull it off like she always does."

"Did you ever stop to think, Marika, how lucky you and I are to be so secure about who we are and from where we come? We don't have to worry about what people think of our backgrounds. We don't have to think about it. It's there—an intangible—you can't see it, but it's there. It's a 'born into' kind of breeding, versus the other kind—the learned kind. And yet the born-into and the learned kind become the same. People are nice or awful."

"I think about it often," Marika said. "We just lucked out by an accident of birth, by virtue of the way we were raised and the educations we received. We are what is known in this upwardly mobile age as 'well born,' yet we didn't do one single thing to earn it, merit it, justify it."

"Marika," the First Lady suddenly interrupted. "I have to go.

The President's car is ready, and he'll be coming over from the West Wing. I must talk to him before he takes off for Denver. Give Georgiana my love, and a big hug for you."

Marika dialed Sand immediately. She would exact payment from the social columnist in return for this prized journalistic scoop that would be hers alone to print. Sand would now *have to* attend Georgiana's dinner and write about it. Georgiana, in turn, would be inviting Sidney and Rachel Miller to "up" their image. Now everyone would be happy—perhaps.

A few days later, four weeks before her dinner party, Georgiana Wilkins telephoned Marika at her office to announce that the invitations were finally in the mail, that very day. "And I called Sand to plead with her on bended knee to come, and Marika, guess what?"

Marika smiled a conspiratorial smile into the telephone receiver and answered, "I can't guess. You'll have to tell me."

"Sand is coming! She'll cover it, too. I told her the invitations were going out, but I wanted her to save the date if she possibly could, and she was smooth as silk back to me. She said, 'I wouldn't miss it, Georgiana.'"

She'd better not, Marika thought to herself.

"She didn't need any persuading at all, Marika!"

"She must have heard how great your apartment is, and she must know that this is going to be the party of the year."

"Oh, I hope so! I want it to be great for Chauncey. I want him to be proud of me! But wait until you see the invitations. Sensational! From Tiffany's, of course, engraved in red and black, which are the colors of the party, with a tiny red and black lace fan at top center. The envelopes addressed in calligraphy, of course.

"And do you know what that pill of a sister of Chauncey's said when she saw the invitations last night? 'What extravagance, my, my,' she said, peering at me down the side of her nose." Georgiana had put on her best exaggerated Locust Valley lockjaw accent as she imitated her sister-in-law.

"She's just jealous she doesn't know how to attend to the little details of a party the way you do, Georgiana. You always send the loveliest invitations."

Georgiana began to laugh. "Could you possibly be referring to my first and third wedding invitations?"

"Well, not the ones for your second."

"Oh, you mean the wedding when I thought I was pregnant and we sent everyone telegrams, because there wasn't a day to lose, to keep me from mortification and shame?"

They laughed, remembering her many marriages. She let Georgiana bubble on some more with excitement over the details of her party, while she finished correcting a press release on a client's fourth-quarter results that one of her young account executives had just given her to approve. It had to be duplicated and disseminated to the financial press by the end of the day. She had learned over the years to listen to someone on the telephone and concentrate on an entirely different written matter at the same time—a skill definitely needed in the world of the media and public relations.

Finally, she remembered the most important aspect of all in this telephone call. Jonathon. He must be invited to Georgiana's dinner. He would meet some interesting people at her dinner. It was also time to take their love affair out of the closet, so to speak, and into the real world to see how it fared.

"Georgiana, can you use an extra man?" Marika knew full well what her answer would be.

"But of course, darling! Can't I always? Who is this delicious creature? Is he eligible for you, or just a walker? Or perhaps an old fart? Or is he young, handsome, and in the employ of an old fart? It would be too much to ask, *n'est-ce pas*, that he be rich, nice-looking and not a *pédéraste*?" Georgiana always asked ten questions before she allowed anyone to answer one of them. She also had a tendency to throw in French phrases, even when her inaccurate accent would inevitably batter the words beyond recognition.

"His name is Jonathon Scher," Marika said, marking a grammar correction on the material before her. "He's just a friend.

He's my age, divorced and"—she laughed to herself—"very definitely straight."

"Next to being straight, and eligible, too, you didn't answer the most important question. Rich?"

"You know that's not an important question to me."

"Good, then that means he's rich. I'm relieved."

Marika did not want her friend spreading the news of a man in her life all over town, but since she was bringing him to the Wilkinses' dinner party, the gossip would be triggered anyway. If she acted offhandedly about him, however, people would think him just an escort and not a real involvement. And this would put less pressure on them.

Marika could picture her onetime college classmate this very minute, a woman of dazzling blond beauty, with two dimples flanking a sensuous mouth, reclining on her pink satin chaise, wearing one of her sexy negligees, probably pink satin, savoring this news. Georgiana wanted all of her friends—particularly Marika—to be happily married, and taken good financial care of by a man. Although she considered herself the prototype of a modern woman, Georgiana was a studied copy of the classic old-fashioned movie-star type—even though she had never been near Hollywood. She dressed to match her pink satin boudoir, having seen more than her share of Jean Harlow and Carole Lombard reruns. Even her boudoir telephone was pink. She had a habit of getting everything she wanted, and of collecting men and jewelry with equal enthusiasm. "Dimples," she once explained as the key to her success in life. "Dimples will do it for you every time."

One thing she had wanted since her childhood was a pink boudoir. It was a perk that should rightfully accompany her beauty and voluptuousness. She had recently married for the fourth time, a man who could give her the boudoir and anything else—Chauncey Bentley Wilkins. Chauncey's grandiose Fifth Avenue apartment had been under renovation for almost a year, and its unveiling was the reason for the dinner party.

"Un vernissage," Georgiana explained triumphantly to everyone as the reason for the dinner. She mispronounced thoroughly the French word for the opening of a new art show. Marika

thought she heard the word "sausage" in there somewhere. "After all," Georgiana kept repeating, "the newly done apartment is nothing short of *un chef d'oeuvre!*"

Georgiana was exceedingly bright, but had been raised by a divorced mother who taught her to hide her IQ. Her mother felt that a college education was a dangerous course upon which to set sail, in that a woman might suddenly sound smarter than her man, which would automatically eliminate any chance of a marriage resulting from the relationship. Her mother's advice on the eve of her departure for Vassar was, "If you have to read Proust, then for heaven's sake, do it on the sly. Don't let a man catch you doing it!" As Georgiana said, not unproudly, "My mother was left behind with the circle of wagons when the women's movement rolled ahead."

The curvaceous blond from Texas was placed as the third roommate with Eve and Marika in a suite in Josslyn Hall. That first night at college endeared Georgiana to Marika—her frankness, her fresh pink-cheeked, dimpled appeal, her warm, sexy voice. She had never quite met anyone like her before, and Marika's father was fond of pointing out that he'd never quite seen a college suite furnished like theirs before, either. Georgiana had decorated the living room with her mother's discards. Twenty years later, Marika could still recall the white satin draperies and Directoire sofa. There was a pink shaggy rug and lampshades with white satin swags on them. The light bulbs were pink, even in the student reading lamps. Charlie once remarked that the Joss suite looked like nothing so much as a bordello in Berlin in the 1930s.

Georgiana dropped out of Vassar before her junior year, when coeducation began at the college. Marika and Eve tried their best to make their lovable, amusing roommate stay in college, to no avail. She left and got a job as a receptionist on Wall Street. Her taste in clothes and decorating flourished in New York. She was now on her own, away from her mother's "bordello taste," and her artistic talent began to show itself. She had a good eye, even if her taste was somewhat flashy, and she read every shelter and design publication she could find. Within four months of starting her job on Wall Street, she was married. It was a *comme il faut* wedding to a young man in the SR (Social Register), complete with Marika and Eve as attendants and a wedding reception at New York's exclusive Colony Club. She was doing just fine.

Georgiana knew what was important in life, at least in *her* life. While her best friends remained at Vassar to obtain their degrees, the new bride audited courses in finance at New York University. Having learned from the mistakes of her mother, she resolved to be knowledgeable about anything pertaining to her financial survival. (As Eve said one day during their senior year, "And *we're* supposed to be the smart ones? Georgiana knows *The Wall Street Journal* back to front!")

On a brief visit to Poughkeepsie after her wedding, Georgiana explained to her old friends that she had "grown lucky and smart," and as a result, her personal fortune had grown by quantum leaps. As each divorce and each remarriage occurred in her life, her assets grew commensurately.

Now in her forties, her marriage to Chauncey was her fourth time to the altar. Clad in an appropriate apricot crepe floor-length Bill Blass dinner gown, Georgiana made a blushing, beautiful bride, with a figure that was still perfection, skin unblemished and unlined, and her head a mass of luxurious blond curls. In the receiving line at her wedding reception, after showing Marika her oversized emerald-cut solitaire diamond ring, she commented, "It's nice that the rings get bigger each time."

"What do you do with your old ones?" Marika had asked, "give them to the Junior League thrift shop?"

"No. It's amazing how easily a solitaire converts to a money market fund." She and Marika had huddled together at a small table at the reception. "You have faithfully come to all my weddings, Marika. You're always here. Will you come to my fifth, if that is in the cards?"

"And the sixth, if necessary," laughed Marika. "The only thing that changes, you may have noticed, is that my wedding gift to you becomes more modest each time."

"Just give me a book the next time. A paperback will do. You're always trying to challenge my mind to make me read more."

"How about a book of marriage advice?"

"I promise I'll read anything you give me . . . You know something, Marika," Georgiana appraised the guest by her side, "you grow more beautiful with each passing year. There is something so serene about you."

"Serene? Ha! With all that I'm trying to juggle, I'm about as serene as Ringling Brothers on opening night at Madison Square Garden."

"Don't argue with me." Georgiana looked at her with a combination of admiration and a little sadness. "You have run your life so well. You sit here now—so handsome in that beautiful pale pink crepe dress with your pearl jewelry. You look so right, so graceful and dignified."

"Georgiana, you are going to make me cry, and I don't want to do that on your wedding day."

The bride patted her friend's hand and rose to rejoin her husband and make him dance with her again to Lester Lanin's band. "Remember that I hold you in the highest of admiration," she said, giving Marika a kiss on the cheek, "because you are the essence of what a real friend is. You cut through all of my glitz and like me anyway."

Now, a year after that wedding, the two women sat side by side upon a banquette at La Côte Basque, going over the guest list for the Chauncey Wilkinses' dinner dance in the newly renovated Fifth Avenue apartment.

"The trouble with Chauncey," Georgiana said, toying with her seafood salad, "is that he just doesn't have any social clout. Here he is, from one of America's greatest and oldest families, and I have to keep reminding him that today such a person has to stand up and show his colors or he doesn't count. He just fades into the woodwork."

"Being in the Social Register doesn't mean much any more, does it?"

"Definitely not, when you look at the names prevalent in the social columns today. They all have lots of money, but no SR listing."

"So which is more important?" asked Marika, testing her.

"To me, both are equally important. Chauncey has both, and that gives me enormous security. You will remember, that is something on which I was short-changed previously. At the same time, it perplexes me that Chauncey is unknown to the social press. He may as well not exist."

It was plain to see that with her dinner dance, she was about to fix all that. Georgiana had brought along her guest list and reviewed it with great pride, savoring the sound of every prestigious name. Marika knew them all, and most of their spouses— including the secretary-general of the United Nations, the CEO's of leading banks and financial firms, advertising agencies, a society surgeon from New York Hospital, a U.S. senator, the president of a broadcast network, two university presidents, a museum director, a playwright, a woman publisher, a leading clergyman, a infamous actress, and the chairman of Christie's in America. There was no doubt about it, she had scored with her guest list, and most of the recipients of the invitations would probably accept. With the demise of the private dinner party in society, guests accepted an invitation like the Wilkinses' with alacrity. After all, dinner in someone's home was becoming a rarity. Society invitations often required a host to ante up anywhere from five hundred to fifteen hundred dollars per guest for the benefit tickets. Here, in America, society's social life was undergoing a change.

Marika had strong reactions to the names of two couples on the list. She was delighted to see that Georgiana had included the Stuart Welltons. Mimi Wellton was another of their Vassar classmates—"a soft, kind woman" was how Eve had described her once. She was also a dedicated literacy volunteer. Her husband suffered from a rare form of epilepsy and had recently lost his job as comptroller of a major sporting goods company. With four children in private schools in New York, things were tough. Marika made a mental note to brief Jonathon on Stuart Wellton, in the hopes that during Georgiana's party, Jonathon could talk to Stuart and perhaps make some suggestions for his finding a new position.

Another couple's name—that of Mr. and Mrs. Henry Bolder—sent a chill down into Marika's hands as she read it off the list. Henry Bolder was married to the meanest, nastiest woman Marika had ever had the displeasure of confronting. With Joan Bolder, it was never "seeing" or "meeting," it was always "confronting." Why anyone would want the Bolders at a dinner party was beyond her.

Georgiana, sensing her displeasure, said jovially, "Oh, come on, Marika, you can put up with the Bitch of River House for one dinner, can't you? Her presence and her jewels will give Sand something to write about." Marika remembered now that she had seen Joan Bolder's jewels, and her jeweler, at Le Cirque recently, Demetri something— Oh, and Georgiana had included him on the list—Marika surmised he was standing in as one of the walkers.

Georgiana called for the check and then she said in the next breath, "Tell me, is this Jonathon chap a nice-looking man?"

"Don't worry," Marika laughed, "Jonathon is a most presentable-looking person." She wanted to add, "And a lot more intelligent than the other single men on your list." Then she caught herself, remembering that available, single, nonalcoholic New York men who were mature enough to carry on an adult conversation, and who possessed clean dinner suits, were almost nonexistent. One filled up one's dinner party with any single men one could find. "That they be *alive* is enough," Georgiana had once remarked.

"I was only asking," Marika heard Georgiana say. "I just want to know if he is a nice-looking man for *you*. In other words, are you physically attracted to him, the way you were to David?"

"Whoa, Georgiana! Yes, I'm attracted to Jonathon Scher, but during the dinner party I promise we won't embarrass you by grappling under the table, or anything like that."

Georgiana's thoughts were now far from Jonathon's appropriateness as a dinner partner for her friend. "I think I've covered the bases for this event. Alain's company is doing the catering. And Norbert the flowers. The salmon is being flown in from Scotland the night before. There'll be four tables of ten, just right for our dining room. And"—her voice was intense—"the best news of all is that I have captured the most fantastic butler for the evening! I mean, he is the *top*, the *ne plus ultra*. He's called

Adams—English, beautifully tailored, looks like an ambassador, and has butled only in the greatest of the Stately Homes of England. He arrives in town in a couple of weeks. Mine is his first dinner party. Can you believe he's charging me more because of that! Oh, well, hang the price. I have him before anyone else does." She paused, waiting for an appropriately awed reaction to this announcement.

Marika reacted as she was supposed to do. "Incredible! What a *coup*, Georgiana! He'll make your dinner an even greater success."

"He'll supervise Alain's food and waiters, even though Alain won't like it one bit."

"For your sake, Georgiana, I hope Alain's prima donna-ing will be under control that night. Isn't it a bit risky to have an English butler overseeing a temperamental French caterer? Is even the European Common Market ready for this?"

As they were about to leave, Georgiana paused in the restaurant's foyer. "Marika, I need you—I mean, I want to count on you helping me. This is very important to me."

"I know it is. I'll have my eyes opened, even in back of my head, for you."

"Will you step in and take care of any problems as they develop? I mean, you're so skilled and experienced, and I'm such a dithering idiot over this. If anything goes wrong, I just won't be able to cope. I'll be up front, greeting people and taking care of my top-ranking guests. Will you pretend you're me and solve any crises occurring behind me?"

"Wow! What a responsibility!" Marika said it jokingly. "Heh, Georgiana, relax. Nothing is going to go wrong, and if it does, Jonathon and I will become mounted St. Georges, slaying the big dragons."

Marika had not seen Jonathon for too many days. On the night of the Wilkinses' party, she was hungry—no, famished is a more accurate description—to see him, touch him, be touched by him, and hear that wonderful laugh. The Scher and Co. jet landed an hour late at Teterboro Airport in New Jersey, and its sole passenger made it across the George Washington Bridge to her apartment with only forty minutes to spare before they were to leave for Georgiana's dinner.

"It is very difficult for a man who is trying to shower and change into his evening clothes," he said, "when the woman standing next to him keeps insisting that he hurry, hurry, hurry, and at the same time keeps seducing him."

Marika finally decided that the only action to take was to leave him totally alone, but only after they both agreed to a bet. In order not to be any later than they already were, whoever touched the other one first before getting into the car to go to the Wilkinses' had to write a check for a thousand dollars, made out to the other person's favorite charity.

When he came into her bedroom he was dressed in his dinner trousers with black braces and ivory silk pleated dinner shirt, carrying his untied black tie in one hand. She sighed, wishing there was no dinner party on the schedule. He smelled of Royal Lyme, his cheeks were smooth-shaven and pink from the hot shower. He held out the tie to Marika, grinning like a helpless little boy. "If I tie it myself, we'll never get to the dinner." She had not tied a man's bow tie since David died. It was difficult remembering what to do, but it all came back.

Marika easily won the one-thousand-dollar bet. Jonathon pulled her into his arms, saying huskily, "I have never wanted anything as much as you right now, in my whole life." She felt her nipples grow taut. He unzipped her green chiffon evening dress and hung it carefully over the back of a chair. Then he took off his own clothes and for the next few minutes it seemed doubtful they would make the Wilkinses' party at all.

Then she remembered her promise. "I have to help Georgiana," she began to protest. "We have to go. She needs me—" He stopped her protests with his lips.

"She doesn't need you one-hundredth as much as I do."

"We *have* to go!" Marika finally found the words and the physical strength. She simply couldn't let Georgiana down. One more moment in his arms would cancel her feeling of obligation.

Jumping off the bed, she went to the bathroom to put her dress on again, and to repair her makeup and hair.

They were silent going over in the car, holding hands and thinking their own thoughts. "I hope you noticed this car I hired tonight," Jonathon said. "It's a non-white, non-stretch limo. In fact, it's not even a limo, just a simple little black car."

"Very simple," she smiled at him in the dark. "Just a simple little four-door Jaguar. By the way, Jonathon, you're sitting next to Sand tonight, because Georgiana needs a friend to sit there and charm her. She has to be lulled into a good mood or she'll write nasty things about Chauncey and Georgiana."

"Shit!" he said under his breath.

"I heard you."

"Do you think it's really fair for me to come back from such a long, hard trip and have to work for my supper, sitting next to that witch? Why can't I be next to you, for God's sake?"

"How about if I say I'll make it up to you later?"

"That'll do it." He kissed her chastely on the cheek.

Just before they reached the Wilkinses' apartment, Jonathon took out a check from his pocket which he wrote up in the darkness and handed to her. When they were in the lobby, she looked at it. It was made out for one thousand dollars to the Literacy Volunteers of New York. It was the easiest fund-raising she had ever done.

They stepped out of the elevator right into the large foyer of the triplex apartment. The air smelled of party—a pungent mixture of perfume, smoke, music, laughter, and the fragrance of the savory hot hors d'oeuvres being passed. The entry hall was a large room of dark textured stone—weathered, ancient looking. The cove ceiling lighting did not dispel the gloom of the space, but it was striking. A large backlit antique Japanese iron vessel sat in the corner; an antique black iron lamp swung on a chain from the ceiling, and a blood-red Chinese vase—spotlit from above—sat on the carved stone altar table, filled with enormously tall branches of white lilacs.

"My God," whispered Jonathon, "a museum—in the foyer?"

"You have witnessed *nothing* yet," she countered.

The fabled butler, Adams, stood just inside the door, greeting each guest. He was very tall, handsome, and aristocratic-looking, just as Georgiana would have insisted he be. Jonathon thought he was the host, and Marika saved him from an effusive greeting. She appraised the butler carefully and found him rather florid of face, and a bit perspiry, in his white tie and tails. She hoped he had a strong enough deodorant to last the evening.

Adams bent low to get each guest's name, and once the name was imparted, he greeted the guest with a proper show of butlerian deference—a gesture accompanied by an almost military click of heels.

"Ma-dawm! Suh!" he would proclaim, as he showed each arriving guest the gold-tooled leather seating plan held in his white-gloved hands. It looked like a leather blotter, with four round tables represented on it, each with slots to hold little white name cards—like miniature place cards. Each person would find his or her seat by looking at the table plan, and then all the guest had to do was remember the table number. One could also see at a glance who else was seated at that table.

It was easy to identify the real social climbers, Marika whispered to Jonathon. They were the ones who spent an inordinate amount of time going over the seating chart, not just to locate their own places, but to study the entire guest list, so as to see who was there, and who should be conversed with at all costs this evening. After all, there was considerable name-dropping to be done for the next few days.

Jonathon suggested to Marika that they wander around and look, if she didn't mind. He turned around slowly in the spacious living room, rather blinded by the art-filled environment around him. It was also Marika's first glimpse of the new apartment.

"A hands-down knockout," she finally said to Jonathon. The designer, Billy Boyd, had done a superb job of rearranging Chauncey's art, antiques, and decorative accessories. He had made the enormous living room into two levels, each subtly different in color and mood, each with its own seating groups and art collections. There was a built-in, illuminated black ebony cabinet for Chauncey's illustrious Famille Rose Chinese porcelain collection. A display table served as a sofa lamp table—its glass top revealing inside the mahogany frame a marvelous collection of small green and white jade pieces, resting on an ivory suede cloth. The decorator had updated the look of the twenty-room apartment with choice contemporary furniture in striking contrast to the antiques deftly inserted here and there. He had embellished the interior architecture with contemporary touches and artful lighting, pinkish in tone, and therefore flattering to women's—and men's—skins. It seemed as though all the shininess of the highly polished pink marble, the brass, smoky mirrored, and stainless steel surfaces bounced back and forth from each other, casting sparkling reflections in surprising places. Every element bespoke luxury, from the deep ivory wool carpets to the thickly textured cream-colored fabrics covering the giant seating pieces. The objects were casually, but tastefully placed. A small Louis Comfort Tiffany iridescent bowl on a table, filled with sprays of tiny pink orchids, caught the reflection of a nearby lamp. Jonathon picked up the gold jeweled dagger from Morocco that sat in juxtaposition with an exquisite piece by Odiot, a small silver gilt sculptured bowl, on the coffee table. "Like your father's," he said quietly, and she suddenly remembered the afternoon of her father's funeral in the house on Beacon Street, now already sold and out of her life completely, except for its memories. "Throwaway chic" was how Georgiana had described Chauncey's little treasures that met the eye everywhere—a throwaway chic Sotheby's and Christie's would have killed for is how Billy Boyd would have described it. Before his marriage, Chauncey's objects had simply been stored in dark corners or behind the doors of secretary-desks. However, each had been carefully listed in Chauncey's prenuptial agreement, which his lawyer had presented to Georgiana the week before the wedding—just in case.

Marika and Jonathon sauntered through the reception rooms, their opaque sculptured Lalique champagne glasses in their hands, inspecting whatever caught their eye—such as a delicate antique French *bergère*, covered in a medieval flame-stitch fabric, and a football field of an ivory suede sofa set on a magnificent blue oriental rug. They wandered through the crowd, Marika leading, Jonathon following her and being introduced every time they ran into a new pair of guests. Marika knew everyone. Since she was in front of him, he would tease her by putting his cold champagne glass on the bottom part of her bare back. Once he put his hand quickly down the inside of the back of her green draped chiffon dress, the sudden cold touch tingling her warm bare skin.

"Jonathon!" she scowled in mock chastisement. "Don't do that. It's—it's naughty!"

"Would you prefer that I put my hand down the front instead of the back?" He made a move with his hand to do just that, but she caught his arm and pushed it back. "Behave!" she remonstrated.

"Why, when I'd rather be home in your bedroom?"

"You'd be there all by yourself. This is a work night for me. I made a promise to Georgiana, you know that."

Suddenly Marika turned and greeted another couple in Italian. She switched to English. "Mr. Secretary-General, may I present Jonathon Scher, a business friend"—Jonathon pinched her bottom at this description, a pinch that made her jump, but she kept a straight face—"from Chicago. Jonathon, this is His Excellency Remigio Casaforte, Secretary-General of the United Nations, and Signora Casaforte." The ambassador kissed Marika's hand and said, "You are more beautiful tonight than ever, my dear. A gemstone in a sea of rhinestones."

"I'd like to know what the dago ambassador does when he's not pouring on compliments like that," Jonathon said gruffly, as they walked away.

"He doesn't pinch female bottoms, I'll tell you that."

They wandered some more, meeting people and looking at the art. Jonathon began to feel the strain of meeting every couple and making inane pleasantries. "It's the thing to do," she whispered. "Horseshit," he replied, but she didn't reply, smiling instead at yet another couple. He would have liked to sit down and talk quietly—just the two of them—but there was a Picasso yet to see, Marika reminded him, two Mirós, an Arp, two small Henry

Moore table bronze sculptures, and a flower still-life painting by Odilon Redon and another by Henri Fantin-Latour. "Theater, pure theater," one guest muttered in adulation of the apartment.

"There's got to be half a billion in this apartment," Jonathon suddenly said.

"I don't look at things in terms of how much they cost," she countered, rather crossly.

"Are you giving me a Marika-style disapproving sniff?"

"No," she said, catching herself. "No, it's just that this collection is so beautiful, rare, and splendid, it should be appreciated for its intrinsic beauty, don't you think, not its worth?"

"No matter how you may try to change me, beautiful, chestnut-haired, sensuous woman," he said, nuzzling her so quickly in her ear, no one in the room could have seen it, "I have the right to go on appreciating the monetary value of things, and you have the right to continue appreciating the aesthetics. I would venture that the Wilkinses are more on my side than yours."

Wanting to change the subject, Marika said, "Come on, let's find Georgiana and Chauncey. We haven't even greeted our hosts yet."

"How terrible not to have greeted our hosts yet! *Cela ne se fait pas!*" Jonathon said. He had learned how to say, "That simply isn't done," in French, in order to tease Marika when she was being overly polite or haughty or critical. She gave him a poke in his ribs. He caught her hand and brought it up to his lips in a swift gesture.

Georgiana and Chauncey stood side by side in front of an immense carved seventeenth-century stone fireplace. Billy Boyd had found the fireplace in a private château in Normandy, and had installed it in the center of the lower part of the main living room. It served as the perfect baronial frame for their receiving line. To Marika they both looked relaxed, handsome, and distinguished. Chauncey was erect and smiling with pride, Georgiana was dimpled and quite dashing looking in a hot Chinese red taffeta gown that hugged her figure tight all the way down to below her knees, where it exploded into cascades of black-lace-trimmed red taffeta ruffles. The same great ruffles cascaded as sleeves down from her shoulders. Her ears and hands sparkled with ruby and diamond jewelry; a large coq brooch with ruby and diamond feathers served as the centerpiece of her chignon in the back of her head. The blond curls tonight were disciplined and restrained into a Spanish-looking chignon—except for a couple of runaway curls that had dared to escape and encroach upon her forehead.

Georgiana's newly done portrait by Clyde Smith hung over the mantel behind them. He had come down from Cos Cobb, Connecticut, she had told Marika proudly, and spent six whole Saturdays painting her. He placed her in front of one of Chauncey's coromandel screens clad in a pale lavender velvet peignoir, hands folded in front of her, blond hair cascading down onto her shoulders.

"Georgiana, it's magnificent!" Marika gasped in genuine admiration. The subject's only jewelry in the portrait was an opera-length string of oriental pearls—a wedding present from Chauncey's sister that had been in the Wilkins family since the nineteenth century—and large pearl and diamond earrings Georgiana had bought herself in a victory celebration two hours after Chauncey had finally said yes to her marriage proposal.

When Marika introduced Jonathon to Georgiana, she looked him coolly up and down, as though she were a butcher inspecting a side of beef. Marika began to laugh at Georgiana's silent but intense gaze.

"Should I bring you a magnifying glass or perhaps a microscope?" Marika finally asked. "Would it help to see his pores?"

"Not necessary. He definitely passes," she said aloud. The two women had their own conversation while Jonathon exchanged pleasantries with Chauncey.

"Did you see Adams at the front door, Marika? Isn't he simply too English peer-like for words? My God, to think that Chauncey and I are having our new home christened with a butler straight from the Stately Homes of England! It makes us feel like peers ourselves."

Then she leaned forward to whisper to Marika while the two men continued to talk about the New York Mets. "Listen, I approve. Nice, very nice. He looks intelligent, and—horny."

"He is. Nice, intelligent, and horny. Georgiana, everything looks superb tonight, and Adams is everything you said."

"I think it's a coup having him. And don't forget, I have a surprise in store for everyone. Marika"—and she grabbed her friend's arm tightly—"I am really counting on you to help me out tonight. I don't know why, there's just something in the air. I can feel it. I just don't feel comfortable. Whatever happens, you'll take care of it, won't you?"

"You are an accomplished hostess. Chauncey is lucky to have you, and everything's going to be all right. You should hear your guests raving over the apartment. So stop this anxiety attack! By the way, you look like a magnificent Spanish gypsy princess."

"That's exactly what I intended to look like, a blond version," she answered happily. "You'll see why—later."

Marika and Jonathon left their hosts and ran smack into Sand, who had been observing the receiving line. She was clad tonight in a silver lamé shroud, her thin black hair plastered to her skull with an oily substance, so that it looked like shiny patent leather. The back had been pulled into a short, thin ponytail, held with something black—which looked more like a shoelace than a ribbon. She wore long sculptured metallic silver earrings that clinked when she moved. She didn't walk through a crowd, Jonathon decided as he watched her, she *slithered* through it, her ebony cigarette holder erect in her hand.

"And this is?" she asked imperiously, pointing at Jonathon with her cigarette.

"It's rude to point," he said.

"Sand, this is Jonathon Scher," Marika interjected quickly.

"From?"

"Chicago."

She pulled out her small notebook, wrote in it, said an abrupt, "Good-bye," and wandered on.

"Don't, for God's sake, tell me that is my dinner partner tonight—that refugee from a Charles Addams cartoon? She gives me the creeps."

"She's America's leading social columnist," Marika giggled, "and not only that, but I think she likes you. She likes spunky men, and when you told her it's rude to point, I could tell she was becoming attracted to you."

"I'd rather have a sea monster."

They watched Sand circling the room. Jonathon was fascinated by the way her body moved, and by the never-changing serious expression on her face, except when she greeted someone she knew head on. Then her mouth muscles would twitch upward for two seconds in a halfhearted attempt at a smile of greeting; then those same mouth muscles would relax back into their natural pout. It was apparently the warmest kind of greeting she knew how to muster for people she knew. Obviously seeing no one of particular interest, Sand slowly maneuvered back to them.

"And what do you do, Mr. Scher?" Sand was determined to find out if this was a serious beau of Marika Wentworth's, and if it was, just what was the cut of his jib.

"Make money," was his short reply. Marika immediately changed the subject. "Jonathon will be sitting next to you, I see."

"Good," the strange figure replied. "And just what do you think we will talk about, Mr. Scher, during dinner?"

"Sex."

Marika shrunk herself down a foot and turned aside, so that no one could see her flaming cheeks.

"Good topics," replied Sand. "Money and sex. I can see this will be an interesting dinner."

"Jonathon, how could you!" Marika said as Sand walked toward a table containing a large platter of raw oysters, reclining on a bed of seaweed.

"I'm not a social animal and I can say whatever I damn please to whomever I damn please."

"Please, just for tonight, behave yourself, will you?"

"I haven't seen you for a long time. I've been dealing only with a bunch of tough, nasty, company brokers in the Far East for thirty-two days, and your only advice to me is to behave myself."

"You are obviously suffering from jet lag. You must feel terribly tired."

"Was I so terribly tired on the bed before we came here?" She blushed.

"Let's go home—back to that wonderful bed. If you love me like I love you, that's where you'd want to be, too."

"You're nothing but a sexual animal, and I adore you," she said, taking his arm and steering him through the guests. "Please help me out tonight, be your usual charming, socialized self, with your libido firmly in check. Just through this dinner party."

A waiter passed by them, carrying a silver tray containing large shrimps, each speared on a sterling silver toothpick. Jonathon took one, dipped it into the sauce, and then grinned at Marika. "What do I do with the silver toothpick, Madam Letitia Etiquette, or whatever the hell she's called?"

She laughed, took it from his fingers and put it in the small silver receptacle on the tray—expressly there for holding the used silver toothpicks. "Why can't I keep it as a souvenir of this party? To pick my teeth with at lunch at the Four Seasons Grill tomorrow?" he asked in a little-boy voice.

"Because the waiter might catch you stealing the family silver and report you," she answered.

"I know why you're worried about that toothpick, you're afraid I'll stick it in Sand's ass at dinner, that's what."

"You just might at that," she said, squeezing his hand and caressing it with her thumb.

The Stuart Welltons had arrived, and Marika threw her arms around Mimi, giving her a big hug. "Jonathon, meet Stuart and Mimi Wellton. Mimi went to college with Eve, Georgiana, and me."

As Marika and Mimi talked animatedly to each other, exclaiming over the apartment one minute, and the latest news on the literacy movement front the next, Jonathon took Stuart aside. Marika kept an ear tuned to their conversation, and discovered from snatches that Jonathon was asking Stuart about his financial experience. She heard him next asking some frank questions about his epilepsy and the status of his medication. She and Mimi kept their conversation going for a full half hour, because neither of them wanted to interrupt what could be a very important discussion. Then she heard Jonathon saying, "Would you ever contemplate a move to the Midwest?"

"Of course, I would," Stuart replied. "In fact, getting out of this expensive city would be the best possible thing for me and my family."

"All right, here's my card," and Jonathon reached into his vest pocket and produced a card which he handed quickly to Stuart, not wishing others at the dinner party to witness a piece of business being transacted in someone's private home. "We'll arrange to have you meet with me in Chicago. There are two small companies I own out there that need a financial vice president. I think a smart person, which you obviously are, could handle both jobs. We'll take a look at it."

When the Welltons said good-bye and walked away Marika put her hand on Jonathon's shoulder. "You are one sweet guy. It sounds as though you can help him."

"He has the credentials. He just had an unlucky break. I think he can do this job."

"I love you for doing that, Jonathon."

"He's a good man. I wouldn't have done it if he weren't."

"I still love you for doing it."

Just then they were separated by a trio of Marika's friends who were full of gossip and chit-chat. Jonathon wandered off for a short while, and then returned, shaking his head in disbelief.

"I just heard the most incredibly loud woman saying the most ridiculous things to her husband. 'Can you believe it,'" he mimicked a high voice, "'that sapphire and diamond necklace came from an ad in a fashion magazine? How gauche!'"

"I know who that is," Marika said. "It could only be one woman, Joan Bolder."

"She went on to attack that cute Mimi Wellton, too. She said that Mimi was wearing an old rag, and that if she couldn't afford to be properly dressed, she shouldn't accept invitations to a party like this. Further, she said, 'I certainly hope Stuart doesn't have one of his fits tonight in our presence. It would be most unappetizing.' It was then, Marika, and I know you'll be proud of me, I took care of this Bolder dame."

"Whatever did you do?"

"Well, I noticed all the big rocks she was wearing, so I just sidled up to her and said, 'Gee, lady, I just had to tell you—those are the best-looking Kenny Lane matched costume jewelry sets I've ever seen.'"

Marika bent over laughing, crying through her carefully made-up eyes. "You are fabulous, Jonathon! You really took care of the Bitch of River House."

"The what of what?"

"Joan Bolder, whom everyone calls the Bitch of River House—that's the fancy apartment house where they live, on Fifty-second and the East River. Joan is mean and wildly jealous of everyone and everything. She is snake-like, has venom instead of human saliva in her mouth."

They wandered over to one large table filled with platters of different crudités and dips. In the center was a large still-life, made from vegetables carved ingeniously into flowers. Just then Demetri, the jeweler Demetri Guardevecchia, his lover Rienzo Doria, each in matching black velvet dinner jackets and black velvet dancing pumps, approached them.

"Marika Wentworth!" purred Demetri, extending his hand and using the occasion to closely examine her green peridot, amethyst, and diamond necklace and matching peridot and diamond earrings. "It is deevine to meet you finally in person. Your dress is so beautiful. By Madame Grès?"

"Jonathon," Marika said, "Demetri Guardevecchia, a great jeweler, and his friend, Rienzo Doria."

"*Incantado*," said Rienzo, bowing low, kissing Marika's hand and clicking his heels simultaneously, then shaking Jonathon's hand.

"Adams and Rienzo obviously went to the same butler's school," Jonathon whispered in Marika's ear as they moved on.

They were being watched carefully from across the room. Joan Bolder and her husband Henry were talking about them.

"Marika and that person she is with are obviously sleeping together. What a cheap, terrible, ignorant man. Ugh! How could she!"

"How do you know they're sleeping together?" was Henry Bolder's tired question. He really hated these dinner parties. Thankfully now invitations for him and his wife were few and far between.

"I can tell the Iron Virgin has found her man," hissed Joan, "and a sorry example, too. A desperate woman. I must find out more about that awful man."

"Let them be, Joan, let them be. He looks like a decent enough chap." His wife's hatchet still upset him, even after thirty years of marriage, particularly when it was used on nice people like Marika Wentworth.

"Look at the way their bodies move together through the room," said Joan. "Some one part of each of their bodies is always touching some other part. Hands, fingers, arms, hips. Something is always touching. If that isn't indicative of a love affair—"

"I think that's rather lovely," he interrupted, almost sadly, as he gazed at the happy symbol of bubbles in his champagne glass. He couldn't remember how long it had been when he was last with a warm, feminine woman. Then he shrugged in resignation. He was married to a woman as hard as the rocks with which she showered herself. It was his profession and his punishment to stay married to her.

Across the room, Marika watched Joan staring at people as though she were doing it through a lorgnette, making critical remarks to her husband all the while. With her short, stylish gray hair, Joan looked like a slender, glittery eel tonight, Marika decided, in her gunmetal-gray mousseline de soie dress, sparkling subtly with gray paillettes. Diamonds set in platinum blazed aggressively from her ears and hands, and in the low center of her décolletage she wore her famous giant weeping willow diamond brooch, with pear-shaped diamond drops hanging like leaves from flexible diamond branches that constantly moved to catch prisms of light.

"Jonathon, I'll be back in a minute," Marika suddenly said. "I'd better take a look in the dining room and in the kitchen. Georgiana made me promise to cast an eye." On her way to the dining room, she passed Sidney and Rachel Miller, and gave each of them a quick hug. They looked very handsome tonight. She could see that Sidney had purchased a necklace of sapphires and rubies for Rachel's new sapphire blue satin evening dress. She knew she had a contented client, for once. Nice—even if paving the way for their social climbing had made her feel like a whore.

How absolutely spectacular the immense space of the dining room looked, she thought, as she entered it for the first time. With lofty beamed ceilings, it was baronial, like a Spanish grandee's might have looked two hundred years ago. The walls were paneled in wood alternating with thin panels of a fiery Chinese red silk. The round, floor-length tablecloths covering the four tables of ten were of a rich red and black brocade, trimmed at the bottom in black tasseled braid. The napkins matched, and so did the seat cushions, tassel-tied at the corners of the little black and gold ballroom chairs. A tall, imposing Spanish black iron candelabrum, holding thick white candles—the kind used on the altars of the old Spanish churches—centered each table. Small antique silver goblets filled with open, velvety, dark red roses ringed each candelabrum's base, and a heavy antique silver place plate sat at each table setting. In the candlelight, the cavernous room glowed in silver, crystal, and shades of red against black. A male flamenco dancer's hat was tied to the back of each man's chair; a black lace mantilla was draped on the back of each woman's chair. Now Marika knew why Georgiana wore a skin-tight, ruffled Givenchy red taffeta dress. It was a flamenco dancer's dress! Georgiana wanted to match her dining room, a relationship everyone would realize upon entering this beautiful room. *Brava*, Georgiana!

There was a sudden commotion in the far corner of the dining room that had to be coming from the kitchen. There was a medley of loud noises, banging of pans and shouts of male voices. Marika rushed through the paneled doors, which swung open automatically as she approached them. Inside the kitchen, pots and pans had been thrown on the floor. She saw Alain, the head of the catering service, his black tie askew, brandishing a large carving knife at a cowering Adams, the butler. The chef and sous-chef were trying to disarm Alain as the Frenchman screamed, *"Crétin! Imbécile! Qu'est-ce que vous faîtes ici, espèce d'ordure!"*

At the sound of Marika's half-scream, *"Alain, arrêtez-vous,"* he put the knife down on a nearby table. At that, Adams, now visibly drunk, lunged for it, all but falling on the floor on top of the knife. Then, grabbing the edge of the pastry chef's table for support, Adams began to pant like an exhausted dog. Alain regarded him with disgust. *"Je m'excuse,* Madame Wentworth," he said softly in his thickly accented voice. "I am sorry about this small encounter. This is not something for a lady such as yourself to witness." He quickly straightened his jacket and his tie, and once again became the smooth, suave head of New York's premium party service.

"I'm glad I witnessed it before we had a homicide here," Marika answered. "Mrs. Wilkins asked me to keep an eye on things tonight. Just what is happening?"

"You can see for yourself, Madame Wentworth, we have a drunken, ineffectual Englishman who thinks he is running this *partee* and who is incapable of running a small children's tea *partee*."

Adams snarled and made another drunken lunge, almost falling again, but he was held up on either side by two of the kitchen help. Marika went over to him, eyes blazing. "You are *not* going to ruin Mrs. Wilkins' party. You were drunk even when we arrived tonight. Please change your clothes this very minute and leave this house. I'll arrange to have you paid tomorrow for your services tonight, even if you don't deserve a cent of it."

Adams began to protest. "Madam, I'll have you know—"

"Look, Adams, you either leave this house at once, or I'll call the police." Marika's voice was firm and he began to back away from her, still supported by the two kitchen helpers.

"Alain, you will carry on, won't you?" asked Marika.

"Mais certainement, Madame Wentworth. I should have been in charge since the beginning, but of course I will now save the party for Madame Wilkins. It will be done perfectly. *Vous allez voir."*

Marika went into the living room to find Georgiana. "I had to fire Adams for you," she whispered. "He was drunk. Everything is under control. I just thought you ought to know in advance that Alain and not Adams will be your *maître d'hôtel* in the dining room." Georgiana looked stricken. "My God, Marika, what happened?"

"I'll tell you later. It's all right. Just carry on." Alain at this moment arrived in the living room, whispered in Georgiana's ear that dinner was ready, and then announced in strong and quite dramatic Gallic tones, "Ladies and gentlemen, dinner is served." He stood at the side of the open portals of the dining room, holding the *plan de table* once again, so that a guest's memory could be refreshed if he or she had forgotten a table number. When Marika walked into the dining room on Jonathon's arm, she found Joan busily changing her table card and various others at nearby tables, in order to assure herself a better seat. Marika went up to her and whispered, "Georgiana has seen you do this. If I were you, I'd change those cards back—fast. Sand is watching you, too. Look, she has her notebook poised!"

Joan straightened up quickly, hatred in her eyes, her weeping willow brooch quivering with movement, and quickly put the table cards back in their original places. "When the day comes, Marika, that Mimi Wellton is justified in having a better seat than *I*, well, hell will have frozen over."

"Maybe the cool climate will be more comfortable for you, Joan," Marika replied, not believing her own bitchiness. That woman brought it out in her, there was no question.

Marika and Georgiana had discussed the table seating during their lunch at La Côte Basque and had decided that it would be better to put Jonathon on one side of the table with Sand, with Marika across from them. In this way, if Sand got out of hand, or if she drove Jonathon to some "act of desperation," which Marika knew Sand was capable of doing, Marika would be able to intervene. Georgiana decided to put young Archibald Youngblood IV on Sand's other side, so the columnist could feel the warmth of the blue blood running through the veins of her other dinner partner.

Everyone finally sat down in the beautiful room, and to the flipping noise of forty napkins being snapped to an unfolded position was added small exclamations and gasps of delight over the Spanish flamenco table designs. Marika watched Jonathon turn toward Sand and stare in speechless fascination as she kept writing in her small gold notebook, her cigarette holder clenched firmly in her mouth, all her front teeth bared as she did so. He looked across at Marika, making comical faces at her pertaining to Sand's actions, including imitating the clenched teeth around the cigarette holder, which caused Marika to look down, clear her throat, and sip from her water glass to keep from laughing outright. Then she heard Jonathon asking Sand, "Why do you suck on that contraption day and night, and never light a cigarette? Does it satisfy your oral fixation?"

Sand obviously loved the question. She turned full face to Jonathon and gave him one of her rare smiles. "Mr. Scher," she said, "you are a very forward and obviously a sexually oriented man. I like that. I don't see it often at parties like this."

"I would think, Sand, if I may call you that, you would present yourself in a different way if you cared about your own sexual orientation. I mean, you are a talented and gifted woman. You are interesting, you lead what many people consider a fascinating life, but why this weird way of dressing, these affectations? You are such an intelligent person, I don't see why you have to do it."

She sucked on her holder. "You don't consider that I lead a fascinating life, do you?"

"No, I couldn't stand it if I had your life."

"And you don't think being mentioned in a social column is important?"

"I never read any of them. That shows how important I think they are."

"You are a very candid man. Very unusual. I like you. In fact, I'll tell you something, Mr. Scher."

"You may certainly call me Jonathon considering I've already made a remark about your sexual orientation."

She laughed a low, earthy laugh. "I have all these trappings around me," she said, grinning and showing yellowed teeth, "because it's good for business. You've been frank with me, so I'm being frank with you. I do not expect you to quote me, not even to your beautiful friend Marika Wentworth."

"It's promised, done."

"I hate parties and I hate social climbers. My job frequently seems like penance. I make good money at this racket of mine, but the entire subject of social life and gossip is thoroughly distasteful. I fax my column every morning to my syndicate and proceed to dislike intensely what I just wrote. So I've learned how to forget it. And forget the people I write about."

"It makes me sad," said Jonathon, "that a woman of your talent should have to confine your daily life—or rather nights—to doing what you hate. That's a long penance of yours. It reminds me of the philosopher Gracián."

"I doubt if Gracián and I have anything in common," she laughed.

"Don't be so sure. The saying goes, 'Let it be a mistake to confide your errors even to a friend, for were it possible, you should not disclose them to yourself, but since this is impossible, make use here of that other principle of life, which is: *learn how to forget.*' "

"So Gracián has words that are truly meant for me. Since I've told you how I feel, how about you, Jonathon, do you like what you do?"

"Yes, I do," and he proceeded to explain his venture capital enterprises to his dinner partner. Sand listened intently, asking questions from time to time.

"You do love what you do, I can see that. Do you also love the lady you brought here tonight in your Jaguar?"

"How did you know we arrived in a Jaguar?"

She smiled and sucked again on her cigarette holder, even while she managed to eat a bite of food from her plate every now and then. "It's my job to know. You haven't answered my question."

"I don't talk about my personal life to columnists," he said, teasing her.

"I take it you do not want your romance imparted to the world in my write-up on this dinner?"

"I would really appreciate your *not* mentioning it, for many reasons."

"The newspaper side of me tells me to ignore your request, but the human side of me—you may have noticed, Jonathon, I have two sides to me—tells me to accede to your request."

"Thank you."

Sand raised her glass to Jonathon. "I wish you both all the luck in this relationship." And with that, she abruptly turned her scrawny back on him and began to talk to her other dinner partner. Another course had been served, and it was time to switch.

A clattering crash from the direction of the kitchen suddenly stopped all conversation in the room. Ashen-faced, Georgiana looked over at Marika and Marika rose quickly, explaining to her table, "I'm the person closest to the kitchen door in this room. I'll go investigate." The conversation level began again, timid, curious, and subdued, but gradually increasing, as the guests decided to ignore the terrible sounds that had emanated from the crash. "It happens to everyone," one person would say. "Trays fall from tables, water pitchers break, wine bottles smash on the floor. It is a common occurrence. It happens at the best of parties." Georgiana's guests were determined to have a good time tonight, and one kitchen glitch would not matter.

The doors swung open automatically as Marika approached the kitchen. There was a mess all over the stone-tiled floor in the center of the area. An oversized eighteenth-century silver platter, bearing the crest of some impoverished English noble family engraved in its center, had been dropped, spilling all of its contents. Marika remembered when Georgiana purchased four of those Georgian platters from the silversmith James Robinson. They had cost a fortune, but as Georgiana said, "How else am I going to serve four tables properly?

Alain was standing over a sea of hot, steaming goo on the floor, muttering epithets in French at the kitchen boy who knelt down beside it—obviously the culprit responsible for the capsized platter. The boy kept moaning, "But what am I going to do? What am I going to do?"

"*Idiot!*" shouted the caterer. "You spoon it all back, carefully, with the sense of an artist. You make it look as though it were meant to be positioned in that manner. You make it look *délicieux*!" With that, Alain knelt down on the floor next to the boy, spooning green vegetables, small roast potatoes, and tomatoes stuffed with a mushroom and sherry mixture back onto the platter. It now looked like beef stew.

"No matter, Alain," whispered Marika. "Just give this platter to my table. No—wait! Sand is sitting there. She would report the food looking like a mess. I know. Have this platter served at Madam Bolder's table!" Alain managed to give her a conspiratorial smile and said, "It shall be done."

Marika returned to the dining room, shot a smile and nod of "It's okay" in Georgiana's direction, and then announced to everyone at her table, "It was nothing, just a pot of the waiter's own supper that spilled." She returned to her conversation with the entertainment mogul on her right, apologizing for being such an inferior conversationalist so far this evening. Sand, however, spotted the upended platter, now reassembled, when it came out of the kitchen. She had been staring at each dish brought out by a waiter. She looked long and hard at the one platter carrying food that resembled beef stew and made another note in her little gold book.

The dinner proceeded without further mishap. The guests, accustomed to formal dinners, dutifully changed conversational partners, by turning from right to left as each course was served. The menus on the table and the place cards had the red and black silhouettes of flamenco-dancing figures blind-embossed like crests at the top. "How clever of Georgiana to have these especially designed by Tiffany's for tonight's theme," Marika said in a voice loud enough to reach across the table. Sand made another note.

After the champagne toasts were completed, and the demitasses had been served in the dining room, dinner was obviously over. The guests followed Georgiana and Chauncey into the living room, taking their hats and mantillas with them, expecting to chat awhile, drink some more champagne, and depart. But a transformation of the double living room had taken place during the meal. The furniture had been pushed back. Some of it had been removed, in fact, and was sitting in a parked furniture van around the corner. An enormous synthetic dance floor had been rolled out. Suddenly, out of nowhere was heard the strong, loud, vibrant sounds of Spanish gypsy music, and out onto the floor pranced twelve black-haired, lithe young Spaniards, six men and six women—a troupe of flamenco dancers from Saragossa, whom Georgiana had flown over just for tonight. Marika grabbed Jonathon's arm with excitement. "This is her surprise! This is what she wouldn't tell me about!" The entire room vibrated with the excitement and thrashing of heel and toe-tapping dancers, skirt ruffles flailing in the air, hands being clapped in perfect strong rhythm to the dancing feet.

Within a minute of their first dramatic entrance, another figure appeared in their midst, joining in the frenzied pattern of moving bodies. It was Adams, now quite florid of face, and having recovered from his alcoholic stupor with a new burst of energy. His white tie, shirt, and vest, but not his undershirt were gone from beneath his tailcoat. He was tapping his heels, clapping his hands, shouting *ole*, keeping his body rigid and moving fast with the others. The Spanish dancers, quite taken by surprise, were too professional to let him bother them. Their haughty expressions did not change. They simply made way for him and continued their dancing. The singers continued their Arabic throaty wailings in accompaniment, as though Adams was part of the group. Marika punched Jonathon in the ribs, and he reacted quickly. The guests were frozen in shock. Jonathon inserted himself into the midst of dancers and grabbed Adams from behind, pinning his arms behind him and propelling him quickly off the dance floor. A voice came forth from the sidelines: "Way to go, Jonathon!"

The musicians played louder to cover the sounds of Adams's protests. Marika went over to a stricken Georgiana and said into her ear with urgency, "Roar with laughter. Everyone else wants to but doesn't dare. Act as though this were the most divine joke you have ever witnessed. Laugh! Then quickly shout for everyone to move out onto the floor to join the Spaniards. Quick!"

Jonathon wrestled Adams back into the kitchen. By now the doorman of the apartment building had called building security, and Adams was being hustled, kicking and screaming, into the back service elevator. Georgiana, holding her hands high and clapping them loudly to the beat of her professional dancers, shouted out, "Everyone join in! Everyone dance! Let our Spanish dancers teach you!" With her jaw set firmly and her eyes bright with a smile, as though she were leading a Conga line, she began to execute a flawless flamenco dance, partnering with one of the Spaniards. She moved her mantilla around her shoulders with great grace. She had obviously taken some flamenco lessons at some point in her education. Another couple then went onto the floor, clapping their hands and clicking their heels, and soon the entire dinner party, wearing their hats and mantillas, had joined the ensemble. Heads were thrown back, arrogant, frowning gestures were made, bodies were held rigid, shoulders moved back and forth, and all ages continued dancing except for momentary rest sessions to down some more champagne. The Chauncey Wilkins dinner guest list had that evening what many later admitted was the best time of their entire lives. "I didn't even have this much fun at my own twenty-four-hour wedding," whispered stuffy Archibald Youngblood IV as he sacheted around the dance floor with Rachel Miller, who by now had shaken her head, flamenco style, so violently, her entire chignon had become undone, letting down her beautiful long hair all over her shoulders and making her look very sexy, young Archibald had decided.

At midnight Marika ignored the crowded room Georgiana had made into the ladies' room for this party, and went into her hostess's pink satin boudoir to fix up her makeup. There were two people already there, looking at themselves in Georgiana's floor-to-ceiling mirrored wall. They were trying on two of her satin negligees. Rienzo wore Georgiana's aqua one, Demetri her pink one with pink maribou trim. He had even managed to put on her matching pink satin mules.

"My God!" said a stunned Demetri. "I didn't think anyone would use this room," he said, his voice hushed with emotion.

"Look," said Marika soothingly, "I didn't see *a thing*. I promise you, this never happened, but I think it would be a great idea if you two hung those negligees back in the closet, made a quick exit, and let me use the bathroom."

"Of course!" said a subdued Demetri. "And thank you," he said in a soft voice, "for not telling. Thank you for that." He paused, "I have to tell you," he added in his high tenor voice, "I love your peridots."

Sand's syndicated story on the Wilkinses' dinner party and the *vernissage* of their new apartment filled her entire four-column spread. It went out over the wire with a photograph of Chauncey and Georgiana that had been taken on their wedding day. Sand managed to get in her digs, mentioning the "gray lady with matching diamonds who tried to change the place cards, thus committing the most serious of all social rudenesses." Nothing, it seemed, had gotten by Sand's cigarette holder, from the platter of food dropped and reassembled in the kitchen to the progressive drunken disintegration of England's most noble butler. She even described the negligee incident without mentioning names. The columnist saluted Georgiana as the hostess with the greatest cool in America, whose "deft handling of an untenable situation made her a heroine in everyone's eyes." Sand went on to say that "Chauncey Wilkins should be proud of his new wife, who obviously has become America's most imaginative, talented, and amusing hostess, one whose invitations will be sought after on an international basis."

Jonathon referred to the column as he and Marika had a quick salad lunch at Reginette's the next day.

"You must feel really pleased," he said.

"Pleased for Georgiana and Chauncey, yes."

"But for yourself, too."

There was something about his tone that she didn't like. "All I cared about was helping Georgiana fulfill the most important goal in her life at this point," Marika said.

"A stupid, vapid goal."

"You're being a little harsh and holier-than-thou, aren't you?"

Jonathon fingered the stem of his water glass, looking somber.

"I don't know, Marika, you and I—we . . ." He was having trouble saying it.

She felt a red alert. "You and I what?"

"You and I haven't had—and haven't sought the same kind of social life. I guess we probably don't even have the same goals."

"What do you mean by that?" she said, sounding irritated. She was not only a little angry at his criticism, but a little frightened, too, at this strange turn of events.

"Look, I don't really mean anything by what I'm saying. It's just that I surveyed that scene last night—*your* scene . . ."

"That wasn't my scene last night, Jonathon," she interrupted. "That wasn't what I crave, what I like to do."

"Oh yes, it is," he said smiling. "You shine like a glittering chandelier over the heads of all those people. They admire you, with good reason. You are so intelligent, so gifted"—he stopped himself to put his hand over hers—"so beautiful, that you enhanced that setting, but it must frustrate you terribly at the same time."

"Frustrate me, why?"

"Because it's all so god-damned phony." He began to think of his conversation with Sand, but checked himself. He had made a promise.

"Everything's phony," Marika answered. "You can find it in any society, any economic group. It's not just in that crowd last night. You can find it in your social life, too. As long as you can see the reality of it, as long as you're not taken in by it, it's all right to partake of it on rare occasions, isn't it?" She hated feeling this defensive. In fact, she couldn't quite believe this conversation.

"Look," he said, "let's not discuss it again, okay? We have better things to talk about, better ways to spend our time." He managed to give her a knowing look and call for the bill at the same time.

Jonathon left for the airport and she went back to the office. She had looked forward to this lunch. She had wanted to hold hands and talk about how lovely it was, making love after the Wilkinses' party. Instead, he had—well, she told herself, let's face it, he had attacked her lifestyle. During the quick taxi ride back to her office from Fifty-ninth and Park, there was time to realize that the surface of the smooth, calm sea she shared with Jonathon was beginning to ripple.

At the weekly staff meeting, Anthony's office, filled with his folding Yale blue director's chairs, was abuzz with laughter and gossip about the Wilkinses' party.

"Great story," commented Anthony on the report by Sand. "Your friend Georgiana must be very pleased. It makes her out to be the coolest, most inventive hostess in America."

"I know she is very pleased," smiled Marika.

A male voice suddenly cut through the atmosphere like a cleaver.

"A cheap story about cheap people" said Greg Willis, slipping down on his spine, and stretching his legs straight before him, so that three people had to move their feet to accommodate him.

Marika was angry. She was no longer enamored of his talent, as she used to be. And she was tired of being the butt of his sarcasm.

"So, Mr. Sourmouth, did we wake up on the wrong side of the bed this morning?"

"I was just giving you the social commentary you're always asking for."

"I didn't ask you to be insolent and nasty," Marika shot back quickly. No sounds were heard in the room except the voices of Marika and Greg.

"I just told you what I thought about the story," Greg said petulantly. "You had asked us directly, if I remember correctly, what we thought of Sand's story. Since you asked for my opinion, I'm merely giving it to you. It sounded like a description of Versailles shortly before Louis and Marie lost their heads."

Silence again. "Greg," said Marika sternly, "this is a staff meeting, not an anger-ventilating session with your psychiatrist. You and I will discuss this later. In the meantime we'll continue the business at hand."

The room temperature was glacial through the rest of the

meeting, and when it was over, Greg stayed behind and apologized to Marika in what seemed like a sincere tone.

"I've been having some personal problems," he explained, "and I can only ask you to forgive me. I'm really sorry for the asshole way I acted in there this morning."

"Would you like me to tell you what your outburst *really* sounded like? Would you like the real truth?"

"Yes, give it to me without embellishment."

"You sounded exactly like a resentful person who had not been invited to a party he had desperately wanted to attend."

"I guess you're right," he said, starting to go out the door. "Am I forgiven?"

"Yes," Marika said brightly. After all, he had apologized. "You know how much I need you and count on you. You're a great talent in this agency."

"Thanks," and within two seconds he was gone, his dark glasses once again in place, covering any expression in his eyes. She wondered why she had felt compelled not only to forgive him, but to praise him.

Greg looked at his watch, discovered he was already five minutes late for his lunch appointment. Throwing his Burberry over his shoulder, he ran for the elevator. There were no empty cabs on Madison Avenue; it was lunchtime and it was pouring. Fortunately, he beat an older woman to a taxi that emptied out on a corner. It was rightfully her taxi, but he successfully ignored her derisive comments. Once ensconced at a corner table in Le Bistro on Fiftieth and Third with his lunch companion, he lost no time and got right down to business.

"Charlie, is the final contract agreeable? Are you ready to sign?"

"Greg," said the other man, "Marika's name isn't even on this document. What's going on here? She created the proposal for Georgetown Electric. It's her firm you work for. What gives?"

"You're overreacting," Greg said, ordering another drink for Charles Mander, president of Georgetown Electric, one of the most distinguished figures in the field of electronic communications. "Marika may have given you the impression the proposal was hers, but it was really mine. She has started to cut back on her activities with the firm—she's involved in a romance and will be turning everything over to me. Besides, I have really been running things for years. Because of my discontent with how I've been compensated—a feeling shared by several of us—Marika is letting me handle certain accounts entirely by myself. I will manage your account and the monthly fees will be paid directly into my bank account. This is the way she is keeping me happy."

"I don't know. Your proposal to handle the financial and consumer publicity for my company was excellent, imaginative, doable. It makes me a little uneasy, however, that your president is having nothing to do with the project."

The waiter arrived with their soft-shelled crabs, and Greg spent thirty minutes persuading Charles Mander that he should place his trust—and his company's future in his, Greg Willis's, hands. By the time they had quickly downed their espressos, the contract was signed, and Greg took it back to his office where he placed it carefully in his personal, locked safe.

CHAPTER

11

*M*arika had become accustomed to stopping by Steve's apartment after each teaching session in her literacy group with Bill Carver. Tonight, as usual, she had picked up some good hot pasta at Trattoria, a restaurant in the Pan Am Building, which was halfway between her teaching session and Steve's building. She had also brought with her copies of the finished artwork for the Imperial Honey Cream products.

"I've been lying here, just thinking about what pasta it would be," Steve said in a voice that sounded cheerful and teasing, but alarmingly weak to her.

"Tonight's *specialità*," Marika answered with an exaggerated Italian accent as she set down a tray on his lap, "is *Tortellini al Prosciutto e Funghi*." She tucked a fresh, large cloth napkin, brought from home, into the neck of his pajama top. She removed the silver foil over the plate of pasta, put it on a tray with a fork and spoon from his kitchen, and poured wine into one of his stemmed glasses. Then she poured herself a glass of wine and drew up a chair close to his bed. She couldn't help but notice that the apartment, usually kept meticulously clean and neat, suddenly looked dirty and disheveled. She had had to wash Steve's eating utensils before giving them to him, because it looked as though he hadn't been washing his dishes. Obviously he lacked the strength to do much housekeeping.

"You spoil me so much," he said, trying to swallow some pasta.

"You were meant to be spoiled. Now come on, Steve, and eat. *Mangia, bambino*," she pleaded.

He laughed, took a large bite, and sighed with pleasure. "It's good." He took a sip of wine. "Very *bona*."

"No, *buono*," she laughed. "*Bona* is a slang word an Italian uses when he's complimenting a woman for having large bosoms." Steve laughed again and continued eating, she was happy to observe, while she filled him in on what was happening with the Imperial Honey Cream products.

"Sarah and I will finish the final corrections on the artwork tomorrow," he said. As he talked, she noticed how slurred his speech was becoming. He had become increasingly forgetful, but his peers managed to cover up for him, with Marika's approval. She saw that the purplish-red spots on his neck and arms were multiplying. She kept on making conversation, but her throat was obstructed with a sob that she managed to suppress. How long will it be now, Steve? How long will you last? How long are we going to be recipients of that sweetness and kindness that emanates from you?

He read her mind. "You can probably tell I'm growing a little weaker, Marika. You have probably noticed a gradual deterioration. But there's a lot of fight in me left. I'm in for the long haul. I'm doing okay, and I think I'm even headed for a period of remission. That's my goal. To buy a little more time. I want to come back to the office *so badly*."

"You will, Steve. I feel you're going to get better, stronger. You're going to be able to come back. You may want to, but we not only want you to, we *need* you."

She felt it now more than ever. She needed her friends. There was evil around. Hortense had run after her in the hall as she was leaving tonight. "Boss, I have to speak to you!" The elevator door had opened and Marika, obviously pressed for time, had said, "Look, tell me about it later."

"No, now."

Marika had walked back into her office with Hortense and closed the door, saying, "This had better be important."

"Greg is stabbing you in the back."

"You have become paranoid. Now snap out of it, Hortense!"

"I'm not paranoid. Marilyn Carruthers, who's Charles Mander's executive assistant, said that Greg has been seeing him about the proposal for Georgetown Electric, and that the accepted agreement is a document with two signatures on it, Mander's and Willis's."

"I don't believe it," Marika said sharply.

"Ask him about it. Just ask him."

"All right, I will. What have you got anyway, a secretarial mafia that feeds information back and forth to each other?"

"That's exactly what we've got," Hortense said, with no little pride. "And if you look at the history of the world of business, you'll find that this information network has been in place as long as business has been."

"I'll ask Greg about this in due time." As she went down in the elevator, she had a sour feeling inside. She had submitted a crackerjack proposal to Charles Mander and had not heard a word since.

On her way to Steve's, Marika had remembered that Greg was leaving for Paris before she was, tonight on an 8 P.M. flight. She checked her watch. There would be no time to catch him. Darn —the sour feeling in her stomach had turned to pain.

Anthony was adamant.

"Take the Concorde, Marika. Save yourself the long trip. It doesn't matter that we sent Greg over in an economy seat. After all, for Christ's sake, you gave him the round-trip airfare as a gift, didn't you? Isn't he going over there to have fun? Is he going to do *any* work for the company at all?"

She shook her head. "No, since we had completed the first stage of the LUXFOODS project, he's gone on vacation, but he told me he'd help me with my research on the Napoleonic bees for LUXFOODS—a little. I don't know, it just makes me uncomfortable to be flying over there like a grand duchess when my account executives always have to go in steerage."

"Tell me, *Madame Duchesse*," said Anthony with a smile that carved the pleasantest of wrinkles around his eyes, "why don't you ever come into this office and sit in one of my nice blue chairs? Why do you always have to sit on the edge of my desk and make me feel the other end of the desk will rise up in the air like an unbalanced teeter-totter?"

"Oh, you're just manic about your Yale chairs," she said, laughing, but then obediently sat down in one of them next to his desk.

"How can I," she said, becoming serious again, "justify the extravagance of the Concorde, which my company has to pay for, when all I ever talk about around here is cutting expenses?"

"Look," Anthony replied, "we are getting plenty of scratch from the Kauffmans and LUXFOODS throughout this year and the next. So take the bloody Concorde—and while you're at it, be sure you make lazy Willis do some first-rate work for you to earn that airfare of his."

"You're not being very kind to him," she said, inwardly grateful that he shared her feelings about Willis.

"I can't help it. He's beginning to get on my nerves. His attitude toward Steve's illness is intolerable, and . . ."

Marika rose from her chair. "Don't worry Father Adviser, I *will* take the Concorde, I'll finish my Napoleonic research quickly, I won't let Greg get away with anything, and I'll be home within five days, including travel time."

She and Anthony did not need to have an extended conversation about Greg because they knew each other so well, they could read each other's thoughts. They reacted to each other's cues with accuracy. Each one had serious reservations about Greg, but the necessary moves could not take place until she was back from Paris. Discussing it now would only make her agitated.

• • •

The telephone rang in a familiar two-beat French rhythm, and she finally heard it in her sleep. She reached over in the dark and removed the slim receiver from its cradle, anxious to silence the loud sounds coming from it. Then she groped for the table lamp button, pushed it, and sat up in bed to figure out exactly where she was. The eighteenth-century French furniture around her, the carved mantelpiece with its gold-leaf framed mirror, and the French doors opening to the balcony overlooking the twinkling lights of the Place de la Concorde finally oriented her. This was Paris, and she was in the Hotel Crillon. She had just spent two arduous days of research for the LUXFOODS Imperial Honey Cream products PR and advertising plans. She had one more day to go. Her head began to clear. She suddenly noticed the telephone receiver in her hand.

"*Allo, allo, oui?*"

She heard Mrs. Matthews' voice and then Jonathon's. He had taken a break from his Chicago staff meeting and was calling from his office.

"Hi, ya, gorgeous."

"It may be five o'clock in the evening there, but do you realize it's midnight here?"

"I just wanted to be sure that a man didn't answer your bedroom telephone."

"Only an exhausted woman is answering."

"You've never complained about my waking you before."

She sighed, "I'm sorry—I'm just tired."

"Is anything wrong?" He sounded concerned.

"It's Greg Willis again."

"Is he helping you?"

"I haven't seen him once. He's conspicuous by his absence. He is on vacation over here, but he was supposed to help me prepare the background material for LUXFOODS. He hasn't called. He probably knows that the jig is up."

"Details, please."

"He is going to be fired. His 'vacation' present is turning out to be a termination present."

"Good. What made you decide on such a momentous action?"

"Hortense faxed me proof of a serious accusation she made against him—something that Charles Mander's secretary told her."

"Good old Hortense. She always comes through. What did she and Mander's secretary uncover?"

"Only that Greg told Mander he was operating now as the real head of my agency, that I was stepping out of the picture."

"Good Lord!" exclaimed an angry Jonathon.

"Not only that, but Mander was supposed to pay Greg the monthly retainer into his personal bank account. In other words, the fees for the proposal which I wrote were all to go directly to Greg!"

"The son-of-a-bitch!"

"I just couldn't believe Hortense when she first told me this. I couldn't believe one man—excuse me, one *person*—was capable of such incredible back-biting, such disloyalty! But when I received the fax from Hortense of the signed agreement between Mander and Willis, that was enough. I erupted like a volcano when I opened the envelope and read it. The Crillon *conciergerie* is still in a state of shock."

"How are you going to handle Mander? Are you going to call him from Paris?"

"No, I'll be home in three days. I want to sit down at his desk, not throw something like this at him over a trans-Atlantic telephone wire. Besides, I'm sure that his secretary has already told him the whole story."

"Smart woman. Did I ever tell you how smart I think you are?"

"Oh, but let's don't talk about Greg Willis anymore. It depresses me. I don't even want to think about him. Tell me nice things."

"All right. Next to being there with you, there's nothing I like more than cutting out of a staff conference to talk to a sexy, luscious woman who's lying sheathed in clinging satin in a great big bed overlooking the Place de la Concorde, every cell of her body aching for me to pay homage to it."

"That's nice!" she laughed, looking down at her sexless flannel nightie. She must remember to rid herself of these nightgowns in the near future, and buy a whole new wardrobe of *charmeuse* and lacy creations.

"I miss you, Jonathon, and I love you."

"I miss you more. Why are you and I always on different continents? Tomorrow, remember, I leave for the Far East. It's getting harder and harder to have to tell myself I won't be seeing you for three more weeks. If we were married, you'd be coming with me."

"I don't know about that!" She tried to sound coy, but it struck a cold note in their conversation.

"You mean, I'd have to travel by myself as always, and you'd be off doing your thing, as always? What kind of marriage would that be, Marika?"

"A fascinating one."

She decided they'd better get off this subject—and quickly. "Jonathon, just think about how much fun it's going to be after the next three weeks, when we're together again. Think of the fun we'll have giving in to all our pent-up longings and frustrations?"

"Look, I have to go back into the meeting. I'll have Mrs. Matthews keep you fully informed of my travel schedule, and I'll call you every night."

"I can hardly wait for you to make love to me again."

"You sure know how to get a guy's attention on a telephone call, Marika."

They hung up, and she frowned as she put the receiver back in its cradle. There were unresolved problems. They never had the time to discuss them, work them out. They were always on a romantic holiday, seeing each other after long absences. They were always enjoying the frosting on the cake. Telephone calls never resolved differences or allowed them to get problems out on the table for a solution work session. But they would work it all out.

She was certain of it, never more than now. They would plan their wedding in a leisurely, orderly fashion and do it right. She fell asleep immediately.

Marika's return from Paris was greeted with unmitigated enthusiasm by Lisa.

"Why are you so excited to see me home again?" Marika asked, smiling at her daughter, whose long legs were encased in raspberry tights, over which she wore a Scottish tartan miniskirt of predominately raspberry, pink, and navy shades, and a navy short-sleeved cashmere sweater top. Lisa was beautiful. Marika decided, looking at her, that one reason for it was her total lack of consciousness of this fact. She was, however, clothes crazy.

"Come on, Mom, come on. Don't keep me in suspense!"

"How do you know I brought you something from Paris? I never mentioned I would."

"Come on, Mom, come on. What's in that package?"

Marika laughed, tossed it in the air, and Lisa caught it. Immediately she tried on the pale blue stretchy fabric jumpsuit with its darker blue wide suede belt, and then the short funky blue matching wet patent-leathery-looking raincoat, which fell from her shoulders in a stiff geometric form. "Neat!" Lisa shouted. "I look like a blue pyramid! Neat, Mom. Thanks!" and she gave her mother a hug and pranced around the room like a spirited Lippizaner performing in the ring. Marika's purchases from the boutique on the Faubourg St. Honoré were hits.

Lisa sat on Marika's big bed with her, perusing all of the fabric samples, menus, and photocopies of textiles from Paris that constituted the main research for tying in LUXFOODS with the Napoleonic era. She asked for an explanation of everything, and showed sincere interest in the way Marika combined the romance of the Napoleonic period with honeybees and the food products. At a certain point Marika caressed her strawberry hair and said, "Hey, wait a minute, could it be that my daughter is professing a slight interest in the operations of the public relations industry?"

"Not a chance!" Lisa laughed. "I'm going to be a vet when I finish college or perhaps a hired revolutionary."

The telephone rang and Marika, hoping it was Jonathon, was only slightly disappointed when the friendly voice of the White House operator said, "Mrs. Watson is calling, Mrs. Wentworth."

The two friends talked together at great length, but Marika was careful to keep the conversation lively, happy, and funny. One did not unburden problems of the business world on the First Lady; she had problems enough. A telephone conversation with a friend should always leave the person in the White House smiling and feeling comforted.

They discussed the latest fashions in Paris, caught each other up on their latest news of Georgiana, all affirmative and happy. Sand's column on the Wilkins's dinner had accomplished Georgiana's objectives. Then Marika asked Eve, "How are things with Mac?"

"Better than ever!" was the very happy answer. "And Jonathon?"

"We see each other so seldom, how could it be anything but wonderful?"

"That doesn't sound good."

"We'll get it all together, don't worry," Marika said, wondering if perhaps she should be a little worried herself, when everyone else seemed to be.

"Spend more time with him. Change your schedule. Give up some of your commitments. Show him who you really are, and let yourself see who he really is. You don't sound really serious, the way you flit around and have warm, loving chats on the telephone."

"All right, Mama, I promise," Marika said, "I'll report back to you."

"What's going on in your bedroom right now? I hear whooping and hollering. Is that the TV?"

"No, just Lisa, enjoying the Paris finery I brought her."

"Give her my love," laughed Eve, but just then Lisa grabbed the telephone from her mother's hand.

"Hi, Aunt Eve! Have you added any sexy young social aides around there lately?"

"I thought you were spoken for. If I remember correctly, he's named Sergio."

"Always room for more," said Lisa, and she handed the telephone back to her mother.

"Remember when we were that age, Marika?"

"Yes, but we had more sense."

"No, we didn't. Remember the night we went into the headquarters of the New York Mounted Police, and said we needed dates for the Vassar prom? Maybe we were naive, maybe not. As I recall," the First Lady said, "they lined up so we could pick out our favorites, and we told them they had to wear their boots and uniforms."

"I've never told Lisa that story."

"And they also had to bring their horses."

"It would have made a great prom."

"Well, what's the difference between the social aides or the Mounted Police? They all do some mounting, don't they?"

"First Lady, you are naughty!"

The two old friends hung up, laughing, which, Marika decided, is the way it should always be.

Marika knocked on Greg's door. When he told her to come in, she noticed immediately the sullenness on his face. He did not rise to greet her, or even offer her a chair. Every time she looked at him lately, his face seemed to be set in a permanent expression of ugliness. It made her task easy. She had no affection whatsoever for him anymore. There was no trust. "I'm sure you know why I've come."

"Yeah, I sort of expected to hear from you today."

"Take off those sunglasses, Greg. This is one time I want to see the 'whites of your eyes,' if you'll forgive the expression." He removed his glasses and fixed his eyes directly on hers, defiantly.

"You're fired, as of this day."

"And to what do I owe this attack?"

"There are so many reasons, and you know them all so well —but the latest little trick you pulled with Charlie Mander is probably the worst thing I can think of a professional doing."

"Oh, come off it, Marika. Don't play that sainted lady role with me. You never gave me a break in this firm. I was never properly compensated, and never given credit for the fact that I was the major reason for the success of this firm."

"I have no time for your delusions of grandeur, Greg. You are a common thief, a disloyal, ungrateful . . ."

"You shouldn't even be running this firm!" He spoke loudly and Marika cringed as she heard several doors nearby open.

"I want you out of here, before your venom oozes out of the door of your office. I had been planning on giving you several months' severance pay. I've changed my mind. You get two weeks."

"I'll tell it to you straight, Marika. I should be running the firm and I'm going to put you and Stuyvesant under. You're nothing but a dilettante."

"You are a sick man. You cannot continue here for one more second. Pick up your check right now, clear out your desk. I will have someone come in to watch you do it. Hortense, I think. She's been on to you for a long time, and I should have listened to her from the start."

Greg Willis was gone within an hour. He said good-bye to no one, and no one came around to say good-bye to him. The minute he got on the elevator, Hortense called Steve to relish the news.

CHAPTER

12

*L*isa read aloud to Marika, as she lay on her stomach on the fragile green silk bedspread, turning it once again, Marika noticed with irritation, into a tormented sea of wrinkled waves.

" 'The seder is our festive introduction to a full week of sacred observance celebrating a number of events and ideas: the birth of the Jewish people, its struggle for freedom, God's role in the history of the people of Israel, and its role in God's purposes.' "

"That's impressive, whatever it is. What are you reading from?"

"A *New Union Haggadah*, prepared by the Central Conference of American Rabbis."

"Wherever did you get it? I must say I'm proud of you. Both of us need to read that before we go to Jonathon's Aunt Ruth's seder."

"A kid at school gave it to me. She heard me talking about how you and I were going to our first seder, and she said it would be helpful."

Marika continued her exercising. "Please go forward. We both need to learn."

" 'The seder is a unique opportunity,' " Lisa continued, " 'for religious sharing with family, friends, and guests; for enhancing the meaning of Judaism and rejoicing in its beauty; and for a personal experience of the mysterious unfolding of our people's story, the wonder of our redemption, past, present and future.' "

"Go on, Lisa," Marika said. She was in the midst of her breathing exercises, lying on the floor, but was listening intently, proud, too, of the beauty of Lisa's voice as she read the solemn description.

"I'll just skip around a bit. The book says that the house must be prepared for Passover, everything cleaned, and the food, dishes, and utensils set aside to use only during those special days. It says you shouldn't eat bread or foodstuffs or matzoh on Passover before the meal. Does that mean us, too, Mom?"

"No, I don't think so. I think we're excused from that."

"It says the Haggadah is not so much recited as it is experienced."

"I'm really looking forward to this," came the voice from the floor, between deep breaths. "Jonathon says it is a very important part of his religion, a very beautiful part."

"I don't know about you, but I'm scared. There's so much ritual. Everyone does certain things on cue. How will we know what to do?"

Her mother chuckled. "I assure you, we'll have plenty of help. Jonathon, his mother Rebecca, his Aunt Ruth and Uncle Jacob, their children and grandchildren."

"Mom," said Lisa, momentarily putting down the book and turning over on her back to stare at the ceiling, painted pale blue with pale white clouds floating across it, "aren't you scared meeting Jonathon's mother for the first time?"

"Hardly!" Marika laughed. "He's very close to his mother and absolutely adores her, so I'm sure she and I will get along beautifully. We love the same thing—Jonathon."

"Any mother-in-law would feel so lucky to have a daughter-in-law like you," Lisa said proudly, "and just think, after she meets me, how elated she'll be to contemplate being grandmother-in-law of a fabulous person like me."

Marika threw a pillow at Lisa's head, and the discussion of the upcoming seder came to an end.

Jonathon picked them up in a rented black BMW and escorted them from the East River to the exact opposite side of Manhattan. The Klugmans' spacious apartment was on an upper floor, overlooking the Hudson River and the New Jersey Palisades beyond. They were greeted warmly by Jonathon's aunt and uncle, Jacob and Ruth, who in turn introduced them to their two married children, Leslie and Daniel and Bonnie and Fred. "They're really all my cousins," Jonathon explained, "but the five little ones always call me Uncle Jonathon."

Jacob had his hands on the shoulders of an adorable four-year-old boy. "This is Roger," he said, introducing him to Marika and Lisa.

"It's a special day for him. You'll see why later. Just keep an eye on Jonathon and that plate of matzoh over there." Jacob winked.

Jonathon's uncle was so warm and easy to talk to. "Oh, I won't have any trouble keeping an eye on Jonathon!" Marika teased back.

Jonathon gave Roger a high five and asked Ruth, "Where's my mother?"

"In our bedroom fixing her hair. She arrived in a state, saying the wind had blown her to pieces."

"I knew I should have picked her up," he said.

"Forget about it," Ruth replied. "After all, you sent a car for her. Her hair would have blown and she'd be complaining if you *had* picked her up. You know that my sister always has to have a lament!"

Marika and Lisa stood in the midst of the happy family, the children teasing and playing with each other, the grown-ups managing to talk on two levels at the same time—a child's and an adult's. Marika's eyes were fixed on the door, and finally Rebecca

Scher came through it, a handsome woman of sixty-seven, slim as a reed, with iron gray hair cut into a short, wavy bob. She wore a long-sleeved tailored gray flannel dress with a multicolored satin scarf tied into a perfect wide bow at the side of her neck. Marika recognized her dress as a Valentino. She wore large round pearl and gold earrings, rimmed with diamonds, two heavy gold bracelets, and classic, high-heeled Ferragamo black suede pumps. She was, Marika decided, *stunning*. Add *intimidating* to that description, she said to herself.

Jonathon's mother had taste, she decided. She admired this all the more, knowing that Rebecca was a self-made woman who had been poor all her life until Jonathon became successful. Now I know, Marika thought to herself, where Jonathon's ambition and energy come from . . . his mother's genes.

Mrs. Scher's welcome was warm. "Marika, my dear, so we finally meet. I am so happy! I have heard nothing but your name for these past few months, and from Jonathon's description, I expected the most fabulous beauty in the world. You're even better than his description," she said. "Men are always so inadequate when they try to describe the woman they love."

"It means a great deal to me to meet you," Marika continued, blushing a little at the expansive compliment, but also feeling a little uneasy about a possible note of insincerity in Rebecca Scher's voice.

"Jonathon is always talking about how close you are to each other, and how much he misses you, now that you live on the West Coast instead of Chicago."

Rebecca and Marika ceased even trying to talk at this point, because the babble of children and the calling of everyone into the dining room had superseded any quiet chat.

The dining room was also a library, all four walls filled with shelves of books. When they sat down at the long, beautifully decorated table, and after the candle lighting ceremony, Jacob explained to Marika and Lisa the meaning of the special seder plate, put in front of him as the leader of this religious observance today. The symbolism was moving, much more so than any book could have described, and Marika found herself emotionally caught up in the spirit of the ceremony. There was a large roasted shank bone resting on the plate, representing the ancient sacrifice of the Paschal lamb, and next to it a roasted egg, representing the burnt offerings brought to the Temple on festival days. Next to it was some horseradish, or "bitter herbs," he explained, "to symbolize the suffering of the Jews." Next came a mixture of apples, nuts, spices, and wine, representing the mortar used by the Jews during their years of suffering in ancient Egypt, when, as slaves, they built palaces and pyramids. The last item on the plate was *karpas*, consisting of parsley, celery, or lettuce, Jacob explained, a reminder that Passover coincides with the arrival of Spring.

"What's that in the center?" asked Lisa, pointing to a large ceremonial cup.

"Ah, that mystery will be revealed soon." Jacob had a twinkle in his eye and it was clear he loved to play the role of mentor to these uninitiates.

"Oh, and one more thing we all must do at this table tonight"—Jacob said solemnly, "we each must drink four cups of wine. Though the Haggadah says this is to remind us of our enslavement and liberation, trust me, it is not. It is to wash down my lovely wife's stomach-defying matzoh balls." Without missing a beat, Jacob raised his glass, and briefly, in half-sung, half-spoken Hebrew, blessed the ruby wine. "Here's to glass number one." As she tasted the sweet red liquor, Marika realized this was her first taste of Passover wine.

Marika and Lisa, flanking Jonathon, watched in fascination as the rituals unfolded, interrupted by the serving of the meal's early courses. True enough, Ruth's matzoh balls were hard as golf balls and just as munchy. After the soup was served, the relaxed conversation began, one thought bouncing off the next, jokes leading into a discussion of politics. Everyone at this table seemed to have an opinion about the state of the world and, inevitably the conversation got around to the Mideast and the contemporary problems of Israel. Each adult at the table had something to say about it, but Marika remained quiet, not daring to comment on a subject that meant so much to these people. This was no time, she told herself, to make a gaffe.

The children didn't have time to fidget, because when Jacob sensed they were becoming restless, he would continue to the next ritual. Finally, before the main course, Marika noticed that little Sara, the youngest grandchild of all, was squirming in her chair and looking more attentive. She seemed nervous and then it became clear why. When her grandfather nodded to her, Sara began to ask "the Four Questions," one after the other, each query addressing the meaning of the ritual they were performing this night. Now her father, Fred, repeated the questions in a language Marika recognized as Hebrew. Then, and only then, did Jacob respond.

And though she didn't know how it happened, Marika felt a new intimacy with Jonathon. Perhaps he felt it too, because beneath the table, with Jacob's voice in the background, he squeezed her hand. Although deeply moved by the feelings of this moment, Marika was suddenly aware of the burning gaze of Jonathon's mother in her direction. She felt its laser sharpness, but she turned aside her negative suspicions, because the beauty of their growing closeness was much more important at this moment, and seemed powerful enough to overcome anything.

Ruth's cooking was incredibly good, and they ate their way through brisket of veal, highly spiced, with a side dish of carrots, sweet potatoes, apples, and prunes, which Ruth referred to as *tzimmes*. And there was stuffing made of matzoh and as a vegetable, simple snow peas. Then Jacob called for Jonathon to hide the *Afikomen*, which he did, having taken the matzoh piece hidden in a white napkin away from the table, and while the others were talking and trying to ignore him, he hid it behind a row of art books. Now Marika had understood why Jacob kidded her about keeping an eye on Jonathon. It was up to Roger to find the hidden matzoh, which he did rather quickly, and exacted his reward from Uncle Jonathon. But not without some negotiating first. Roger and Jonathon finally negotiated a price of $5.00, which Jonathon removed from his money clip with much fanfare. Marika noticed that he had a number of these crisp 1989 $5.00 bills, and now he gave each little cousin a gift of one of them. How, she wondered, had he managed in his hectic schedule to arrange for the new bills for his cousins? Then Jonathon held out one to Lisa. She blushed. "Jonathon, that's silly, I'm an adult."

"At this table, you're a child." He gave her the bill affectionately. "Remember this evening. It's important to me . . ."

Lisa smiled. Her skin glowed beneath the candlelight and in that moment, she looked as young as any of the five young cousins.

Through it all, the deep baritone voice of Jacob would call forth reminders of the purpose of this event:

"We were slaves to Pharaoh in Egypt, and God freed us from Egypt with a mighty hand. Had not the Holy One, praised be He, delivered our people from Egypt, then we, our children, and our children's children would still be enslaved."

After much singing, at the conclusion of the meal, the cup in the center of the ceremonial plate was filled, and two of the children went to open the doors of Aunt Ruth and Uncle Jacob's apartment to welcome Elijah, the prophet, should he be coming by. Such was the evening's magic that Marika could have sworn she felt a presence enter the room.

Everyone got up from the table and wandered about in conversational groups. Rebecca took Marika to the master bedroom where they sat down on the Klugmans' big bed, full of the guest's coats.

"I love your son very much," Marika said with utter simplicity.

"I'm sure you do," his mother said, "but somehow—somehow—that's not enough."

"What do you mean?" An alarm went off inside Marika, and she could feel her eyebrows arching half in hostility, half in fear.

"You saw today, in the seder, what we're all about."

"Yes, I saw it and I was deeply moved. I truly was. I loved every minute of it."

"We are an old traditional family, and we are better off when we marry our own people."

"Jonathon is not devout in his religion, you know that."

"It doesn't matter. He once was, and will be again—one day. Marriage, my dear, is difficult enough, without adding the chasm that exists between Jew and Christian."

"There is no chasm between *us!*" Marika answered sharply. "Do not imply something that does not exist."

"He had a very unhappy marriage, I'm sure you're aware of that," Rebecca Scher said sadly.

"Yes, and she was Jewish. So you see, just because two people are of the same religion does not guarantee success and happiness."

"The reason they were not happy had only to do with her selfishness and her refusal to have his children."

Marika did not answer, so Rebecca continued. "I want so much for him to be blessed with children. Now is his chance. He deserves to have—to have what Ruth and Jake have—children and grandchildren. He does not need an older woman—a woman who is not Jewish—as his wife."

The words rang out like sharp slaps to the side of her face. She felt her cheeks to relieve the terrible stinging of her skin. What was Rebecca Scher saying? How dare she? Then she pulled herself together.

"I am not, Mrs. Scher, just an 'older woman.' I am close to Jonathon's age. I probably won't have any more children, but I fail to see why our happiness should be wrecked because you want grandchildren."

"Jewish grandchildren," she said. "It is the children of the daughters of the family who pass on our Jewishness from one generation to another. My friends are not frank when their sons marry women who are not of our faith. I believe in frankness and honesty. You are an intelligent woman, Marika Wentworth, and a fine person. I feel in your heart you understand me—and even agree with me."

"I do not!" Marika felt as though she were fighting for her life. The tears welled up in her eyes, and she did her best to control the emotion which showed up in her voice the minute she began to speak.

"I love your son, with my whole heart. My only ambition in

life is to make him happy. Not only that, but I consider myself a darned fine catch for him. I am proud of who I am and what I have accomplished. So is he. We love each other, but we admire each other, too. I can't believe you are talking to me like this—not accepting me! Never in my wildest dreams would I have envisaged that you would be acting this way toward me. I thought you would walk in here, accepting me, full of happiness just because of our own happiness. Instead you are outright rejecting me!" She stood up angrily and began walking up and down the room, in a fashion she had seen Jonathon do many times when he was upset about something.

"Marika, my dear, if you truly love Jonathon, then you will have to admit that he is what he is and you can't take his Jewish tradition from him."

"I'm not trying to!" Marika's tone was one of heated anger by now. "I'm not trying to kidnap your son away from some nice young girl of whom you would approve. We are two people who happened to fall in love, quite by accident, but you can't take that away either, Mrs. Scher. We have something very powerful that unites us, not divides us!"

"I must say, I admire your spunk," the other woman said. She walked over and got her coat. "I'm sure you'll try to make Jonathon very happy." And with that, she left the room.

Jonathon walked with Marika up and down in front of her Sutton Place apartment. Lisa had gone off to meet Sergio right after the seder, and Jonathon felt his energy level subsiding rather quickly in view of the force of Marika's fury.

"I'm not considered such a bad deal by most of the people I know," she said defensively. "In fact, a lot of people would say I was extremely eligible, they would say 'lucky Jonathon,' and here your mother says, 'Fuck off.' "

"My mother would never say that."

"And I would never talk like that if I weren't so *incredibly* upset, disappointed, frustrated!"

"You are not marrying Rebecca Scher. You are marrying me,

remember?" Jonathon was feeling not only tired, but defensive about his mother. He had not expected her to make a scene, but he certainly hadn't expected his future wife to be so uncomprehending of his mother's nature. With time, his mother would come around. Why couldn't Marika sense that?

"Well, then, repudiate her. I want to hear you say it. I want to hear you say, 'Marika, my mother was a bitch to talk to you like that.' "

"You have to understand my mother. I am all she has. Her life begins and ends with me."

"Well, what about me?" she retorted angrily. "Look, Jonathon, if your mother means that much to you, why don't you marry *her*?"

"Marika, I'm asking you please to calm down first, then to realize that I could kill her for having talked to you like that, and third, to realize that she is consumed by loneliness, by having had only one child—a son with no children for her to love and fuss over. She has been wild with jealousy of her sister Ruth all these years. She feels imprisoned by her own fate."

"That has nothing, repeat *nothing* to do with me," Marika said, even angrier now. "I was expecting her to say, 'Welcome into our loving family. We're so lucky to have you, Marika.' Instead I get, 'Why don't you drop dead, Marika, because you're not one of us?' "

"I repeat what I said before, you are marrying me, not my mother. Once we're married, she will not only accept you but *love* you. We have already discussed how I would have to be with her every year for the High Holy Days and Passover, and you said that would be all right. You said that, remember?"

"Of course I did. And of course it will be all right." Her tears now streamed openly down her face.

"Well, then, that's the only pact you have to make. Nothing else matters except you and me. I don't give a damn that we won't have any children, and Mother will forget about that point once we are married and she sees how happy you have made me."

Marika buried her head in Jonathon's coat and clung to him in full view of the doorman of her building.

"Everything's going to be all right. There, there," and he soothed her and stroked her hair as if she were a child.

"I'm sorry, Jonathon, if I made you really sad with this—with this miserable meeting with your mother. I wanted it to go so well." Her voice trailed off.

"You will understand her a little bit more, once you get to know her, Marika, I promise."

That was not what Marika had wanted him to say. She had wanted him to say, "I'll never forgive my mother for acting that way." But he hadn't. She went up in the elevator to the penthouse, trying to understand what had occurred on this strange, sad day.

Marika agonized for weeks about the problem with Rebecca. Every day, no matter how she tried to forget it, she would replay the scene in the bedroom, trying to think what she could have done differently. Perhaps she should have tried harder, turned on the charm, but the truth was, no matter what she did, she would have been an "older" woman, incapable of delivering grandchildren. She promised herself that if she met Rebecca another time, she would rebuild their relationship. She could do it—somehow. Still, anger and hurt stabbed at her; she needed some validation of her relationship with Jonathon that was obviously not going to come from Rebecca Scher. She and Jonathon needed support, like any couple, from their families, not only from Lisa, but from others as well. And suddenly Marika felt again, as though it had just occurred, the death of Charlie Russell. It was always like that; when she least expected it, she was flung back to those terrible days of sadness. If only Charles Russell were here to help her.

This morning, in her office, as she did her neck rolls, the scene came unbidden to her mind once again. She wanted to talk to someone other than Jonathon. At the stroke of nine, she dialed her Great-Aunt Victoria's number.

"Aunt Victoria, I long to see you. I've lost sight of you these last few months."

"I long to see you, too, my dear, to learn the reason for this call. Something is obviously up—or down—I don't know which."

Marika smiled as she imagined her great-aunt having breakfast in bed that very moment, clad in a shower of lace and propped up against a gaggle of pillows, all trimmed in lace, too. Marika pictured her pale blue wicker breakfast tray, with a blue and white Pratesi flowered linen place mat and napkin, and one of her exquisite Cantonese blue and white porcelain breakfast sets. There would be a fresh garnet rose on the tray, in a tiny crystal teardrop bud vase. Great-Aunt Victoria still lived like a tasteful aristocrat *should* live, complete with maids in black uniforms and starched white organdy aprons. Her cook, with her since her wedding day and now, like Great-Aunt Victoria, eighty-nine years of age, still turned out delicious meals in the kitchen on a big Garland stove, worthy of being in a restaurant kitchen.

"Can't I want to see you without a specific reason, just because I like to touch base and see how you're coming along?" Marika asked playfully.

"You know perfectly well that you know that I am fine, except for my regular arguments with the rheumatologist at the Hospital for Special Surgery. He and I still have at it once a month, and the situation is forever the same. Whatever he tells me I must do for my arthritis, I do exactly the opposite. That's why I am still functioning better than most people."

Marika laughed again. "I can picture you right now, Aunt Victoria, with your left arm bolstered by one of your mother's crocheted Irish lace pillows, and you're having tea, orange juice, a soft-boiled egg, dry whole-wheat toast, and honey."

"You are meticulously correct, as always, Marika. I might also add everything is getting cold, so get on with it."

"May I drop by to see you late this afternoon?"

"Of course you may," she answered, sounding very pleased. "But I haven't been out in a week now. Instead of coming to this musty old place, let's have tea at the Stanhope, down the street."

"Wonderful. What time should I pick you up?"

"Four o'clock would be fine, and don't pick me up. Meet me there. Eleanor will walk me down there. It's only a few blocks, and she can do the grocery shopping while we're having tea. The walk will do me good."

"Aunt Victoria, you just referred to your apartment as 'this musty old place.' Why won't you let me arrange for your apartment to be freshly painted, and some new upholstery and drapery work done?"

"And spend all that money to make the place nice for the next person who lives in it after my body is carried out feet first? I should say not! You may be the most accomplished woman in the business world in our family, but you don't know everything about spending money wisely, and you never have known."

Marika smiled again at the affectionate rebuke that Great-Aunt Victoria felt privileged to give everyone in the family, regardless of his or her age or position. Victoria, the last surviving member of her mother's clan to bear the Stuyvesant name, was worth several million dollars. No one had ever counted her assets, so no one knew exactly. Her Fifth Avenue apartment, high up overlooking the reservoir and the Metropolitan Museum in Central Park, had not been redecorated for perhaps thirty years. It was kept scrupulously clean by her staff, but was now threadbare and lugubrious-looking. At every window hung lace curtains that had been darned in several places; heavy garnet velvet draperies, tied back with tired gold-fringed swags of velvet, flanked the sides of the windows. Priceless orientals covered every floor of the fifteen-room apartment; there was even a seventeenth-century oriental runner down the servants' hall. The furniture was baronial, dark carved oak, some of it Gothic in design, much of it looking like the furnishings of the robber baron Gould's house, "Lyndhurst," above New York on the banks of the Hudson. Large beautiful bronzes of panthers and elephants, complete with real ivory tusks, were scattered through the apartment, and so were Chinese bowls full of Victoria's favorite potpourri. There was always a distinctive exotic fragrance in Victoria's apartment from her potpourri, sometimes so strong one could barely taste the fragrant, spicy tea she served her visitors.

Victoria, who had married a Stuyvesant at age nineteen, had been the unchallenged queen of Boston society for half a century, but after her husband's death, she moved herself to New York, and never went back again, except for the funeral of her beloved

nephew-in-law, Marika's father, Charlie Russell. She was still tall
and erect, her snow-white thick hair expertly coiffed into a chignon
every morning by her maid. Marika had always been her pet,
because, as she was fond of saying, "Finally there's a woman in
the family who knows how to take care of herself, regardless of
what the men in the family are up to." When Marika married
David, she sent them around the world for three months on their
honeymoon, and every year she would give Marika a piece of her
jewelry, saying, "Save them all until you have enough to turn them
in and have them redesigned into something magnificent!" Marika's jeweled Schlumberger fish and the amethyst, diamond, and
peridot necklace and earrings were the result of four Christmases
of Victoria's generosity.

At 3:55 P.M., Marika's car service dropped her off at the
Stanhope. She would never have allowed herself to be late for her
great-aunt. She saw her now, only a half-block away, walking tall,
in spite of her arthritis, with one hand on her ivory and jewel-
headed cane and her other arm in faithful Eleanor's. Marika ran
up to greet her, and embraced Eleanor whom Victoria then sent
off to the Madison Avenue food shops. They walked together into
the lobby of the Stanhope and to the tea place, *Le Salon*, on the
left.

The grand lady set herself down in a gingerly fashion on one
of the ivory Louis XVI chairs, upholstered in pale green and white
striped fabric to match the fabric on the walls. "I like this place,
it's warm and cozy," she said approvingly, as she looked at the
green flowered geometric carpet and the painted green trellis
ceiling overhead. A sparkling crystal chandelier cast light on the
paintings of occasional French landscapes and beach scenes hanging on the walls. The room was soundless except for the gentle
hissing of the boiling water for the tea and the occasional scurrying
of waitresses' feet across the carpet. There were only two other
tables occupied at that hour.

The two women studied the menu of teas, from Fortnum &
Mason, House of Twining, Jacksons of Piccadilly, and Grace Rare
Teas, while the waitress in her black uniform with white organdy
apron patiently stood by, her order book ready. Before Marika

could ask Victoria which tea she would prefer, the old woman blurted out from behind her menu, "I suppose we are going to discuss Mr. Scher. I'll have the black currant tea, please, and scones with Devonshire cream, finger sandwiches, and a strawberry tart."

Marika swallowed quickly and entered into the rhythm of ordering. "I'll have the Lapsang Souchong, please, and the finger sandwiches. That will be all."

"What makes you think the purpose of this tea is to discuss Mr. Scher?" Marika asked, amused.

"Because at your father's funeral, when you weren't shedding all kinds of appropriate tears, you were looking absolutely lopsided over this stranger. I tried to figure out who he was and couldn't. Then I tried to reason why he was there and couldn't. Now maybe those mysteries will be solved." The graceful matriarchal head with its intense lavender eyes turned to face Marika, in order to give her her absolute attention.

"I didn't think I was that obvious about Jonathon's presence at Daddy's funeral."

"Perhaps I overreacted, but I thought it was strange, with your father freshly dead, to have someone there, in the bosom of your family and close friends, someone whom your father never even met."

"I'm in love with him.

"That is quite apparent."

"He is Jewish."

"I know that. When we talked on Beacon Street, he told me he was of the Conservative Jewish faith, and we had an interesting discussion about the different burial customs. I found his to be far more interesting than ours—the sitting shivah customs, for example."

"No one in the family has ever intermarried before," Marika said without being defensive, "and it's high time we descended from our holier-than-thou Episcopalian niche."

"That was for me to say, my dear Marika, not for you to say."

"Sorry, Aunt Victoria. I'm thinking out loud, I guess."

"Are you ready to cope with discrimination?"

"There's no discrimination in New York."

"How you can be so worldly wise and totally naive at the same time absolutely astounds me. What about private clubs' discrimination? Are you ready never to take it out on Jonathon if the going gets rough? If some 'society' bigot idiot called him a 'kike' behind his back, are you ready to turn the other cheek?"

"Sticks and stones may hurt my bones, but names will never harm me. And as for private clubs that don't want me because of him, they are the last place I want to be. That is *no* loss."

"I'm just testing, just testing," Victoria said, pretending to ward off imaginary blows from Marika, and shifting her weight to sit more comfortably in the chair.

"And what do his parents think of your marriage," Victoria continued with her interrogation. "How do they feel about you?"

"His father is dead. His mother—well, his mother—" and she did not finish, but looked at her tea, steeping in its pot, waiting to be poured into a Limoges china teacup.

"I take it Mamma is not all that thrilled."

"She is not."

"Well, I don't blame her."

Marika's eyes lit up. "This is not the reaction I expected from you, of all people."

"From her point of view, you are most unsuitable, my dear Marika, and I'm sure, from your point of view, you would be suitable for anyone."

"Aunt Victoria, why are you taking this position?"

"Because I want you to understand how a devout Jewish mother, who is widowed and has no other children, how she would feel about her son marrying out of her faith. Don't ask to be accepted with open arms."

"You weren't even present at my meeting with Jonathon's mother, you have no idea what happened."

"No, but I probably could write the scenario. I'm asking you to look hard at what you are entering into, so that you do not take it out on your future husband, so that you never blame him for any—however small—acts of discrimination committed against you, and so that you realize that to your future mother-in-law, you're not a gift from God. And you may have to work a lot harder than you want to earn her affection."

"*What* kind of discrimination are you talking about? For goodness sake, this is New York!"

"There is hidden, secret discrimination nonetheless. Racial and religious discrimination are insidious; they hurt, and they're *there*. You are mature enough to know how to handle it, I would presume? And your love is strong enough to buttress you against it?"

"Aunt Victoria." Marika felt her voice rising with emotion in the small salon, so she lowered it immediately, not wanting the entire Stanhope Hotel tea salon to partake of such an emotional moment. "I love Jonathon so much, there is nothing that could ever happen in our lives together that would affect our relationship or cause me to desert him. I would work hard to compensate for any sorrow he might feel himself. I would be there for him. We are not going to have any trouble whatsoever."

"I like your answer. I had to joust with you a little, Marika, to see just how really much you love him. You've been sheltered all your life. You've had the right name, gone to the right schools, always been accepted everywhere. Your credentials have always been 'in place,' so to speak. Now you are marrying someone from a different background, but you maintain you love him enough to overcome any problems that may ensue."

"I *do* love him enough, and more. I wanted you to know about him and welcome him into your life, Aunt Victoria."

"You know that there is no question of my welcoming him," the old lady replied. "I liked him when I met him at the funeral and it's high time there's another wedding in your life."

They sipped their tea, and the waitress approached to put down two empty plates on their table and a platter of small, assorted, crustless sandwiches—watercress, cucumber and dill, egg with chives, tomato, chicken breast, and smoked Scotch salmon. She quickly returned with Victoria's hot scones, the Devonshire cream, butter, and assorted jams. "I'll bring you the sweet in a bit," she announced, and returned to her serving post after inspecting the two teapots, to see if more tea or hot water were needed.

"I shall welcome this young man with enthusiasm into the Stuyvesant family, Marika," Victoria said, reinforcing her approval. "And now that the food has arrived, you may spend the next twenty-five minutes, before Eleanor arrives to walk me home, extolling the brilliance and the virtues of Mr. Jonathon Scher. Tell me *everything* about him."

After Marika had finished speaking nonstop about Jonathon, her great-aunt reminded her of an open invitation she had often extended.

"As you know, I can no longer travel as far away as Switzerland. My chalet is sitting there in Saanenmöser, kept clean, and, my housekeeper there assures me, with fresh water ice cubes and a well-stocked bar ready for use by anyone I should send to the house. When you are next in Zurich on business, remember to use it. Perhaps Jonathon would," and she gulped at having even suggested such an immoral invitation, "would like to go there with you before the wedding."

A half hour later, when Marika said good-bye to her Great-Aunt Victoria, she stood watching for a minute as the old lady and her companion moved painfully back up the avenue. She had her aunt's blessing. Victoria would never know how much that meant to her.

"It's so damnably frustrating," he said gruffly, tracing the lines in the palm of her hand, "seeing you in bits and snatches, on weekends between long trips, as though we were both married to other people and having an illicit affair."

"I know, I know," she said soothingly, moving over on the black leather sofa in his Michigan Avenue apartment to snuggle closer to him.

"We just don't have enough time. I'm always jumping on a plane, and you are, too. We can't even finish a conversation. I'm angry that you only told me yesterday you could get away this weekend." There was no doubt about it. He sounded seriously upset.

"Jonathon, we can't rush things. We have to go *piano piano*."

"Why don't you speak English, for God's sake? We have arrived at the point where your throwing around your precious European phrases that I don't understand doesn't make sense anymore." He was both tense and furious now, she decided. A little mean, too.

"Why can't we just relax? We're together now, that's what matters. We have the whole weekend to ourselves and I want you to myself." She tried to sound relaxed and happy herself. "I love every minute I'm with you. Soon we'll have more time together. We'll go away this summer, and we'll also meet all your friends —small groups, big groups, anything you want."

"You are content, aren't you, just to let matters ride as they are now?" Jonathon got up from the sofa and went over to the bar to pour himself a glass of soda. "Want some?" he asked, distracted.

"No, thanks. Jonathon, you're pacing around like a nervous lion in a cage. What's the matter?"

"It's just that—it's—" He stopped, flushed in his face, and sat down on the sofa again.

"Go on, get it out. You have something to say that you're having trouble with."

"We seem to be going nowhere," he said, looking very glum. "I can't bear to be without you, yet I always seem to be. And you don't seem to be bothered by these continual separations."

"I *do* care about these separations, Jonathon." She spoke passionately, and cupped her hands around his face. "I think about you day and night. I hate it every time you walk out my door, or every time you go off in that car of yours, leaving me on the sidewalk, on your way to some foreign country or other. But you have to realize that I have a daughter—as well as a business to run. I have even more responsibilities than you, Jonathon."

"If you said that to make me feel better, you're doing a lousy job of it."

"I'll say it this way then." Marika leaned forward and kissed him long and hard on the mouth.

Then she put her head on his shoulder, snuggling into his neck. He smelled so good to her. His sweater felt so soft and his neck was warm and comforting. She knew he liked it, too, when she nuzzled him. "You're like a puppy dog," he had told her once.

"We're not going forward," he said in a husky tone of voice. He was full of desire to have her, right then and there, but there were many things left unsaid. He had had a dream last night—and the thought of it made him laugh outright—in which he was talking to himself in a mirror. He had held a conversation with himself, chiding himself on not getting things settled with Marika. "If you spent less time fucking and more time talking, you might get things straightened out," the mirror image had said to him.

"Look," he said, "I've told you many times that I love you. I want to marry you. I want you to be my wife and to live with me, not off in another city from which you take as many planes to other destinations as I do."

"I can't just change my life that abruptly," Marika answered, pulling away from him so she could face him. She couldn't have a conversation like this one with her face buried in his neck. "I have a home for Lisa. I have a payroll of thirty-six employees to meet. Jonathon, give me time."

"Lisa is a grown-up young lady. Maybe you haven't noticed she's with Sergio much more than she's home. Maybe you've forgotten that many college students live away from home, in dorms or apartments."

"It takes time to arrange all that," she pleaded.

"But you're not even starting to move in that direction. You're content just to have this long distance romance. I, for one, am not!"

"You really are upset, aren't you?" Her tone was now more sympathetic. "Look, Jonathon, help me out. Help me think through what I'm going to do with my company. It can't run by itself. I'd have to live in New York half the time."

"The company comes ahead of me, obviously."

"Look," she said, now feeling her own cheeks inflame, "you're putting the whole blame on me. What about your mother? How do you think I feel about her disapproval?"

"Marika, for God's sake, what my mother feels about you does not enter into our plans whatsoever. Don't bring my mother up again! She shouldn't be made the scapegoat for whatever isn't going right between us." He was completely angry now, and began to pace up and down the length of the living room, staring at the pattern in the Portuguese green and yellow abstract rug.

She knew she had been wrong to bring his mother into this discussion. Why was she so vindictive on this subject, so ungiving? Well, she was.

"Jonathon, look, sit down. I can't bear to see you this upset." She patted the sofa beside her. He stayed where he was.

"I am an impatient person. I've always been a man of action. I don't pussyfoot around. I know what I want, and I happen to want you. If you don't want me, then I'd better hear it right now, and we won't waste any more time. I'm not a kid, Marika. I'm lonely without you. I want you—all the time. I don't want the damn telephone receiver to remind me of how you look, how you feel, how you smell—" He threw himself down beside her, took her in his arms, and kissed her.

She drew back. "That was a kiss with more roughness than sweetness to it."

"I'm sorry, God, I'm sorry, Marika." He put his head in his hands.

"Jonathon, Jonathon." She tried again to calm and soothe him. "We're going to work this out. That will happen. Please. Just a little more patience. Let me work through some things. Let me have the time to make plans, work out solutions. It's not that I don't want to hurry, it's that I can't. Look at what I'm going through now with the company," she pleaded.

It was true, she rationalized. With Greg gone and Steve so ill, decisions had to be made. She couldn't just separate Stuyvesant Communications from her life, but deep inside her a voice seemed to be warning her, *Don't push him, Marika, you'll be sorry.* She waved the voice away. Why couldn't he understand that she had pressures, too?

"Jonathon," she pleaded, "you promised to take me on your architectural tour of Chicago. We're both emotional, heated, upset. Words aren't going to help us at this point. Let's put on our coats and get out in that cold, bracing air. Show me all those great buildings."

"That's it, Marika," he said wearily, "escape confrontation. Never decide. Never make a move. The status quo is always your choice, isn't it?"

She thought that the only way to handle this situation was to get his mind away from it, so they could both approach it again gently, calmly, rationally. Now was not the time. Perhaps tonight in bed. Right now, they should do something—anything—to change the nasty direction of this conversation. They could throw themselves into the vigorous Chicago School of Architecture tour he had promised her. He was such a good guide, so knowledgeable about architecture. They would see everything from the Frank Lloyd Wright house at the University of Chicago to the Adler and Sullivan buildings to the Mies van der Rohe experimental work in steel and glass on Lake Shore Drive to Pei's jewel of a small synagogue out in Highland Park. Her mind raced ahead almost hysterically, counting off the list of "must sees." *Anything* to get off this conversational track.

Marika was full of anticipation as she took Jonathon's arm and they left his apartment for the tour. She would make everything up to him tonight in bed. Between now and then she would find the time to sort things out, think with clarity, and decide what they, or at least *she*, should do. The ball was in her court.

Jonathon's thoughts were not half so cheerful and bright. In fact, not even a quarter as bright.

It was the first time they had not made up for it in bed, she thought to herself on the plane back to New York from Chicago. They had had a delightful time, but— A certain air of detachment, just a slight coolness, had suddenly entered the picture. He was sweet and considerate to her as always. After a wonderful dinner of veal and champagne, back in his apartment with its magnificent view overlooking the lake and up Lake Shore Drive, sparkling with the lights of the apartment buildings, she had thrown herself into bed next to him with joyous abandonment. He had made love with his usual careful tenderness, but something was missing. Something simply wasn't there. She tried to put her finger on it. She had been warmer to his touch than ever before, but the responsiveness, the appreciation was—well, just a bit lacking on his part. She dismissed it, because he was exhausted and under a great strain. She had put him under even a deeper one by not being decisive, by not making definite plans to make their marriage the number-one priority in her life.

She went back to *Vanity Fair* magazine, resolved to finish it and leave it behind on the plane before landing at La Guardia. She always did that with magazines on planes. She hauled them aboard in a big heavy tote bag, skimmed through them quickly, and then walked off the plane with a light tote bag. Today, there was a new pervasive feeling around her—one of uneasiness. She pushed it aside. Think positive. She and Jonathon would be married within the year, she was sure of it. Decisions would be made, she would move Lisa into a smaller apartment and keep Geneviève to watch over her. The apartment would have a large bedroom for her, too. After all, she would have to keep a New York base for herself. She would keep Stuyvesant Communications, Inc., not only in operation, but she would expand it. She would open a Chicago office, take Hortense with her, and see who on the staff would like to move out there. She would recruit in Chicago— good people. She would keep the New York clients and increase those in the Midwest. It wouldn't take more than a year. There was a lot of business out there in Chicago.

Then she remembered how Jonathon's words in his Chicago apartment had stung when he had said, "The difference between you and me, Marika, is that I love you enough to make the commitment, to go whole hog, to get married and to make it work. If I wait around long enough for you to come to grips with all of your concerns, all of your problems of juggling that grow more intense every month, it seems to me, by then we'll both be in our seventies. I don't have that kind of patience. You either love me enough to compromise, to accept, and to resolve, or you don't."

Lisa wasn't there when she opened the door to the apartment

on Sutton Place. She turned on the lights and went upstairs to her room. The house seemed cold and empty, and she wondered why she wasn't dancing a light step of joy, the way she usually did when she returned from seeing Jonathon.

"I feel better about Jonathon," she said to herself, as she did her exercises at 6 A.M. on the floor of her pale green bedroom. She had fallen into the habit of concentrating on him always when she did her boring morning exercises. The time went much faster, and thinking about him gave her a far greater sense of purpose than counting how many times she managed to get through any particular floor exercise. His call from Taiwan last night had been full of the old Jonathon, a certain tenderness that he was able to transmit over the telephone unlike any man she had ever known, including David Wentworth.

"I really hate the fact," he had said, "that I could miss anyone as much as I do you. I dislike being that enslaved to a human being."

"What would you prefer," she had asked, in a little girl's voice, "that I be your slave girl instead?"

He had roared into the telephone at that. "Marika, you're not that good an actress. For someone as independent and as much in charge as you, you'd never get away with that little slave girl stuff."

"I just thought I'd try it. I miss you, too. I lose my feminist independence when you're away for a long time like this."

"That makes me very happy," he said in a soft voice. "Maybe I should stay away longer."

Then she said to herself, "I must be doing something wrong, when Jonathon and I seem to fight now only when we're together. When we're continents apart, it's as though there had never been a hint of a problem between us." She did her scissor kicks with agile grace. Talking aloud was another way to get through her exercises.

Then she remembered how testy he had become when she corrected him the night before he left for the Far East with one of her "Marika sniffs." She had jumped on him for constantly using the word "folks."

"Don't use 'folks,' please, Jonathon, it sounds like a hick. It's so—I don't know—so uncultured," she had said.

She remembered that instead of making a joke about it, or leaning over to kiss her and say, "Yes, teacher," as he always did, he had remained absolutely silent. He had not said a word. So she had leaned over and kissed him, and said, "You are a wonderful, warm, cuddly sexy man, and I don't care if you use 'folks' or not." That had done it. He took her in his arms and forgot about her criticism.

With legs up straight, hips in the air, while she did her rapid bicycling motions, she reached with her toes toward the ceiling and pulled every muscle in the back of her thighs. She decided she had better watch those criticisms. He was no longer the eager puppy, striving for love and approval. She had better watch her step with him.

Marika waited for Jonathon in the Diplomatic Reception Room on the ground floor of the White House. He had just returned from another long Far Eastern trip, and was flying into Washington to meet her at the White House. In ten minutes the Watsons would descend to the Diplomatic Entrance from their personal quarters. The President's own helicopter sat proudly peacock-like outside on the South grounds, as it did every Friday afternoon, ready to whisk the Watsons away to the peace and quiet of Camp David.

Marika went over in her mind the dialogue that preceded the invitation from Eve to join them at Camp David this weekend. Eve, during her usual long weekly chat, had said, "Marika, I don't like it."

"Don't like what?" was Marika's reply, totally surprised.

"Something is going amiss between you and Jonathon. I can tell. Something is wrong."

"No, nothing is amiss, really. We're just having quite normal mutual butterflies involving our plans, that's all."

"Look," said the worried voice on the other end, "how about you two coming to spend a quiet weekend at Camp David with us, immediately after Jonathon returns from the Far East? We never take any friends out there, but Mac has promised to see staff only for a few hours on Saturday, and the rest of the time he'll stay free—for you two. We'd really like you to come."

"I can't imagine anything more exciting than that," Marika replied enthusiastically, "and I know Jonathon will want to say yes, too. I mean, what an invitation! A moment of history—"

"You can cut the crap," Eve said. Marika knew her friend didn't talk like that to anyone else, which is why she liked to cuss every so often in front of Marika. "Be here at four o'clock on Friday the eighteenth. Bring only slacks and sweaters—warm stuff. No jackets or ties out there in the Maryland mountains. It's cozy and informal."

Now Marika heard a stirring in the corridor outside the Diplomatic Reception Room, its walls lined with historic scenic Martin Buber wallpaper of the early nineteenth century. She had been sitting on the Duncan Phyfe sofa, upholstered in lemon yellow satin, staring almost hypnotically at the colorfully hand-painted wallpaper, fascinated particularly by the scenes of marching cadets at West Point Academy on the Hudson. How did an Alsatian manage to capture something so wonderfully, sentimentally American?

Suddenly, the door from the hall burst open, and in came Jonathon, with two White House doormen behind him, carrying his and Marika's bags. Two secret servicemen were also with him, to announce that the elevator signal had been given, that the President and the First Lady were on their way down from the private quarters. Jonathon gave Marika a peck on the cheek, all that was appropriate for the occasion, with so many people standing around, and within seconds, the Watsons appeared. Mac and Eve embraced Marika, shook hands warmly with Jonathon, and then they all rushed out the door to the waiting helicopter. The Watsons turned to their right and left to say good-bye to their staff, who were lined up outside on either side of the doorway to wish them farewell and a happy weekend.

Once inside the helicopter, the Watsons engaged in their own conversation, while Jonathon and Marika sat mesmerized by the view of the Washington monuments beneath them, the choked Friday afternoon traffic going over the bridges, and then finally the Maryland suburbs and the rolling countryside. At last they were over the gentle Catoctin Mountains. Spring had touched the mountainsides with a virgin green. Even though the air was cold outside, they all felt the warmth of the sun working hard to awaken and energize the landscape beneath them.

As always, the camp commander, a naval officer, saluted his commander-in-chief when the Watsons and their guests emerged from the helicopter. Jonathon and Marika were shown to their own cottage by a naval seaman. It was decorated in warm, bright colors. Giant logs made snapping noises in the large stone fireplace, and toasted the interior. They looked at each other and then threw their arms tightly around each other's neck. "We have exactly ninety minutes until we have to dress for dinner," Marika said.

"Then let's talk, let's sit down here," he said, untying her arms and leading her over to a country plaid wool sofa.

"I can think of better things to do with the ninety minutes," she said.

"I haven't seen you. We never have any time to really talk seriously."

"My, my," she said teasingly, "a gremlin's come between us."

"Marika," he said, toying with a strand of her hair and looking at it with seeming fascination, "I have worries about us that don't seem to abate. I can't see you cutting back all that much on your career when you marry me. And although I have met many of your friends, you have met none of mine. This isn't the first time I've brought this up."

"I'm sure I'd adore all your friends," she said, snuggling up to him.

"No, you may not 'adore' all my friends. You never stay long enough in Chicago to give me the chance to introduce them to you."

"If they're like you, how could I not think they were great?"

"They're different from—well, from Georgiana and Chauncey, the Stuart Welltons, certainly from Eve and Mac."

"From the way you acted about Georgiana's dinner, I'm sure they are." She looked him straight in the eyes. "That kind of high-flying party is not what I crave or need. I very seldom go to a party like that. That's not the life I need."

"But you seemed to fit into it like the last piece in a puzzle."

"No, you read me wrong."

"Maybe I don't know you as well as I should."

"I don't think you do. I manage to lead two separate lives. One is as the serious head of my company, and a mother, and the other is the social side. I fit into Georgiana's world, but it's not mine day in and day out. I just enjoy dropping into it once in a while—for a big party, for something fun."

"I don't do that as well as you do."

"Since you have the wrong idea about the parameters of my social life, let's move to the other point you raised, your friends. Why don't you give a party for me in Chicago, to introduce me to them?"

"This time your problem solving is off base," he said. "A big party is not how you become friends with your—your husband's friends. You spend time with them, get to know them, couple by couple."

"I don't have that much time," she said with an edge of irritation in her voice, "to keep dashing out to Chicago to have dinner with your friends, couple by couple, Jonathon."

"That's just the trouble, you don't have time for anything."

"Now come on," she said, really irritated. "Don't make me the heavy in this. You haven't been burning up the days and nights in New York, meeting my friends, spending time with my family."

"How will it work when we're married?" he asked. "Will you spend one night with me, and five in your business pursuits? Is that the way our marriage will be? One out of five?"

She pulled him up off the sofa. "Come on. Our marriage will be great. I promise you that! Leave it to me, and stop worrying," and she began to undress him. They still had seventy minutes until they had to get ready for dinner.

He didn't resist her and their bodies were as much attuned as ever. But afterward it seemed to Marika that Jonathon hurried out of her arms to dress for dinner.

The next morning Mac took Jonathon skeet-shooting on a special range he and the Secret Service agents enjoyed using together, in a competition that was obviously one-sided. Eve and Marika sat in the living room on the white linen sofa splashed with giant red and purple anemones, their feet up on the coffee table. A small silver tray sat on a purple silk pillow between them, holding white porcelain coffee cups, the gold of the rims and the presidential seal glittering in rays of sunshine that intruded through the glass French doors.

"You have no idea, Eve, what a treat this is for Jonathon and me. The fact that you two, the two busiest, most pressured people in the entire world, would think about two old pals, exhausted and burned out, and offer us the rest and exhilaration of this weekend, well—"

"It's great for us," Eve interrupted, "but I've gotta tell you, old friend, that for two people who are supposed to be madly in love, you two sure don't look it."

"We're just tired. Too much travel, too many things to decide, too much in our separate lives that don't concern the other person's life. It all presses in on us."

"You're looking great," Eve said, appreciatively eyeing Marika in her hunter green suede pants and matching tunic top. "I just wish I felt as admiring of your emotional insides as I do of your physical outsides."

Marika laughed. "Look, don't worry about us. We're going to be just fine." Her voice broke on the "just fine." She picked up her coffee cup and stared down into it.

"Last night at dinner you were testy with him, did you realize that?"

"What do you mean?" Marika felt on the defensive now.

"You made fun of him. I don't think you even realized it, but that sermon of yours!—that he should know enough to pick up firm asparagus branches and eat them with his fingers, if the sauce is only on the tips . . . For God's sake, what does his cutting his asparagus with a knife and fork while the rest of us are eating it with our fingers have to do with anything? Mac said afterward that if you had done that to him, you would have been the first woman he ever slugged!"

"I sounded *that* critical? It—it sounds downright bitchy."

"Well, it was. And then you made three snide innuendos about his mother's disapproval of you. That Passover dinner was weeks ago, yet you still ride him on it. It was unnecessary, uncalled for. I don't care how much the old girl hurt you, you should have just put that behind you. You should have forgotten it. That was the *only* way to handle it, just never refer to it again. Next year, you can let him go without you to Passover dinner with his family, and you can go to a contemplative convent to ruminate on the fate of the world, or something." Eve stopped short. "I'm sorry. I'm being hard on you, aren't I?"

"I can't help thinking," Marika said, serving herself another cup of coffee from the silver pot, with its graceful dark wood handle, "that there's something you're not telling me. You suddenly seem to be aware of all kinds of things going wrong between Jonathon and me. Why?"

"Because Jonathon called me from the Far East. That's when I invited you two to Camp David for this weekend. He is upset, Marika."

"I didn't even know you had spoken to him," Marika said crossly. "He didn't mention it. I just extended the invitation to him in one of our telephone calls. That's downright devious. He never mentioned talking to you from Taiwan or wherever."

"We had a short conversation, but it seemed to mean a lot to him to come here for the weekend. He said he could never pin you down for longer than forty-eight hours, and you were always going somewhere, doing something else during those forty-eight hours, involving people, people, people."

"Sounds like he's whining and complaining." Marika frowned, not liking the conversation at all.

"Sounds like he's hurting," Eve countered. "I just think you should be sensitive to him. You've got something good here. Don't let him slip away.

"Look," Eve said, changing her tone of voice, "I didn't ask you up to Camp David to lecture you and give you a hard time. Mac and I want you and Jonathon to have a wonderful, romantic time, so let's don't discuss it any more."

"Fine by me." The two friends went back to reading the *Washington Post* and the *New York Times*, each wanting to read the section the other one happened to be reading at that particular time, just like the days when they sat together on the sofa in their college living room, reading the papers. At a certain moment, Marika had the "Style" section of the *Post* on her lap, and was just ready to pick it up, but Eve made a quick sideswipe and snatched it out from Marika's lap before her friend could stop her. "You always used to do that to me at Vassar," Marika laughed in mock irritation.

"You haven't gotten any swifter on the defense, either." The two old friends decided to put the subject of Jonathon Scher down on the table and leave it there—for the time being.

Eve and Mac talked for a long time in bed back at the White House Sunday evening, going over the weekend in retrospect. Eve was much more depressed about Marika and Jonathon than Mac was.

"Look, Eve," he said, trying to sound positive, "those two are in love. They have great sex. It sticks out all over them like a pair of blasting sirens. I've never seen anything like it—for people, that is—our age." Eve reached over at this and punched him in the stomach. "They'll make it. They're not children. They have a real love for each other. It's apparent. You fault Marika for trying to shape up Jonathon. Well, it's just her way. She's always tried to shape up everyone within her reach. And he understands her. He obviously loves her, her bossing him, everything. He eats it up."

"Oh, how I wished I agreed with you. I think they're over-competing with each other to a perfectly ghastly degree. Well, we shall see. I have a foreboding about it all. I think they're falling apart—away from one another. A couple of Humpty Dumptys sitting on a wall, each one too pigheaded and selfish to compromise."

"Why, may I ask, are you so damn single-minded about Jonathon and Marika getting married? Why can't they just go on as they are? Then the difference in religion and her insistence on her career won't matter."

"Because there's *no one else* for her, that's why."

"Oh, forget it. There are a million men who would just love to get into Marika's pants, and certainly a million lovelies who would like to get into Jonathon's trousers."

"Don't be so disgusting," she laughed. "I'm talking about there being no one else to *marry*. I'm quite serious. Marika hasn't met a man she could marry since David died, and she's a woman who needs *marriage*, not an affair. There aren't any available good men around. Plenty of bad ones, but no one," and she turned to kiss Mac's nose, "of substance, charm, and intellect, like you, for example. They just don't exist."

Mac took the neat piles of files he had been studying on the bed and placed them on the floor.

"If anyone ever asks me why I married you," he said, before turning off the light by the side of the bed, "I'm not going to say it's because of your cooking."

This should not be happening, Marika thought to herself, sitting next to Jonathon at a big fund-raising dinner for a Jewish cause and toying with her *poulet chasseur*. For Jonathon's sake, because this was an important night to him, she had dressed with great care, wearing her hot red draped chiffon dress. He had not even noticed it.

They were growing apart, the chasm was widening, and they seemed to be standing forlornly on either side, watching in helplessness. She felt waves of tension, not support, emanating from him now in the seat next to her.

She remembered Sarah's admonition of a week ago. "Watch out, Marika, watch out. Mercury is in retrograde again!" She didn't know about the influence of Mercury, but everything did seem to be falling apart. Greg's absence from the firm was greatly missed—not his personality, but his contribution. Steve's illness was becoming more serious every week. None of these factors mattered, however, in comparison with the possibility of losing Jonathon. They were sniping at each other. The great energy level they had shared and exulted in had gone into a negative drive. Her nerves were rubbed raw, exposed like electrical wiring when the baseboards are removed.

She was tired. The fast march forward of Marika Wentworth's career was veering in another direction. The seemingly endless path upward to success, love, and admiration was suddenly zigging backward. For the very first time in her life she was feeling like a loser, and she did not like that feeling at all. To have this perfect man in her life, this supporter, comforter, lover, starting to back off and away made her feel as though everything around her was dismal, slippery, and sliding.

She also did not want to be here tonight, in the Waldorf's Grand Ballroom, at a jam-packed fund-raiser. She was out of sorts with everything. She hated it when people stood up, gave their names, and mentioned vast sums of money they were donating. To her, it was just bragging, flaunting wealth, inviting praise.

"I hope that if you are going to donate to this good cause, you don't plan on standing up and announcing it to the world like that, Jonathon."

"And why not?" His voice was sharp, combative.

"Because—"

"Because what?"

"Because charity is best when it is anonymous, not when everyone pats you on the back because you've publicly announced it, and says gee whiz, Money Bags is really coughing up tonight. It makes me feel—uncomfortable."

"This is your polite way, Marika, of saying that you do not wish me to stand up tonight and announce my donation publicly?"

"Exactly."

"And if, in your eyes, it is vulgar to do this, then you are saying it is a Jewish vulgarity to make your generosity public. May I remind you of all the buildings around the country bearing the name *Rockefeller*, or *Carnegie, Astor,* or *Ford?* Do you call that anonymous philanthropy?"

"I didn't mean it the way you took it, Jonathon."

"Marika, we've got to have a talk."

"We can't—here," and she looked around the table at the other guests in their black ties and evening dresses, engaged in animated conversation.

"Let's go," he said, and with that, he pulled her chair back and took her by the arm, propelling her at some speed out of the ballroom, into the east elevators of the Waldorf, and down to the main lobby.

"Let's go home," she said wearily, "where we can relax and get on even keel again."

"Oh no," he said. "I'm putty in your hands in that apartment of yours, you know that. Too many times I've wanted to have the conversation we're about to have, and you sit down next to me and I forget every damned word I was ever going to say to you. Tonight let's stay on very neutral, nonphysical territory." He steered her by the elbow into Peacock Alley, the bar and restaurant on the main floor where Marika was first brought by her mother and father when she was four years old.

They sat on a banquette against the wall, Jonathon ordered a bottle of champagne, and then he turned to look at her.

"Funny, isn't it, that I automatically ordered champagne, because I know how much you love it, and so do I, and it's supposed to be a symbol of celebration?"

"Yes," she said, smiling at him and feeling a warm surge of love in her heart for him.

"Well, tonight, it's going to represent something far different. Marika, let's face it, we're not going to make it."

"What do you mean, we're not going to make it?" She had sat bolt upright and grabbed his hand in both of hers, gripping it so tight, it hurt him.

The waiter poured two glasses of champagne and left the bottle in a bucket of ice on their table.

"We should have had this conversation long ago."

"Why? Jonathon, what's happened? Why are you talking like this? Every couple has difficult times in a relationship, but they talk it out."

"You don't talk anything out!" he said sharply. "You know damned well things haven't been going well between us, and I'm not talking about problems that can be solved. I'm talking about basic fundamental differences that are irreconcilable."

"All right, let me have it, both barrels. I'm waiting."

"No one," he said with great earnestness, now holding both her hands and looking deep into her eyes, "wanted this to work more than I. I was madly in love with you—no, let me correct that—I *am* madly in love with you, but we're too different, and we're just not going to make it."

"I always felt that the differences between us made us more attracted to each other."

"No, they don't, frankly. Look, I'll speak straight from my heart, and it's going to hurt, I warn you. It's going to hurt a lot."

"All right, I'll put on my suit of armor. Go ahead," Marika said quietly and sadly, looking down, unable to face him while he was on this verbal rampage.

"Look, I didn't come from your background. I didn't go to St. Paul's or Deerfield, I didn't go to Harvard, Princeton, or Yale—"

"Jonathon!" she interrupted sharply, "what difference has that ever made? Why are you bringing up such a trumped-up excuse?"

"I asked you to listen to me. I'm asking you again. Don't interrupt. Let me speak, and then you can speak, okay?"

"Okay."

"We have different backgrounds, and instead of accepting me exactly as I am, you have been unconsciously trying to mold me into your idea of a perfect man from the right background, with the correct mannerisms. At first it was amusing. I stopped wearing my diamond ring, I changed from the white limo, I corrected my table manners, I did all the little things you faulted me on."

"We laughed about that, for heaven's sake," she said, breaking her promise not to interrupt. "It's not fair of you to hold that against me now. That wasn't serious. That was all a joke between us."

"Marika, you just didn't realize that underneath, it hurt. It wasn't a joke to me, even though I pretended it was. You remember when you made fun at Camp David of my cutting the asparagus when everyone else was picking up the branches in their fingers, well, I absolutely *hated* your doing that. You didn't know it, but it was damned humiliating." He paused and then continued, because Marika was unable to speak at this point.

"You are you. You want everybody to be like you, because you've heard all your life that you do the right thing, say the right thing, and are the right thing. I was grateful at first for all those little 'Marika sniffs' of yours. But then, all of a sudden, I didn't like it any more. It began to grate on me. You weren't aware of it, but you should have been."

"Why didn't you let me know? Say *something*? I had no idea it was getting to you that much. It was stupid of me not to know, unfeeling of me, too, I guess, but why didn't you say something?"

"Because every time I resolved to talk to you about this, you'd turn those beautiful green eyes of yours on me, and I'd touch you and turn to melted plastic, and I could never even think about discussing it. I am physically addicted to you, to put it mildly, and that's why I have to keep at a distance in order to talk frankly to you. That's why we're having this talk in Peacock Alley, for God's sake."

She took her glass of champagne and drank the entire contents in one gulp.

"Heh," he said laughing, "*piano piano*, to use your favorite expression. . . . But then," his expression grew serious, "other things happened. You didn't even try to understand my mother, Marika. She had no right to attack you the way she did. I understand your anger and disappointment, but I can't help feeling that if there was real love between us, you would have said to yourself, I'll tame that Rebecca Scher. I'll *make* her like me, just to keep peace in the family."

"I could have. I would have, Jonathon. I will." She was pleading now, and there were little sobs interrupting the rhythm of her words.

He stopped her. "But you didn't. I looked down the road and saw nothing but problems there, even though my mother lives on the West Coast. It wasn't the problems so much—it was the lack of love on your part to head them off at the pass, before they were blown into big crises."

He watched her for a moment, as she struggled to hold back those tears that always seemed to come. Damn her, he thought, so emotional, looking so tragically beautiful and desirable at this very moment. He made a fist, as if to drive away the love he felt for her.

"Look, Marika, we're in our forties. If we were in our twenties, we could work out all kinds of things and grow together. Instead we grew by ourselves in different directions. What happened tonight, upstairs in the ballroom was, from my point of view, absolutely unforgivable. Marika, you've got to face it. You're basically anti-Semitic!"

"Jonathon!" She said his name in a shocked, angry voice, and suddenly, she had no more words to follow.

"You haven't tried to comprehend, understand, adapt, and accept, which is the basis of a relationship between a Jew and a Christian who marry. Two people have to work at it, not one. Marika, I love you, I probably will never forget you through my whole life, I will probably miss you every single goddamn night I can't either feel your body next to mine or hear your voice on the telephone. But our life in bed isn't the only important thing. Other things matter. You're a powerhouse all by yourself. You're a raving success in life. You attract people like flies. You don't need me, and I expect to be needed. I expect to be loved, needed, and adjusted to. I want a wife by my side, not off in Zurich in a chocolate factory, for God's sake. In our relationship, I did all the adjusting. It's worn me out. I want out, Marika, it's as simple as that."

She had no words to express what was in her heart. Protests, excuses, promises weren't relevant tonight. He had issued an ultimatum, an unqualified one. He did not leave the door open a crack. He had locked it. They talked for a few minutes more, and then he dropped her off at her apartment. It was over—like that, she thought. A beautiful flame had just been extinguished like two fingers snuffing out a candle—pinching the burning wick. What was left of the wick was now cold, charred, brittle.

She expected to hear from him by seven the next morning at home, before she left for the office. They were so good on the telephone, she and Jonathon. They had laughed over the fact that no two people in history, because of the distance separating them and their competing schedules, had ever put in so much time whispering words of love over telephone wires. Those pillow chats. They would make it all up over the telephone this morning, even though they were facing their office days, not bedtime. And the next time they were together, bedtime would be sweet. She would see to that.

The telephone did not ring. She managed to get to the office, but she told Hortense to hold all calls unless one came from Jonathon. She sat for two hours, her head on her arms on the desk, eyes closed, trying to reconstruct why this disaster had suddenly happened. Then, in a complete non sequitur, she remembered how she had felt at eight years of age, when her precious four-foot-high doll's house collapsed without reason in a corner of her bedroom, leaving only rubble and broken objects, each and every one of which had been so loved by her. She remembered sitting there on the floor stunned and uncomprehending. It was the very same feeling now.

Hortense knew what had happened without questioning her. Hortense read her face and simply left her alone, reassuming her guardian position outside the boss's door, waving curious staff members away, holding all the calls, and fingering the sterling silver beads of her necklace like a rosary, praying in vain for Jonathon Scher to call.

Marika finally raised her head from her arms and once again took action. She wrote Jonathon a long, long letter which Hortense then took down to the Federal Express office in the lobby. It was a letter written from her heart, with total spontaneity, without thinking it out ahead or correcting it, a letter exposing raw emotions, in which she told him she was wrong, that she loved him too much to lose him, that *she* would be the one to make all the changes in their relationship. He would not have to do anything. It was a humbling experience to write those pages. She had laid her total vulnerability wide open, on the record. She had taken all the blame, but she kept thinking that perhaps there was at least a little blame on Jonathon's part—wasn't there? There was strength to her pride, not just fallibility.

No answer came, no calls, no response to her letter. Marika's pride then took over. Since Jonathon had shut the door on her, she closed out what had happened between them. It was like throwing all of the undone household chores and office work into an empty closet, so the house looks straight before the guests come. Hide the mess and forget about it.

When Marika's Great-Aunt Victoria called the Sutton Place duplex in the evening two days later, Lisa answered and said her mother simply wasn't taking calls for the moment. When a worried Victoria asked why, Lisa stated with great simplicity, "You remember the love of Mom's life, Jonathon? Well, Mom blew it." Victoria didn't question her further. She simply sent over a basket full of bright-colored anemones for Marika, with a card that read, "This too shall pass."

Funny. Two weeks had passed since that night at the Waldorf. A fortnight is a short time, Marika said to herself, but somehow it seemed like the first forty years of her life all over again. She had managed to speak of Jonathon to no one. Not even Eve and Mac knew what had happened. She would tell them in due course. Lisa knew only that Jonathon had vanished from her life because her mother had "screwed up." Hortense and her staff knew without interrogation that the romance was over, and it was better left without editorial comment, either to her or about her.

Yet she hardly knew herself. She couldn't believe that there was still no word, no sign, nothing from Jonathon, after they had meant so much to each other these past months. Either she had meant absolutely nothing in his life other than a bright drawing room comedy, or he was too embarrassed and chagrined to be able to approach her. To her, either reason for his refusal to contact her was unacceptable. He had slammed the door; she would bolt it tightly.

There was no joy anymore in her work at Stuyvesant Communications. The usual ebullience she felt upon arising in the morning and preparing for the day at the office was gone. The delightful curiosity she had always felt, the anticipation of what the day would be like and the surprises it would bring, was simply not there. It had become a chore just to rise and start her day. She had not even been exercising the past two months because of worrying over the course of their affair. Now the course had been decided. They had broken up. She felt an unwelcome softness to her waistline and thighs. She would not go to pot physically, for God's sakes. No man was worth that. She put a big sign up on the inside of her full-length closet mirror: DIET AND EX-ERCISE!

She had two options, after all—either to enter a deep depression or to become a take-charge person again. The latter course was obviously the one to take. She would get on with her business life and suppress her personal one, if that's what it took to become a well-functioning human being again. Who needs a man anyway? She had lived happily and well without one since David's death. She could do it again.

On Marika's next trip to Washington for a Flairhotels meeting, Eve asked her to lunch at the F Street Club. They lunched alone in the privacy of the high-ceilinged, cozy library of the great nineteenth-century house.

Eve looked at her watch. "It is now 12:55 P.M. I made a firm promise to Mac that must be upheld, that I would give you the third degree about Jonathon for exactly five minutes and no more. Mac is of the opinion that you don't pry when your best friend is hurting, that you let it come from the other person. He and I happen to be of different schools, so I'm compromising. I expect you to tell me about this mess, but no more than you want to. I won't make a federal case out of it."

Marika laughed. "God bless Mac."

"All right, I'm timing myself. Question number one: What remedial action, if any, have you taken in regard to this unfortunate turn of events?"

"I wrote Jonathon a letter that very night, after the Peacock Alley episode, and Federal-Expressed it the next day to Chicago. I said that I had acted in a shameful, selfish, bigoted manner," Marika continued, "that everything he accused me of was true, but that I loved him, adored him, would do anything to get him back, and would never again displease him, if he only would give me a chance. I told him he was perfect as he was, and that my trying to change him had been a mistake—a sad, sorry one. I told him I would make his mother accept me, that I could do it, I knew I could."

"My God! You gave away the store and everything in it! All right, what was his response?"

"Nothing." Marika made ridges in the white damask tablecloth with her fork.

"Didn't he answer in any way? Any word at all from him in these past two weeks?"

"None whatsoever."

"Bad. Let's go a little further. After all this, shall we say, 'dose of bitter reality,' do you still want to marry the guy, move to Chicago, put up with his mother, put your career on hold in deference to him?"

"I would gladly do all of that."

"My God, you must hurt really badly then."

"I've been a good actress around Lisa, around the office. I'm *dying* inside. Everything seems to have gone wrong at once. Funny, I can handle all the company stuff, but Jonathon has left too big a hole. I just can't seem to pull myself together."

"Bad. Okay, the inquisition is over. No more questions, no more discussion about Jonathon. I found out what I needed to know, and now it's time for you to heal, to put him behind you, and think about the wonderful positive things that have always surrounded you. You had a great life before he ever appeared on the scene. You'll have a great life after him."

Richard, the maître d' of the club, brought them a piping hot cheese soufflé, and the two old friends talked rapid fire until two o'clock about Mac, the White House, Marika's clients, Lisa and Sergio—everything but Jonathon Scher. When they arrived at the North Portico of the White House, Eve got out. Her car was to accompany Marika to her next appointment. Before she started up the steps, she leaned into the car to give her friend a kiss on the cheek. "You know," Eve said, "for someone who's glued together with weak library paste, you're doing a pretty good job. We love ya, I hope you realize that. I'll call you this week to check up on things."

CHAPTER

13

The day had begun badly for Marika. At six-thirty her telephone rang. It was Georgiana.

"Chauncey and I are off to Palm Beach, but I know you're always up at this God-awful hour," she said. "You are, aren't you?" suddenly worried that she had called too early.

"Always up. How are you?"

"How I am is beside the point. I know you are devastated, because I talked to Eve and it was she who said I should give you a call to cheer you up. So I was going to do just that—when we got to Palm Beach. But then—but then—last night Demetri called me to tell me he had heard that you and Jonathon were finished and that Jonathon had a serious new girlfriend, someone almost half his age. Just like that! I thought you ought to know, damn it. I think a woman needs to know these things so she can hold her head up high and say to the world, 'I don't give a shit.'"

"Well, I don't, although I'd use a substitute word."

"Don't try to be heroic or even well bred with me. Go ahead and cry or something."

"No, Georgiana, I'm all right. Do you—do you know her name or anything?"

"Only that she's very young, unemployed, and smashing look-ing. And husband-hunting. Her name is something like Barbara Frankel."

"I'm glad to know. One should know things like this, Geor-giana, but I'm all right, and I'm not hurting, and life goes on full force at this end."

"I'm glad, darling. You're brave and strong, not like the rest of us. I'd be a sniveling idiot if it had happened to me. In fact, it *has* happened to me so many times that I should have invested in a tissue manufacturing company. I would have been a rich woman by now."

"You are a rich woman by now," Marika reminded her.

"Oh, that's right!" Georgiana's laughter tinkled like a chan-delier's crystal droplets moving in the breeze.

"Listen, I know you have to rush, that Chauncey is waiting for you. Thank you for the intelligence report. Just think, you won't have to give them to me anymore, since I'm really not interested."

"Yeah," she said sarcastically, "don't give me that stuff. When a man hurts you, it hurts for months and months, like an insect's stinger under your skin that becomes infected."

"And on that heartening, cheerful thought," Marika said, smil-ing through the telephone at her passionately caring friend, "I say thank you for being so concerned, Georgiana, and have a great trip to Palm Beach. Love to Chauncey, and you were really nice to call me. I mean it—I really appreciate what you've just done."

"How I wish I could do more for you," she said sadly. "I did as you once told me to. I started calling Eve at the White House twice a month and actually got through each time. I guess she likes to talk to real people on the outside, and last time, we spent half an hour telling each other that this should never have hap-pened to you, of all people. And we both had thought he was so divine! Show me a divine man who doesn't turn into a rat," she said bitterly.

"Good-bye, Georgiana."

. . .

The depression had been obvious to everyone since the breakup with Jonathon. It had affected her work, too, something that not even pneumonia or a broken leg had ever done to her performance in her past. She had let some matters slip between her fingers. She had even forgotten some deadlines, unacceptable behavior no matter who did it. It was, however, her demeanor that upset those around her the most. The spark was gone—as were the fire in her eyes and the energy in her movements. She had become listless. Lisa and Hortense talked to each other each day about it, and today, at seven in the morning, were chatting to each other from their respective bedrooms at home.

"You say that Mom's work is hurting, too?" asked Lisa, almost not believing it.

"Definitely yes. But I don't care about that. It's her heart that's hurting the most. Every time I think of what that Jonathon Scher did—walking out on her! He's not good enough to serve as a rug beneath her feet." Lisa laughed at this remark, but Hortense went right on with her emotional diatribe. Her boss could walk out on a man, but no man could dare do it to her.

"I keep sticking imaginary pins in a voodoo doll, hoping it will hurt him," she added.

Lisa chuckled again. "Look, I'm upset about Mom just as much as you are, but don't forget, she's strong. You know perfectly well *how* strong she is. And she'll come around. She'll mend from this. We'll help her. She always helps me with Sergio, so now I'm going to turn the tables."

Now it was Hortense's turn to smile at Lisa's comparison of her spats with Sergio to Jonathon's desertion.

"What tack do you think we ought to take, Hortense?"

"Let's get her busy. I'm doing my best to get her involved in office stuff, but we don't have much new business around here, and it's the new projects that challenge your mother. She's not very happy servicing Greg's and Steve's old accounts, which is what she's doing now."

"I wish I could do something about her social life," commented Lisa pensively, lying on her back on her mother's bed, having totally messed up the light green silk bedspread as usual with her impromptu calisthenics. Her legs were now straight up in the air as she performed a tensing exercise with them.

"Lisa, what is that awful noise?" Hortense asked.

"Oh, sorry," she replied, "I've been blowing and drying the new nail polish on my other hand, the one I'm not holding the telephone with. . . . We've got to get Mom away from this apartment. She's here night after night, won't accept any invitations, just won't go anywhere."

"Why don't you and Sergio take her out to dinner to Le Cirque tonight? It would do her good."

Lisa laughed again. "Can we charge the dinner to Stuyvesant Communications? I assure you that Sergio and I can't afford to take her there on our own credit."

"*I'll* pay for it," Hortense said firmly. "Her birthday is in a couple of days, and she deserves some diversion. Tell her dinner is on me, my present, and then I'll call Le Cirque to have them send me the bill."

Marika came back into her room from her morning shower to find her daughter hanging up the telephone abruptly. She also noticed that Lisa had totally decimated the bedspread again.

"Lisa, I had just made that bed! You know Geneviève is off this week. Now get off the bed and put the spread to rights, will you?"

Her daughter half-straightened the coverlet and then saluted her mother in a mock military style. "Mom, Sergio and I request the honor of your presence at dinner at Le Cirque tonight. It's Hortense's advance birthday present to you. She insists on paying for our three dinners."

Marika laughed. "I am impressed by such a formal invitation, and by Hortense's generosity, too. I love your thought of cheering me up, but I'm really very tired." She brushed back an errant strand of her daughter's strawberry hair. "I think I'll just have a tray in bed and turn in early."

"But you've been doing that for the last three months," Lisa protested, and then in as provocative a voice as she could muster, she said, "I bet Jonathon Scher isn't staying home every night, having a tray in bed."

Marika finished dressing quickly. Ever since she heard the news that Jonathon had a serious girl, she had been pushing it down into her subconscious, ignoring it as a piece of non-news. Lisa's words about Jonathon not staying home every night galvanized her into action. She grabbed her alligator handbag and her snakeskin briefcase, and called over her shoulder as she ran down the duplex apartment stairs: "Make it a table for four at seven-thirty at Le Cirque. I'll ask Hortense to join us, because I know she has never been there and it would be a real treat for her. We'll call it my birthday party, but dinner is definitely on *me*, not Hortense."

It was a busy night at Le Cirque. The three women and the young man were enjoying themselves thoroughly at their corner banquette table. A potpourri of delicious fragrances wafted toward them—white truffles in hot pasta, rack of lamb lightly flavored with garlic, chocolatey things, a variety of cheeses, hot cheese toasts, and sweet fruits. Sergio took very seriously his assignment as the escort of *"le mie tre belle donne,"* as he referred to them. On sure ground, he ordered only Italian wines for their dinner —among the very fine ones in Sirio Maccioni's cellar. He talked to each of the three in a private, flattering, and totally charming way—half naive and half sophisticated. While Lisa was telling Hortense all about life in the classrooms of Columbia University, Sergio took it upon himself to cheer up Lisa's mother.

"What does it feel like, Signora Wentworth, to be the kind of woman whose beauty makes every man in the room stare at you? They all look over at you—*segretamente*—furtively, as if they don't wish their women to know."

Marika laughed with pleasure. "That's an old line, Sergio, but I know you're trying to make me feel good—and I want you to know"—she turned now to the two women—"that it's working. I believe every word of it."

Hortense laughed along with Marika, trying to disguise the

fact that she was holding her frog's leg limply by one ankle, and didn't really know what to do with it. Marika signaled with her fork and knife that she should use them to deal with the frog at this point, and continued speaking.

"I've been selfish—feeling sorry for myself. There's no time for that, so I'm going to snap out of it—as of now. You three are terrific. Tonight was an inspiration and I thank you. Mission accomplished," and smiling, she made a brushing-off motion on the front of her dress, as though she were using a whisk broom to rid Jonathon Scher from her thoughts.

The conversation continued on a cheerful note as Marika explained the decor of Le Cirque. "You know, Ellen Lehman McCluskey did this interior several years before her death. Sirio commissioned her to do it. She was so clever, she found a château in France full of eighteenth-century paintings of monkeys masquerading as people, so she had them copied for the murals on the walls of this restaurant. Ellen used gray and apricot colors— and pinkish lighting—because she knew how to make women look beautiful."

Sergio looked at Lisa and whispered, "That's why you look even more beautiful than usual tonight." Then, afraid that the others may have heard him, and ever the diplomat, he added, "and it makes you, Signora Wentworth, even more *deliziosa*." Knowing he could not omit Hortense, he added, "and it makes you, Signorina O'Malley, with your dark hair and eyes, resemble *una bella Italiana*, even if you are Irish!"

They were eating their entrées when Jonathon walked in with a stunning young woman on his arm, her heavy dark brown hair cascading below her shoulders. Barbara Frankel's large brown eyes were carefully made up, framed by blended colors of gray-blue eye shadow, and long black mascaraed eyelashes. As they walked through the narrow aisle to a table on the other side of the restaurant, her arm was wrapped inside Jonathon's, close to his body. Everyone in the restaurant stared at them, because she was so stunning.

They were seated by a confused Sirio, who could not understand what this young woman was doing with Jonathon, when *la*

Signora Wentworth was with her daughter and friends on the other side of the room. *Curioso.*

Jonathon did not see their table for at least three minutes, because the captain was standing in front of the new arrivals, taking their drink orders. The foursome at Marika's table tore at their white rolls in silence, eating little pieces and staring glumly at their plates. They were all aware that Jonathon sat on his banquette, gazing with complete attentiveness into the dark eyes of his beautiful young companion. She had smooth olive skin, full lips reddened with a high-gloss lipstick, and her wonderful, long, luxurious hair made a sensuous frame for her face.

Lisa noticed Sergio gaping at her like a schoolboy and kicked him in the shins under the table. Marika bravely made conversation, taking a quick glance across the room every few seconds. The young woman, dressed in an expensive black crepe sheath that was cut low enough to expose half of her generous-sized breasts, wore large, magnificent diamond earrings. No wonder, Marika thought to herself, that Demetri could pass on to Georgiana the gossip that Jonathon had a new girl. Those earrings must have been purchased at Demetri's. Who knows, the purchaser might have been Jonathon. She was glad of only one thing on this terrible night—that she had followed her good sense and had not worn Jonathon's butterfly brooch.

Then she suddenly realized with a great sense of irony that this woman was to be Jonathon's wife, the mother of his children. Rebecca Scher must be overjoyed, Marika reasoned, because from the looks of the girl, she could bear many children with ease. The heavenly taste of Le Cirque's *gigot d'agneau* had suddenly turned bitter in her mouth.

For lack of anything else to say, to break the stillness, Lisa noted aloud that Jonathon had lost quite a bit of weight. "He's much thinner," she said to no one in particular. "It's probably his lousy conscience."

"He obviously lost all that weight trying to satisfy the *bambola*," Sergio blurted out, referring to Jonathon's companion. Lisa kicked him again and whispered, "You are so tactless!" Sergio reddened after realizing how callow his remark must have seemed to the others. He turned to Marika, "You must forgive me, signora. I tend to look at the world in physical terms. It's a bad habit of mine—and I meant not to cause anguish. *Mi dispiace!*"

Marika patted his hand. "It's perfectly all right. It was a witty remark, nothing more."

Across the room, she saw Jonathon sip his drink. Marika paid much attention to her meal, but something compelled her to glance up. Jonathon's shadow fell across her plate. He had came over to their table. It seemed a long time before anyone spoke. Out of the corner of her eye, Marika saw the young dark-haired woman watching them.

"Jonathon—it's, well, it's been a long time!"

The others at the table might as well have not been there. Marika's voice seemed to reverberate back at her.

Jonathon's blue eyes, backlit by the dining room's famed subtle lighting, turned to gray.

"Marika, Lisa, Sergio, Hortense—it's good to see you all. I can't stay to talk, unfortunately. We're—we're late for a special cabaret performance." Sweat began to form on his forehead. He had been holding on to Marika's hand without realizing it. He let it go quickly. Then, nodding to all four occupants of the table with as wide a smile as he could muster, he turned and went back to the table. Sirio was pulling it out to let Barbara emerge from her banquette seat. They walked quickly to the coatroom, got their coats, and left, the young woman again tucking her arm under his and moving close to the side of his body.

"Jesus," said Lisa quietly, addressing the small bouquet of flowers in the center of the table.

"Don't talk like that," said Marika irritably.

"This didn't happen, this didn't happen," chanted Hortense miserably.

"*Managgia la miseria!*" exclaimed Sergio.

"Perfect touch for Mom's birthday party," proclaimed Lisa.

Marika was busy asking herself, Could that girl be better in bed with him than I am? No, not possible. I have more experience, she comforted herself. I know more. Let him teach his young student all he knows about pleasure, she still won't be able to please him back the way I do.

Suddenly, she began to laugh.

"What's so funny, Mom?"

"Nothing, just a private joke," and then she laughed again, because she had known only two men *that* way in her entire life, and was probably one fourth as experienced as *la bambola*.

"Tell us!" Lisa prodded, "we can use the laugh."

Marika smiled at her daughter and took her hand. "Life is funny, that's all—and love is even more so."

"You said a full mouth, as you Americans say," Sergio said, and his eyes found Lisa's across the table.

"It's Mathilde Kauffman, *Frau Chok-o-lad*," Hortense mimicked the German pronunciation into the intercom. Marika picked up the receiver and spoke cheerfully, because she had good news to impart to her caller. "Good morning, Mrs. Kauffman. You are psychic! I was just this second about to call you. We're ready to go with our proposal, on schedule with your three months' delayed product launch. I'm so glad you have solved your technical problems with the new products. It's better to have everything perfect before introducing the new line. When may we come to present our really exciting plans for you?"

The voice on the other end was glacial. "There's been a change in—the—the way in which we will proceed with our new group of products at this point in time."

Marika's pulse rate jumped ten beats. "Mrs. Kauffman, I don't understand. What do you mean, 'a change in the way in which we will proceed'? Haven't we been performing satisfactory work for you? You've never said otherwise."

The Swiss woman interrupted her. "You have done excellent work in laying the groundwork over the past few months. It was a disappointment to us all that we had to postpone the big launch for almost a year from our original schedule, but these things happen. Your company's liaison person at White Plains has worked out well, and we have absolutely no complaints about the servicing of our account during these preparatory months."

"Well, then, what—?" This time it was Marika who interrupted.

"In reference to the next step, the big plan for the launch, we have already received a proposal, a very fine one, five days ago, which we have accepted."

"But you chose my company for this. We have a contract! You accepted my overall outline submitted at the start, and now I have the final, budgeted, polished one all ready to give you, as we agreed. Not a day late either."

"Mrs. Wentworth, I am under no legal obligation to continue to work with you when there has been a—a—shall we say a question of malfeasance?"

"Malfeasance!" Marika was almost shouting now. "Explain what you mean by such an accusation."

"Your former associate, Mr. Greg Willis, came to see us ten days ago. The story he told was not a pretty one, not pretty at all."

Marika suddenly felt warm. Her face was flushed and her pulse accelerated again. Her tone changed from one of distress and confusion to one of cold anger.

"What do you mean, Mr. Willis's not so pretty story?"

"Let's be calm, Mrs. Wentworth." Marika wanted to interrupt and say, Would *you* be calm about losing a multimillion-dollar project?

"Be calm," the Swiss woman repeated, "you are first and foremost a lady."

"I am first and foremost a businesswoman," Marika corrected her quickly, "and I am waiting for a total explanation of Greg's conversation with you."

"We—my husband and I—have agreed to accept Mr. Willis's fine plan for the launch of our new products, along the French Empire theme that your entire staff came up with jointly."

"What do you mean, my entire staff? It was my idea from the very beginning!" Marika shouted into the receiver. Then she checked herself, picturing Mrs. Kauffman wincing and holding the telephone a foot from her ear.

"That proposal is *mine*, Mrs. Kauffman, and not Greg Willis's."

"He has told us otherwise, Mrs. Wentworth, and convincingly so."

"I fired him. If he gave you a proposal, it was stolen. His input on the entire format was minimal. He did not do what I asked him to. He was not part of the final planning. He did not contribute to any of the creative work whatsoever."

"He warned us you would say just these things," Mathilde Kauffman said calmly. "He predicted a strong reaction on your part, but we believe in justice, and he has convinced us that the plan is his, not yours."

"You believe a former employee, rather than me?" Marika asked incredulously. "You trust a disloyal employee—why he doesn't even have an office, a staff—how could he have prepared the proposal and how can he service your account?"

"Oh, but he can," Mathilde Kauffman interrupted. She was quite disliking this turn of events and wanted it to be over with as quickly as possible. She had been dreading this telephone call all morning. "He has a staff of four, a fully equipped office already in operation, and he has shown us that he can handle our account with maximum effectiveness and efficiency, and at a cost savings, too, with reduced overhead."

"Mathilde"—Marika called the Swiss woman by her given name for the first time, something she never did until the new client requested it—"Greg Willis is a thief who stole my entire plan. How can you let him do this? Do you have no sense of ethics and fairness yourself? Is this the way the Swiss do business?"

"I find that last remark unnecessary and very unworthy of you, Mrs. Wentworth."

"I'm sorry, I did not mean it the way it sounded."

Mathilde Kauffman continued, now nervously munching one of her company's chocolate bars, a supply of which was always available in her second-from-the-top desk drawer. "My husband

and I sincerely believe Mr. Willis's story, Mrs. Wentworth. He is an earnest, intelligent young man. He said that all the basic ideas were his, and that you told him he would receive no credit." She continued in a dispassionate voice repeating Greg's litany of grievances against Stuyvesant Communications, Inc., all of them total untruths. Marika listened, stunned into silence not only by Greg's outright lies, but also by the fact that he had persuaded this smart Swiss businesswoman of his veracity.

"Mrs. Wentworth, there is nothing more to say," Mathilde Kauffman continued, now chewing on the hard, nutty part of the chocolate bar, so that the sounds crackled loudly in Marika's ear. A chocolate bar becomes a security blanket, Marika thought to herself, to help her through this difficult telephone call. She could picture the woman's rolls of fat straining against the seams of her too-small dress.

"My husband and I," Mathilde continued, "heard a very compelling story from Mr. Willis, a rather dramatic story of your theft of his brains and talent since six years' time. He told us of how you never gave him any recognition or compensation commensurate to his value to the company. What finally forced him into coming to us was when you fired him—after he formulated all of the plans for our product launch, after he did *all* the important work on the project. His proposal for the 'Imperial Honey Cream' launch is of genius quality. We will be proud to work with this gentleman, and worry not. I will never tell any of this—of your —dishonesty—in treating his role in the project. This sad story will rest between us. I shall never tell anyone else, and I will make sure that Greg does not repeat it to anyone either. After all, you have your reputation to think of. I like you. We shall remain silent about all this. I don't want you to be hurt permanently by this— this mistake on your part."

"I am so stunned," Marika managed to say weakly at this point, "that I would like to terminate this conversation right now, and call you back later." She needed time to think. Engaging in a losing battle over the telephone because of these absurd allegations, made by a woman eating chocolate bars in her ear, was something with which she did not wish to cope.

"I see no reason whatsoever for further conversations, Mrs. Wentworth," was the cold reply.

"I do," Marika shot back quickly. Then her intuition told her she would have to flatter Mathilde Kauffman to regain even one bargaining chip with her. "Look, Mathilde, you are a very fair person." The nervous munching on the other end ceased. Good, at least the Swiss woman was listening to her. "You are recognized as an extremely smart, sophisticated businesswoman, who commands great respect in the food products world." She could almost see Mathilde Kauffman smiling and nodding agreement with these fine words of praise.

"Therefore, I know you will be just and talk to me again about this situation. You will take my call."

"Of course," answered a mollified woman on the other end, "I will take your call."

They hung up, and Marika told Hortense what had happened and asked her to call a quick emergency staff meeting.

"I can't ring the ship's bell," Hortense said sadly. "I guess I'll have to blow the trumpet to assemble them."

"What's that?" asked a perplexed Jennie Lee when Hortense's trumpet blew a few discordant notes.

Sarah looked up from her lettering chore at her desk, "Jesus!" she exclaimed. "Bad news, Jennie Lee. Just as a bell ringing calls a staff meeting to celebrate a new account, so a trumpet blowing calls a meeting to mourn a lost account. Let's go find out what's happened." Sarah grabbed a crystal and put it in her pocket as they both headed for Anthony's office.

Marika knew it was necessary for staff morale to keep her sense of humor, which she did. The meeting was filled with a chorus of "that son-of-a-bitch," but Marika moved quickly to reassure them that "we'll get it back." She cautioned them not to mention to anyone what had happened outside, in case there would be a court case. "We must keep this within these walls— not only because of possible legal proceedings—but because of the fact that the press might crucify us. Greg has probably already told lies about us to some of his buddies in the media."

"Let's keep this out of the courts, if possible," Anthony added.

"It would be very expensive, and by the time it would pass through the judicial system, some other marketing firm will have brought the LUXFOODS new product line to the marketplace. We have to be ready to move—and move fast—on this matter."

"If anyone can fight back fast and effectively, it's you, Marika. Whatever you decide to do, we're with you," Steve added. She noticed how gaunt he seemed, sitting perched on the end of Anthony's desk. Even his voice was weak now—and as slow as his body's movements. He was disintegrating right before their eyes. She walked over to him, put an arm around his thin shoulders, and said, "Thanks. You're all a great group. We'll get over this—this brief little—glitch." They all laughed at her description of the crisis and went back to their desks.

Later that night, Marika lay for a long time in the dark, analyzing what had been going on in her life. She seemed to be getting nothing but F's—for failure—a new grade for her. Sure, she had lost out on various projects. But this total failure stage of her life was so *ugly*. There was nothing redeeming about it whatsoever. There was no bright side, no positive energy emanating her way. She had first of all lost Jonathon, not because of events, but because of her own stupidity, lack of vision—even meanness. She had cast away the greatest thing that had come into her life since the death of her husband. She had chased away a man who was kind, who made her laugh, who loved her. She had thought that she, Marika Stuyvesant Russell Wentworth, was such hot stuff that everyone else in the world would conform to her ideas and accept her decisions.

And now she had lost what would have been a multimillion-dollar account for her company because of the outright crookedness of the bad apple on her staff. Where was her judgment, her creativity, her savvy? Why hadn't she acted immediately? Where was her old fast-thinking, fast-acting philosophy—the zip?

It had gone—gone with her self-confidence. It had never been like this before. She had *always* been on that fabled success curve, ever since she moved the company to New York. The invincible, charming, beautiful, talented, makes-no-mistakes Marika Wentworth, she thought to herself with bitterness. What a sham!

She would get back the LUXFOODS account, she knew she would. But how? Her self-esteem seemed to have dried up, like flower petals, and blown away. Where was the determination and firm grip on things she had always had? Where was Jonathon Scher, damn it? She could have used his strong arms around her this very minute—how she could use his arms around her right now.

Strange, not rising to a crisis brandishing a fiery sword, which had always been her way. She felt punched out, lifeless; the energy for combat simply wasn't there. She thrashed around on the bed, trying to find a comfortable way in which to make her head and pillow compatible. Then she looked at the late hour on the clock, glowing in the darkness, and tried to relax and do deep breathing. She tried visualizing herself skiing down a virgin white open slope, her tracks the only marks on the mountain. Nothing worked. Finally, two hours later, sleep came while she was doing something she had done every single night for weeks, as automatically as brushing her teeth and taking off her makeup before going to bed—crying herself to sleep over the loss of Jonathon Scher.

Marika left the office earlier than usual for her literacy lesson with Bill, because she wanted to stop first in a bookstore to buy him a present—a reward for having made such incredible progress with his reading. She purchased a wittily illustrated version of *The Wizard of Oz*, because she remembered Bill having said he had seen it on television several times and wanted someday to be able to read the book.

He thanked her effusively, and as she helped him with the beginning of the book, he said shyly to her, "You know, ma'am, a pretty lady like you shouldn't look so sad."

"What do you mean, Bill?" she asked, knowing darned well what he meant.

"You have looked so hurtin' these last few weeks. I know it's not my place to say nothin', but I've been wantin' to."

"Well, go ahead, say it. You and I are friends."

"It's some man, isn't it? You got that sad woman-look that can only be caused by a man."

She smiled at him. Here she had discussed the breakup only with one person—Eve—and here was a hillbilly forcing her into admitting it now. It was obviously because he was a man, she told herself quickly, and an attractive one at that. Her student was the impetus to make her suddenly admit that it had all happened, that Jonathon had not been just a mirage. This man sitting opposite her sincerely admired and appreciated her. It felt good.

"Yes, it was a man. But we all lose lots of people in our lives whom we—whom we—" She couldn't finish the sentence.

"Whom we love. Yes," he said solemnly, "sometimes we lose 'em, and sometimes we just can't have people we love neither, but we make do." He reached over and patted her hand. "You'll make do, Marika. You're a beautiful, strong, wonderful woman. Any man in the world would be lucky to have *you*." His hand tightened on hers, and then quickly withdrew.

They finished the lesson, and after saying good-bye, Marika went into a little closet-like space off the bank's cafeteria that had a desk, lamp, and telephone. It served as the office during the nights the volunteers gave their instructions at the bank. The director of their section, Tracy Hayward, had asked all the volunteers to assemble in that tiny space at the end of the teaching session, before they left that night.

"I have something to tell you," she said, her eyes glittering with excitement. "You remember when I said we couldn't make a down payment on the building we needed as our new center in the Bronx?"

A few of the volunteers, Marika among them, nodded a vigorous yes.

"Well, we were just about to lose our option and the money we had already invested, when today, as I opened up this cafeteria for our evening teaching session, along came—out of the sky— some angel Gabriel or some messenger from God, I swear. There was an Express Mail package, and inside, without a name, address, or note, was a cashier's check made out to us. It's an anonymous contribution. I mean, I looked at that check and said, 'Man, you've got to be kidding!' "

One of the volunteers interrupted. "You're forgetting the important part, Tracy. How big was the check?"

"How big? I'll tell you how big. Two hundred fifty thousand dollars big, that's how big."

There was a stunned silence in and around the closet. Then a peltering of questions. "Who is this donor?" "You must have some clue." "It's impossible not to know when the donation is *that* big." "How can we find out?"

"I called an officer of the bank in Chicago that issued the check, and was told that the person wishes to remain anonymous. It's bank policy to protect that wish."

All Marika had to hear was "a bank in Chicago." An anonymous donor from Chicago. It had to be him. It was an act of love, even though they no longer belonged to each other.

"Tracy," Marika said, "I have an idea. We can't ever thank this individual in person, so why don't we put a message in the Personals ads in the *Chicago Tribune* and the *Sun-Times*? Just a couple of lines saying, 'We wish to thank the compassionate and generous donor of the check who saved our building for the literacy project. We want that person to know how much it meant to us. Even if the donor doesn't see the ad, someone in his or her family or office might see it."

"Great idea. I'll do it tomorrow," replied Tracy.

Surely he would know, then, that the donation was not anonymous to her. She wondered if he was married yet to the beautiful young woman she had seen him with at Le Cirque, and if so, if his wife would ever be told by him about a woman he once knew who believed in anonymous donations.

Hortense waited until she knew Marika had left for the office before her early morning call to Lisa. "Now I'm really worried about her," she said.

"Me, too, Hortense. I'm just as worried."

"She hasn't come to the office all week, and it was like pulling wisdom teeth to get her to come today. She simply isn't coping very well and can't seem to get out of bed without being urged. However," Hortense suddenly seemed to brighten, "she is a fighter and she bounces back with more resilience than anyone I've ever seen."

"Now you have me *un*worried."

"Good. We'll get her going down here. There's lots for her to do. We haven't even had a staff meeting in two weeks! We need her. Staff morale is terrible."

"Will that get her over the blues?"

"Not exactly get her over it, but help. And I know Mrs. Watson is calling from the White House this morning. That will be good medicine, too."

"Don't you love it, Hortense, the wife of the President of the United States calling to cheer up my mother? Isn't that a bit of history, or something?"

"It's something you will always remember, Lisa, but don't forget your mother called up Mrs. Watson plenty of times to cheer *her* up."

"Maybe we ought to take that trip to Budapest we've been talking about since Grandpa's death. Maybe this is the time to get her excited over finding out about my grandmother's Hungarian . . ."

"Hungarian beau," Hortense finished the sentence for her. Lisa burst out laughing. "You're great! But it wasn't her Hungarian 'beau.' It was her 'lover'!"

"You shouldn't speak about your natural grandfather in that disrespectful way." Hortense's tone was disapproving.

"Ah, come on. I meant no disrespect. It's just that the word 'beau' is antediluvian. Istvan was no 'beau' of my grandmother's. He got her knocked up, that's what he did."

"Lisa!" Hortense's Victorian sense of morality had come unglued.

"Don't give up on me," Lisa laughed. "Look, I have to go to class. And I promise I will treat Grandfather Istvan's memory with more respect."

"You better had," said her mother's assistant gravely, "just remember his seed is in you."

"Pepper seeds—paprika—hot stuff! Bye." Lisa hung up quickly, knowing that Hortense was probably fainting on the other end. But she knew Hortense loved to be teased by her. It was a game they had played since she was a little girl.

Hortense, shaking her head and laughing to herself, dialed Steve.

"Yes?" a weak voice answered.

"It's Hortense."

"Oh, Hortense, wonderful. Nice to hear from you." His voice cheered up perceptibly in her ear.

"And today?"

"Like yesterday and the day before."

"No better? Not a tiny bit better?"

"Okay, better." He gave in to her. She was willing him so hard to feel a little better that he actually did feel a little better. He knew there was one thing Hortense could not stand—to see people suffer.

"Want to help out our boss?"

"Crazy question. I'd do anything for her, you know that, including getting out of this bed and carrying it downstairs, if she wanted it done."

"She's finally coming into the office this morning, the first time this week. Really depressed."

Steve mumbled something unintelligible under his breath.

"I want to tell her when she comes down here that she should go see you right away, that you're feeling down, and that she should cheer you up."

"Okay. And what happens then?"

"Then she'll come over to cheer you up, and that will cheer *her* up and get her out of this funk she's in. It might even cheer you up a little."

"Well reasoned, Hortense. Any ideas on how the cheering process might begin?"

"Yes. Get her going on recapturing the LUXFOODS account—away from Greg. It is ridiculous that she hasn't moved

mind of yours, the strategy you plan to use to get the account back."

"Flattery will not get you very far today."

"It seems to me you're the one who's not getting very far. What's the plan? What are you going to do to get back the account?" His voice became stronger as he held her hand tighter.

"I'll think of something, don't worry. He won't get away with it."

"But he is getting away with it. You've delayed a week already. You're not getting the staff geared up to do anything, you're not talking to Mathilde Kauffman, you haven't shot an arrow into shit-head Willis's heart . . ."

"Hey," protested Marika. "I'm not that bad. I've been doing a lot of thinking. I just can't go off like a wild pistol shot. I have to act with a cool head."

"No, you don't. You should act with a head full of the usual Marika Wentworth passion. That's what everyone's waiting for. I would have been in the office if there had been a call to action today . . ." And his body was suddenly racked with coughing.

"Steve, is the doctor coming today?" She went to get a glass of water and stood over him, a worried expression on her face.

"Yes, he's coming in an hour."

"I feel I can't go to the office and leave you alone like this."

"I'm perfectly all right. Just a little cold or something. I'll be fine by tomorrow. I'll be back in the office by tomorrow. That is . . ."

"That is, what?"

"That is, if there's a reason to go back to the office tomorrow."

"Now you're laying it on me, is that it?"

"You're damned right. Sit down again, let's discuss strategy."

"I told you, didn't I, that Hortense had a talk with one of the night cleaners who told Hortense that she had seen Greg Willis the night he was fired, working long into the night at the copying machine? He had returned to the office after everyone had left, like a thief in the night."

"Yes, I heard. The shit-head copied every single document in the files with the name of LUXFOODS or Imperial Honey Cream. But, Marika, I've been lying here and thinking—didn't I once see you with a suitcase full of photographs, fabric swatches, and things from the research trip you made to Paris?"

"Well, yes. They're in my apartment as of this moment in my bedroom. On the day Mathilde Kauffman called me with the news of Greg's dirty dealing, I had been transferring the material into background material for the press kit."

"Greg was in France the same time you were, but didn't you tell me he did absolutely no work on the project?"

"Yes, that's true. I paid his way over and back, and he was supposed to go on some of my research expeditions, but he didn't accompany me. He was off with his friends the whole time. Of course," and she paused for a second, "I was really very happy not to have him with me."

"But that's it!" Steve said excitedly. "You're way ahead of him. You have all that research and planning that Willis doesn't have. You can catch him on all kinds of things—that he doesn't have included in the stolen copied documents."

The light came back into Marika's eyes. "Of course, Steve, I've been blind. It's been sitting right there on my bedroom desk, staring at me. It's stuff I have written and information from France that no one else has even seen!"

"He has an out-of-date press party plan for one thing."

"He sure does. The one he stole from the files is full of holes. It never would have worked."

"You also said fat Mathilde agreed to talk to you again, didn't she?"

"Yes, but what does that have . . ."

"Just tell her to give you and Greg a test—an exam—to prove who knows the most about the launch plan," he said, interrupting her, and coughing pathetically between words.

"Get back to the office, fast, Marika, and tell them you have the key to unlocking this mess and getting the account back into our shop."

"You're right, Steve—as usual. You've got to get better, old friend." She looked up a telephone number in the little black computer in her handbag and, after finishing her conversation, went to bid Steve good-bye. "I have a home care person coming by this morning to stay with you during the day until you get over this cough," she said. "She'll tend to your meals, change your sheets, run errands—things like that. It's a little present from me."

When Steve began to protest, she interrupted him. "You must follow the boss's orders and do it docilely. And don't forget, I am in your debt. You've just opened my stuck-together eyes about how to proceed on LUXFOODS. I probably would have sat vegetating, feeling sorry for myself, until Greg Willis had completed the assignment. You deserve a raise, old friend!"

"I don't want a raise. I just want you to sink shit-head into a pile of mud, where he belongs."

Hortense dialed LUXFOODS from her boss's desk, and handed the telephone to Marika as soon as the Kauffmans' secretary answered. This was a tradition in the office. Marika felt that it was always much nicer when the boss, not an assistant, was on the line when a client picked up. It was a rule Marika made everyone in the agency follow.

Today, Hortense's presence by her desk lent a certain moral support she needed to make this difficult call. Under normal conditions, there was no need for outside moral support, but lately—well, lately, things had not been normal. Her self-confidence had eroded to a thin veneer.

"Mathilde," Marika said warmly, "thank you for taking my call."

"You're welcome, Marika." Her voice sounded slightly suspicious.

"I'm asking you and your husband to be judges in a contest to see who is telling the truth and who is therefore the true originator of the Imperial Honey Cream proposal."

"I don't quite understand."

"What I'm asking you to do is simple and fair. I'm proposing that you ask Greg and me the same questions, separately, and then you can judge who originated the Imperial Honey Cream ideas."

"What kind of questions?"

"I'll leave that up to you. You, not Greg nor I, should decide on the quiz questions. They might pertain to how Napoleon became the key figure. How was the logo conceived, for example? What are the exact plans for the press party launch? Things like that."

Marika realized she had already installed two questions in Mathilde Kauffman's brain that the Swiss businesswoman would now think she had thought of herself.

"Very interesting idea, *un petit examen*." Mathilde Kauffman began to mull it over in her mind. "Very interesting." She thought in silence some more, and Marika did not interrupt, knowing she should let her concentrate. "Yes, we'll do it," came the answer. "It's only fair. And I believe, as you know, in being fair."

"You have a reputation for fairness in all your business dealings, Mathilde." Marika knew Mathilde would love being reminded.

Marika noted in her wizard the date and time of the *"petit examen"* and notified Hortense to call a quick staff meeting. Hortense stepped out into the hall and alternately rang the bell and blew the trumpet Marika had ordered by telephone from the music store.

"What are you doing that for?" Marika laughed.

"Because you're back and working again."

"But why the rather horrifying sound combination?"

"Because the trumpet symbolizes an account we have lost, and the ship's bell symbolizes an account we have won, and this occasion is sort of in-between the two of them."

"I should have known not to doubt your logic."

Marika was early for her appearance at LUXFOODS. She wanted to be calm and collected, so she had left New York with a half hour to spare. The Lincoln she reserved was driven by the same man who had taken Steve and her out to White Plains the first time. She felt it was a lucky omen. After all, she and Steve had left the corporate LUXFOODS offices that time with the account in their pockets.

She missed Steve terribly this time. His cough had persisted, and he had been able to return to the office only half a day every other day. Anthony and others had offered to accompany her, but this was an "exam," and she would go it alone. There was no question she could not answer. If she had ever felt confident in her life—or at least prepared—it was now.

The driver helped her carry in the visuals, her copious files, and research materials. She had also tucked into her handbag a ten-minute cassette tape made at the Château de Compiègne. She had noticed when she and Steve first went out to LUXFOODS that the Kauffmans had a VCR in their office. If the opportunity were to present itself to show the tape, she would be ready.

She soon found herself in the large office shared by the Kauffmans, confronting them seated at their own desks, which seemed to be laden with files. She laughed to herself at the air of the inquisition the Kauffmans were trying to instill in the atmosphere. Mathilde Kauffman turned on a tape recorder and said quietly, "Our lawyer advised us to do this."

"Of course," Marika replied. "I have my own, too," a remark that was certain to make them feel either admiring or intimidated.

At the beginning of the meeting, Luke Kauffman did nothing except show signs of faint disapproval. She felt intuitively that he preferred dealing with a man, and that was why he probably stood on the side of Greg Willis.

"The first point we will discuss," Mathilde said primly, like a stern schoolteacher, "will be the logo."

Marika wanted to laugh, it was all so theatrical and ridiculous, but it had been her idea, and she must take this very seriously. She began to discuss the Napoleonic bee symbol that had been worked on as the logo for the new food products.

"Where exactly did the idea for the bees come from?" Luke Kauffman asked.

"Well, of course, it was logical, once the theme of the bees' honey was seized upon. The classiest bees in history were Napoleon's. For some reason, he had a fixation on them." Marika was now totally absorbed in her subject. "His favorite bee was the queen bee, who destroys all her workers when their work is done. However, even before we began studying the Napoleonic concept, I had seen a double bee ring—in diamonds set in gold —on the finger of a guest at a state dinner at the White House." Marika could hear a muffled gasp at the mention of the White House. It had to have come from Mathilde.

"That was the real inspiration for the logo of the bees," she continued, "because the ring was so extraordinarily beautiful. I thought to myself after spending that first afternoon with you in White Plains that the diamond double bee ring would be fantastic sweepstakes prize with which to launch our new products. A small version of the bee ring could also be a sales incentive prize for your national network of salespeople and retail employees."

She saw the Kauffmans nodding to each other. It was obvious the origins of the bee logo had not been part of Greg's proposal.

Luke Kauffman handed her a mock-up of what must have been Greg's designer's version of a bee logo. It was a standard Napoleonic bee, facing down, drawn in gold on a pale blue satin ground. Very pretty, very feminine, she thought to herself.

"Is this your concept of how the logo should more or less look on the packaging for the products?" he asked.

"Hardly," Marika said, laughing and perturbing them as she did so. They did not find this a laughing matter. "You will have to excuse me for laughing, but if there was one thing that was definite in the Napoleonic era, it was that the bees were always rendered turned up, never presented down, like this. If you had used this on your logo and packaging, you would have been in for a lot of derision by the French *savants*."

The Kauffmans turned to each other and whispered what Marika described later to her staff as a "Swiss version of the Japanese 'Ah, so' sounds."

She decided to drive the nail into Greg's coffin a little harder. "I also went to the Museum of Textiles at the Louvre," she said, "and spent two whole days closeted with the head curator and the librarian. They were very cooperative." She threw on each Kauffman's desk a pile of photocopied pages from the huge eighteenth- and nineteenth-century books of fabrics from the royal palaces she had located tucked on the top shelves in the Louvre's textile library. "Here," she said, "the proof of Napoleon's love of the bee design—but notice how all the bees are facing up. It's too bad Greg didn't bother to do the work I did when he was in Paris."

Marika went over the plans for a tie-in with the "Empire Era of Taste and Decoration" with Tiffany's, and then gave the format for a national tour of an Imperial Honey Cream spokesperson to appear on local TV shows, armed with excellent visuals and nutritional information on honey of interest to the general public.

"Let us turn now to the press party at Malmaison," Mathilde Kauffman said, checking down her list of questions in a businesslike fashion. "I care most seriously—and my husband does, too," she said, nodding deferentially to her husband, "that these products be launched in the most upscale, socially acceptable, and artistic way possible—in some manner so as to impress the entire world, not just America." Marika could see a copy of Greg's two-page typed summary on the press party in her hands; her original memo on the press party at Malmaison was the same, but, of course, the entire picture had changed since she wrote that memo, and Greg was unaware of it. She felt as though she had just downed a delicious glass of sparkling cold champagne.

"Oh, I'm afraid we can't have the press party at Malmaison," Marika said, with an unmistakable note of superiority in her voice.

Mathilde's face fell perceptibly from disappointment. "And why not? What better place could there be than Joséphine's favorite abode—and so close to Paris—just a half hour away? I thought Greg's idea was genius. Such a famous, beautiful house, so tasteful and representative of the Empire period."

"It was my idea, Mathilde, to have it at Malmaison, but when I went to Paris—Greg would have known all this, if he had cared enough to accompany me on any of the research trips—I discovered, upon calling that treasure of a museum, that they did not have any bees in their fabric or decoration. Nor would they have allowed us to have our commercial press launch there. It was out of the question, but I consoled myself, because a young friend, Anne Brandstrom, knew the curator of the Château de Compiègne, and they had bees there, so off I went."

"What's this Château de Compiègne?" asked Mathilde skeptically, even though impressed at this interesting turn of events.

"A magnificent place, little known to us Americans, but well known, of course, to the French. It was designed in the time of Louis XV as a hunting château, finished in the reign of Louis XVI, and used and enjoyed by him as well as by Napoleon I, II, and III. It was built on the sixth-century remains of other royal residences. It's only an hour and fifteen minutes' drive from Paris, when it's not rush hour. When the court was there in hunting season, usually for six weeks at a time, one hundred royals and their guests were in residence, and nine hundred domestics were also in the château or nearby to take care of them!"

"Go on, go on, this is full of promise," urged Mathilde.

"The gardens are unbelievable. It's like a small Versailles, absolutely enchanting. Marie Antoinette had a bedroom there—Napoleon and Joséphine had magnificent rooms there—Joséphine for only a short time. She was replaced, as you will remember, by a young woman, the Archduchess Marie Louise of Austria, who was to bear Napoleon the heir he needed. In fact, Marie Louise's and Napoleon's first encounter—when she came to marry him—took place at Compiègne, in March 1810. Even though she towered over him, he found her immensely attractive and it was love at first sight."

"How romantic!" sighed Mathilde.

"I was fascinated by Marie Louise's classical white and gold bathroom—complete with a green marble tub, with gold swan-head water spigots."

"A green marble bathtub with gold swan-head water spigots!" parroted an awed Mathilde Kauffman. "Perhaps part of the soirée could be held there . . ."

"I think not," Marika countered, trying to temper her client's wild flight of fantasy—a press party in the Empress' bathroom.

"Of course," she continued, "the château has witnessed the unfolding of the history of France, having been under attack in four wars. All the damaged parts have been restored lovingly and authentically. The royal residence is exquisite—with some of the most beautiful fabrics I have ever seen . . . One entire bedroom of Napoleon's was ablaze with a crimson fabric, printed with the gold imperial bees, and with a large bronze bee at the top of his bed hangings."

"Think of what prestige to associate our honey-cream products with such a historic place, and how romantic it is!" Mathilde Kauffman sighed again. "Go on," her husband said gruffly, "about this château and how we could hold our press party there."

"Well, the Louis XVI theater is being restored and will most likely be ready by 1991, so we can hold our dinner in and around the theater—which is really part of the château, and is reached by a bridge from the château across the narrow street. Of course," Marika interjected, "LUXFOODS would be expected to make a generous donation to the château for its continuing refurbishment. They really need the funds to keep it looking so magnificent. It is a costly project."

"But of course, but of course!"

"We could get Paris's best caterer to come out to do the dinner, so that the LUXFOODS products served look and taste magnificent. We'll use reproductions of Napoleon's handsome china and stemware for the table settings—I already have a source for that. We would have a performance of something in the theater—perhaps a ballet, so there would be no language problems for the guests. The dinner tables would be set under beautiful Empire-style tents beneath the great trees around the château. We could have tablecloths made to match the fabric in the château—a smashing pattern in one of Napoleon's rooms—purple, chocolate brown, and fresh green stripes. An incredible color combination. We'll put down a fresh green outdoor carpet to match the green carpet in that room of the château."

"But of course, but of course!" cried Mathilde Kauffman, completely under the spell of the thought of herself, dressed in a low-cut Empire gown as Empress Marie Louise of Austria, and Luke Kauffman dressed as—well, not as, but perhaps to *look* a bit Napoleonic.

Marika felt like an orchestra conductor with her entire orchestra and audience mesmerized by the magical movements of her baton. "Our invitations," she continued to an enraptured audience of two, "would be copies of those used by the palace in the time of Napoleon, with the 'Château Royal de Compiègne' and the Emperor's seal bumped embossed at the top center. Every person would receive his or her own invitation, not one addressed to a couple, just as it was done then. It would be authentic, with '*Billet d'Entrée, Bon pour une Personne*' engraved on it, announcing that this invitational ticket allows only one person to enter.

"Our guest list," she continued, "would comprise top magazine and newspaper editors and TV personalities from America, France, England, Germany—the entire Common Market, with special emphasis, of course, on the media from Switzerland."

"Of course," nodded Luke Kauffman, going over in his mind the leading media figures of Geneva and Zurich who would all be lobbying for an invitation like this one, from a Swiss company.

"The list would also include top French social and business figures," Marika explained, "and some of the greats of the American business and social worlds, and, of course, the top Swiss VPs."

"And maybe some TV or movie stars?" Mathilde asked, excited beyond her usual enthusiasm.

"Some might attend. They love to party and some search for publicity."

She slipped over to the VCR in the corner of the conference room, inserted her cassette, and played a magnificent photographic tour of the Château de Compiégne, with its exteriors, interiors, and gardens. She had dubbed in background music of the Empire period. Every so often, the camera changed from an indoor scene to an outdoor table set with what looked like one of the new food products. The camera would switch from a mouthwatering close-up of a dessert on an exquisite porcelain plate to a long lens shot of a palatial ballroom, complete with shiny parquet floors, satin benches, and chandeliers that sparkled in the rays of sunlight from the windows like thousands of fireflies.

The camera showed close-ups of Marika's favorite fabrics in one of Napoleon's private rooms, with the furniture upholstered in warm chocolate browns, purples, and green stripes. She would use that combination for the table linens at the product launch dinner, she explained to the Kauffmans, who had never imagined such a royal treatment of their dairy desserts.

The camera went lovingly over the crimson fabric covering the walls, bed hangings, sofas, chairs, and footstools of Napoleon's bedroom—making the immense room seem filled with a swarm of precious gold bees. The camera then showed close-ups of bees in the bronze dore wreaths that embellished gray marble fireplaces in another room, and a large bronze dore bee surmounting the white *baldocchio* over the bed in another First Empire blue and gold room.

"Of course," nodded Mathilde Kauffman. She was so emotionally strung out at this point, it was all she could say or do.

"But logically," added Luke Kauffman.

Not wishing to relinquish the floor at this point no matter what, Marika went on as the cassette continued. "Our press kit holders would be covered in a reproduction silk of the crimson bee fabric in Napoleon's famous bedroom—bees facing up," she added with a trace of wickedness. The grand finale on the cassette was very simple. With the background of the château, the camera stayed on the foreground action—a delectable crystal pitcher of golden honey being poured into a big bowl of cream, while being stirred with a wooden spoon. *"Mein Gott!"* cried Luke Kauffman almost orgiastically as the spoon continued to stir the golden stream into the creamy crater, enriching its texture and color all the while. Honey and cream now belonged together, there was no doubt about that. The nail in Greg Willis's coffin was in so far, it was no longer even visible.

Marika arose with the graceful dignity of Empress Marie Louise being received at court at the Château de Compiègne. She knew she had won.

"Thank you for your hospitality this morning," she said. "And on that yet. She won't take action, she's acting like a quitter rather than a fighter, and that's not the Marika we know."

They hung up, and Hortense picked up the snapshot of Charles Russell. "I told you, Charlie, that I would take care of her. And I'm doing my best."

She put down the frame quickly, because she heard the elevator doors open and saw the figure of her boss coming toward her.

Marika rang the buzzer, heard a weak "come in," and pushed in the door, which was ajar.

"Steve," she said, putting down a tiny gold tote bag full of Godiva chocolates on the table next to his bed, "how goes it, my friend?" She kissed him before he could answer, and then pulled up close to the bed a little Victorian-tufted armchair that his mother had lent him when he first decorated his apartment. It was her favorite piece of Steve's family's charming antiques that filled his apartment.

"Not so hot," he finally answered, "but much, much better now that I see you before my eyes. I just couldn't drag myself into the office all yesterday or today."

"You're not to worry about that. You know perfectly well you're under orders *never* to come into the office unless you feel like it."

"You make me sound very unnecessary to the operations of the office."

"I didn't mean that," she said putting her hand on his arm. "You know you mean everything to us."

"I still can't believe what that shit did with the Imperial Honey Cream proposal," he said, watching her reaction intently.

"I know," she said with an air of distraction.

"Is that all you're going to say? 'I know'?"

"What else am I supposed to say, other than what a stinker Greg Willis is?"

"You're supposed to say plenty. You're supposed to give me, Steve, your old friend and cohort, the musings of that brilliant

I'm sure you will agree that this was *my* project, not Greg Willis's. I hope to hear from you soon."

She picked up her documents and materials, which she had not even had the time to discuss, tossed the cassette that had been in the VCR onto the table, and said, "I hope you will enjoy looking at this again. After all, we should be there, holding our press dinner, a year from September." And with that, she turned and left—but only after dramatically throwing a piece of crimson satin on the table—a large piece of fabric printed with gold bees in an upright position.

Before Marika's car brought her back to the office, Mathilde Kauffman had already called, and left a message with Hortense that, "Of course, the account belonged to Stuyvesant Communications, and would Mrs. Wentworth please go forward at once with all plans and projects, without further delay?"

Hortense rang the ship's bell even before Marika's return, and there was the sound of cheering and shouting on the fourteenth floor of the Madison Avenue building.

CHAPTER

14

*L*isa looked up from the pile of Hungarian tourist brochures on her lap and stared out the jet's window. The
September sun dripped rays of honey on the cotton
candy clouds surrounding them. It was an exciting feeling. They
were finally on their way to Budapest—or, as Sergio had taught
her to pronounce it, *Bud'-a-pescht*.

She interrupted her mother's study of brochures. "Do you
wish, Mom, when you were growing up, that you had known
him?"

"I can't really say, because I loved Charlie Russell so much.
My mother's great Hungarian passion wasn't exactly a subject of
conversation around Beacon Street. In fact, I never heard Hungary
mentioned in our house until I was eleven or so, when my father
ranted and raved about the uprising against the Communist regime
in 1956. I remember watching the horror of people in Budapest
being slaughtered by the Russians—in the 'shorts,' black and white
newscasts we watched on television in those days. Daddy kept
muttering about how we Americans had promised to support the

patriots when they rose up against their persecutor, but that we had done nothing to help them." She stared out at the clouds, thinking. "I can see now that Daddy was probably more involved emotionally with the 1956 uprising than most people, because he knew there was Hungarian blood flowing through my veins."

"So other than that, Grandpa never mentioned Hungary to you?"

"Correct. Though, I do remember our having *goulash* every six months or so, laced with paprika, so hot it required a drink of water after every bite. And, of course, it was goulash with an Irish flair, made by our cook, Mary O'Houlihan."

Marika was silent for a minute and then said, "I'm sure Mama would have told me about my Hungarian father when I was older. . . . I wish my mother had not died when she was so young," she said, her voice coated in sadness. "It seems as though I— never—really knew her at all." Thoughts of her mother disappeared as Jonathon intruded on her mind once again. It seemed there was no way to forget him and it angered her. They had been apart now for almost four months, and for all she knew, he was already married to his beautiful young friend. She wondered how long it would take before she stopped measuring every thought and action in terms of how Jonathon would react to it. She was certain that she had lost one of the greatest joys of love . . . being able to communicate with someone on the most or on the least important of levels.

She gave Lisa an impromptu hug of affection. Without Jonathon she was still rich. She had her daughter.

They were greeted at the busy airport by their English-speaking guide/driver the minute they walked through customs. "Mrs. Wentworth and Miss Wentworth?" the handsome, dark-haired young man asked with a little bow. "I am Laszlo Horvath, at your service." He wore camel-corduroy trousers and a Hungarian version of a white polo shirt.

"Doesn't look like much of a Communist," Lisa whispered to her mother, who promptly shushed her.

Marika, curious, asked the driver, "How did you recognize us so quickly? There were at least sixty women on our plane."

"I was told to meet an important-looking pair of attractive American women. There was no question as to your identity when you walked through customs."

"And he flirts as well as any European," Lisa whispered again.

He loaded their luggage into his silver Citroën, and they drove off down a modern highway, through the countryside of ugly, modern factories and apartments, typical of most rides into the city from airports the world over, Marika explained to her disappointed daughter.

"What did you expect, Lisa? Oxen by the road, folk dancers along the way, dressed in local costumes, boots, and peasant embroideries?" They were now on the outskirts of the flat, business part of the city, called Pest, crowded with grimy buildings. Laszlo explained what they were seeing, but his passengers kept interrupting him with personal questions. They learned he was married, with two small children, and living, like so many other Hungarian families, with his wife's parents in a small apartment.

"How is it that you speak such perfect English?" Marika asked him.

"It helps to have had an English mother."

After a while he spoke again. "You know, the new winds of freedom blowing through my country are very exciting. Have you read much about what is happening in your press?"

"Yes," answered Lisa first. "There are headlines every day. And soon you will become a republic, a *real* democracy, won't you?"

"We are moving quickly in that direction. The Communist party has lost much influence. Different parties are now about to campaign in freedom."

"Why? How could such a change come about so fast?"

"Because we have hope now. To have hope means everything."

Marika interrupted at this point. "Do you worry that things have gone perhaps a little too fast, that your government won't be able to handle this rapid breakthrough to the West?"

"We are used to disappointments, if that is what free elections will bring us. We take them well."

"I certainly hope these new winds will bring you great success, not disappointments," Marika said, "and I hope happiness, too."

They were stopped by hastily thrown-up construction barriers in the main road. Laszlo muttered an oath in Hungarian and explained that they were forced to make a big detour because of sudden repairs being made to the highway, construction that had started without warning, just in the last hour.

"Since we have to leave the main road," he said, "do I have your permission to digress a bit further, and to take you through a nicer neighborhood, to my favorite little park in Budapest? A very special park?"

"Of course," replied Marika and Lisa in unison. They had been exposed to such ugliness on the main road coming in from the airport, it would be a welcome diversion.

Laszlo parked the car in a street bordering the small park. There was no one around. In the center of a peaceful, tree-lined lawn stood an imposing statue.

"It's fairly new," Laszlo explained. "Though it is a Hungarian shame that it was not erected forty years ago."

Puzzled, Lisa looked hard at the giant bronze figure of a man in a trench coat, standing flanked by two giant slabs of red marble. "But who is he?"

"It's Raoul Wallenberg, the savior of the Jews in Hungary during World War II," said Laszlo reverently. "A great man."

"But what did he do?" Lisa asked.

Laszlo seemed surprised, almost offended, by her question. "He was a Swedish diplomat here during the war, a Lutheran who managed to save over a hundred thousand Jews from Nazi concentration camps. He was captured by the Russians in January of 1945. They thought he was an American spy. He supposedly died in a Soviet prison camp, Miss Wentworth, but no one really knows what happened."

Marika was moved by the statue in this quiet little park. Clearly the driver had an emotional attachment for this Swedish hero she had heard about only vaguely in her study of history of World War II. Lisa, in the meantime, was beginning to care more about getting to a bathroom, dinner, and a bed than she was about paying homage to heroes from a long time ago.

Laszlo suggested they go to their hotel. He drove them from the Pest side of the city over an ancient bridge. "You are crossing the Danube now," he said, "on the Chain Bridge, which is lit up at night like a diamond necklace strung across the neck of the city. It makes for an extremely romantic walk at night."

"Tell you what, Mom," Lisa commented, "you and I will cross this bridge some night and pretend that Sergio and—and—"

"And some dashing Hungarian hussar are with us," laughed her mother. She knew that Jonathon's name had been on her daughter's tongue.

"We have crossed to the Buda side of the Danube," said Laszlo in his best tour guide's voice. "We are now climbing 'Castle Hill,' up through curving ancient streets, lined by houses often destroyed in wars, always rebuilt, and lived in today by the very rich—including your American ambassador. See—up there!" And he pointed to a large house sitting atop a multiterraced hill, each terrace adorned with large lanterns. Most of the luxurious villas they passed were hidden behind stone walls or lush gardens that were still enjoying a late summer's warmth.

At the top of the hill, they found themselves in a vast space —Trinity Square—centered by a lofty stone monument. "It was erected by the citizens in the late seventeenth century in gratitude for having been spared the Black Plague," Laszlo informed them. On a corner of the square sat the imposing Church of King Matthias, complete with flying buttresses and spires, which were tiled in bright-colored patterns of mosaics.

"It looks like Ozland," said Lisa in awe.

They checked into the luxurious Hilton situated in the center of a medieval square and followed the bellman and his shiny brass baggage cart through the hallway. They passed a glass wall with a breathtaking view out over Castle Hill and down to the Danube. Across the river on the other side loomed the giant, gray, ghostlike Parliament buildings. In the twilight, their domes and spires looked like a procession of silvery ghosts. Jutting out at a right angle from the hotel's window wall was a free-standing wall, several stories high, painted terra-cotta red and ending in soaring Gothic arches. It was startling, a remnant of antiquity interjecting itself into the side of the newly constructed hotel. The bellman informed them that the wall was a part of a thirteenth-century abbey.

They were tired so they decided to order dinner in their suite from room service. The meal arrived on a table pushed by two waiters who served them with great flourishes. First a clear soup—consommé with quail eggs and sherry—then a fillet of veal, with goose liver and dill paprika cream sauce. Then came a fruit sorbet. Lisa tried to write down the names of each course in her diary in phonetic English, but it was difficult to decipher the complete Hungarian pronunciation. Besides, she was famished! So she put aside the diary and ate her meal.

By nine o'clock both were fast asleep. The bell tower of King Matthias's Church tolled the hours in sonorous chimes, but Marika was only vaguely aware of the sounds of time passing by—time drawing nearer to begin their search for clues to the life of Istvan Bokanyi. She did not want to be disappointed, to have their search lead nowhere, yet they were probably on a fruitless expedition. In her dream Jonathon was saying to her, "Your imagination is not up to predicting how this will turn out tomorrow. Good night, sleep tight, my love."

At seven the next morning the Wentworths enjoyed a breakfast of strong, memorable coffee and delicious warm pastries. But the orange juice made Lisa wrinkle her nose with distaste. "Gross, totally gross."

"Lisa, have some compassion. This is a poor country. The food here is excellent, but they can't afford to import fresh oranges. Maybe you can make this 'sacrifice' and still survive your trip to Hungary."

"Heard you, Mom," and she rolled off her mother's bed and into the shower.

Marika dialed Anthony's office direct line, and was glad to hear that all of the accounts had been going well. She had not been in the office since the previous Thursday, but the thirst for work had returned to her since the day she had decided she had no time for a real depression. There was even an important new account brewing, Anthony reported—a travel business account recommended by the senior management of their client, Flair-hotels, Inc.

"The Kauffmans are very pleased with how our agency is handling the product launch," Anthony related, "and they said to tell you they'll send a car to meet your plane at the Zurich airport. The driver will be holding up a 'LUXFOODS' sign. They are looking forward to your visit to their headquarters. That was a genius move, Marika, to combine your trip to Budapest with a quick stop in Zurich on the way home."

"I wanted to see the Swiss operation anyway, and it only takes two days out of my life. It also gives me a chance to use my great-aunt's chalet near Gstaad for the weekend. *That's* the really genius part of my planning."

"You deserve some R and R," he said solicitously, "after the schedule you've been on, and considering the things you've been through recently."

Oh, but you can only guess at what I've been through, Anthony, she wanted to say.

He transferred the call to an eager Hortense, who plied her boss with questions about the hotel, the flight, the driver, and Budapest in general.

"Boss, this is so momentous, I am a nervous wreck for you."

"I'll report to you tomorrow on what happened, but Hortense, is something wrong? Your voice sounds strained. Is there something I should know about?"

"You are uncanny in reading me."

"Just as you are uncanny in reading me. All right, tell."

"It's Steve. He's a lot worse. It's in his brain. The doctor says there's not too much longer to wait. He's hallucinating much of the time. But two days ago, when you and Lisa were in London for the weekend, a moving van pulled up in front of his apartment. The movers took all of the family possessions—the antiques, the oriental rug, the tables, lamps, chairs, everything. His terrible parents left poor Steve just his bed."

Marika found it hard to summon her voice. "How could they?"

"His parents didn't want any of Steve's male friends to get his furniture when he dies. When I came over to see him, I found his clothes lying in neat piles on the floor—not even a bureau to put them in."

"Lord! Hortense, what did you do about it?"

"You would have been proud of the team. We moved fast, lent him pieces of our own. Anthony ran down to Conran's and bought him everything he needs that we couldn't scrape up. In one day, we put his apartment back together again, but I can tell you, I've never seen such maliciousness, such evil heartlessness—"

Marika interrupted her. "I want to call Steve right away. I'll talk to you tomorrow sometime."

"I don't know if that's such a good idea, Boss."

"Don't be silly, Hortense. God bless."

Marika hung up and dialed Steve's number. After several attempts, she got through the Hungarian telephone system to New York. One of Steve's friends answered. She lost no time with polite conversation.

"This is Marika Wentworth. How is he?"

"Not good. The home care person is with him all the time now, thank God. I understand that's a gift from you. It's—it's very nice of you, Mrs. Wentworth."

"What's happening?" she said.

"I just dropped in to see Steve a little while ago. I hadn't seen him in a month. The nursing aide told me what his parents did to him. Jesus Christ, it just about killed what's left of him. Sort of like giving him a *coup de grace.*"

"I want to speak to him."

"He doesn't make too much sense right now."

"I still want to speak to him."

"Sure. Heh, Steve old pal, here's a friend of yours, Marika, who wants to say hello."

She noticed how pleased the faint voice sounded when he said hello to her. Then he began to babble.

She listened to him for several minutes. Try as she might to interrupt him and get his attention, it was in vain. Finally she said,

"Good-bye, Steve, I love you," and hung up, just as Lisa came dancing into the room, pulling an oversized beige mohair sweater on top of her jeans. "Mom," she said laughing, "you look really beat. Must not have had much sleep last night. I just took a *thirty*-minute shower. Twenty-eight minutes of trying to make that complicated thing work, and two minutes of water coming out of it!" She laughed again and said, "Hurry up, you have only fifteen minutes until it's eight o'clock." She saw Marika's tears and her voice wound down. "Mom? Mom, what's happened?"

Marika pulled her daughter into her arms. "Oh, I love you, Lisa."

"I love you too, Mom. But, what's this about?"

"It's Steve."

"Is it over?"

Marika shook her head no. "Oh, Lisa, it's so sad what's happening to him." The young woman gave her mother a tissue and Marika made a little honking sound as she blew her nose into it. Her daughter held her in her young strong arms.

"I'm sorry, Mom."

"Come, no more today. There'll be time left to cry."

Laszlo was waiting for them in the lobby, his silver Citroën parked right at the front door. "I know the doorman *very well*," he said proudly, "I am the only driver allowed to park this close." The two Wentworth women entered the back seat of the car, sharing an ambivalence of anticipation and dread.

"We should relax and enjoy this drive," said Marika, "because what very well may happen is that we will find out nothing. It could be a great anticlimax, a washout. We must prepare ourselves for that."

"I know," said Lisa, "you're right. It's better to let it all happen, rather than try to second-guess the outcome."

Laszlo, intent on making the right turn out of the city, wondered what the American ladies' strange conversation signified.

Lisa studied Laszlo from the back seat and made a sign to her mother about how good-looking she thought he was. With dark brown curly hair, flashing green eyes, and an engaging grin that created two small dimples every time he smiled, he was definitely a handsome man. Marika looked over at her daughter and said in a low voice, "Fickle one." At that, Lisa laughed in embarrassment and stared out the window.

They passed vestiges of a Roman aqueduct, and even an entire Roman town that had been evacuated. Rolling meadows and fields dotted with trees made the countryside a luxurious palette of greens. Laszlo stopped giving his tourist guide's *spiel* as they neared their destination, because he sensed his passengers would satisfy his curiosity about them if he prodded. What were they doing in Hungary, anyway? They did not seem to be normal tourists. He summoned his courage.

"Mrs. Wentworth, Szentendre is not so much a tourist spot as other places. Why is it your first priority, if I may be so bold to ask?"

"We are not telling anyone why we came to Hungary, Laszlo, but I feel you will be able to help us more if you know why we are making this trip. My father, whom I never knew because I was—adopted—was Hungarian. My adoptive American father, when he died last December, told me my blood father was a Hungarian who died in the war. My mother, who died when I was quite young, had no knowledge of his whereabouts, except that he came from a place called Szentendre. And that is all I know. I want to learn more about my father as you can understand. I have decided to start by investigating the town's birth records."

"Oh, Mrs. Wentworth," said Laszlo, obviously moved, "that is a very interesting development." He said no more for they were entering the small town of Szentendre, which was alive with the energy of people going about their daily affairs. Serbian in heritage and with a pretty church near the center, the town sat placidly on the Danube. There were wide quays for promenading, which were bordered in bright-colored flowering plants. Marika and Lisa were fascinated by the twelfth- and thirteenth-century buildings, splashed with a centuries-old palette of rainbow paints that Hungarians seemed to love. Laszlo parked the car off the main square in town and led them through quaint, narrow cobblestoned streets, lined with pink-, yellow-, blue-, green-, and paprika-colored buildings. The town hall turned out to be a late nineteenth-century pair of buildings in need of a good painting. One was a deep pink in color, the other a marigold yellow. They followed Laszlo past a portion of a Roman column that had originally formed the entrance to a building of another era. They passed through a courtyard and entered a small office on the right. It was a typical *fonctionnaire*'s whitewashed office, crowded with inexpensive modern blond wood desks, tables, chairs, and shaggy-looking plants. The smell of cooking and the ever-present smell of cigarette smoke mingled exotically in the air. The registrar came out of her tiny inner office to greet them because Laszlo had explained that these were two "very important American ladies." A woman in her forties, she had a definite air of chic, Lisa decided, with her leather sandals, white cotton pants, and a long khaki bigshirt, cinched at the waist with a woven belt. Lisa whispered in her mother's ear, "Someone gave her a Banana Republic catalog," which made her mother laugh.

Laszlo explained to the curious registrar that Marika and her daughter wanted to look up the birth records of a "male friend of the family's." As a courtesy to the Americans, the conversation took place in English.

"When was he born?" the registrar asked.

"I would say between 1918 and 1923," Marika replied. The woman went to get the books of that era and reappeared bearing a few heavy volumes.

"And the name?" the woman asked.

"Bokanyi," Marika replied. "Istvan Bokanyi."

Lisa, who happened to be looking at Laszlo at this moment, was surprised to see him look startled. Then he said "Oh!" almost imperceptibly.

"Are you all right?" she asked.

"Oh yes," he said. "I was moved by the sight of those old books, documenting the lives of so many people—young and old, important and unimportant, now all just names, birthdates, and dates of death. No longer people, just statistics."

After about ten minutes of turning the heavy yellowed pages slowly and with great care, the registrar and Laszlo had an excited exchange of conversation.

"She's found Bokanyi," he announced to the Americans triumphantly.

Marika and Lisa leaned over them to examine the page. "Mom," Lisa said, "how do you feel right now?"

Marika did not answer, but squeezed her hand for support. The registrar took Marika's finger and placed it on a horizontal line that crossed the page, under the name *Bokanyi Istvan.* Laszlo translated the different column headings: *Birthdate*: October 4, 1920. *Place of Birth*: Szentendre. *Parents' Names*: Tamas and Vera Bokanyi. There was a final column on the far right. Laszlo translated it as, "Died in the War, December 1944."

"Is this all I can find out!" Marika asked, disappointed there was no more. Laszlo asked if there were any other surviving Bokanyis in the book, and the registrar said there were not, that the rest of the family had obviously been born elsewhere, and that their births and deaths were thus not reported in this town hall. The registrar and Laszlo talked some more, and he turned to Marika. "She says there is a possibility—a very small one—that a restaurant owner near here who was about Istvan's age in the war, would remember him."

They drove to the café on the outskirts of town and found the owner. He and Laszlo talked for five minutes and then he wrote down a name and address on a paper napkin and handed it to the tour guide.

"We go back to the center of town," Laszlo said.

Marika and Lisa followed him to a door set in a long whitewashed wall, which was covered with flowering green vines. Once inside, they found themselves in a narrow alley that was like a separate street, lined with whitewashed stone houses on both sides. Men were tinkering with cars in small garages, women were sitting on their tiny porches, chatting and preparing food for lunch. The sounds of everyday chatter resonated through the alleyway. Laszlo called out the name of Latki and a white-haired man quickly appeared, looking very curious, his face wrinkled and tan from a long summer in the sun. Dressed in a clean white T-shirt, his belly protruded over his gray work pants. Yes, Marika thought, he would be about the same age as Istvan.

The two men conversed, repeating the name Bokanyi several times, then the stranger ushered them through the door of one of the houses. They found themselves in a small, meticulously clean living room, with a worn oriental rug on the floor, two daybeds in opposite corners, covered in gold rayon spreads and further embellished with some pillows and a teddy bear, and a series of chairs, all upholstered in the same drab brown plush fabric. A floor-to-ceiling caramel-colored ceramic stove loomed in one corner. They were joined by Mr. Latki's robust wife, who with her gray hair, gray eyes, gray skirt, and white blouse, and gray leather oxfords reminded Lisa of many teachers she had had in Boston and New York schools. The large black family dog of dubious ancestry also formally joined the group and sat himself down on his haunches with a large sigh, as if he knew this would be another boring session in which he received no attention.

The shelves of the four-tiered bric-a-brac stand, Marika noted, were jammed with small bottles of liqueurs and liquor. Laszlo was to explain to her later that they served as decoration but were also gifts from Communist official friends—people who traveled freely in and out of various countries. The little bottles of liqueur available on airplanes had become a symbol of freedom to the Latkis.

Laszlo performed like a well-trained ambassador as he introduced them all to one another. Mr. Latki pronounced to the Americans one of the few words he knew in English, "Please," as he motioned them to sit down. Laszlo and their hosts proceeded to have an animated discussion in their own tongue, while Marika and Lisa looked around at the little objects visible everywhere on tabletops and shelves. There were pieces of porcelain, odd demitasse cups, a candy server, some religious items, and small boxes made of different materials, everything carefully dusted. The tables were covered with freshly laundered white linen embroidered cloths. Hanging on three of the four walls of the room were two rows of shelves, sagging under the weight of a full load of books.

"This man knew Istvan Bokanyi," Laszlo reported to the American women in English. "I did not tell him you were his daughter, but just that you were inquiring for friends of his in the States."

"Go on," Marika said excitedly. "Tell me every word he says."

Laszlo continued to talk to Mr. Latki, a few sentences at a time, and then would report back in English to his eager listeners. Bokanyi, he explained, had attained the rank of captain, whereas Latki was only a lieutenant. He had seen Bokanyi in front of the Swedish Embassy two or three times, and Latki, who knew nothing of Istvan's family, had asked him what was the connection, and he had replied that his mother was a Swede. The old man went on, saying that Bokanyi had died, he heard, near a Swedish Embassy-owned house, full of Jews living under Raoul Wallenberg's protection.

Laszlo grew agitated, and Marika kept pressing him with more and more questions to translate and direct at Mr. Latki . . .

"How did he die?" Marika asked.

"He says that he does not know for sure. The story is that it was the Arrow Cross who killed him."

"What's that?"

"I will explain later."

"Ask him if Istvan was a Jew."

More talk between the two men.

"He says, no, that he was Swedish Lutheran, like Wallenberg. He also remembers, Mrs. Wentworth, that everyone in the regiment was curious when Bokanyi was able to go to London for a short time in November 1944. No one could leave their regiments to go anywhere in those days."

"Then how did he manage it?"

Laszlo kept turning to Mr. Latki to ask a question, wait for an answer, and then translate it.

"Evidently, he had a Swedish passport, that's how he managed it. He obviously went there to do something for Wallenberg, perhaps involving funds, rumor has it."

Marika looked over at Lisa. They read each other's thoughts. This Istvan Bokanyi was indeed her father, the man who made a trip to London in 1944.

Laszlo continued talking to Mr. Latki. Excited, he announced dramatically that the word in the regiment was Bokanyi died a hero's death fighting for the Jews and that "your friends in America should be very proud when they learn of it."

There were tears in the eyes of both mother and daughter. They reached for each other's hand. "Laszlo," Marika managed to say, "one more question. Does he know anything about Bokanyi's family? His parents?"

Laszlo answered very quickly, "He says he knows nothing about his family, that they moved away from Szentendre after the war, because he tried to look them up one day. Perhaps his mother went back to Sweden, who knows?"

Lisa, more objective than her mother in this emotional moment, noticed again Laszlo's own state of tension and excitement. He feels things deeply, she thought to herself, and she liked him all the more for it.

"There is not one more drop of information to be had?" Marika asked Laszlo plaintively.

"Quite unfortunately, no."

Marika and Lisa arose and Marika instructed Laszlo exactly how to express her gratitude to the Latkis. Her final words were "Bokanyi's friends in America will be so pleased to learn he was a brave man." The only sounds in the room as they left were the heavy breathing of the dog and the ticking of the wall clock, which, although it gave a totally inaccurate time, made a very comforting sound.

As they walked toward the car, Marika saw a rustic building that was obviously a flower shop. She went in, purchased a bunch of long-stemmed roses, and coached by Laszlo, printed some words of thanks in Hungarian on a card, transacted the cost of the flowers in forints, and asked that they be delivered right away to the Latki house. Laszlo then asked his passengers if they would mind strolling nearby for a few minutes, because he had an important call to make.

The line was busy for three minutes, then it finally became free.

"Clara, it is I, Laszlo."

"Oh, dear man," she said affectionately, "do you have some nice rich customers to send my way today?"

"Not exactly. No one in my car is exactly in the mood for buying your expensive dresses today."

"Pity. So what is on your mind?"

"Clara, my passengers are an American woman named Marika and her daughter Lisa, from New York."

"Marika. A Hungarian name. How nice, and from New York."

"Clara, she is Istvan Bokanyi's child."

On the road back into Budapest, all three people sat for several kilometers, lost in their own thoughts, unable to speak . . . Marika was the first to compose herself.

"We have had so much thrown at us today, but I still must find out more. What about this Arrow Cross group that killed my father? What are they?"

"In October 1944, the Germans, who were being hard-pressed by the Russians at this point in the war, abducted to Germany and imprisoned Horthy, the Hungarian regent, and put a band of renegades in power. It became the Szalási regime, and the men were called 'Nyilas' or 'Arrow Cross' in English. They were the worst kind of people, Hungarian, not German, Nazis. They had cross arrows on the armbands of their black uniforms. They were hoodlums and criminals."

He had paused and Marika pressed him, "Go on, go on. Tell us everything."

"In December of that year, the Arrow Cross took all the Jews from the houses under Wallenberg's protection and marched them down to the Danube quais and slaughtered them. Your father was there, obviously, from what Latki said. The Danube 'ran red' that day, as they say. It was an awful, unforgettable black mark in Hungarian history."

"How did the Arrow Cross or the Nazis or anyone else know who was a Jew and who wasn't?" Lisa asked.

"They knew," Laszlo said sadly, "just as the Nazis knew. They had made them sew patches on every sleeve of every garment. Star of David patches. Wallenberg kept issuing fake Swedish passports to the Jews until he got caught by the Nazis for doing it too often. He used his family's jewels, and his mother's friends' jewels, to bribe the Nazis to leave the Jews alone."

"Do you know anything more?" Marika asked softly, her whole body shaking with a quiet kind of sobbing.

"There is no more. I have told you everything," he said, hating himself for lying so blatantly. There *was* more. There was a widow named Clara Bokanyi who years later was to own an elegant dress shop on the Vaci Utca. Her husband was Istvan Bokanyi. Yes, there had been more than he had told Mrs. Wentworth. May God forgive him for keeping it from her. But she would know it soon enough.

When they reached the hotel, Marika invited Laszlo to join them for lunch on the outdoor terrace behind the Hilton. It was time for everyone to lift their spirits and become positive again. They had a light lunch of smoked meats, cheese, and cucumber salad, facing the gray turrets of what looked to Lisa like a Disneyland small fortified castle with ramparts. Laszlo explained that it was called the "Fishermen's Bastion" when it was built in the late nineteenth century to replace the medieval castle wall that had originally been there. A group of fishermen had been slaughtered there defending the town, and that is how it got its name.

They sipped Hungarian beer and watched the people scrambling all over the curving ramparts, amusement-park-style, in order to gain a splendid view of the Danube, Parliament, and Pest on the other side. Flute and harmonica players, as well as violinists situated around the vast open space, were playing to the indifferent ears of some twenty nationalities of tourists.

After lunch, there was only an hour left to sight-see on foot around Castle Hill with Laszlo, before he had another client to pick up in his car. He led them through a maze of cobblestoned streets, showing them fragments of Roman, Gothic, medieval, and eighteenth-century houses. Marika and Lisa sat down to rest for five minutes on two of a series of uncomfortable stone seats, set in Gothic niches, in the barrel-vaulted entry of a great house.

"You are sitting where the noblemen's bodyguards sat many centuries ago," Laszlo laughed. "If only these medieval stone walls could talk to you."

Finally, he had to leave them. "You can wander around these *utcas* some more by yourselves," he said, realizing by now they would know the Hungarian word for "street." "There is lots more for you to see around the top of Castle Hill. Trinity Square and the Hilton are close by, so you can wander by yourselves and not get lost. I will see you tomorrow." By now he had become their friend.

"I'm tired, Mom," said Lisa. "Can't we sit for a moment longer in these 'comfortable' stone guard niches?"

Marika laughed. "Of course, though I'm not tired at all. It's probably the adrenaline flowing through me—left over from this morning in Szentendre. I still can't digest it all."

"Do you know what totally perplexes me? I've always considered myself a hundred-percent American, right?"

"Well, aren't you?"

"No, I suddenly realize I'm really not, nor are you, Mom. Look, when Grandpa Russell told you about Istvan and you told me, I had to get used to considering myself three-quarters American and one-quarter Hungarian. Now, today, I find out my grandmother on my father's side was Swedish. That means I am three-quarters American, one-eighth Swedish, and one-eighth Hungarian. How's that for a mishmash?" She paused for a second, "Actually, I think it's kind of cool."

"That makes me one-half American, one-fourth Hungarian, and one-fourth Swedish," laughed Marika. "We are like a bowl of goulash. C'mon. There are still places to see. There'll be plenty of time for you to sit and rest on the steps of Columbia when you're back home."

They peeked into the thirteenth-century interiors of the "Red Hedgehog Inn," poked into the eighteenth-century "Fortuna Inn," and inspected the old ovens and kitchen implements in the Commerce and Catering Museum. "What a great promotion could be done for an American gourmet chef in this place," Marika mused out loud.

"Mom, how can you think about public relations at a time like this? Look, I meant it when I said I was tired. I want to go back to the hotel."

"I want to go back, too, but just one last place. This beautiful baroque villa—or manor or whatever it is—looks interesting. Let's go inside."

The sign on the building announced in Hungarian that it was a music foundation. The words were enough like English for them to understand.

They stepped into the entryway, past magnificent carved iron arched doors on either side. Lisa recited from heart a passage she had read about Hungary's famous ironwork.

Then they entered the courtyard. "A perfect space!" cried Marika. It was—a beautiful square courtyard, surrounded by the inner walls of a perfectly balanced baroque château. Beneath them the small pebbled courtyard had been made into a handsome circular design. They continued to profess their admiration for the courtyard when a male voice called down to them through an open window.

"Americans!" They looked up and saw a handsome man. Marika figured him to be in his mid-thirties. He was leaning out of the casement window and laughing at them. Then he asked in accented English, "What can I do for you?"

"Well, who are *you*?" asked Marika. "Are you an official of this foundation?"

"No, I am an architect, but I am lucky enough to have my office here. I do a lot of restoration work on Castle Hill, so an office here allows me to be near my work."

He bounded down the stone staircase and was suddenly standing next to them.

"We were just admiring this space. It's—it's beautiful."

Lisa whispered in Marika's ear, "Have you *ever* seen anyone descend a staircase that fast?"

The two women appraised him shyly. Marika noticed his tall, muscular build. He was trim, and his dark gray flannel trousers, white shirt open at the collar, and sea-green V-neck sweater made him look like someone who had just stepped out of a Ralph Lauren ad. He had ash-blond, thick, wavy hair and smiling gray eyes. She noticed his beautiful hands, which moved as he spoke. A family gold crest ring glinted in the afternoon sun. So did his very white teeth, she noticed. A lovely smile.

"I'm at your service, ladies, to show you the building, if you would like. My name is Janos Margitay."

They introduced themselves to him, he kissed Marika's hand, and they were soon following behind him on a tour of the baroque building. Marika chattered animatedly with him, but Lisa began to lag perceptibly. Finally, they walked back to the hotel. Lisa swore she could not walk another step. They sat in the bar and drank iced tea. It was now five o'clock. The manager of the hotel came by, pummeled Janos affectionately in the back, and they exchanged greetings in Hungarian.

"Mrs. Wentworth, you are in the company of one of the finest young architects in Eastern Europe, and, I might add, a member of one of the great old families of our aristocracy."

Janos immediately chided him in Hungarian. "I have been censured quite thoroughly for having said that," the manager smiled, and moved on.

"I would be very honored," Janos said, looking at his watch, "if you two ladies would allow me to take you to dinner. Fate obviously sent you to me, and she must be treated hospitably."

Marika answered quickly. "No, you're very kind, but we have been in the countryside all day and are very tired."

"In Budapest, the way you make yourself *un*tired is to go out to dinner, listen to some gypsy music, and forget what it was that made you tired."

"I don't think I can forget what made me tired," Marika said quietly.

"Mom, let's go. It would do us good." Lisa was suddenly like a puppy dog, straining at the leash.

"All right, that is nice of you, we will," Marika said, but then added a little hesitantly, "However, you must let us take *you* to dinner. I insist on that."

"When you are with Janos, you do not manage the evening. I am the manager, and I pay, not you." That was that.

They made an appointment to meet in the lobby at eight o'clock, and he bid them good-bye, taking the stairs that led from the bar to the lobby three at a time with the grace of an athlete.

"*Mamma mia!*" Lisa exclaimed after his retreating figure, "that is one gorgeous hunk of man."

Back in their suite, Marika threw the key in her handbag, kicked off her shoes, and collapsed on the bed.

"I have never before made a dinner date with a stranger in my entire life. It's the kind of thing you're not supposed to do. Do you realize he might be a white slave trader?" She laughed, and then said in a more serious tone, "Do you realize we know absolutely *nothing* about this man, and here we are, going off to dinner with him?"

"Mom, you heard the hotel manager. Janos Margitay is a friend of his. You've been a worry wart all your life, but frankly, I don't think we are at risk."

"Somehow it feels very safe to go out with a stranger in this country. It's not like being picked up at Forty-second and Ninth Avenue in New York."

"After the number of dinners you and I have eaten lately without an escort," Lisa stated, "I think we'd go out with Janos even if we *had* met him at Forty-second and Ninth Avenue."

It was much more difficult packing into their new friend's little car than it was into Laszlo's much larger Citroën. Marika and Lisa questioned Janos about his life and learned that he was thirty-five and had never been married. He had an aunt, who lived with his family after the 1956 uprising. The aunt, to whom he was very close, was an English teacher at the university, and she had taught him to speak it—and taught him well.

Marika, sitting next to him in the front seat, noticed again his wonderful smile, rather like that of an older, less handsome man in Chicago. His eyes crinkled in the corners, and his smile illuminated his entire face—every facial muscle seemed to be involved.

"Have you had enough of how do you call it, the third degree?" he asked. "Any more questions?"

"Yes," Lisa answered. "I'm starving and it would be nice to know where we're going."

"To a place you will love," he answered. "All the tourists love it."

"But do we want to go to a place that the tourists love?" Marika asked, an edge of irritation showing in her voice.

"You'll be glad I took you to this place," Janos replied. "Have trust. In order to appreciate this city, you must trust."

They entered the Café Hungaria and walked through the crowded bar area. People were standing at the bar, dressed in dark executive-type clothing, Marika noticed, like any expensive New York restaurant at night. Her ear picked up at least five languages being spoken, and the air was thick with cigarette smoke—including a heavy intrusion of smoke from the French Gauloises. Janos led them through a set of marble and bronze archways and columns, everything curving in bursts of baroque energy. Lisa whispered to her mother, "What is this place anyway? An opera house? Catch those cool balloons."

Marika laughed. "Cool balloons, my foot," she said. They had come to the top of a long stairway leading down into a cathedral-like space, where large clusters of white electrified globes hung from the frescoed ceiling.

Marika suddenly became aware of a warm hand on her bare elbow, guiding her down the stairs. She blushed, wondering if Janos could possibly sense that his mere touch had sent a sensual thrill through her. It had always been that way when Jonathon touched her. It felt nice to have this tingling sensation again inside her, and Jonathon's words came back to her: "I have never known a woman with the extraordinary sensory reactions you have when your skin is touched. It's so easy to get you excited, and that is so pleasing to a man."

She was embarrassed remembering his words, and she wondered if Janos was aware of her blush and her warm cheeks. Her daughter was. Lisa was looking at her slyly.

My daughter reads me far too well, she thought.

"This place is almost a *monument historique*," she heard Janos explaining, and she was grateful that he, at least, was unaware of her adolescent behavior. They sat down at a narrow table covered in a salmon pink linen cloth. Janos pointed out the framed caricatures hanging on the walls of the renowned journalists, writers, and poets who had congregated here since the mid-nineteenth century. "They still do," he told them.

Giant menus were placed in front of them, with dishes described in English as well as Hungarian. "Here, let me recommend our dishes you might enjoy."

They ate quail, wild-boar sausage, stew of carp in red wine with cottage cheese paste, and finally ended the meal with one order of *Palacsinta Gundel* and three forks. These were thin pancakes folded into triangles and smothered in a thick chocolate sauce.

Marika observed Janos and Lisa talking about American sports and Columbia University. By the time the conversation turned to Hungarian politics, she found herself attracted to this young man with his intelligent and zealous way of expressing himself. Young? Well, he was nine years younger than she. Not *much* younger— but still. However, he was seventeen years older than Lisa.

Perhaps she had consumed too much red wine, Marika thought to herself, to be even considering such things. Lisa wouldn't want Janos. She had Sergio. Marika caught herself again, stifling a giggle in her wineglass. Here she was, after this day of all days, putting Janos Margitay on a scale, weighing whether mother or daughter was more suitable for him.

Still, he was terribly attractive, she thought. That ash-blond hair, wonderful body, those nice eyes. An intelligent face and a lovely manner. She tried to think of whom he reminded her. That was it. Janos had the coloring of a northern Italian—a Milanese, like Sergio. No wonder she had pictured him with Lisa.

A gypsy musician began playing his *cimbalom* intently, and they were suddenly surrounded by violinists who had come to serenade them.

Marika and Lisa loved the intense music played by the group. It was Hungarian, Janos assured them, not gypsy music. When the musicians in their black velvet costumes finished and started to leave them, he pressed some forints in the hands of the lead violinist.

When the bill came, Marika once again thanked Janos for his generosity in taking them both to dinner, which she knew was expensive by Hungarian standards, but certainly not by New York ones.

He shrugged off her gratitude. "It is not every day that American women like you come into my office courtyard, rhapsodizing over its Baroque architecture. Therefore, you honor me by having dinner with me.

Once back at the hotel, Lisa went up ahead to the suite. Marika couldn't decide if Lisa was motivated either by extreme fatigue or by diplomacy. Whatever the reason, Marika was grateful. She stood talking to Janos in the front lobby of the hotel, and it was obvious neither wanted the conversation to end. They finally sat down on a comfortable sofa by the elevator, and talked over a demitasse about their jobs and what they hoped for the future in their careers.

"You are so much further than me in success and achievement," he said sadly.

"I've had more years in which to achieve," she said smiling, "but more importantly, I've been in a free country."

"No, I didn't mean what I said at all in terms of your being older than me," he said, obviously discomforted by her implication that he was too young for her. "A few years makes no difference in the scheme of things. What I meant is that you are obviously a star in your profession, this public relations business."

"And you are a great architect," she said shyly, "that's what the Hilton manager said."

"Maybe someday, now that things are beginning to be or hopefully will be—different in Eastern Europe, I'll be able to visit the great architecture of the world. Much of it is in your country, Marika. Who knows, maybe someday I'll pop up on your New York doorstep and say, 'Educate me, Marika. Show me all I should see and study.' "

Oh, Janos, she thought, that would be nice. She felt an indescribable tenderness for this man sitting close to her on the Hilton sofa.

He stayed for an hour. It had grown late, and he apologized. She walked with him down to the lobby and out to the tiled street in front where the doorman usually holds court. It was so late that for the moment no one was around. He took her hand as if to kiss it, but then just held it in his. It gave her a strange feeling of excitement, his hand was so warm and strong. "I could not take my eyes off you tonight," he whispered. "I must see you again."

She was embarrassed, so she laughed off his comment. "You are just overwhelmed," she said, "by suddenly finding yourself the meat in a sandwich of two generations of American women."

"No, I am overwhelmed by nothing more than you," he said. "You can't possibly be here for only two more days. I must see you. Tell me you will have dinner with me tomorrow night."

"*We* will have dinner with you tomorrow night, Lisa and I."

He laughed and she could see the straight white teeth and the beautiful smile, even in the dark. "All right, we will all three have dinner, but afterward—I must see you alone."

He kissed her hand this time, looked in her eyes, and caught her own smile.

"I saw you just now. The darkness does not eradicate a smile like yours. You felt something, too, tonight, with me. I know it from the feel of this," and he turned her hand over and kissed the inside of her wrist. "Until tomorrow night, then—at eight."

Marika and Lisa ordered breakfast early, so that they would not have to hurry their enjoyment of it. This time no canned orange juice, which Lisa claimed must have been imported from Siberia a half century ago. There were, however, large potfuls of delicious strong coffee again, which Lisa had described to Sergio in her daily telephone call as the "coffee for the resurrection of the dead." There were also soft white rolls with crispy crusts and *dios kifli*, which they learned from the waiter was the Hungarian name for the irresistible croissants filled with walnut paste.

Lisa watched her mother over her coffee cup. "You just stretched now, like someone in postcoital contentment." She knew her mother had been smitten by Janos. Her attraction to him had been in the air all around her last night, like a romantic mist. If Janos had not noticed it, she, Lisa, could not help but notice it.

"Postcoital. Is that the kind of education I pay all that tuition for?"

"Mom, wouldn't you rather have a daughter who can discuss the realities of life in direct, clear terms, than a daughter who can prattle on about Doric versus Ionic versus Corinthian capitals in ancient architecture?" Marika threw her towel at her, as they both heard the bells of the Matthias Church ringing the hour: nine o'clock. They were late.

Laszlo was waiting for them by his car.

"Can you stay with us until three today?" Marika queried, warmly shaking hands with him in greeting.

First stop on the day's exploration tour was the old Hotel Gellert, so that Marika and Lisa could see the famous spa there, one of fifteen in the city. The women entered it from the hotel by means of an old-fashioned iron cage elevator, and stepped into what Marika saw as a Felliniesque Art Nouveau movie set. The giant indoor pool with its green-colored waters had been built in a Beaux Arts palace-like area, with a high vaulted glass ceiling, carved stone columns lining the sides, second-story balconies— for *kibbitzers*—overhanging the pool, and water gushing from fish-head fountains.

They walked past the Gellert's world-famous outdoor swimming pool. "In the summer, every half hour or so," Laszlo explained to them later, "or when it jolly well feels like it, a machine sends immense artificial waves rolling down one end of the pool's surface for a couple of minutes. That's so we won't complain we don't have the sea at our door. It's completely mad."

Marika and Lisa then inspected the adjacent marble and tile thermal bath for women. Lisa read aloud from a tourist guide as they inspected it—" 'Its misty warm medicinal waters are produced from the hot spring running beneath the Danube.' "

"Mom," Lisa suddenly announced, "if I were as corpulent as

the females are around here, I wouldn't let even other women see me without my clothes."

"If you lived in this country and ate the amount of whipped cream and pastries the Hungarians do, you would eventually look just like the ladies in there."

"But most of the women on the street are slim," Lisa protested.

"You are looking at the young on the street," reminded her mother. "These women are all much older. Look at the less advantaged women in America, too, the ones who get no exercise but who eat junk all day. Is it any different?"

"I wonder why poor women seem to be fat. I don't understand it, if they're hungry all the time."

"Poor women can't get raspberries, melon, fresh vegetables, and lean meat and fish to eat, the way you can, Lisa. They are lucky if they get bread and potatoes."

"I never knew anyone like you, Mom, who can turn a visit to the baths of Budapest into a lecture on the inadequate diets of poor women. You should teach a course along with art history called 'Social Conscience 105.' "

"There are worse things you could say about me." Marika looked at her watch and made Lisa walk faster.

They told Laszlo later about the women they had seen in the baths, and he said, "You should see the baths for men only. Fat old men with many layers of stomachs sit like Buddhas in the steam, saying nothing, but playing very serious chess. It's incredibly funny!"

Marika asked, "Why are there so many baths in Budapest?" The day before they had driven by a sixteenth-century domed bath along the Danube, still functioning.

"The Turks had to leave us one good memory," he joked with cynicism. "Legend has it that one homesick sultan had a large steamed bath facility constructed within three days of his arrival down by the Danube, to satisfy his homesickness for his country."

Laszlo drove them on a quick "culture tour," past the opera house, and to the Museum of Fine Arts. "If you see nothing else," he said, as he waited with the car outside, "you must see the Madonna by Raphael from the Esterhazy family's collection of

Old Masters." He made them go into the Hungarian National Museum to see the symbol of the country's identity: St. Stephen's crown and royal scepter, which Pope Silvester II purportedly gave the country's first crowned king in 1001.

Laszlo then drove them out to the *Margit Sziget*, which he explained was "Margaret Island" in English. "This mile-and-a-half long island, situated in the middle of the Danube, is one of the most pleasant aspects of life in this city," he said proudly.

"Why are we going here?" asked Lisa, who was beginning to feel over-sightseen.

"Well," he answered, "for one thing there are two first-class hotels here, beautiful outdoor cafés, a Japanese garden of note, a zoo, and acres of meadows full of wildflowers and gardens to stroll in. In fact, it is in this romantic spot that my wife and I"—he stopped himself, and then chose his words carefully—"we fell in love here."

"Now I know why we came here," Lisa whispered to her mother. "A taste of Hungarian schmaltz."

"Quiet!" shushed Marika.

Laszlo continued his tour, giving them the history of every part of Budapest they passed. Because he had two such extraordinary women in his back seat, he felt he should tell them about some of the famous women of Hungarian history, like the mother of the beloved Ferenc Rakoczi.

"Ferenc," he explained, "was a fiery prince of Transylvania."

"Goody!" interrupted Lisa. "Dracula came from there. I love to hear about Transylvania."

"Most Americans do," said Laszlo in a tired voice. "It's the power of Boris Katloff, or whatever his name was."

"Karloff," corrected Lisa, "but George Hamilton did a good Dracula, too."

The trio lunched quickly in a small restaurant in the open-air half of the Malomto Restaurant on the Frankel Utca. They sat at a table covered with a green cotton cloth, overlaid with a white square cloth printed with little red hearts.

"No tourists here?" asked a delighted Marika.

"No tourists here. This is a characteristic eating place for the people of Budapest."

"This place won't win any *Interior Design* magazine competition," Lisa remarked to her mother, "but it's clean—and delicious. What is this fish, Laszlo?" They had let him order for them, because they could not understand one word of the menu in Hungarian, and he could not explain the dishes either.

"You're eating a traditional dish—*fogas*—a Lake Balaton fish served with salad."

When Marika paid the check for the three meals, she discovered she had spent only fifteen dollars' worth of forints.

"Laszlo, ask the owner if I could have a menu, will you?" When he went off to request one, she said to Lisa, "I must send one back to the office, with the prices converted from forints into dollars. They won't believe it. A turkey sandwich costs five dollars at our corner deli in New York, and here for five dollars apiece, we had a delicious meal and a glass of wine each."

"Wouldn't it be more effective, Mom, if instead of sending it to your office, you sent the menu to Sirio Maccioni of Le Cirque?"

Laszlo drove them around the beautifully restored nineteenth-century royal palace, then into the vast Heroes' Square, which to Lisa looked like the inside of two football stadia laid end to end, with a bunch of columns and porticoes where the hotdog stands would normally be located.

Then they walked up and down the aisles of the big Central Market Hall, past hundreds of food stalls.

"Mom, I may not be a great sight-seer," Lisa commented, "but when it comes to food, I become one."

"How jealous other Communist countries must be of these food markets!" Marika said to Laszlo, both her hands deep in mounds of fragrant, brilliantly colored peppers of all sizes and shapes. Some of the peppers were strung like Christmas tree garlands; others hung from the booth ceiling like fat necklaces; ropes of sweet garlic were used like Sheraton swags for decorating the stalls. There were stalls full of sausages as small as fountain pens or as large as rolling pins. There were goose livers fatter than any they had ever seen, the size of loaves of bread, and round mush-rooms the size of frisbees. Racks of apples, paprika packed into cotton sacks, strips of bacon, and rows of potatoes and onions filled the cavernous market, underneath its soaring ceiling of iron-work that supported the roof. Peasant women from the farms tended their stalls, the younger ones wearing bright-colored sweat-ers and scarves, the older widows usually clad in black dresses and head scarves, perhaps adding a dash of color in a sweater.

"It's three o'clock," Laszlo said. "I must go. I will drop you off right near the Café Gerbeaud but first, a treat as we leave." He stopped in front of a stall that had a round plastic five-gallon-sized container, filled with fresh uncooked sauerkraut. The woman in attendance gave each of them a small paper bag of sauerkraut, which tasted pungent and sweet, and which they ate with their fingers while walking through the building.

"Mom," Lisa said, her mouth full of sauerkraut, "don't ever give me a hard time again about eating on the street in New York. It's acceptable to eat this on the street."

"When it becomes the fashion to eat sauerkraut on Fifth Av-enue, I promise I won't say a word about your doing it."

They drove to the outside rim of the great square on the Pest side of the city where the Café Gerbeaud was located, historically a famous coffeehouse for everyone who was anyone in Hungary, meeting at any time of day, for coffee and a mouth-watering sandwich or patisserie. "Café Gerbeaud," explained Laszlo as he said good-bye to them in the parking lot adjacent to the square, "has three hundred seats inside and four hundred on the outside terraces. This is where the country's main pleasure—gossip—is engendered."

"I'll take the dessert instead of the gossip," Lisa replied, al-though the taste of sauerkraut was still in her mouth.

"Everyone is always ready for dessert here," laughed Laszlo. "And the big shopping street Vaci Utca is right over there. You can take a look in the shops, if you wish. They even have Benetton, Estée Lauder, Adidas, and a McDonald's now, in case you're homesick. You can easily find a taxi back to the hotel from here. I will see you tomorrow, to take you some more places. At what time, Mrs. Wentworth?"

Pickup time was settled for nine o'clock the next morning, which was their last day. The two women then made their way through a throng of tourists and Hungarians strolling in the warm late summer sun. Marika kept thinking about dinner tonight, when they would see Janos again. It was just a pleasant thought that made her feel happy, a slight anticipation. Perhaps she had a very small crush on this handsome young man. Maybe even a minor sexual attraction. She smiled again, not hearing Lisa's comments on the slim young people in jeans everywhere surrounding them —some Hungarian students, others tourists from other countries, all bowed down by huge backpacks that made them waddle like ducks.

A great carved stone balustrade protectively enclosed the Gerbeaud's outdoor café tables from the people strolling by. The acoustics in the large square, Marika noticed, seemed to increase the volume of human voices. The hum of chatter combined with the water splashing in the fountains, the fluttering of the hungry pigeons' wings, and the click-clack of high heels over the stones made a lively concert of sounds.

They entered the enormous coffeehouse and found themselves in a large, quite formal space, with inlaid wood and marble surfaces, mirrors and crystal chandeliers casting reflections of light on the tiers of glass shelves crammed with the pastries—fruit tarts and crepes, puddings, cookies, strudels, and small sandwiches. Waitresses were replacing items fresh from the kitchen as soon as the patrons requested them from the shelves.

Marika and Lisa decided to order two double espressos, after a long discussion about whether or not to give in to their desire to try one of the coffee selections brimming with flavored whipped cream that were dancing by them on trays. They could not resist the pastries. Lisa succumbed to a *Meggyes Kosar*, a boat-shaped pastry stuffed with sour cherries. Marika ordered an *Anna Bombe*, a light pastry filled with strawberry cream and coated with burnt almonds. In perfect English, the waitress mentioned the fact that

Lisa had chosen the favorite patisserie of the Queen of the Netherlands, which Marika noted in her mini-computer, to add to her collage of impressions of Hungary. The fact that certain pastries were famous because they were the favorites of notables was another bit of trivia to remember.

They gave their order inside the café, and then sat down outside to await its arrival at their little table.

"What fun, to have absolutely nothing to do except stretch like cats in the late afternoon sun, notice people, and vegetate," Marika said after a moment of silence. They were fascinated counting the number of people wandering through the square eating ice cream cones—one out of every four. They noticed, too, how the ever-present gray cloud of pollution in Budapest, caused by the burning of diesel fuel oil, managed to change the color of the sunlight playing over the square and turn it into a silvery haze of light. They watched gleeful children climbing onto the backs of the stone lions in the fountain, riding them like competing jockeys on their horses. Then the children would slip off the animals' backs and drink the cool water that gushed from the lions' mouths.

"Mom, you are attracted to Janos, aren't you?" Lisa said, after yawning and stretching again.

"We just met yesterday. What are you talking about?"

"It's the way he looks at you. It's the same way Sergio looks at me, and you loved it."

"You're going to have to help me out with this conversation, since I really don't know what you're getting at."

"It's the way Janos kept leaning forward on his side of the table across from you last night. I began to wonder if he'd get through his meal." Marika blushed with pleasure, but didn't know how to reply.

"It's that lovely little smile around his eyes and mouth," Lisa continued.

"You are romanticizing an ordinary dinner into a dramatic love affair. It's ridiculous!" said Marika, rather sharply.

"Relax, enjoy Janos," Lisa said, in a maternal voice. "Since Jonathon took a walk, you deserve every bit of happiness you can get."

"He did not walk out on me!" Marika protested. "It was a mutual fifty-fifty decision."

"Come off it. I'm your daughter, remember?"

Marika had to laugh. "All right, so he did walk out on me. And, yes, I find Janos very attractive, but he's only thirty-five."

"What does it matter if he's thirty-five or fifty-five? Mom, you could use a man right now in your life."

"Lisa, I don't need sexual therapy as a cure for all my problems."

"It helps, it helps." They both laughed, and then began to giggle at the action taking place next to them. A couple of German tourists seated close by, in the café adjoining the Gerbeaud, were trying to stand up to leave. They were unable to get out of their small aluminum armchairs. They simply could not free their girth from the confines of the arms of the chairs, so they both arose, with their chairs stuck to their rear ends, and then struggled to help one another out of their predicament, swearing in German the whole time.

Then Marika and Lisa became aware of a figure approaching and staring at them. They watched silently as a wrinkled woman, her skin dyed bronze from the sun, glided through the square as if on ice skates. There was no motion of her body as she came toward them. She was totally enshrouded in black, like a mummy, no sign of her hair showing beneath her veil. Her black eyes darted to every side of her, mistrustful, watching, fearful. She came straight toward them.

"The Black Madonna," Marika said half-aloud, remembering the famed black likeness of the Virgin Mary in a Kraków, Poland, church. "There's something about her, almost magical, Lisa."

"Scary, you mean. She looks like a dirty old gypsy to me," was Lisa's answer. "Come on, Mom, don't look at her. Don't pay her any attention, or she'll come to us."

The gypsy sat down at the table of an English couple a few tables away, and began reading the young woman's palm in a soft, low voice. They strained to listen.

"She speaks English, Lisa."

"Mom, I don't care what she speaks," and Lisa shivered and buttoned the top of her denim jacket.

In the meantime, they heard the Englishman exclaim his amazement at what the gypsy was telling his wife.

"Extraordinary!" he cried aloud. "Amazing. Really unbelievable!"

Lisa squirmed in her chair. "The Englishman is probably a shill. Don't ask her over, Mom."

It was too late. The figure in black, clutching her shawl tightly around her thin figure, came to their table. Without an invitation, she sat down in one of the two empty seats. She smelled of oil, spices, and strange things.

"You Magyar—" she said in a rasping voice, pointing a bony dark finger, yellowed with nicotine stains, at Marika.

"Half," answered Marika lamely, not knowing how to respond to this mysterious creature. She noticed Lisa tightening her grip on her handbag.

"Klara, you must find Klara," the gypsy said huskily. She saw one of the managers of the café coming in her direction, and she arose hastily, pointing at Marika's handbag. She repeated "Klara," and Marika gave her some forints quickly, without looking to see how much she gave. The gypsy fled into the crowds of the square.

"She is not supposed to bother people in this place!" the manager shouted, obviously upset to have his patrons approached by this woman.

"She did not bother us," Marika said calmly. "But tell me something, what does "Klara' mean?"

He shrugged in almost a Gallic manner. "I have no idea what is ever on a gypsy's mind—unless—it's the shop 'Clara.' It's a boutique on Vaci Utca—just over there. French dresses and accessories. It's been there for years, but it is very expensive. Until this month only the wives of the Communist leaders could afford to go there. But never would that shop employ a gypsy to advertise it." He shuddered at the thought and hastened back inside the café.

They paid their check and walked over to the Vaci Utca, peering in the shop windows, and marveling at the paved brick streets with their magnificent polished bronze manhole covers, carved into floral designs. Clara's was easy to find, because it was on the ground floor, with a mannequin in the window, smartly dressed, and with scarves, handbags, and costume jewelry around her. They stepped inside. The shop's interior was luxurious, far removed from even a hint of socialist deprivation or dowdiness. Marika first noticed the thick robin's egg blue carpet, and the Louis XV painted chairs with blue silk cushions. The petals of the large white-flowered Venetian chandelier were traced with the color of blue glass. Panels of white moiré silk set into the walls and framed in dark wood alternated with panels of smoky mirrors.

"I feel like a damn fool," Marika whispered to her daughter as a *vendeuse* approached them, smiling.

"You *should* feel that way," said Lisa. "Just what are you going to say now? Mom, this is ridiculous. I think you're losin' it."

The saleswoman asked in German if she could help them, but she quickly slipped into English when Marika said haltingly, "I —we—would like to see the manager, if that is possible."

"But, of course, I will call the directrice, Madame Bokanyi, if you will please make yourself comfortable for a minute."

Marika and Lisa looked at each other in shock.

"This is too weird," said Lisa. "Why don't we get out of here?"

"No! We must meet her. We can't walk out now." Marika's voice was so faint, Lisa had to lean close to hear. "I don't understand. The gypsy knew somehow—"

A slim, very chic woman in her mid-sixties came down the curved stairway, lightly holding on to the white iron railing. She wore a teal blue crepe suit, the jacket nipped in at the waist and with a small peplum. Her legs were long and slender, sheathed in sheer black hose; her shoes were black French kid pumps. She wore turquoise and diamond earrings set in gold, and smelled, Marika decided, of Guerlain's *L'Heure Blue* fragrance. It was a perfume she knew. Her mother had used it all the time, and it was the first scent she grew to recognize as a little girl.

Strange. The woman's thick, lustrous gray hair was pulled back softly into a chignon, which was embellished at the back with a small gold rope ornament. She was stunning, and both Marika and Lisa were affected by the glamor and charm of this woman who bore such a recognizable name.

"My name is Clara Bokanyi. What may I do for you?" She spoke in perfect English, with a recognizable, but nonetheless pleasant, Hungarian accent.

"I am Marika Wentworth, and this is my daughter Lisa. We have always heard of your shop in New York," Marika tried to gather her wits.

"I felt we should pay our respects," Marika continued, "because a mutual friend in the U.S. told us to be sure to look you up."

"Oh, and who is that, Madame?" she asked in a warm, spirited voice.

"I have—oh, dear, how is it possible? Madame Bokanyi, I've pulled a complete blank. All of a sudden the name is gone. Completely. But it will come back. I'm so sorry!"

"It does not matter whether the name comes to you or not. I'm happy to have you both here—and from such a long way."

"Do you suppose we could see your dresses and suits? May we look around?" Marika was desperate for time—desperate to discover something, find out who this woman was, without having to go into her own story.

"Of course, you must look around. But first, let me give you a cup of tea upstairs in my little office. I have a pot full of tea steeping this very second."

She motioned for them to follow her up the curving stairway, and they did, feeling guilty and intrusive. Madame Bokanyi's office was like a small boudoir of beige silk, with its walls lined with the moiré. A French writing desk sat in a corner, holding three telephones, a basket of fabric swatches, and one of sketches. A beige file cabinet sat in another corner next to a beige typewriter on a stand. There were three small antique chairs covered in beige and brown silk, where their host asked them to sit down and make themselves comfortable.

Lisa remained silent, and Marika knew she would have to do all the talking. She had already made some command decisions. She would not confide in this woman; she would not tell her about Istvan, but she would try to find out more about this woman named Bokanyi.

The directrice served them tea in the white Herend porcelain teacups and saucers, decorated with colorful little birds. Then she passed them a small silver plate filled with chocolates. "Hungarian chocolate is calorie-free, did you know that?" Her laughter made the joke seem more effective than it was. Lisa began thinking about what she had recently put in her stomach, including lunch, the sauerkraut in the market place, the pastry at the Gerbeaud, and now the chocolates, while Marika and the directrice talked uninterruptedly about fashion in New York and Paris, and how successful her shop had been in Budapest. Madame Bokanyi spoke kindly and graciously, but kept looking closely at Marika, as if to try to fathom her purpose in being here. She explained to her American visitors how difficult it was for women to find and be able to afford good clothes after World War II. "Now that we are free to leave the country again, for the first time in so many years, and with trade being restored, it will all be much easier—and better."

"I find the Hungarian women on the street very well dressed," Marika said brightly, "amazingly so in comparison to women in other Soviet bloc countries.

"Yes, that is true, but Budapest will probably never return to what it was in the early 1900s—the most elegant, fashionable, and luxurious city in the world."

Marika decided she could not lose any more time. "You have always lived in Budapest, Madame Bokanyi?"

"Before the War I lived in a little town in the country that you will probably never hear of, called Szentendre. After the war, my life has been Budapest—and this shop."

Marika was now positive that the hunch she had was correct, that this woman was the wife of Istvan Bokanyi.

"Are you married, Madame Bokanyi? Forgive my being so

forward. I picture you and your husband making the handsomest couple in Budapest."

"You are very kind," she said, and Marika felt her eyes were penetrating right through her. "I lost my husband when we were both very young—in the war—late in 1944. We had only been married two years."

"Did you have any children?" The Hungarian woman stared at Marika before answering.

"No, sadly, we did not." Marika realized she had reached the point of no return. She could press no further.

"We've taken up too much of your time, Madame Bokanyi. Lisa and I will take a quick moment to look at your beautiful things downstairs, and I promise to send you some customers from the States. You have exquisite taste."

"Our clothes are French, but our prices are much lower than in Paris," she said proudly. "Please come back to see me one day—on your next trip to Budapest, perhaps."

"That's a promise."

They shook hands warmly and then Marika and Lisa took a flying tour of the racks and closets downstairs. As they left the shop, they were both conscious of the fact that Madame Bokanyi was watching them from the top of her curving stairway on the second floor.

When her shop assistant came to find her, she found Madame Bokanyi on the telephone. "Yes, Laszlo, the gypsy woman was too silly but it worked!" The assistant quietly closed Madame's door and returned to her duties.

When Madame Bokanyi returned the phone to the receiver, she stared for a while at the photo she kept in a silver frame on her desk. Her husband had betrayed her, perhaps, but she could easily forgive him. Istvan had been a wonderful husband and he would have been proud to have fathered this wonderful American woman.

Marika and Lisa rode in a small Soviet-made taxi from Pest up to Castle Hill in Buda, too emotionally spent to talk. In the lobby of the Hilton, a large number of International Bibliophile conventioneers awaited the elevators. Their chatter filled the area with loud noises echoing off each other. Lisa finally spoke. "Are you going to tell her you're Istvan's daughter?"

"No. Her husband died a hero. Nothing should take away the luster from that."

"Are you disappointed in Istvan—I mean, that he had a wife when he was in the sack with your mother?"

"Lisa, your way of putting things is crude, to say the least. No, I am not disappointed. Men and women do things in a war they do not do otherwise when they don't even know if they'll live to see the next day."

"Next time you give me a sermon about Sergio and me, Mom, I'm going to remember these words of yours."

"You and Sergio are not living in a world war, Lisa," and with that they were able to squeeze into an elevator.

"Hurry, Lisa. Janos is picking us up at eight, and we must be on time. He can't park out front with all this confusion of cars and buses."

"Where are we going for dinner?"

"To some really characteristic Hungarian place."

"Would it upset you if I didn't come? I've had so much to eat today, my tummy isn't quite right. I'm not up to another rich meal."

"You don't have to eat. You can just sit and drink Apenta Mineral Water. There'll be lots to look at and listen to."

"I'd really rather not go. Do you mind? What I'd really like to do is order consommé and crackers from room service and do some reading."

"Well—it's all right. Are you sure you're not really sick? Do you need me to stay with you?"

"Mommm! I'm fine. I'm a big girl now." Then Lisa put her arms around her mother and gave her a hug.

"You've been so strong and brave these last two days about Istvan. I love you. I bet all five of my grandparents are seeing all this and are proud of the way you are handling yourself."

"Thank you, darling. I've been holding in a lot of things, but everything's been happening so fast, I just want to live through all of this and then when I'm back home again, I'll sort it out."

"Knowing you, you'll cry it through."

"Probably right." She kissed her daughter good night, put an extra squirt of perfume on her neck and wrists, and left to join her dinner date, feeling exuberant at the thought of seeing him again.

"You look so beautiful tonight," were his first words. "Just stop a minute. Let me look at you."

She smiled, embarrassed. "Lisa is sorry she won't join us. She's not feeling up to par."

"I knew there was something of a genius in that girl. She did that for my sake. Wonderful Lisa!"

"I think your expectations of this evening are too high."

"I don't." He put her in one side of his car and they left Castle Hill. The pleasure she felt feeling the strength of that male body driving the car next to her was undeniable. She could feel the muscles on his thigh and his arm as he shifted, and she began to feel some of the sensations she felt when Jonathon touched her, made love to her. Damn you, Jonathon, she thought, why did you give up on me? Why didn't you have patience and wait? We could have worked it out.

She felt the presence next to her as a very comforting one.

"You're quiet tonight, Marika," he said, patting her hand fraternally.

"It's been an overcharged day, that's why. And you? I bet your day was a full one. You've been working all day, I've just been playing. What has gone on in your life today?"

"Well, first of all," he grinned, "I persuaded the music foundation to rent an office to Stivesoot Committee on the floor above my office, so you can open your first international branch here. Then when we're both not working, we can send each other messages from one floor to the other, and we can make love during any mutual free time we have. As you can see, I have been giving you a lot of thought the past twenty-four hours."

Marika laughed. "In the first place, my company is Stuyvesant Communications, not Stivesoot Committee."

"I don't think that's such an error."

"It's not. But in the second place, I couldn't possibly open a branch in Budapest. In the third, you're thirty-five and I'm—well—over forty. You need a beautiful young woman in your life to send those messages to when you're not busy in your office!"

"You will always be beautiful to me. Besides, I like older women."

"Wait a minute," Marika protested. "I'm not that much older!"

"I wouldn't desire you if you were my mother's age, I assure you. But I admire that fabulous body of yours. I want to see it without any of those elegant clothes you wear, that so successfully cover it up."

"Lisa really should have joined us this evening," Marika laughed.

"If she had, it would have made me happy. I would have waited until dinner was over, driven her back to the hotel, and then you and I would have gone on—for a drink, let us say, at my flat."

"Can't we do that anyway?" she found herself asking. He said nothing, but reached for her hand and raised her fingertips to his lips.

They dined at the *Kiskakukk Etterem* restaurant, a charming, simple place, spotless, with an extensive menu and an enthusiastic Hungarian upper-class clientele. They listened to four gypsy violinists, sipped their wine, and discussed Hungarian history, politics, and economics.

"You make me feel shy," Marika finally said, conscious of his eyes unabashedly riveted on her all through the meal.

"You know, I've been looking at you and thinking you look more Hungarian than American," he said.

"I'm complimented."

"With a name like yours, Marika, you must have some sort of Hungarian background. Maybe some Hungarian passionate blood?"

"Way, way back, yes," she replied. Something in her voice must have told him not to question further—instead, he called for the check. "Now we go home," he said in a husky voice, "*my* home."

"I keep thinking that we just have just met, you and I, and that this is so fast." She hated the fact she was using the exact same words she had used with Jonathon some nine months earlier.

"I know you're not the kind of woman who throws herself at a man," he said. "That is what makes you so delicious. Your shyness is totally wonderful," and putting his arm around her back, he guided her out of the restaurant, into his little car, and later up three flights of stone stairs to his apartment. A miniature slide rule served as the knocker on his door.

Once inside the door, she began to protest softly. "But this isn't going anywhere. We're leaving tomorrow afternoon."

"Does everything *have* to go somewhere? Can't you enjoy this moment? Look," he said, cupping her chin in his warm hand, "do you find me a little attractive, just a little?"

"More than a little."

"Well, we're even. I find you attractive, intelligent, amusing. I want to repay you tonight for some of the pleasure you have given me with your company these past two evenings. Is that so bad?"

"No. It isn't the way I've run my life, but it's not so bad."

"Has anyone made love to you just for the sake of pleasing you? I mean, a man who was not your husband, not someone you planned on marrying?"

She knew that question had set off the color in her cheeks. She didn't have to feel them to see if they were warm.

"No."

"You have missed much, my little American. You work so hard, you read so much, you do a man's work, and yet you miss so much pleasure out of life."

"I was raised with moral standards," she protested.

He tried not to laugh, but his face was lit with the broadest of smiles—perhaps even a very controlled laugh.

"You are old enough to have a man make love to you just to please you."

She felt suddenly bold. "What about you being old enough to have a woman like me please *you?*"

This time he really did laugh. "Marika, Marika, you're wonderful. Look, let's draw a plan for tonight. Tonight you are *my* guest. I will please *you*. This will be my hospitality. You can show me your hospitality another evening."

His arms around her felt so absolutely, perfectly superb, she was not going to argue with his premise.

They had climbed the three floors in the stone tower where he lived, and he had opened a heavy carved oak door—probably from medieval times, she judged, having seen so many other medieval doors in Budapest that day. The apartment inside was a startling contrast—very contemporary—with white-washed stone walls and black slate floors. There were bits of woven African rugs and pieces of African primitive art spotlit here and there. A tall black metal stool was pulled up to his oversized white architect's drawing table, over which a black metal lamp hung, making an arched curve in the air. The room was furnished in a minimalist manner, the furniture all black and striking against the white walls and vaulted ceiling. Her eyes searched the room, and he noticed it.

"The bed is over there."

It was not all that visible in the corner—a large bed covered with a chalk-white coverlet that blended into the wall.

He turned on the stereo to Bach music, and asked her if she would like a glass of wine. When she said no, he began to undress her slowly, kissing her first in a teasing way that made her frustrated, because she couldn't find his lips to return his kiss. Then he kissed her with a soft pressure that soon changed to an urgent one, and soon she wanted him deep inside her. He had not shaved since that morning, and his light beard tickled and lightly scratched her skin. The touch of his face on her body was pleasurable to the point of being almost unbearable. She gave in to her feelings with total abandon and a lack of self-consciousness. She could not believe she was the same person as the Marika Wentworth who lay in that bed. For several hours he made expert

love to her entire body, waiting for the perfect moment each time
to bring her to full climax, and holding her afterward like a child
in his arms, caressing her hair and whispering words of love in
Hungarian.

He taught her new ways of kissing him, of pleasing him, and
their bodies moved back and forth in rhythm as they spoke to
one another in their own languages, but mainly communicated
with one another via their hands, lips, and bodies. Time passed
with cruel swiftness and they lazily experimented, bent on pleasing
each other. Marika pushed everything and everyone out of her
mind—including the only two men who had ever made love to
her—David and Jonathon. Janos Margitay had transported her
into quite another world from any she had inhabited before.

"I may never see you again," she said wistfully as she dressed,
"but you must know that you have given me more pleasure tonight
than any man has ever given me."

"You were thirsty and hungry, that's all," he said, enjoying
the sight of her body. "Somewhere, back home, there is a man
waiting to awaken all of this in you again, you'll see."

"You will go on with your busy life and I with mine. It is so
sad that we didn't have more time together."

"Ah, but time goes fast. You'll be back next summer! I'll take
you horse trekking with me? Do you ride?"

She nodded, "Yes, I used to all the time, but not for years."

"Promise me then, Marika, you will practice this year, because
you must be a good rider to go horse trekking. We will go off
with a group in June—but we'll really be by ourselves, riding all
day through unbelievable wild flower-filled meadows, lunching
and dining under the trees on great estates, sleeping together every
night in some castle bedroom, and making love until the dawn
comes—when it's time to move on with our horses."

"My God, Janos," she said, nuzzling into his neck, "that's a
prospect that will keep me alive through this entire coming year."

"Come back to me, Marika, next summer. I want to keep you
in my thoughts all year, too."

It was four o'clock in the morning when he drove her back
and she tiptoed into her hotel suite. Lisa's bedroom light was off,

and she was sure she had not awakened her. She had insisted on coming back to the hotel so that Lisa wouldn't think she had stayed out all night with Janos. She still had old-fashioned principles, even though her daughter did not.

Lisa and she breakfasted together before going off with Laszlo on their last morning of sight-seeing before catching the plane. They did not exchange many words during the meal, but as they left the suite, Lisa handed a scarf to her mother.

"Mom, I know this is the land of Transylvania and Dracula, but even so I think you'd better wear this scarf. It might be a good idea to cover that considerably large love bite on your neck."

Marika and Lisa found the smoky airport, with its long lines waiting for customs and passport control, hot and miserable. They said a warm good-bye to Laszlo, kissing him on both cheeks and exchanging addresses. It truly felt like they were leaving. Then he surprised Marika by slipping an envelope into her hand as they passed through the security gate. A thank-you note to me, she thought, but then he said, "This is from a lady who told me to give it to you just as you leave, and to make you promise not to open it until the plane lifts off the ground."

She put it in her purse and almost forgot about it in the confusion of leaving. They had been in the air for an hour when she suddenly remembered it and took it out. Inside, without a note or explanation, was a yellowing snapshot—of a handsome, brown-haired army officer in a Hungarian uniform, light-colored jodphurs, and shiny leather riding boots. His dark, long tunic jacket, with its wide leather belt, was buttoned up high and handsomely collared. His tall, visored officer's hat was dashing, she decided. He had a thick, full mustache and flashing eyes.

"Look, Lisa," she said softly, handing her the envelope, "here is a picture of your grandfather."

"The gypsy, Clara, Laszlo—a chain linked to Szentendre, isn't it?" asked Lisa.

"Perhaps, but you know, I'd prefer not to really know—it's more fun to think it all came together through magic."

The two women spoke very little on the flight to Zurich. When they landed, Marika quickly hugged her daughter and said good-bye. The plane was to continue on to Kennedy Airport and would take Lisa back to her classes.

The driver sent by Mathilde Kauffman met Marika in the passport control part of the Zurich airport, and once her suitcase appeared on the conveyor belt, they headed straight for the LUX-FOODS headquarters outside the city. She had days of hard work ahead on the honey cream products with the Kauffmans and their research and home economists staff.

As she sat in the back of the gray Mercedes, thinking of the past few days, she tried to take stock. So much had happened so fast, she felt as though she had been doing a whirling dervish dance and was still spinning from it. Yet, through the entire landscape of the excitement of finding out about her father, the shock of meeting his wife, the joy of discovering Hungary, the exciting, warm, and comforting touch of Janos Margitay's lips and hands, there was a discomforting shadow that still dominated everything. There was an intense ache inside her where love used to reside—love for a man named Jonathon Scher. He was not the lover Janos was. But at one time he had something far more important than skill at love-making. He had truly loved her. . . .

CHAPTER

15

"Mac darling," Eve came into the upstairs sitting room where he was going over some papers on the desk, "I saw Jessica Davson today at the Senate Ladies' Luncheon for me."

He gave her a quick glance, then a second more appreciative one. She looked like a confection, her ash-blond Garbo-like hair radiant, her eyes shining—as they almost always did these days—with happiness. He had learned to love her more than before, because she gave him back more than before—and he needed it, oh, God, how he needed it, wrestling with affairs of state in the official prison in which they lived. He loved this woman, all warmly wrapped in a butterscotch cashmere sweater, skirt, and silk scarf.

"What about Jessica?" he feigned polite interest in the senator's wife, but he had become engrossed again in paragraph three of a White House assistant's report, from which the sight of Eve had distracted him.

"She said that Jonathon Scher, darling, has dumped his luscious young beauty."

Mac left paragraph three at these words and looked up again at his wife. God, she was beautiful. "What happened with Jonathon?"

"I couldn't really ask for details. It would have tipped my hand to be too eager. I just asked her one question that I had to ask, to satisfy myself for the next six months."

"And, that subtle, quiet little question of yours was . . . ?"

"I said, 'Jessica, is it positively, unequivocally over?'"

"And?"

"It elicited just the information I wanted. She said, 'I'll say.' She said Barbara was furious with Jonathon, said he kept stalling about when they were going to walk down that aisle. She had warned him that he would lose her if he continued his delaying tactics, and finally, she met a rich young man at a cocktail party when Jonathon was out of town."

"What does that mean?" he said skeptically. "Everyone goes to cocktail parties without their dates, mates, lovers, whatevers."

"Only that they fell in love, those two, that very night at dinner. The next night he popped the question and they set their wedding date—all while Jonathon was away on business. And it took them only two days to make their plans, whereas Jonathon had kept her waiting and wondering for months. Of course, Jonathon is still in love with Marika. He never would have made final plans with that Frankel woman."

"Fast worker, that Barbara. I like to see a woman go get what she wants." He got up from his desk, came over to her chair, leaned over, and began kissing her on the neck. "She is almost as fast a worker as you were with me."

"*You* were the one who worked fast on me!" Eve retorted, rising from the chair and putting her arms around him.

"It's too bad," he said, his face in her hair, "that Jonathon and Marika probably won't even try to make a go of it again. They're both too hurt, too strong-headed, too unused to compromising with anyone." By now his hands had pulled up and over her head the First Lady's cashmere sweater, and she had already removed the shirt from the back of the President of the United States.

"I haven't given up on them," she said thoughtfully, trying to find the right option key in her computer mind that would open the right file.

"Don't spend any time on it," he whispered, blowing on the inside of her ear, his hands cupping her bare breasts. Their clothes were coming off, piece by piece, and lay now all over the floor.

"Maybe I can let lie the subject of Jonathon and Marika for a few minutes," she said, laughing and wrestling free from him to lock the sitting room door. He pulled her down with him onto the sofa and the two bodies began to make lazy, langorous, and very satisfying love—right beneath a framed copy of the Declaration of Independence.

Jonathon's shoeless feet reclined on his large early nineteenth-century Empire desk, the legs of which were "encased in glorious ormolu mounts," as the antique dealer in San Francisco had described it when he purchased it. In deference to the beauty and great value of the desk, although he still put his feet up on it whenever he had some thinking to do, at least he did it without shoes.

Two weeks ago Eve had called him as he sat in this same pose to invite him to a White House dinner—on short notice.

"You're getting the big treatment, Jonathon," she had said, "I'm calling you myself, instead of having the Social Secretary's office do it. Consider yourself the recipient of very special VIP treatment!"

He had laughed and said, "I am properly awed."

"Good!" she replied. "Are you going to be in the East any part of next week? Before you can say no, let me mention that I have not one, but *two* state dinners to cope with in the same week, for which we have invited twenty-three widows and divorcées, and as of this moment, only fourteen single men. Only fourteen so far! I am seriously thinking of putting up a sign in the Georgetown University student placement office, stating that any young man who has his own dinner jacket and a decent haircut can get a free White House dinner anytime he is hungry."

"My God," he laughed, "I feel I must serve my country and come."

"Yes, it would be an act of patriotism. Now, what's your schedule?"

"It just so happens, Eve, that I have a board meeting on the fourteenth—in Philadelphia. Does that help?"

"Perfect! Have that gorgeous jet of yours fly you into Washington the night before, Tuesday the thirteenth."

"I'm delighted to do that. Tell me one thing . . ."

"You mean, tell you if Marika will be there?"

"Yes."

"Well, she won't. I have enough sense when two people who never should have broken up, who were idiots to break up—I mean, I have enough sense not to invite two cretins like you two together. Tell me, Jonathon, you really *have* broken up with that young woman, haven't you? I mean I heard you did—from Jessica Davson."

"Yes," he said wearily, "it was a magician's trick—a relationship that materialized like magic, and disappeared in the exact same way."

"Well, I'm relieved," Eve said. "I mean, I need an extra man like you to help out in emergencies, just as you are doing right now. If you were still involved with her, I would have to invite her, too."

He was laughing now. "Eve, you are the epitome of politeness. No, I am very uninvolved and I can be invited solo any time— any time I happen to be in your neck of the woods on business. In fact, I love it. I am honored."

The state dinner on the following Tuesday night was for one of the African presidents. Jonathon had always been fascinated by Africa, had a lot of business interests there. Yet on this night he felt so depressed being in that house without Marika that he could not even hear the toasts or care that he was not paying attention. Jesus, he felt down, down, down.

Eve had come and sat by him after dinner during the Rolling Stones' performance in the East Room. Guests were seated at small tables; it was like an informal cabaret.

"I'm highly flattered, Madam First Lady," Jonathon whispered, loud enough for her to hear, but not for those around them to hear as the screaming beat of the Rolling Stones filled the gold and white room. "But aren't you supposed to be with President What's-his-name?"

"First of all, he's a real Stones fan. He doesn't want to talk to me. And if I can cause gossip for leaving him for five minutes, I rather like that. The White House press corps will wonder what you and I have cooking, sitting here in the back of the room in the dark. It's all the more fun that we have *nothing* cooking! Just wanted to know if you have heard anything from Marika at all, since—well, since everything went—kerplooey."

"No, Eve." He knew damned well that she knew he hadn't.

"Well, then, you probably don't know she's in Budapest."

"Budapest?"

"Yes, she finally did what she has wanted to do ever since Charlie Russell died. She took Lisa with her—to seek her Hungarian roots. I just talked to her in her suite at the Budapest Hilton."

"Must be an interesting trip." His voice sounded a little too artificially bored with the discussion.

"Well, what's great is—now that you two no longer care about each other"—an arrow had pierced his flesh at that point in the conversation, he now recalled—"I can tell you freely that, although it's unofficial as yet, she has a new love. Mac and I are thrilled."

"What?" He kept his voice low and bored, as though he didn't really care about her "new love," God damn whoever it was.

"Yes, there's some madly attractive Hungarian—a dashing type—and you know what a fantastic reputation they have—who's fallen head over heels in love with her, and she sounds pretty smitten herself."

He didn't know what to say, but he didn't have to respond, because Eve had risen and was saying a whispered good-bye in the darkness of the back of the East Room. "I have to go back to my duty, Jonathon, both to officialdom and the full decibel sound of the Stones. Wonderful to see you—thanks for coming . . ." and she slipped away from him.

He didn't care, he said to himself now, rolling his *Wall Street Journal* into a tight and then even tighter roll, relaxing at his Empire desk high in a skyscraper overlooking Michigan Avenue. Then he began playing with his handsome sterling silver library shears that sat on his desk in a leather holder. He twirled them around and around on his forefinger while gazing idly at the fading light through the windows. He sat fascinated by the fast-changing textures of the burnished facades opposite him, and he remembered how he and Marika had talked about that. They would both sit in their offices at the end of the day, watching the play of light, shadow, glimmer, and color on the stone, glass, and steel opposite them. They had thought about so many things in the same way, at the same time. Suddenly his reverie out the window was interrupted.

Just what *was* this "fantastic reputation" the Hungarians had anyway? If it means they are great lovers, something he had heard before, he would like to cut off the balls of whoever it was who might possibly lay a hand on Marika Wentworth.

Then he laughed aloud at his symbolic gesture, put the scissors back in their holder, reread Marika's letter to him after their breakup for the eightieth time, and went back to work.

CHAPTER

16

Hortense's voice was decidedly cool. In fact, Jonathon felt his face might become chapped from the iciness of the voice coming at him through the receiver in the Brussels airport.

"Why would you think she'd want *you* to have her number?" she asked haughtily. "You have not exactly been a *persona grata* around here these past few months, you know."

"Hortense, I know how you feel about me, but I feel worse about myself than you could possibly feel about me. Look"—she could hear the sounds of flights being called on the loud-speaker—"this is not a good connection. I've just *got* to know where Marika is. We may be cut off any second. It took me a half hour to get through to you."

"*Why* should you know?" The Fu Manchu guardian dog at the gate was doing her job, and bristling with antagonism toward the man calling from Belgium, the man who had hurt her boss so much. "You may not be aware of it, because men like you seldom are, but you really hurt Marika. And she doesn't need to go through it again, so why don't you just leave her alone?"

"I'll tell you why I should know where she is. I love her, and I can't live without her, and nothing's going to stop me from getting to her and telling her. I know she's been in Hungary, and . . ."

"Who told you she was in Hungary?" Hortense interrupted with irritation.

"Eve Watson. She said Marika was still in Europe. You've got to tell me where she is, before I get on a goddamn flight back to Chicago when I should be on a goddamn flight headed wherever she is over here."

There was a perceptible change in Hortense's voice. Mrs. Watson had told him her boss was in Europe. She obviously had a purpose in that. Things were becoming a little bit clearer.

"Not only do I want to see her," he said pleadingly, "but if she is really mixed up with some Hungarian, I've got to stop it —before it's too late."

Hortense smiled to herself. Congratulations, Mrs. Watson. You've made Jonathon Scher frantic and jealous. Well done!

Her tone became warm and confiding. "You'll find her at her Great-Aunt Victoria's chalet in Saanenmöser, outside Gstaad, in the Bernese Oberland. The number is 030/8 30 30."

After she had finished talking to Jonathon, Hortense went outside the office and rang the big bell. When the staff poured out into the hall and wanted to know what new account had just been won, Hortense announced with a large grin that united her two enormous sterling silver abstract sculpture earrings in a strong upward curve, "I just felt like ringing it, that's all."

Marika stretched out on the small kilim rug in front of the stone fireplace like a dog awakening in the morning. She had donned her olive-green, long-sleeved leotard to do her exercises. The smell of the coffee in the percolator was enticing, the sound of Great-Aunt Victoria's stereo with its tape of Wagner's magestic *Tristan and Isolde* was thrilling, and the crackling sounds of the fire made a perfect accompaniment to it all. She saw the window boxes of bright red geraniums nodding in the late September wind outside the windows, and she looked around appreciatively at the rustic light oak hand-carved furniture that filled the living room. What a perfect Saturday morning! She felt in a state of physical exultation. She sprang up in one leap from a seated position on the floor to do some *tour jêtés*, just to prove to herself she could still do them well. The living room shook as she landed on the floor with each one, and she continued dancing around, laughing and touching the black iron chandelier to make it twirl some more.

She had had a good night's sleep, after a wonderful meal of *fondu* generously laced with white wine, which had been prepared and served to her by Victoria's housekeeper. The rosy-cheeked, gray-haired lady would not accept Marika's protest that she did not have to stay to cook her dinner. She had been instructed by Mrs. Stuyvesant to take care of her great-niece, and that was that. Marika had stirred the pot of melting cheese over its alcohol stove fire with her long fork, enthusiastically spearing and eating pieces of good Swiss white bread, after swishing them around in the bubbling cheese. Then there were the generous sips from her glass of cold white dry wine. For dessert, Frau Rüchti served her home-made macaroons and a delicious compote of fresh fruit.

Renting a car and driving herself down to Gstaad from Zurich on Friday afternoon had been the best idea yet. She had before her an entire weekend alone in which to relax, write some reports, and get her life in order, at least in her thoughts. All this free time and all this peace!

Marika felt completely content. This was the first time since Jonathon's abrupt departure from her life that she had been able to be by herself and to reflect. She was now able to stand aside and look clinically at what happened between herself and Jonathon and to realize that part of the intense pain she had been feeling stemmed from the humiliation of sheer rejection. Strange, she thought, how a few romantic days in Hungary had brought about so much healing and understanding of her self. Learning about Istvan and meeting his wife had been an exciting experience and a soothing one. She felt something deep in her heart she had never been able to feel before—intense pride in her Hungarian father. She now knew him, knew that he had been a brave man, an attractive man. She smiled, thinking of her proper Bostonian, lovely blond mother, overcome with physical desire for the young Hungarian officer who had probably made love to her in a way that Charlie Russell never could have done. Even if her mother had never known that Istvan was married, she felt sure it would not have mattered. Their affair was meant to be a momentary passion brought on by the emotions of war, in a country foreign to them both.

She thought about the uncanny similarity to Janos, how he had come along at just the right moment in her life, an incredible tonic to her spirits. He had made her feel like a beautiful, desirable woman again. He had taught her new mysteries of sex. She had learned from him. She smiled, suddenly wondering if Istvan had instructed her mother similarly. Then she laughed out loud, realizing that her Hungarian blood was a source of the new passion she was capable of feeling.

She could think about Jonathon now with happy remembrances, concentrating on the good things of their relationship, rather than the bitterness and rejection. She even felt a mellowness in her heart. She would not dwell in her mind on their arguments, their fights, and personal criticisms. They had shared too many exquisite times, and those were what she would think about . . . She even almost wished him happiness with his new bride.

Jonathon. She automatically touched the side of her neck to brush some hair away, and suddenly remembered his touch, the way he kissed her neck without any warning. He would just do it, to tickle her, surprise her, give her a small feeling of sexual pleasure when no one was looking—sometimes in the back seat of a car, or when she was going through a doorway, often just sitting next to her on a restaurant banquette.

Life was beginning to look up again, because she was in charge of it. She was healthy, lucky, sexually renewed. Things were going to get better. She would spend more time with her daughter, she would devote even more of her time to the literacy movement. She would use that energy she had expended on loving, wanting, and needing Jonathon—and harness it to new projects. She needed to be happy and productive, to create.

Fortunately, her days in Zurich with the Kauffmans had been successful and very productive. But at night, in her hotel room at the Dolder Grand, she did a lot of contemplating and decision-making. Viewing her life objectively, it was obvious she was working too hard, and there were other things in life to do in the mid-forties than just working. She would stay at the helm for a while during the implementation of next year's plans for all their major clients, but her staff should begin assuming more of the executive decision-making. She envisioned stepping back—just a little—to allow them more authority, more responsiblity. She had trained them well, they were smart, capable, and could do as well as—well, almost as well as she.

There were gaps in her table of organization, and they were handling more accounts than ever. She would have to find, hire, and train three more senior account executives. There were many good ones available in New York. The major PR firms had been trimming their staffs—unfortunately for them, fortunately for her, just when she needed to staff up. Her company had several new accounts, and with the loss of Greg and Steve, it was almost an emergency situation.

Steve. A sharp thrust went through her heart at the thought of how they would now have to get along without him, without his cheerful, wise-cracking ways, his intuitive creative mind, his unswerving loyalty. . . . When some people go, she thought, they leave larger holes, bigger vacuums to fill than others. . . . Trage-dies!

She heard the sound of airplanes flying low, so she walked outside the front door and looked all around at the mountains that encompassed her. They magically changed their colors and textures according to the whim of the sun and its shadows—from velvet browns to verdant greens—a striking contrast to the clean, sharp blue sky above them. The mountain peaks, dusted snowy white from the recent storms at high elevations, looked like mounds of ice cream shredded by coconut. The air was so pure, it made her suddenly sad to think of the contrast with the gray veils of dirt New Yorkers swallowed every time they breathed their air. Budapestians, too. Lisa should be here, she thought, instead of in New York, breathing this exquisite air into her lungs.

Marika hugged herself in the chill air, wishing she was wearing a sweater over her leotard. On Monday morning she would drive the car back to Zürich, turn it in at the airport, and fly to New York. The stillness around her was comforting, soothing. The only sounds she heard, now that the planes had left, were the clangs of the cowbells, signs of herds being brought down from the high summer pasturelands to the farms below for the winter. Occasionally, she could hear the sound of an automobile motor, struggling up the steep road that went from the little town of Saanenmöser, straight up the mountain a few miles to Victoria Stuyvesant's chalet and other farms nearby.

The house was a typical, charming structure of white stone on the first floor with a second story, balcony, and roof of carved wood. Its many windows were framed in green shutters, and boxes of geraniums hung from the second-story balcony as well as on the window ledges. Frau Rüchti took great pride in keeping the house and gardens alive with blooms for at least five months a year.

The shrill sound of the Swiss telephone interrupted her musing. She just knew what this telephone call would be. She entered the house quickly, picked up the receiver and did not say hello.

"He's gone, Boss. Steve is gone." She could hear Hortense struggling for control against the sobs that constricted her throat. "It was for the best. He's at peace now."

"Of course he is. He's in a much better place, but I feel terrible I wasn't there. Oh, God, who *was* there?"

"They called us from the hospital. Anthony and I were by his side from then on. He had suffered enough. He went at midnight. Sarah had returned from a shoot and was in the room with us, too. He knew we were there, I think. Just before the end he became more lucid, though his eyesight and hearing were gone."

"Thank God it's over for him," was all Marika could say. The two women remained silent for a full minute.

"We have already been in contact with St. Thomas's church

on Fifth Avenue for the memorial service. You remember he told you that if he ever did a 'chic thing' in his life, it would be to have a memorial service in that church."

"I remember."

"Of course, it will take place after you return."

"You'll get the paid announcement into the *New York Times*?" Marika asked. "And can you try to get a paragraph on him into the obituary page?"

"Anthony has a friend on the obit page. He's already at work."

"And his parents? Have they been notified?"

"Notified, yes. They showed no interest."

"How can flesh and blood mean nothing at a time like this?" Silence again. Marika, choking, said, "Tell the staff about Steve Monday morning at a staff meeting for all the employees. Then close the office at noon for the rest of the day. Instruct everyone in what to say to people who call from the outside. Have all the details buttoned up on the memorial service, as to time, place, et cetera. Put that information also on our answering machine tape. And, of course, our office will be closed all day the day of his memorial services. Has his lawyer been notified? Have his wishes about instant cremation been relayed to the mortuary?" Marika was firing off questions in an effort to have some semblance of control.

"They have. How do you think of everything so fast, Boss?"

"Because I have gone through this scenario many times before your telephone call—in my mind. If only"—and her knuckles gripped the receiver so hard, her fingers turned several shades of color—"if only I had been there."

"I'm glad you weren't."

They finished talking about other matters, and Marika put down the receiver and gazed at the telephone, musing over the fact that so many of the joys, sorrows, and moments of love had been communicated in their entirety through this damned instrument. She slumped in Victoria's old Dutch wood rocker, with its cheery cushions of red cherries, and thought about Steve. The tears did not come. She was happy for him that everything awful and negative was finished. He was another one she would see again, up in heaven in the next life, and she had to smile, remembering her thoughts in Boston's Trinity Church, at her father's funeral, when she wondered how all of her late relatives were going to fit together up there, out there, or wherever heaven is.

She entered the glass shower stall, only faintly aware of a motor straining to climb the mountain road. She showered quickly and put on her aunt's long white terry cloth robe. Her hair and skin were still damp from the steam when she heard the front doorbell. It would be Frau Rüchti with the provisions and the morning mail, because this was the hour she was expected.

It took her a full ten seconds of just looking at him before she reacted at all. He stood immobilized on the threshold, too, looking out of place in his dark gray pinstripe suit, conservative striped tie, and black wing-tipped shoes.

He finally said, "Am I allowed inside the door, or would you prefer that I just stand here, on the outside step?"

"Come in, come in," she said with as much affability as she could muster, still feeling her entire being in a state of shock. She could not react or think properly. She was simply a parody of someone frozen to the spot, yet dripping wet from a very hot shower, unable to think, move, or speak. She suddenly became very self-conscious. "I—I look a mess. I just had a shower. My hair's wet. I . . ."

She looked like an embarrassed little girl to him, so very sweet and desirable. He wanted to crush her in his arms, but now was not the time. She was very vulnerable, he could see that.

"I've seen you coming out from the shower before," he said quietly, with a small smile, thinking of the morning after her father's funeral in Boston.

"That's right, you have." She still could not summon the words. She did not know what to say. Finally she motioned him to one of Victoria's chairs and sat down across the room from him, her bare feet making a small puddle of water beneath them on the floor.

"Are you cold?" he asked solicitously. "Maybe you ought to put on some warm clothes. I'll fix the fire."

"That would be nice," she said, and she watched him in silence as he laid two logs on the now almost quiescent fire, used the poker, put some small kindling pieces beneath the logs and got things going again. He stood and looked at it, watching the flames flicker higher and the little crackling sparks spit out from them. The room seemed to spring to life with the awakening fire.

"I had to see you," he said.

"After such a long time of not having anything to do with me, why?"

He laughed. "You and Hortense sound just alike. That's the question she asked me when I wanted to know how to reach you."

"I just talked to Hortense," she said, the tears finally beginning to run in small rivulets from the corners of her eyes. "Steve— Steve is gone."

He moved swiftly to embrace her, she arose from the rocker, and they stood in total silence, arms around each other, while the tears came. His face became wet from her tears. She pulled back and smiled, "Here, I'll get some tissues for both of us."

When she returned, he was still standing in the same place. She dried her face and his, too.

"I'm not going to grieve for him," she said, "he suffered too much for that. He's much happier now. I will save my crying for the day of his memorial service."

"You always do everything right, you figure everything out right, Marika."

"That is not exactly true. There were a lot of things, Jonathon, that I didn't figure out 'right' concerning you." *Oh, Jonathon*, she thought to herself, *why aren't you telling me right now that you love me, that we should spend the rest of our lives together, that we were fools to stop something that was meant to happen?* Instead, she said to him, "I'm surprised, frankly, to see you."

"Do you mind? Do you hate my being here?" He sounded to her like a little boy, unsure, timid, even afraid.

"I'm a fool," he continued, poking at the fire, "I love you and I've missed you every day and every night. God, especially every night. I want you. And I'll be damned if I'm going to lose out to your Hungarian."

She wanted to laugh. "Her Hungarian." She was certainly not, however, going to tell him the truth about her Hungarian. Let him puzzle and suffer—just a little—perhaps.

"And how did you hear about the Hungarian man I—my Hungarian acquaintance?"

"Eve told me. I attended a White House dinner this week."

"Oh." She tried to sound serious, but inside she was enjoying a great laugh. That devil Eve, using the old trick of making the man jealous. Well, it had worked!

"What does he mean to you?" he asked, almost defiantly.

"I had—an—an interesting time in Hungary," was her non-committal answer.

"Marika, tell me, for God's sake, that I'm not too late."

"You're not too late—perhaps—but tell me, what happened to your *grand amour?*"

"We never got anywhere. I tried. I wanted to forget you. She was a sweet, nice young woman. She didn't have your fire, your intelligence, your . . ." He stopped, unable to find words to continue.

"Why," she asked coldly, "didn't you answer my letter, call me, react, do *something*? Do you know what it took to write that letter? Do you realize how humiliating and humbling it was?"

"I did realize. And I couldn't face you. I read that letter so many times, it was shredded around the entire border. I started to call you so many times, I tried writing you, but I couldn't. I was ashamed. I felt beaten, inadequate. I handled everything wrong, and I couldn't face what you'd say to me. I've always been a coward about you. I've never been able to face you."

"You're facing me now."

"Yes, because I felt I really had a chance of losing you this time. That's what it took to get me to look at myself, and realize what a weak-kneed jerk I've been. I'm sorry I did it. God knows why. I was scared, but there was never—ever—one minute that I did not love you."

"You were so much a part of my life," Marika said, feeling her courage coming back into her. "You just dropped out of it as if you had never been there. It's hard for me—remembering that."

And then he cried. Jonathon Scher sat down again in his chair, put his head in his hands and cried. "I can't believe I'm such a blubbering adolescent. I can only say to you, Marika," he said, trying to force the words out, "that you have meant more to me than anyone or anything in this whole world. You are all I want in life and I'll do anything to get you back, if you'll just forgive me, if you'll just give me a chance."

She couldn't stand seeing him cry. He was made of strong, tough stuff, like Sheetrock, a man who never let a tear form in the corner of his eye. Suddenly she knew that he really did love her. He really had missed her, and whether it was pride or shame or whatever it was that had kept him from coming back before, it didn't matter now. She went over to him and pulled him up from his chair. He put his face in her hair and held her close, so close she felt his body almost suffocating hers. They stood in the oak living room of Victoria's chalet for half an hour, the man in the pinstripe suit and the woman in the terry cloth robe, holding each other in front of the fire, as though it were the last chance on earth for them to be together.

They waited to make love that morning until after Frau Rüchti had come—and left. They also agreed they would do their talking over dinner that night, but that first things should come first. They went into the bedroom and fell into each other's arms on the nineteenth-century massive carved four-poster bed. At one point Jonathon said he had never seen her make love with such abandonment, and when he remarked about it again later, with great happiness, she said, "I have Hungarian blood, remember?" This made him question her again about her experiences in Hungary, to which she replied mischievously, "Someday—not now—I'll tell you about Hungary. At that point you can tell me what you've been doing the last few months, and I'll tell you what I've been doing, and we'll compare notes."

He looked at her and said, "It's no fair. I can tell you've had a hell of a lot better time. I've been suffering and agonizing over you, and you obviously have *not* over me."

"And just who left whom?" she asked.

"Your grammar is impeccable," Jonathon replied, and then he made love to her again, and she did not know if he was seemingly insatiable, or if he was trying to outdo the Hungarian. Frankly, his motivation did not matter.

They managed to get dressed and leave the chalet in time for a quick visit to the shops in Gstaad, where they laughed their way through purchases of hiking boots, corduroy slacks, polo shirt, and ski sweater for Jonathon, who had only business suits with him. Then they went to the rustic Restaurant Sonnenhof, high up the mountain between Gstaad and Saanenmöser. They walked around on the mountain for an hour and then went inside for an early dinner. There weren't many people there on an off-season night, so they sat comfortably in their wood slat-back chairs at a table for four, using one hand for drinking and eating, and the other to hold hands. Jonathon laughed. "I knew I'd find one time in my life when being left-handed was helpful." The owner, Frau Berchtold, came to their table to announce the specialities of the evening, including her famous wild game and steak dishes, but since the couple was not listening and wouldn't concentrate, no matter how many times she tried to get their attention, she finally said, "May I please just bring you something I think you'd like?"

"Splendid idea," said Jonathon, squeezing Marika's hand and telling her that there was no woman ever born who was as beautiful and wonderful as she. Then with an impish grin he jumped up, pulled Frau Berchtold out of the kitchen, and in front of eight other startled patrons of the restaurant, said to Marika, "Madam, you are a most beautiful, wonderful, and superb woman." With that, he put his arm around the owner's waist and galloped around the room in a fast and very graceful polka. At the end of this performance Frau Berchtold collapsed in one of her chairs, and Jonathon addressed the room: "You will have to excuse me. I am very much in love—with this lovely lady," he said, pointing with pride at Marika, who was laughing with embarrassment.

"Now, let us all drink to our happiness with champagne. Frau Berchtold, your best champagne, for everyone—and for everyone in the kitchen and the waiters, too!"

By the time dinner was over, Marika looked at Jonathon, who was now slightly bleary-eyed, and said with a grin, "Two things, lover. First, we'll do our talking *tomorrow* and not tonight, and second, I'll drive."

The next day they were exhausted, from eating, drinking, and making love.

"Is there any feeling so wonderful?" Jonathon said to her, his arm across her breast, imprisoning her as he lay beside her. "I mean physically, mentally, spiritually, is there anything so wonderful as feeling exhausted, sated, deliriously in love?"

"You're a poet," she said, kissing the end of his nose.

When they got dressed and went into town, Marika said, "I want to say some prayers for Steve. Let's find a church."

At noon, on this Sunday, the only service they could find was at the pretty, rustic Catholic church in Gstaad. They attended Mass in their slacks and sweaters, and then wandered across the street to have lunch.

"The next service we attend together will be at the synagogue," she said.

"Agreed." There was a spirit of compromise in the air.

At the restaurant, after ordering the first course of hot *Zuppe* with vegetables, they fell deep into a conversation about their plans. It was now one o'clock.

They would get married within a month's time, with only Lisa and Sergio, Great-Aunt Victoria, Jonathon's mother, his secretary, Mrs. Matthews, Mac and Eve, Georgiana and Chauncey, and Marika's top staff in attendance. They would marry in Washington, so that the Watsons could attend with ease. For the President and the First Lady, they both decided, you make things easy. You bring the wedding to Washington, not to the White House, but to Washington.

By the time the soup was consumed and the plates of veal schnitzel with noodles arrived, they had embarked on the subject of Jonathon's mother. Jonathon had already talked to her and put the fear of God into her about giving Marika a hard time. Marika, on her part, had already assured Jonathon that she was going to make his mother not only accept her, but be delighted that Jonathon was married to "that nice sweet Marika."

When she told him about the role Istvan Bokanyi had played with Wallenburg during the war, Jonathon smiled broadly, leaned back in his chair, and replied, "That should shut up my mother for the next twenty-five years, at least."

"Jonathon, let's get a pad and write down all the hurdles we have to leap over in this relationship of ours. I'd feel better about seeing them all written down and checked off, one by one. If we can't jump over them right now, at least we will have discussed them, and they aren't hidden away in some closet, with one of us festering with resentment."

He borrowed a large pad used by the owner for marketing lists, came back to the table, whipped out his fountain pen, and confessed he would rather be back in Great-Aunt Victoria's bed, catching up for lost time, than making lists in a rathskeller.

"No, this is important," she said.

"I know."

By the time the salad and cheese course had arrived, they had decided that their Washington wedding would consist of a small ceremony at an Episcopalian church, with a large reception afterward at the F Street Club, using a tent over the back terrace.

"My mother will be on the warpath about the Episcopalian church, but it doesn't really matter—unless you could see your way clear to doing it in a nonsectarian place."

"I couldn't," she said firmly. "But I'll meet her more than halfway. Not only will it be an ecumenical service, with a minister and a rabbi in attendance, but we'll get the most terrific rabbi there is!"

He laughed and crossed off that problem on the notepad.

Marika had marked "Lisa" on the pad in capital letters.

"Would it help set your mind at rest," he said, holding her hand tightly, "to hear not only am I proud to become the stepfather of Lisa, but that I love her as your daughter, and that I see in her things that I love in you? And furthermore, I swear always to love, protect, and take care of her as if she were my own?"

"That is very dear of you," she said, and then she penciled in another name next to Lisa's on the list and laughed. "Does that proclamation include Sergio as well?"

He put his head back and laughed along with her.

By the time the dessert arrived, drowning in the envitable sea of whipped cream, they had gotten down to the heavy stuff on the list, too—such as where they would live and what Marika would do with her company.

By the time the espresso was served, it was decided that Marika would keep the Manhattan apartment for Lisa, and for herself and Jonathon to use when in New York, and that Sergio would be told he couldn't officially move in while Marika was in Chicago or away with Jonathon, but he would probably move in anyway.

By the time they had really delved deep into Stuyvesant Communications, Inc., they were having a cognac and Jonathon was longing to be back in Victoria's big bed, where problems, big and small, seemed so easily solvable.

"No, Jonathon, we must stay and finish—right here," said Marika firmly. It wasn't easy for her to say that, because he was kissing her neck at this point. Jonathon sighed and they continued talking out every point. They were drinking decaffeinated coffee by now. When Marika felt Jonathon was capitulating too much, she warned him, and he would adopt a momentarily strong position. Inevitably, however, he would kiss her and say, "We'll do it your way," but she noticed how often what she thought was her way was really his. No wonder he was so smart in business.

Jonathon finally felt compelled to give the owner of the restaurant a large wad of Swiss francs so that the two of them could hold their table. It was now seven o'clock. They had now been in the restaurant for six hours, and it was filling up with dinner guests. They talked, held hands, made frenzied notes, and then held hands again. The proprietor mopped his brow, paced back and forth in the kitchen, decried love, romance, and anything having to do with sex. "It takes forever!" he cried to his pastry chef, who was still working on the Napoleons for tonight's dessert. The pastry chef shrugged his shoulders and remarked that everything took forever, including his pastry.

The owner finally gave up and went home to rest for an hour. He was not used to marathon hours in his restaurant. He left his establishment in the hands of the *Suisse Romande* salad chef, who read *Paris Match* every week, and who had read a long article on prenuptial agreements, American-style.

"*Pardonnez moi, m'sieur at 'dame*, but are you working on a pre-nupt-iale accord? I was just fascinated to know."

"No," replied Jonathon. "That is for settling financial concerns. We are working on emotional concerns."

"There is a *différence?*" asked the pastry chef.

By eight-thirty, Marika and Jonathon had struck a written pact that she individually or they as a couple would:

- Move to Chicago as her main base.
- Make things very attractive for Lisa in the new apartment the Schers would purchase jointly in Chicago, but that Marika would decorate with all new things. "I don't want to sleep in a bed that Barbara Frankel has slept in before," she said, twitting him.
- Make weekends so enticing in Chicago that Lisa would want to join them all the time. They also figured out a barter-work arrangement wherein Sergio could do work for them in New York in return for his round-trip plane fare for those Chicago weekends.
- Keep the Sutton Place apartment, so that Lisa would still feel she had a home in New York. Marika would stay at the Sutton Place apartment whenever Jonathon was away from Chicago for more than three days.
- Make herself chairman of the company and appoint Anthony as her president and CEO. He would therefore run the main New York office.
- Open an office in Chicago, small but elegant, not too far from their apartment, with a strong (not too strong, interrupted Marika) senior account executive, who could easily manage the agency when Marika was elsewhere.
- Seek new business opportunities that would allow her the flexibility to travel with Jonathon when he would be gone for a week or longer—particularly to choice spots.

He agreed not to make her accompany him to unchoice spots.

· Use her own name during the day, but be Mrs. Scher at nighttime and on weekends.

· Spend Christmas with Great-Aunt Victoria and New York friends. Yom Kippur and Passover would be spent with Rebecca Scher, wherever she might be.

· Nights out were not to exceed two a week.

"Of course," Jonathon interjected at this point, "we might just never get out the door at night. We have better things to do."

They took turns adding new points to the ever-growing list, arguing them out, and finally compromising on them. Finally, she smiled and said, "We haven't mentioned the word money once."

"I'm rich," he said quickly, "you'll always be taken care of."

"You mean . . ." she interrupted.

"I'm sorry. That was a gross way to put it. What I really meant is that you'll always have security, Marika, I promise you that. There, does that sound better?"

"And if you can't provide it, I can for both of us," she retorted. The competitiveness between them would always be there.

"I know. But remember, Miss Oh-so-secure, you can't make love to a bank."

"I know," she said, grabbing his thigh under the table.

"Are we almost done?" he asked, "I don't think I can stand much more talk. I need rest—bed rest."

"We're done," she said, "for today. We have many more ahead of us."

"Hey, beautiful, you know something? We're going to make it."

"Yeah, handsome," she said, putting her arm around his neck in a wrestler's hold and putting the tip of her nose to the tip of his, "I think we're going to make it."

"I've always loved the way you're a 'nose person,' you know that? And promise me that the next time you go back to Hungary, you'll take me with you?" He was now kissing her hard on the mouth, in full view of the fascinated diners and waiting staff. The room became deathly quiet. Everyone in it wanted to hear what the lovers were saying.

"I won't return to Hungary without you," she said, and then she couldn't help adding, in a devilish manner, "except perhaps to go horse trekking." It was to be forever her own inside joke.

"What the hell is horse trekking?"

"I doubt if you'll ever find out."

"All right, but promise you won't go back there without me?"

"Promise you'll never ever say again to me, 'I don't think we're going to make it?'"

"We *are* going to make it," he said, and the other people in the restaurant, led by the owner, began to applaud.